# A Grand Day To Get Lost

■ ■ ■

*Kris Radish*

ISBN-10: 0-615-78171-3
ISBN-13: 978-0-615-78171-6

Also by Kris Radish

———

The Elegant Gathering of White Snows
Dancing Naked at the Edge of Dawn
Annie Freeman's Fabulous Traveling Funeral
Searching for Paradise in Parker, PA
The Sunday List of Dreams
The Shortest Distance Between Two Women
Hearts on a String
Tuesday Night Miracles

Non-Fiction:

Run, Bambi, Run
The Birth Order Effect

# The Beginning

*Thirty miles is a long time for a woman like me to keep her mouth shut. But Charles and I here in this luscious middle-of-nowhere territory, uprooted from everything we have ever known, jobless, and the two of us fighting as if we have never been in love has made me long to throw myself out of the open car window. Silence may save my own life.*

*Charles finally parks the car, or rather leaves it in the middle of what appears to be a driveway. We have not seen another vehicle since we left the train station in Gainesville and Charles has done nothing but complain. I see this southern jungle as a unique and absolutely beautiful world. Mr. Charles Rawlings does not agree.*

*Two smiling images of Charles, his brothers, met us at the train and insisted we immediately drive to this abandoned farm. Charles dreams of winning the damned Pulitzer Prize and they suggest he become a farmer! I had to bite my lip to keep from laughing and reminded him that we had agreed to accept whatever happens. Right now that means this dusty, palm lined, driveway and what appears to be a house that may fall over if one of us gives in to a wild sneeze or cough.*

*Charles steps out first but not before he looks at me with those lovely dark, and now hate filled, eyes, slams the door, makes a grand gesture of wiping the dripping sweat from his face and then leaves me to my own discoveries. And they come very quickly.*

*I swing my feet from the car, my ridiculous hose clinging to my thighs as if I were a cow in heat. The wide brimmed hat, which has shaded me on the drive, seems ridiculous now. I throw it on the seat as I exit and my feet finally touch ground.*

*The door closes and I am standing on sandy, hot, floral scented earth. There are birds everywhere I look—peeping, singing, shouting, welcoming me, so I think, to a land that is as foreign to me as the far away landscape of my once-dear husband's heart. The flowers—red, white, purple, yellow, a rainbow of sincere beauty, and shrubs and trees as vibrant as the July fields up north, are everywhere, as is a constant surge of heat that makes me feel as if I am standing in front of my Wisconsin grandmother's black-as-hell cooking stove.*

*I can hear Charles pounding through what must surely have once been someone's house; slated weather beaten gray boards haphazardly linked to form a building, and finally his raving no longer concerns me. I have suddenly gone blind with the beauty of this place.*

*The hot air has captured me, brushed its seductive head alongside my own in a way that makes me giggle, as if I had just consumed six glasses of my favorite whiskey. I blink twice and can see the rotting oranges in the trees next to me spring back to life. There is a long porch that needs to be built, neighbors to meet, a land to claim as my own, and as I walk blindly towards my future, dozens of stories are already boiling inside of me.*

*I raise my head into the hot afternoon sun, smile, and feel as if I have just been baptized, and then I do not so much step forward, as fly. Hardship be damned! I am rolling up the sleeves of this ridiculous blue dress as I barge past a startled chicken, pray to God there's an outhouse, and laugh so loud a flock of small black birds rise, and then join me, with a chorus of their own frightened hellos.*

—*Cross Creek Prelude* - MKR - 1941

# 1

The alligator appears so quickly Emily wonders for an insane moment if it can fly. The blink of an eye, a long breath of the intoxicating swamp-like air, a sharp corner carved out of the heart of a jungle, and the creature arrives as if by magic. She instinctively jams the brake to the floor, skidding on the loose tar-coated gravel, and the car's rear end swings so that Emily is almost parallel with the alligator. When she looks down, leans into the steering wheel and feels her heart pounding as if she has just sprinted, the alligator twists to look at her, blinks twice, and drops its head. The great black prehistoric-looking reptile is not moving and there is no way around him. Emily is trapped by an alligator and has absolutely no idea where she is or where she is going.

These three facts make her laugh, a low fear-lined rumble that rises from the top of her stomach, as she backs up her aging grey sedan and pulls as far to the right side of the narrow highway as possible, so she won't get rear-ended. Not that she's even seen a car since she turned down this unnamed primitive road. The last town or city, or whatever in the world you call places in the middle of nowhere in Florida, that she remembers before she lapsed into a driving trance was Ocala. She turned off the major highway several times for reasons she will never be able to explain. There would be an interesting-looking country road, a narrow stretch of pavement covered in a tunnel of towering oaks and waving palms, and without thinking, as if someone else were actually steering, she would quickly turn the car and be creeping down its bumpy carpet of old asphalt. There were several lefts, a couple of rights, and Emily imagined if she pointed the car back up north, where she supposedly belonged, she'd eventually get someplace, maybe even home.

*Home.* Emily snorts. Home has mostly been her car for almost two weeks and the other home, a condo in Columbus, Ohio is surely decaying at its sixty year-old foundation as she starts looking around her car for a weapon.

She sticks her head out the open car window, feels a wave of solid heat that is like a delicious warm facial, and looks at the dark monster that has decided to take a sunbath in the middle of the road.

Emily Weaver, 57, on an extended vacation from her job at Ohio State University, where she plows through endless stacks of donated historical documents, takes a breath and waits. She's very good at waiting. This woman has an extraordinary amount of patience, which often makes others think of her as easy, slow, and lacking in personal empowerment. These assessments are only correct on one account-Emily has never been able to figure out how to light her own fire. Perhaps an alligator encounter is the reason why she's where she is. Emily looks out the window and decides the very long animal is simply resting. The road isn't wide but perhaps it's a long haul for this short-legged creature. Actually, when she really looks at the width of the road, she realizes that it would be a feat of driving dexterity to not collide with an oncoming car.

"How hard can this little journey be, Buster?" she asks the unmoving critter, wondering what it would be like to be brave enough to reach out and touch it.

Emily turns the engine back on for a few seconds so she can roll down the other three car windows. She's certain alligators do not jump, even if they might fly. The hot air blows into the car and she notices a deep earthy scent that makes her limbs go weak and her eyelids drop.

The rich scent of eucalyptus surrounds her and as she breathes in the glorious scents, Emily feels as if she is sitting in the middle of a spa.

When she opens her eyes, she sees so much more this time than just the alligator. The slim road has really been carved through the center of a dense, luscious jungle. Mere inches from the edge of the highway, the world is dark and the foliage is so thick that a human would need a machete to go more than a few feet. Before the lush darkness there are so many shades of green that Emily is transfixed and closes her eyes.

When she opens them again and looks up, she is startled to see a car approaching from the opposite direction and she instinctively starts blinking the car lights to warn the driver to slow down.

There's a cloud of dust rolling behind the vehicle, and in spite of her flashing lights, the driver does not look as if he sees her.

"Damn it! Are you blind?"

Emily quickly glances over at the alligator. The wild thing is absolutely not moving. The thought of it lying dead next to her car emboldens her. She starts to beep her car horn, leans out the window, and moves her hand up and down, pointing at the oblivious black animal in a frantic wave.

"Slow down!" she screams, risking the amputation of her own arm if the driver does not see her, or what he's about to turn into major road kill.

The car is not slowing and Emily bravely decides to open her car door. This also semi-exposes her to the alligator and she hopes the grand gesture will somehow endear her to an animal who clearly owns this piece of Florida highway and who doesn't seem to be at all bothered by her gawking at him, or the approach of a speeding car.

Her open door blocks just enough of the narrow highway so that whoever is driving, unless he or she is blind, must slow down, stop, or rip her car door off its hinges. The on-coming driver finally jams on the brakes, gravel spews out both sides, and the tail end of the car wiggles back and forth and appears as if it might tip over. Then the engine dies.

"There's an alligator on the road!" Emily yells out the window as she closes the door. But when she looks down, she sees the alligator has disappeared.

Emily can see now that it's a man driving a red SUV. He opens his door for a split second, looks down the road, and she can hear him shout, "You stupid bitch!" The man looks as if he's going to lunge from his car and Emily finally realizes how absolutely insane it is to suddenly be protecting disappearing wildlife miles from civilization.

She quickly rolls up her windows and is holding her breath. Then the crazy man starts his car, slams his door so hard Emily can feel her steering wheel shake, guns the engine, and roars past her fast, throwing gravel all over the side of her car. All she can see through the haze is his middle finger sticking out of the window as he speeds past and leaves a trail of dust.

Breathless, she rests her head on the steering wheel for a moment. The alligator frightened her much less than the horrid man in the fast-moving red car. Emily knows many people blame behavior like his on testosterone. She prefers to call it simply crass.

A moment later she rolls the windows back down, lifts her head, and looks into the rear view mirror as the lingering trail of dust floats down the road. When she drops her gaze, she notices a lovely green leaf, as wide as an elephant ear, which must have blown in through the back window when she was trying to save the ungrateful alligator.

She picks up the leaf, raises it to her nose and swears it smells of perfume—something light and sweet, with a hint of lemon. Emily twirls the leaf in her hand, spins her head from side to side and doesn't see a bush or tree with matching leaves anywhere close to her car. Where in the world did it come from? She tucks the leaf into her unused ashtray so that it's brushing against her right knee, starts the car, and realizes her hands are shaking.

Before she shifts the car into drive, Emily rests her head on the steering wheel to steady herself, and the moment she closes her eyes she is suddenly overcome by a feeling of déjà vu. She's positive she's never been on this highway before but the spinning sensation now gliding through her, that perfume smell, the leaf, the heat caressing her into confusion, the alligator and the awful man, have her wondering if something's seriously wrong with her-physically and mentally.

When she turns the car back on and spies the alligator safely lying in the grass alongside of the highway, covered in a thin layer of dust from the marauding car, she has an unsettling feeling that sends a shiver up her entire spine, as if a cold breeze has just entered through the open window.

Emily shakes her head to dispel any seemingly-ridiculous notions of time travel, ghosts placing leaves in open car windows, and alligators who move out of sight in the literal blink of an eye. And when she looks behind her, before pulling back onto the road, she's absolutely certain she sees that the red car has stopped its dusty exit so the man driving it can watch her out of his rearview mirror.

## 2

Driving like a snail, lest she plow into a relative of the brazen alligator, Emily turns around a wide corner and within
minutes she's relieved to see a house. As she gets closer,
she notices that it's not just one home, but several, a cluster
of small houses and every single one of them has a slanted
metal roof that is steaming in the hot noon sun. Emily laughs
because the buildings look like huge house-shaped coffee
cups.

Slowing even more, and glad for something to take her
mind off of what has just happened, she notices that the last
cottage is surrounded by several cars and there are perhaps
five or six people milling around its yard and looking as if they
are preparing to leave.

She wonders what this nameless place might be; she
slows even more, raising her eyebrows so that her entire face
looks like a question mark. Maybe she's stumbled upon the
end of a country breakfast party.

Then she sees the sign, "Estate Sale," hand-painted on
what looks like an old wooden door, and without hesitation
Emily pulls the car over to the side of the road and all but runs
toward the house.

Surely this faded beauty has a treasure, if someone else
hasn't wandered by and scooped it up. It's an old wooden

house that is covered on the outside in peeling yellow paint. A wide porch looks as if it runs all the way around to the back of the house and the depth of the glass in the windows, thick, wavy, and glowing like a rainbow, helps Emily correctly guess that the house dates back to the 1920s. Her historian's heart, blocked by sidestepping into a safe university job, feels as if it's about to fall out of her chest. If she didn't know better, Emily would be rushing to the hospital to stop a major heart attack.

But she knows this feeling is something else, even if it's been as foreign as the waving palms in this gorgeous jungle. Years ago, before she put her unfinished thesis in a box and sealed it shut, she felt this way when she was in the library or doing field research. Her passion manifested itself in such a physical way that she was often embarrassed. She would begin to sweat, her racing heart would make her weak, her hands would shake, and even if she were doing something as simple as reading an important letter, an ancient manuscript or a lost document, it was magic to her.

Those feelings and discoveries have all but vanished over the years but now, standing by the porch while her pulse races and a screen door bangs, Emily has to force herself to focus, to remember where she is, to find whatever treasure or ghost has lured her to this remote location.

"Hey there! Where did you come from, Missy?" a male voice asks from the top of the steps, as the other cars leave.

Emily looks up and sees a tall man dressed in a white shirt and blue tie looking down on her from the top step. He could be her own tall grandfather except he has dark hair brushed to one side like Donald Trump, unlike her bald grandpa, and a wide smile that offers nothing but kindness.

"I have absolutely no idea," she says, smiling, and placing her hands on her hips. "I suppose I'm lost, but all roads go somewhere."

"Ain't that the truth," he responds, with a hearty laugh. "Let's see now. From the look of things you aren't from these parts, are you now?" Emily gazes down at her bare white legs, the toenails she painted bright red before she left Ohio, the bug bites on her arms, and realizes that she must look like she's from anywhere but wherever she is right this moment.

"It's pretty obvious isn't it?" she admits, brushing the sweat off her face, certain that he likes her anyway.

"Hell, no, it don't matter as long as you're here to shop."

"I'm shopping!" she shouts, anxious to start looking through the house.

The man comes down the steps, sticks out his hand, and introduces himself. "Bob Landers. I'm kind of the real estate, auction, yard sale, do-whatever guy in this part of the county."

"Emily Weaver. I'm the wonderful niece who drove her cranky Aunt Rena to her condo on the beach, started daydreaming on the way north, and ended up in this yard."

"Welcome, Miss Emily. This is a grand day to get lost."

Bob is a charmer. Emily has to restrain herself from spontaneously hugging him as he sweeps his left arm in front of her and invites her into the house. Not all men, she knows, are jerks.

The wooden porch slats creak when she steps on them and Emily immediately wonders whose feet wore the boards so thin. Her hand is on the screen door when she stops and turns around.

"Out of respect, Mr. Landers, can you please tell me who lived in this house that I'm about to enter?"

"I knew you were a gentlewoman," he says, moving to hold open the door. "Some folks just barge in and have no respect. This was someone's home, a special place for the woman who lived here."

Before Bob continues, she closes her eyes and imagines the woman who lived in the house. This is a sweet game she has been playing her entire life. When she went on road trips with her brothers and sisters, they would pass the time by imagining the lives of the people in the houses they passed. Their creative game has remained a part of her life. Emily still loves to imagine the lives of others, especially the lives of men and women who are no longer alive. A good part of her life's work has been piecing together the clues they left behind.

Today, perhaps because she's just survived a fairly harrowing incident with a man and a reptile, Emily feels something simple and vague about whoever lived in this house. Kindness. Quiet. Relief. When she opens her eyes, Emily shakes her head so she can focus. Perhaps she's thinking about herself.

"Leslie Kincade lived here for a very long time," Bob tells her, looking directly into her green eyes. "She moved here years ago from New York City. She was one of those almost-famous kind of writers, I guess, who left it all behind and wanted the peace that only a place like this can offer."

Emily doesn't move. She holds her breath.

"These other houses are people who came to be close to her. She was a smart, smart woman and I'd say just about everyone who was anyone in the writing world passed through here. I hear this was quite the place, and yet those of us who lived close by in these swamps and on these remote lakes, we let them be. People who come here come for a reason, and we only bother them if we're invited. We're all here for a reason, aren't we, Miss Emily?"

"I suppose that's true," she agrees, eager to get into the house. "But I'm just lost."

"Exactly," he says, smiling even wider as Emily pushes past him.

The house is quiet, musty, and there isn't much left to look at. Most of the furniture has apparently already been bought and when she walks through the bare living room and into the kitchen, there's nothing left but the old wooden cupboards that are attached to the walls, a few jars on the counter, and an old grocery note pinned where the phone must have been.

Emily smiles. Her grandmother and her mother did the same thing. When her sweet grandma died, Emily stood in her kitchen and watched as her mother lovingly took the last note off the wall, kissed it, and then held it against her heart as she sobbed. Emily can't help herself. She pulls the note off the wall and gently puts it in her pocket. Then she turns to stand in front of the kitchen sink, looks down into its yellowed bottom, and imagines all the dishes and hands and hearts that danced around it.

"This is so much more fun than looking at papers in the library," she says out loud, not caring if Bob or anyone else can hear her. "Talk to me."

Place always tells a story. Emily knows this. It is the foundation for her professional life. She knows that houses and objects and surroundings can hold secrets of the lives that passed through them. There are tattoos of life everywhere if people take the time to stop and look at them. Low scrapes on a door where a cane might have banged it open several times a day. Pencil marks near the phone where someone took notes. A tiny slice of potato peel lodged under the edge of a counter. A list or note tucked inside a cupboard door that someone forgot to remove; a note that can say pages-worth about its author.

This old house has seen a lot of life and is talking to her as if it is still alive and not waiting for its new owners. *When was the last time she was on a treasure hunt like this?* Emily sticks her head inside of the small pantry and almost staggers when she takes a breath.

"Sage. Whiskey. Onions. Earth."

The smells mingle and during her second breath there are about a dozen more; meat, licorice, grease. Lots happened in that small room. Someone loved to cook. There are three lonely jars of canned pickles swimming in long slivers of dill on the top shelf, dying to be claimed. Emily scoops them into her arms and walks toward the back door.

The backyard is nothing but garden, and when she turns her head to the right she can see a long screened porch that must be attached to the other side of the house.

Bob is outside talking with his hands to a man who is sitting in his truck. She seems to be the only person left inside the house. Emily sets down the jars by the front door and walks back to investigate the other rooms. There's a small bathroom that she ignores, and a long hall that almost looks as if it curves. Maybe it's the shadows, or perhaps the carpenter who worked on this section of the house was a drinker. Halfway down the crooked hall, there's a small bedroom on the right that is empty except for several stacks of newspapers and a dresser that's been painted bright red. Someone was a bit flashy.

Emily leans in, picks a random sheet of paper, and notes the date: January 25, 1973. Someone was also a bit of a hoarder. She moves the entire stack into the hall. She wants them all. Then she starts opening the dresser drawers. Apparently, no one else thought to do this.

There's a small box of jewelry in the top drawer, filled with assorted gold and silver necklaces, rings and bracelets, all knotted into a tangled mass. That will go with her for sure. The other drawers are stacked with clothes. Emily notes the size and decides rather quickly that she's taking everything in the dresser. If she could get the dresser in her small truck, she'd take that also.

She imagines herself as a medium even as she sucks in a stomach that has been dangerously close to more than large for several years. She's always eager for a bargain, and because of her archaeological mind, thinks it's interesting to see what someone forgot to take out of his or her pockets. This is going to be fun! But it's the next room, and what she sees on the porch, that drive her almost insane with excitement.

The entire room looks as if someone just rose from bed, pulled back the multi-colored quilt very quickly, and then left the room. Emily can also see several stacks of cardboard boxes on the porch. Before she can move, Bob sneaks up behind her and when he says, "This room's taken," Emily is so focused on her treasure hunt she screams.

"You scared me!" she shouts, bending over to catch her breath.

"Sorry, dear," Bob says, stepping around her and into the room. "I didn't want you to get too excited about this here bedroom because someone bought the whole room."

"Seriously?" Emily says, dropping her shoulders in utter disappointment.

"A woman who lives around here ran right to this room and said she wanted everything in it before I had a chance to even say how are ya."

"Everything?"

"Yep. She told me she'd be here tomorrow at noon with a truck and begged me not to touch or remove one single thing. She gave me five hundred dollars in cash, too. That's a lot of money around here. And the funny thing is, there was just a guy here a few minutes ago who was desperate to get in this room too."

Emily wants to know what the man was looking for and Bob tells her the man wouldn't say, but he was incredibly upset when Bob wouldn't let him into the bedroom. He tells Emily that the man tried to push past him and get into the bedroom and that he finally made him leave.

"I'm sorry." Emily can't imagine anyone being rude to Bob. "I suppose everyone is looking for a hidden treasure. It's been my experience that being nice gets you past the door. And it's also much easier than being nasty."

"You've got that right, sweetheart."

"So does that gain me entrance to the bedroom so I can just look?" Emily is busy moving her eyes around the room. Everything she sees is speaking to her. There's a tattered pink and blue bathrobe still hanging on the bedpost, stacks of magazines and books on the right side of the bed that no one obviously slept on, handwritten notes lying all over the table next to the bed, and a small collection of ceramic birds lined up on the windowsill.

She looks up at Bob, who's at least six feet three, and decides there's no way she can take him out if he says no.

"What are you thinking there, Miss Emily?" he asks her, moving his large hands to his hips.

"I was thinking of jumping you so I could look around the room."

Bob starts laughing so hard that he has to bend down and put his hands on his knees just like Emily did when he frightened her.

"This is my big chance," she sort of jokes, taking a step forward.

"I just don't get why anyone would be interested in these things," he says, coughing to clear his throat. "It's simply what I call *living material*. There can't be one thing of value in this room."

Emily could give Bob a twelve-hour lecture on the importance of *living material*. Museums are filled with toothbrushes, buttons, old jackets, beds, the last pencil someone remarkable held before they died. She looks at Bob, who is staring at her, and she guesses he probably has a few things to tell her about life around here as well. Living in the middle of a Florida jungle has got to hold some serious life lessons.

Before she can ask him who bought or inherited the house, what the woman looks like who purchased this bedroom of memories, or any of the other fifty questions that are lined up on her mind's runway, Bob turns and points to the screen porch.

"The woman who bought this stuff didn't say nothin' about wanting the boxes on the porch," he shares, shrugging both shoulders. "I don't know what's in those musty boxes but if you want 'em, just take 'em. After all, you have been polite and sweet. I'm havin' to lock this place up pretty soon because my wife's ordered me home for early dinner. Take a peek and I'll be back in a few minutes. If they spark your interest, I'll help you haul them to your little car out there."

Bob pounds down the hall and she can hear him locking doors and windows. Emily takes four large steps and pulls open the screen door. Suddenly, nothing but the stack of boxes matter. Later that night, Emily won't be able to remember that the porch was painted light blue and that all the holes in the screens had been sewed closed with small pieces of dental floss. She won't recall the tiny stool sitting in the corner, all the cactus plants that were perched on top of a broken wooden table right next to it, and the lovely collection of empty wine jugs lined up on the floor that looked like backwoods trophies.

Emily kneels by the boxes as if she's in front of an altar. The wooden floor is surprisingly cold and she can feel a chill go right into her bones. There are six boxes stacked in three rows, one box on top of another. The cardboard cartons are about twenty-four inches deep and each one has been taped shut with small strips of clear tape that has turned brown, as if it's been years since the tape has been applied.

Emily's hands are shaking again as she pulls the tape fastened on the top box and it doesn't budge. "My kingdom for a knife," she says, pushing the box backwards and tugging on the flap of the box beneath it. The tape pops instantly and Emily quickly pulls back the flaps and looks inside.

Without thinking, she holds her breath, dips her hands inside and pulls out a stack of typewritten papers, loosely held together by a rotting rubber band. The manuscript is in remarkable condition. It's three inches thick, the pages are double spaced, typed with a typewriter that had a lopsided *E* and a *T* that had a drooping right side, and the title, *Lost Hearts in the Swamp of Life* makes her smile.

But what erases the smile and makes her heart race and her hands sweat are the name and the date on the bottom of the manuscript. It says *Marjorie Kinnan Rawlings—1963, Big Cotton Hollow, Florida.*

Emily's head is full of fairly useless historic facts. Over the years she's trained her mind to focus, to latch on to something others might think is peculiar and keep it stored inside of her brilliant and underused mind. One of those seemingly useless facts, gleaned from her days and months and years doing research, is that Marjorie Kinnan Rawlings, the Pulitzer Prize-winning author who forever changed the literary landscape with her brilliant prose, died unexpectedly in 1953, ten years before this manuscript was written. She's almost certain of it.

Totally awestruck by her discovery, be it real or not, Emily excitedly dances out of the room to find unsuspecting Bob so she can load her treasures into the car.

But her joy is quickly erased when she finds him, red-faced and standing on the porch with his hands clenched into fists. Bob tells her that the rude man who tried to get into the back bedroom was outside circling the house in his red SUV.

Emily's heart all but stops. A red SUV? A rude man? Could this be the same man she saw on the highway? She swallows, takes in several deep breaths to slow down her heart and then gently puts her hand on Bob's shoulder, not simply as a gesture of kindness, but to calm herself as well. When she quickly turns to look down the road, she sees the orange taillights blinking as they disappear into another cloud of dust.

"Bob, are you okay?" She can see that the man must have pushed Bob to the edge.

"I'm sorry," he says, unclenching his fists. "I'm fine, but that young man was downright ignorant to come back here."

"I wonder if he was the same man who frightened me on the highway. He was in a red car too, and just as nasty."

"You didn't tell me about this," Bob says, clearly upset. "What happened?"

Emily tells him about the alligator and her encounter with the man not so far from where they are standing.

"Don't worry, Miss Emily. He's gone now," Bob reassures her, touching her hand. "We don't tolerate that kind of bad behavior around here. I should never have let him get the best of me."

Emily tries hard not to worry as Bob helps her load the boxes into the car but when she goes back inside to grab the clothes and the pickles she notices Bob looking down the road as if he's worried the red car and the man inside might return.

She can't imagine being rude or unkind to the gentle-giant of a man who has been so kind to her, but Emily knows the rest of the world doesn't operate using the same rules of life. When Bob sends her off, with another sweet smile and an unexpected hug, Emily decides to believe him and suddenly all she can think about is what's inside the heavy worn boxes that are soon resting inside of her smelly old car trunk.

# 3

*"...Then I followed the light home, blazing a trail through thick bushes and storming past doves who were too shocked to remember how to fly and then I saw the first orange tree bending against the wind and my heart beat like a wild drum."*
—*Lost Hearts in the Swamp of Life* - MKR - 1963

The first sound wakes her. A wild cackle that could be a big-mouthed bird, a witch, the flying laugh of a long dead spirit. Emily opens her eyes and is trying to decide if she should leap to her feet in terror or glide back into a dream that had her commanding an army of women dressed in long skirts who were holding burning lanterns. Then, she hears gunfire.

"What the hell!"

She falls out of bed, landing with a crack on both elbows, rolls onto her right shoulder, and is desperately trying to remember what might be happening and, for the second day in a row, where in the world she is at this particular moment.

Before she can move her mind forward, there are several more shots—*bam, bam, bam*—and then she hears men shouting. Shotguns! Emily looks down at the worn speckled linoleum floor, the boxes she has hauled from the truck that are scattered everywhere, and finally at the old mothball-smelling nightgown she's wearing that she has pulled from one of her estate sale bags, and it all comes rushing back.

She is in a roadside cabin somewhere in central Florida, where there is no cell phone reception, where people laugh when you ask them about Internet access, and where a room that includes cotton sheets that have been ironed, a hot breakfast, a semi-view of a river, and people who don't ask you questions costs only forty stinking dollars a night.

Emily raises herself up on her bruised elbows, looks at her ridiculous red toenails and says, "Duck hunting." Then she imagines she may be having fried duck and eggs for breakfast at the tiny lodge kitchen not far from her front door. *Happy Hollow*. Emily's lying on the floor of a cabin at a rustic resort called Happy Hollow. This is so perfect from what she's seen so far, the mere thought makes her smile as she struggles to her feet.

She staggers to the small antiquated bathroom, looks at her bloodshot eyes, her dark shoulder length hair that is now sticking straight out in every possible direction, and wonders how in the world she even managed to fall asleep. Does the nice woman who walked her to this cabin know she is sharing space with a crazy woman?

Emily pulls at the skin under her eyes and remembers driving away from what she thinks may be the find of a lifetime, after getting directions to these cabins from gentle Bob. She was so desperate to start going through all of the boxes that she forgot about dinner, forgot about the alligator, forgot about the man in the red car, forgot anything that had happened before she was lured into the backwoods of this *Deliverance*-like county by some unseen force.

And she is beginning to believe something mystical is happening to her. From the moment she turned off the highway yesterday, everything that she has done has been so unlike her that she can only think she's been possessed by some old swamp goddess who has jumped out of the manuscript she has discovered. It is the only explanation she can come up with for her present set of circumstances.

How many frumpy middle-aged women show up out here? The woman who took her forty dollars looked at her as if she were an alien. Emily thinks she looks plain and usually normal. "I'm so damn average it's pathetic," she jokingly whimpers, splashing water on her face. But she was in such a hurry to get to the boxes, she could have been just as rude as every other tourist who doesn't bother to share a few words with the innkeepers.

Right now, brushing her teeth while wearing a stranger's well-worn flannel nightgown at a remote hunting lodge in Central Florida, Emily actually does look about as normal as it gets, fifty miles from the interstate. But she always sees herself in judgmental ways that others do not. Emily has emerald eyes, absolutely perfect features that accentuate her high cheekbones, light olive skin and naturally curly hair that acts as if it has been trained to dance around her lovely face and kiss her shoulders by a very strict hair authority. Her straight white teeth never needed braces, and until menopause slapped her upside the head; her weight has rarely gone over the 140 pound mark, which has been just right for her five feet and eight inches. She's recently developed a small muffin-top stomach and hasn't cared enough about that reality to do anything about it.

Her friends would say that Emily's not outdoorsy or indoorsy; she's just Emily, which she sees as part of a lifelong problem. "I'm sick of blending in with the crowd," she shouted to her best friend, Bev, the night before she took off with Aunt Rena for Florida.

"Well, shut up about it and do something," Bev shouted back. "Christ, Emily, you've been on auto-pilot since you divorced, what, sixty decades ago? I love you and everything but this whining about not having a life or never doing what you want is bullshit."

Sweet Bev, not one to mince words, went on for another ten minutes, reminding Emily that she was single, her son was long gone from the nest, she wasn't too old to get the graduate degree she's been whining about for thirty years, it's been three years since she's been laid, her long lost dream of moving to New York to be close to the big museums isn't as dumb as she thinks it is and the people who really care about her are on the verge of becoming violent because they are sick of listening to her whine like a baby.

Spitting into the sink, Emily wonders if that's not why she was driving aimlessly yesterday, when she should have been picking up fresh pecans on her way back to Ohio.

Or not.

Boxes of manuscripts and Leslie's interesting house, and a lingering sense of fright, in spite of what sweet Bob said about not worrying, have Emily wondering if she's slipped into an unseen dimension, as she wipes her mouth with the over-sized nightgown sleeves.

She leans in again close to the sink. Emily knows that lately she looks distracted, which is the absolute truth. It's hard for her to be unkind, even when her friends are correct, and equally as hard for her not to be hard on herself. Her mind constantly craves a feeding of new facts and so much of what she does at her job is tedious and borderline boring that more and more she's been feeling robotic. The people with the advanced degrees are the ones who get to do the good stuff. Emily doesn't blame anyone but herself and a life path that got erased and re-drawn more than a few times. Aren't lost dreams, and the drive that propels them, part of the deal?

She's at least proud that when no one stepped up to haul her eccentric aunt south on her annual snowbird pilgrimage, she spontaneously took all her unused vacation days in one lump-a month's worth-and had absolutely no clue what she was going to do with the last two weeks.

Until yesterday.

Emily steps away from the mirror and bends down to glance out the small window, just to the left of the sink, that looks like an afterthought. It's so tiny, only a very short person would be able to stand and look out of it at eye-level. Everything that is happening seems so surreal she needs to look at something solid, something more tangible than her own reflection.

There's some kind of flowering bush planted right outside the window. It has long green stems, white flowers, and Emily braces herself against the wall and stares at the flower's bright yellow centers.

Impressed by everything she sees, Emily pushes her face up against the window and smiles, causing a small round fog where her breath hits the cool glass.

Her stomach growls, reminding her that she's famished, and of her intense reading session last night.

The first manuscript she discovered in the box while still at the estate sale appeared to be just the beginning of reams of typed pages. Emily paid for her room and all but ran into it with one box after another, so eager to see what else she had that she hadn't realized she'd all but offended her hostess, who stood slack jawed as she slammed the tiny office door in her face, then rushed back to ask about the cell phone, then the Internet, and then she didn't even turn to acknowledge it when the woman said breakfast was at nine in the lodge. And nestled into her cabin, Emily wasn't happy that her door didn't have a lock. It's one thing to be at a remote lodge where the owner convinces you everyone is safe, but Bob wasn't sleeping in her room to protect her from an angry stranger.

But the three boxes she managed to get through before she all but passed out around 2:00 a.m. were filled with notes and writings that took Emily's breath away, and distracted her from any potential danger. Were they really from Rawlings? Were some of them from Leslie Kincade? Who was Leslie Kincade? Were all the notes signed with Rawlings' initials, MKR, forged? What were these documents doing in a remote cottage in the middle of nowhere?

Emily was desperate to get to a computer by midnight, when she realized what she might have sitting in her cabin. The small bits and pieces of information she could dig out of her brain about Rawlings were limited. All she could remember was that Rawlings had won the Pulitzer Prize for *The Yearling*, a novel that was still one of the best-selling books of all time, and that she had died the year Emily had been born. Why she remembered the second detail is as bizarre to her as the fact that she is crouched down and watching flowers dance in an early morning breeze at a lodge in Florida.

And then, well past midnight, when whatever creatures live here started their nocturnal wanderings, she couldn't help but think of the man in the red car. The scratches against the side of the cabin, rustling leaves, small gusts of wind-every sound suddenly became the evil man in the fast red car. It wasn't as easy to be brave, once the outside world turned into total darkness.

Emily forced herself to focus. Her own work and life have proven to her that anything is possible. Many deceased writers and famous men and women from the past had old undiscovered manuscripts, lost writings and important letters surface years after their deaths. The word "death" is suddenly a very important word. She has to stay focused, calm, and to make certain she evaluates the boxes of papers as a professional, and not just as an overheated woman who is looking for adventure because her own life is boring as hell. She doesn't want her emotions to override the meticulous and painstaking work that will be needed to authenticate the papers she has discovered. There's a process that needs to be followed, steps to take, clues waiting to be pieced together.

"Get a grip, Agatha Christie," Emily says looking at her own eyes in the bathroom mirror. But then she strides from the tiny room, and like a junkie, is about to start obsessively reading again when she hears a dinner bell clang. A dinner bell! Breakfast must be ready. She strips off her nightgown, dives into the clothes she wore yesterday and is out the door in less than five minutes.

The walk from her cabin to the main lodge takes her all of two minutes, but Emily may as well be flying into outer space, because she's about to enter a world unlike any other. She steps lightly on round well-worn bricks that wind around towering palms. There's a huge fenced garden behind the lodge and it looks as if the owners must grow half of their food. Tomatoes, carrots, patches of green herbs and dozens of other vegetables that she doesn't recognize are planted in neat rows. It's organic farming and Emily is impressed.

The door handle on the outside of the log building where breakfast is being served is a huge deer antler. Emily smiles when the soft bone touches her hand; she can't wait to see what's inside. When she pulls open the heavy door and steps up into the large room, she's greeted by a sea of eyes. Male eyes. Male duck-hunters' eyes. The chatter she heard when approaching, the sound of silverware rattling, plates sliding across tables, and men laughing comes to an immediate halt.

Before she can figure out what to do or say, there's a gust of wind that all but pushes her inside of the lodge. It feels as if someone has come up behind her, placed both his hands on her waist, fingers pointing up, and shoved her. Emily stumbles, bangs into a table, regains her balance, and is greeted by a choir of whoops and then a lovely round of applause.

"Thank you!" she manages to shout into the room. Emily has to restrain herself from turning around and running back out the door to see if someone actually pushed her.

"Come on in," the woman who checked her in says, quickly rushing up to rescue her. "I think you were exhausted last night. You and your boxes were so distracted. My name's Beth, but everyone calls me Dessie."

"Dessie?" Emily can't see the connection.

"It's a long story. Let's get you some coffee and breakfast. You even smell like you're starving. Set your rear end down here, ignore these jackasses, and I'll bring you some food."

Emily has totally misread Beth, or Dessie, or whoever in the world she is. She's definitely not a quiet wallflower. She must run the entire lodge and maybe even owns it. How interesting there would be a woman, way out here, feeding duck hunters and probably fishermen, and maybe a wild recluse or two from the big city. If it's all true, then this Florida adventure may get better and better every day.

Before Emily has time to imagine what might happen next, Dessie sets down a platter of food in front of her that could feed half of Iowa. Eggs, pancakes, potatoes, ham, sausage and what Emily assumes are grits-a white blob perched on the edge of her plate that looks like starched oatmeal. A thermos of coffee and fresh orange juice also appear. Emily is so awestruck she can't move.

"Oh my God!"

"You'll eat it all," Dessie tells her, standing beside her with her hands on her hips. "Eat up. I'm coming over in a few minutes to have coffee with you. You're my last mouth of the morning."

Sitting at a small table for two by the window, Emily all but falls into the food and by the time Dessie is sitting across from her she has eaten everything but the plate. The hunters leave one by one, and soon it's just Emily, Dessie, and someone in the kitchen banging pans who is obviously on clean-up duty.

"Talk to me now that you're full," Dessie orders, sipping coffee and gesturing a come on with her left hand.

Emily finishes chewing her last bit of sourdough pancake and sizes up her breakfast partner. Dessie looks like she's in her forties and she obviously likes to eat what she cooks. She's about ten pounds past plump, wears her dark hair twisted in a bun and shoved under a red bandana, and she's got kind, wide and very beautiful dark blue eyes. Her large hands cradle her coffee cup as if she's holding something fragile; there are no rings, and she's got a demanding swagger that already has Emily wondering what she's going to say when she asks her why she's at the lodge.

"That was amazing," Emily says, closing her eyes in a post-food orgy salute.

"Screw bland oatmeal and whole wheat bread," Dessie laughs. "We eat real food here and just about everything is made from scratch."

"I haven't eaten like that in a while. If you weren't sitting here I'd lick the plate," Emily says seriously, picking up the plate and looking at it as if she's going to kiss it.

Both women laugh. Emily fills up both their cups and waits for the dreaded question, which comes immediately.

"What in the holy hell are you doing here, woman?" Dessie leans across the table and looks as if she's waiting for a big announcement.

Emily wonders if she should tell the truth. The truth being she has absolutely no idea what she is doing at Happy Hollow in rural Florida with a mess of duck hunters. She's surely not ready to reveal the secret that's inside the boxes in her cabin.

"I got lost after I dropped my aunt off at her condo."

"Sure," Dessie scoffs.

"It's true."

"Right." Dessie hasn't budged. She knows there's more to the story. "Who sent you to me? I don't even advertise and unless you know the road you would never have found me."

Emily tells her about Bob and the estate sale and how now that she's here she might stay another night or two.

"Satisfied now?" Emily hopes that's enough information.

"That'll do. It's odd to have someone just drive up. Odd for it to be a woman. Odd for me to even have an empty cabin. The fishing and hunting business is amazing. And by the way, it's nice to have a conversation with someone who doesn't wear Old Spice and..."

Dessie trails off for a moment. It's as if she's trying to figure something out. She looks into her coffee cup and then looks back up at Emily. "You're not running away from a guy who's about six feet tall, with scraggly brown hair, really straight white teeth and a bad attitude by any chance, are you?"

Emily is startled. "Good Lord, I haven't even had a date in about six years. What are you talking about?"

"It was the strangest thing, but last night after you escaped with all those boxes to your cabin, someone else drove up. An obnoxious man who wanted to stay here, and I'm out of cabins. We're full now. After he walked out, totally pissed that there wasn't room, I saw him looking in your car window."

Emily has been holding a sip of coffee in her mouth that she almost spits right into Dessie's face. She manages to swallow as she moves her head from side to side.

"Was he in a red car?" she squeaks out.

"Hell if I know," Dessie says, handing Emily a napkin for the coffee that is dripping down her chin. "I rolled down the window and told him to get out of here, and I never saw what he drove. I think I scared the living hell out of him."

Emily decides to tell Dessie about stopping the man in the road and what Bob said about the red SUV circling and how the man was so rude, and absolutely not about what she has been reading all night in her cabin. She's mad at herself for not asking Bob what the guy looked like so she can compare notes with Dessie.

But sensing her worry, Dessie quickly reassures her that the swamps are full of angry men who will follow someone who made them stop in the middle of the road. "He'll go home and kick the side of his house and forget about you. Don't worry about it. I'm sure it was just a coincidence."

Emily tries fairly unsuccessfully not to worry and chastises herself for not being more aware as the women talk, laugh, and drink way too much coffee. Emily shares her Ohio world and Dessie launches into her life story, which reads like an *Amazing Race* sidebar. She grew up on a ranch, dropped out of college, worked on a fishing boat in Alaska, went to a cooking school in California, hiked the Appalachian trail and then, ironically, driving through Florida, she also got lost, found this rundown lodge, fixed it up, and is living happily ever after.

Emily is impressed and jealous. Talk about opposite lives. She almost wants to apologize for being boring. She glances at her watch and is astonished to see how long they've been talking.

"Shoot! I have to drive back to the estate sale and meet someone," she says, jumping to her feet. "Can I stay tonight?"

"Sure thing darlin', as long as you agree to sit and chew the fat with me again. My God. I must have gotten a bit lonely. The testosterone level around here is sometimes overwhelming but these guys are all aces."

Emily is by the door when she remembers to ask Dessie about her name. "Dessie. By the way, how did you get that name? It's not even close to Beth."

Dessie turns slowly, pushes to her feet, crosses her arms and smiles.

"Do you by any chance remember who Marjorie Kinnan Rawlings was?"

Emily feels her entire breakfast move up about an inch in her stomach. "Of course."

"Well, she lived in this part of the state, and people still talk about her as if she never died," she shares, wondering why

Emily's face has gone white. "She had a wild, independent friend named Dessie who owned a fishing lodge just like this. Dessie and Marjorie had some adventures that would make wild women today faint. People say I remind them of Dessie. My God, those two women were fearless!"

"Dessie..." Emily whispers.

"I sort of like the nickname. The more I find out about Rawlings and her escapades, well, it's like an honor."

Emily can't move.

"Are you okay?"

"I'm fine," Emily lies.

"Get out of here," Dessie finally says, because Emily is frozen in place. "I've got to throw a huge hunk of meat in the oven for dinner."

Emily can't remember grabbing her purse, locking her cabin door, and getting into her car. All she can think about on her way back to Bob's estate sale house are the boxes waiting for her on the cabin floor, and the growing sensation that someone or something else is suddenly holding the reins to her life.

She's also convinced that this part of the world is absolutely riddled with secrets, and at least one frightening man.

There's a medium-sized covered truck backed up against the front steps when Emily skids to a halt in front of the yellow house.

"Damn it!" she yells, slamming the car door and squeezing up the steps of the house when she finally arrives. "I got here just in time."

As she walks through the front door, two men push past her carrying the bed from the back room that has been taken apart. Emily can hear someone barking at them to hurry up.

"She is something else," one of the men growls, holding onto each word as if there are marbles in his mouth.

"No kidding," the other man agrees.

Emily holds the door for them and though they don't even bother to ask who she is, both offer a relieved, "Thank you," as they struggle down the steps and hoist the metal bed into the truck.

Bob is nowhere to be seen, although Emily notices his car parked out front. Maybe the woman yelling in the back room has him locked in a closet. She tiptoes down the hall and when she gets close to the bedroom, she can see the woman standing in the now-empty room with her back to the door, hands on her hips, inhaling as if she's a lion about to attack.

"Excuse me…" Emily says timidly, taking a step into the room.

The woman whirls to face her, and Emily feels as if she's watching a human top. She is a blur of color and she's spinning and before she says a word, Emily can feel that the woman is a powerful force.

They size up each other for a few moments, and Emily can't help but smile and let down her guard. This woman is beautiful. She is black, extremely tall and her deep-set chocolate-and very large-eyes are shining. Her hair has been made up in dreadlocks and they hang past the middle of her back and are still swinging back and forth. Emily has a feeling she's also getting analyzed before they introduce themselves. The seemingly brazen woman is wearing a brightly colored long skirt, a sleeveless orange shirt covered in a red vest and both arms are filled with bangles and bracelets halfway to the elbow. Emily thinks that this woman, whoever she is, looks like a party waiting to happen.

"Can I help you?" the woman asks, still standing with her hands on her hips. She looks as if she's not at all happy to be bothered.

"I was here yesterday and Bob told me you'd be coming back..."

The woman cuts her off with a loud roar. "You took the boxes!"

Emily isn't so much startled as defensive. "Pardon me, but Bob gave me the boxes. He said you purchased this room and its contents and that I could have the boxes."

The woman steps forward until she is directly in front of Emily. "Do you have them? Did you keep them?"

There's no serious fear in this encounter as Emily realizes she has the power position now. This crazy woman is acting desperate. Emily decides to throw the woman off-balance because it's obvious she's used to being in charge. She smiles, extends her hand, and introduces herself.

Taken aback, the woman shakes Emily's hand, says her name is Silver, and when Emily says, "Of course it is," Silver breaks into a laugh that rolls out of her mouth like a cannon.

Emily can't help herself, and starts laughing too. She's always found other peoples' laughs infectious. Silver's laugh hits her right below her own throat and she swears she's either heard the same sound coming from her before, or this woman looks vaguely familiar.

"So," Emily says, boldly avoiding the question about the boxes. "Who is Leslie Kincade, why do you want her bedroom, and who in the world are you?"

Silver hesitates. She's looking Emily directly in the eyes and Emily notices something soften in this woman's face. It's subtle. Silver's eyes turn up, her jaw loosens, and then she drops her arms off her hips. She's obviously thinking and trying to decide how hard to push.

"Please tell me you're not some snoopy reporter."

"I'm not some snoopy reporter."

Silver closes her eyes; Emily guesses she's trying to decide if she should step forward or backward with this conversation. Suddenly the door leading onto the porch where Emily found the boxes bangs open, and then shut, as if an invisible ghost has just passed in or out of the room.

"A sign," Silver whispers, opening her eyes.

"Or wind," Emily says.

"It's a sign," Silver says forcefully.

The door miraculously bangs open and then shut again.

"It's a sign," Emily agrees, looking at Silver, then the door, and then back at Silver.

Silver walks away, grabs a huge beaded purse, takes out a notebook and starts writing. When she finishes she hands Emily a piece of paper.

"I was going to come find you. Bob told me you were staying at Dessie's. These are directions from Happy Hollow to my house. I have to leave right now. Come by tonight. I'll cook. And you can keep this little encounter of ours to yourself, if you don't mind. "

Emily, absolutely speechless, looks down at the directions as the door bangs again. Silver smiles and walks out of the room and Emily feels as if she's just been run over by a road grader. So much for standing her ground and being in charge for three seconds.

She walks to the banging screen door, pulls it open, closes it and then pulls it open again and walks out. She convinces herself that the wind kept pushing the door open, even though there isn't a breeze within fifteen miles of the house, and the air is thick and hot. The small stool that was in the corner of the porch yesterday is still sitting there, as are all the empty wine bottles.

Emily pulls the stool to the center of the porch, sits down, rests her elbows on her knees, and the very second she looks up, a huge white bird with a curved orange beak lands right outside the screen window.

"Another sign," she mumbles, and wonders what a white bird suddenly landing in a yard in early afternoon could possibly mean.

And then the screen door bangs again, and Emily, absolutely terrified, picks up the stool and runs straight out the porch door to her car.

**4**

*"The light in the window was an invitation. It lured me onto the porch where I swayed back and forth with the early night wind trying to decide if I should move ahead, or if I should disappear, yet again, heart and soul, into the dark night behind me."*
—*Lost Hearts in the Swamp of Life* - MKR - 1963

Emily has no clue what time people named Silver sit down for dinner. What she does know is the moment that she drove back into Happy Hollow, and was all but running toward her cottage to paw through the boxes with the stool in her hand, Dessie shouted at her from the lodge and demanded her attention.

"Hey, Ohio! Come in here."

This is how she ended up in the kitchen peeling potatoes, sipping some fabulous French white wine, and listening to Dessie unsuccessfully try to explain to her who Silver, the mystery woman, might be. Thus far Dessie has been about as revealing as a fifteenth century nun.

"It takes a while to get to know her," Dessie says, sticking her head out the back door to light up a small cigar. Dessie reveals absolutely nothing else as she puffs away.

"You smoke cigars?" Emily's certain if she hangs around long enough she may see one of everything. "Do you wrestle alligators too?"

"Smartass. I love cigars. Probably because I'm not supposed to. People think that anyone who doesn't live in the middle of all that chaos called a city must be an unrefined hick. And here you are Ohio, drinking fine French wine with a chef who won every award on the West Coast when she was in culinary school."

"You're right," Emily admits. "People chose to live in places they love if they can. Look at me. I've already gotten the nickname 'Ohio'. No one around here uses his or her real name. 'Dessie'. Now 'Silver'? What the heck! I'm going to have dinner at Silver's house, if I can find it."

"Maybe that's her real name," Dessie says, putting out her cigar and then immediately breaking what's left of it into little pieces and putting it inside of a flower pot. "Great for planting," she explains before Emily even has a chance to ask her what she's doing.

A succession of questions about what Silver does, why she's so interested in Leslie Kincade, and how long Dessie has known her, are met with simply no answer at all. Dessie does confess that she's surprised Silver has invited her to her house, and for dinner, too.

"Let's just say around here, unless you run something called Happy Hollow, people don't usually invite strangers over for dinner after giving them directions to their private homes," Dessie offers and then makes it clear by turning her back that she's done talking about the mysterious Ms. Silver.

Emily totally surrenders. Everyone here seems to be twenty paces ahead of her. Apparently there's some kind of secret backwoods code that doesn't allow anyone to say anything beyond something vague to outsiders. If Dessie knows Silver, she probably won't admit it until Silver tells her it's okay. Emily finishes her wine, peels three more potatoes, and announces she'd better shower so this Silver person will let her in the door.

Dessie is already distracted with the rest of her dinner preparations when Emily realizes she hasn't even bothered to ask her if she knew Leslie Kincade. They've been chatting about hunters and menus and Emily's been blabbing about what she does and doesn't do at work. She turns to ask her but decides Dessie will start talking about firewood or how she makes grits-anything but who Leslie Kincade was and how she came to be what people around here consider a neighbor.

As she says goodbye, and then steps out the door, Dessie turns, lets out a huge sigh and says she has a small bit of bad news for her. "I didn't want to spoil that nice glass of wine we were sharing."

"What is it?" Emily is afraid to hear the answer to her question.

"Your room is rented starting tomorrow afternoon and I'm totally booked," Dessie explains, looking as if she might cry. "I feel horrible about this, but I'm asking around to see if someone has a room for you. Are you staying for a while?"

"I have absolutely no idea," Emily says, disappointed at the news but also finding her situation somewhat humorous. "I thought I'd be back in Ohio by now. I'm kind of going day to day, which is sort of exciting for a boring librarian."

"Something will happen," Dessie reassures her with a wink. "You just wait and see."

Emily believes that's beyond true, although she's not convinced she's ready for what the universe might have up its sleeve for her here. She actually hesitates for a moment before she opens the screen door because she's certain the mystery wind is going to open and close it for her.

Two hours later, she's showered, thumbed through a few more papers in her cabin and is stopped at the entrance to the lodge. Emily's clutching Silver's hastily drawn map in her hand and wants to make certain that she heads in the right direction when she leaves. According to the map, she's about fifteen miles from Silver's home.

As she turns and heads north, which she now realizes is also left, Emily can't help but imagine what Silver's house or mobile home-because there are a lot of them, everywhere she looks-might be like. If the house looks like Silver, she may be heading towards a circus tent.

It's still light out, but Emily can glance over the tops of the far trees, mixtures of pines, palms, and lots of swaying clusters of bamboo, and see that the night is descending fast.

Everything looks new and different to her. Ohio's rolling hills, cornfields and often-frozen tundra look nothing like Central Florida. She laughs as she comes to an intersection without a stop sign, and thinks about how most people have the impression that Florida is one long orange grove surrounded by pristine white beaches.

Emily finds the landscape oddly enchanting and comforting, which is also why, she realizes, she keeps getting lost. When she comes to the next intersection, she simply stops in the middle of the road because there's no traffic. She doesn't want to get lost again but stopping for a moment also makes her remember what happened yesterday. She looks out her window and doesn't see an alligator or an approaching red car and is totally relieved.

Just then her cell phone rings, and startles her so much that she screams. It's not just the sudden sound of something that frightens her, but the uneasy reality of how absolutely vulnerable she is driving without knowing where she is going or who she might run into-—*again*. It's been two days since she's even thought about her phone, texting, and a computer, except when she's wanted to do some research. Dessie told her that reception and service are so sporadic that most people still have landline phones and couldn't care less about keeping in touch with each other 24-7. Emily declined Dessie's offer to use the phone in the lodge; she's been too focused on what is in her precious boxes to worry about checking in with anyone. And the quiet has been oddly soothing.

Fumbling in her purse in a slight panic, and astonished that the uncharged phone is even ringing, she picks it up, sees that it's Bev, and is immediately overcome with guilt and relief to be talking to someone while she's out in this wilderness.

"I know, I know," she says as she takes the call. "I'm sorry."

"What in the hell happened to you?" Bev shouts. "I've been worried sick for two solid days!"

Before she speaks, Emily has to decide what she's going to say. If she tells her about the boxes, Marjorie Rawlings, Silver, French wine in the kitchen, angry men, magical doors-pretty much everything that's happened to her-Bev will probably organize an intervention and have her committed. The truth is terribly complicated. So she decides to tell another half-lie.

"I found this very funky lodge and they don't have cell phone reception and the woman who runs it is very cool and so I've decided to stay because as you know I don't have to be back to work for almost two weeks." Emily is talking fast because the light is fading, and she doesn't want to get lost, and she really wants to get off the phone so she doesn't have to lie too much to her best friend.

"Jesus, Emily, I've been imagining the worst. People down there are serial killers, backwoodsy conservatives who just wait for innocent women to drive through the state and get lost," Bev says in all seriousness.

Emily snorts into the steering wheel and almost drops the phone, which is about to die any second. "Honey, all those people moved to California."

"Smartass," Bev says, still shouting. "Are you okay and safe?"

"I'm fine," Emily realizes she's lying now because she's still a bit terrified. "But my phone is going to die and I'll try to find a place to email you, because this is remote and the cell towers apparently haven't gotten everywhere here yet."

"Okay, but stay in touch and don't be any more stupid then you already have been." Emily knows Bev's worried and her voice has finally quieted.

"This is good for me. I kind of like it here," Emily admits. "I'm thinking about a lot of things."

Bev chuckles with relief. "That's something new!"

"I have to go. I'm sorry, honey."

"Do not bring home an alligator purse—"

Emily's phone clicks off; she's not sure if a cloud shifted or her battery died. She opens up the glove box, tosses in the phone, checks her map and makes a right-hand turn.

She's not certain if she's on Silver's driveway or a county highway. The asphalt has turned to gravel and she knows she's getting close when she sees an abandoned barn that Silver has drawn on the map, an old tractor, a grove of abandoned orange trees and then a huge sign that says, "Private."

Relieved that she's almost to her destination, Emily wonders who in the world bothers to drive out this far and trespass.

The private sign is hilarious. It's not like cars are backed up to take a look over the fence.

Silver's house is set back from the gravel road and there are outside lights twinkling in between the trees when Emily slows so she can take it all in and keep from arriving in a cloud of dust. There's a weathered wooden fence that runs parallel to the road now, and someone's taken great care to make certain twirling vines dotted with white flowers are growing on almost every section of it. When she gets close to the house, she decides that Silver, or perhaps someone she lives with, must have a very green thumb. The yard looks like a botanical garden. There are plants and flowers everywhere and when she steps out of her car she discovers a small brick-paved pathway that leads up to the front steps and ends at a lovely wide porch.

If houses speak of their owners then this house is saying, "Come on in, sit down, and make yourself at home!" Emily feels transported again. There is so much green, but even in the two days since she's actually paid attention to her surroundings, Emily can see the various shades of green, only something someone who seriously looks could see.

Mesmerized by the house and vibrant colors everywhere, Emily walks up the steps and stands by the front door. The house is painted a pale green and almost disappears into its surroundings. There are bright flowers and tall plants inside pots that are lined up and down the steps and all over the porch. Emily wonders who comes to sit in the fading canvass chairs. Dessie? Bob? Silver's children? Gypsies?

She has a sudden urge to sit down, put her head back, and watch the rest of night descend on this mysterious land, when she hears the unmistakable bellow of Silver from inside the house.

"Ohio! Get in here. You can sit out there later if you're a good girl."

Emily almost drops her jaw onto the porch floor. Well, of course Silver and Dessie know each other. It's not as if there are a few thousand local residents out here. More like a few hundred. Half the county already probably knows she drives a beat-up sedan, found the manuscripts, is staying at Dessie's, has been nicknamed Ohio, is having dinner at Silver's and has absolutely no idea what she's doing. Some of them might even know the guy in the red car.

"Coming!" she shouts back, then quietly adds, "Enough of this Southern intimidation."

Emily talked Dessie out of one of her bottles of wine just before she left so she wouldn't feel like a piker. She's ready to meet Silver on her own turf, produce the wine, and get to it when she's stopped dead in her tracks the moment she walks in the front door.

Silver's house isn't just a house-it's an entire world.

Color schemes be damned, because the moment she steps inside, Emily feels as if she's just arrived on the back-side of a rainbow. One red wall here. A blue wall there. The ceiling in the large living room is yellow-and not just any yellow but bright, bold yellow. Emily is stunned into silence. She rotates her head and realizes that Silver has also brought the outside into her house. There are piles of rocks, plants, strands of moss draped over the two very slow-moving ceiling fans she can see from just inside the door.

Emily feels as if she's been drugged. Silver is cooking something pungent and so flavorful, even if she can't identify what it is, that she has to close her mouth to keep from drooling.

"Are you shy or what?" Silver shouts from the next room.

"This isn't a duplex in Columbus for God's sake," Emily responds. "Give me a moment to compose myself and pick up a rock."

Silver laughs and the echo of it feels as if it's riding up Emily's leg, her stomach, her arm and right into her hair, almost as if it's something physical.

"Get in here, city girl. You'll get used to the colors and this grand world soon enough."

Emily obeys and simply walks forward and makes a sharp turn left. She's glad to be off the lonely highway and safe inside this wild planet. The kitchen is a steamy paradise that's obviously been remodeled. The back wall has been punched out; it looks as if the kitchen's been expanded. There's a huge glass window facing the backyard, which even in the fading light looks out onto a magnificent expanse of gardens, walkways, and what Emily thinks must be a path towards the river she noticed zig-zagging through the fields close to Silver's house.

There's a large round oak table on the far side of the kitchen, stacks of books everywhere, a huge sliding glass window in front of it that that looks as if it adjoins another back porch, and suddenly there are one, two, three dogs yipping at her from that very porch and jumping up and down like little balls on strings right outside the window.

"Girls!" Silver shouts, clapping her hands, "Settle down! This is Ohio. She's been invited. Now go play."

"They're all yours?" Emily has moved into the kitchen and is leaning over to look out the first window.

"Unfortunately, and they're all teenagers. I don't let them into the kitchen when I cook. They think they own the place, and, honestly, they do. I need to throw my weight around now and then."

"I grew up with tons of hunting dogs," Emily shares, still cradling the wine. "Our dogs were always kenneled outside but my brother used to sneak them in all the time when my mom was gone."

Silver is stirring something in a huge cast iron pot on the stove and looking over her shoulder. She laughs and says that she's certain Emily's mom knew. "My dogs are all mutts rescued from here and there, and I finally had to stop myself because I'd have a hundred of them," Silver admits. "They're little guard dogs, friends who keep me from talking to myself when I'm lonely, and just like me, they have a pretty good way of telling when they think someone or something's good or bad."

"I hope the jumping means they like me," Emily says, bending down to put her hand on the window, as if she's about to pet them.

"They're still deciding," Silver says, smirking.

"It must run in the family," Emily fires back.

Even with the sarcastic give and take, Emily feels absolutely at home. There are candles burning on the back counter, soft lights above the table, and brightly-colored braided-rugs on the shiny wooden floors. Everything is comforting and comfortable. For an insane moment, she feels as if she could lie down in the middle of the table, curl up, and sleep for a week.

"You okay, Ohio?" Silver has stopped stirring and is staring at Emily.

Emily imagines she looks dazed, drab, and confused to this together-looking woman. Silver is dressed tonight in black tights with small silver buttons running up the sides, a long blue cotton tunic, the same bracelets she had on earlier, and a dark-patterned blue scarf holding back her gorgeous hair while she cooks. She looks as if she has just wrapped up filming her latest country cooking show.

Emily quickly looks down at her seedy flip-flops, baggy white T-shirt, bare arms, and her faded denim driving shorts and knows she's totally outclassed. How did this happen to her? She looks like an under-employed middle-class white geek from the Midwest.

"I feel like I've been here before," she answers, standing right where she is. She doesn't want to let on that she's a big baby and afraid to drive alone on a country highway and that the tension from the past two days has finally caught up with her.

"You mean, here, in this house or this state or this time or...?" Silver has now set down her spoon and is walking toward Emily as her words fade.

"I suppose all of the above," Emily replies.

There's something about Silver that exudes confidence. She's a strong, tall, obviously bold woman who lives in the middle of nowhere, collects dead women's furniture, and invites strangers over for dinner.

Silver stands in front of her, puts one hand on Emily's shoulders in a quick gesture of kindness and says, "I don't believe in that reincarnation bullshit. I think you're tired. Everyone loves this house because it's so me, and everyone-well, most everyone-loves me too. I'm pretty much a 'what you see is what you get' kinda woman, and I can't stand being pushed around."

There's no way Emily can stop herself from smiling. Silver is towering above her like a female giant. "You're absolutely nuts aren't you?"

"Pretty much," Silver agrees, dropping her hand. "And if you aren't going to open that wine, then get the hell out of here."

Emily salutes and shakes her head to keep herself in the moment; the wine flows as easily as the conversation, even if neither one of them immediately begins discussing the boxes Emily discovered, or the entire bedroom Silver purchased. The two women are dancing around each other, cautiously, while the dogs finally lie quietly outside on the porch.

Silver has made seafood gumbo and the rich scent of garlic, unknown spices, simmering sausage, shrimp, scallops and whatever magic she has put into it is making Emily's mouth water. She's dying of curiosity and would love to see the rest of the house, but Silver doesn't offer. What secrets are down the hall and behind closed doors? Emily hasn't noticed telltale signs of anyone else living in the house and yet she gets the feeling that everyone she's met seems to be holding in secrets.

The women sit at the kitchen table drinking wine for a half hour, making small talk while the dogs occasionally whine, bark, scatter and do it all over again as if they have been practicing the routine for years.

It doesn't take Emily long to realize that Silver is being just as evasive as Dessie. They have talked about Happy Hollow, the weather, the roads back and forth between this house and the next town over, dogs, alligators and banging screen doors. But Emily doesn't really know anything about Silver's life beyond that. Who is she, really? Why does she live out here? Why did she buy a dead woman's furniture and most importantly-what in the world is Emily doing eating gumbo while this woman's dogs fly around outside her window?

Silver is explaining the nuances of cooking gumbo when Emily decides it's time to act as brash as her hostess.

"Okay, Silver, I feel as if I'm in the middle of some kind of mystery that everyone knows about but me," she begins, setting down her spoon. "We're chit-chatting like a couple of old ladies, but I have no idea what I'm doing here, who you are, where those damn boxes came from, or what in the world I should do or say next."

The word boxes lights up Silver's face like a summer sunrise. "Did you open them yet?"

"Partially."

"And...?" Silver's leaning so far across the table she's almost in Emily's lap.

Emily hesitates, and for good reason. She's not going to give away anything until she gets more than a bowl full of gumbo and a walk though this fantastic kitchen.

"How about if we trade information? I have no idea how to get anyone around here to tell me anything but what's for dinner or which road to take."

Silver throws back her head and laughs into the ceiling. The table shakes, the dogs jump, and Emily almost feels like barking herself. Silver starts to explain what the people are like who live in the backwoods, what's left of the evergreen hammocks, along the creeks and isolated riverbanks in this part of Florida, and then stops herself. "It's complicated," she admits. She tells Emily that this part of the world is riddled with secrets and with people who have embraced quiet in ways that people in other places have not. She says there's really no written code of secrecy here but it's something newcomers, many who don't last long, come to understand as time passes-if they manage to survive.

Emily tells her it sounds like a cult. Silver doesn't disagree but says it's so much more than that. She tells her that an understanding grows, not unlike a plant that is tended and fed and cared for with great affection. People in the backcountry are not trusting by nature; the trust has to be earned and that takes time.

She explains that someone might help change a tire and then drop off a pie and then a month or two later they'll offer a neighbor-—a neighbor in these parts being anyone who lives within a five-mile radius- —a drink. And she's not talking about water. She's talking about bourbon or whiskey or something called corn jack that is made in just about every garage or backyard shed this side of the state line. Then more time will pass, and someone might feel as if they need to ask a neighbor a favor. It might be something as simple as getting a ride to the clinic in Gainesville, or borrowing an extra bale of hay. It could be that someone needs money before the next paycheck, or just to sit and talk over a cup of coffee.

Nothing ever happens fast here, Silver says, especially relationships and the trust needed to sustain them. She says the sun sets and rises slower, the seasons-and there really are seasons-are longer, and the wind is so slow that even on days when you think a door won't bang-there's a slow, secret, unseen movement of air.

"So what you're saying is that if I move here, that maybe in five or ten years I'll get my questions answered?" Emily is absolutely serious.

"Well, there are exceptions to the rule," Silver says with a grin as wide as her gumbo bowl, as she leans back and places her hands behind her head.

"It seems like a good place to get lonely though." Emily isn't really asking a question, but observing what she thinks is obvious.

Silver hesitates for a moment, drops her head back, and then pushes it back down and says, "Yes. It can be a lonely place."

Then it's as if a mask is lowered over Silver's face. Her eyes close for a few seconds, her jaw tightens, and it's obvious to Emily that she's not interested in elaborating.

Emily decides to back away from discussing emotional issues, like isolation and loneliness. It's impossible not to like Silver, but it's also clear she's not the kind of woman you push for direct answers if those answers aren't ready to be released. While Silver is on pause, Emily is also thinking about how her own life of semi-isolation, her practiced routines, and the way she has limited her own relationships have cut her off from engaging conversations and the professional talents she developed years ago when she was studying.

Beyond searching for clues in abandoned houses, and sifting through the physical remains of a life, you can also observe a person silently and get to know them. Do they like to touch you when they speak? Is there eye contact? Do they hesitate before they answer a question or are they spontaneous? Emily is remembering all those physical clues and how exciting it was when she had a class assignment that turned her into an unseen reporter. One day without warning in anthropology class, the teacher dispersed them around campus and made them observe two different people sitting in the commons area outside the cafeteria. Unlike half the class, Emily loved the assignment, and now observing the way Silver closes her eyes, shifts her weight, uses humor to warm the room makes her long for a new assignment, which is exactly what she has sitting in front of her.

Emily smiles as Silver opens her eyes and instead of pressing forward with an emotional interview when Silver clearly does not want her to, totally changes the subject. She asks Silver if she knows a guy who owns a fast red car. Silver tips her head, looks puzzled, and wants to know why. After Emily explains, Silver looks concerned. She's pushed herself forward and is drumming her hands on the table.

"You're the second person who's asked me about a guy in a red car today," she shares. "Apparently, whoever he is, he was at the grocery store buying a mess of food, all kinds of supplies, and asking a lot of questions."

"Does anyone know who he is?" Emily is trying hard to calm the quiet rumble inside of her mind.

"No," Silver tells her, shaking her head back and forth. "But lots of people come here to hunt and fish and be alone. We watch each other, though. You might not see us watching each other, but we do. The very fact that someone else told me about him means he's being watched right now."

"Should I worry?" Emily realizes this means she's also being watched.

Silver closes her eyes, moves her hand band and forth and says to forget about it. "I think a woman always has to be cautious," she advises. "Be alert and aware but don't stress yourself out because of this. You know what they say about men who have to drive around in big flashy, fast cars."

Emily's not certain how she feels about everyone watching everyone else, even if it's out of protective kindness, and her newly awakened professional and personal interest in details has her about to ask what else the man had in his shopping cart besides milk and eggs, but she lets it pass. When Emily leaves an hour later, she only knows two more things. Silver isn't married and she left an entire and as-yet-unmentioned life behind when she moved to what she now calls Jeeter's Old Hammock. Who Jeeter is-or was-Emily has yet to know. But Emily has met the jumping dogs, had the best gumbo of her life, can't help but like the illusive and apparently lonely Silver, and still has the secret contents of the boxes all to herself.

Emily is almost certain Silver has no idea what's in the boxes. She's surely interested in finding out but unwilling, so it seems, to part with some of her own secrets to do so. Maybe she knows something Emily doesn't, or she could simply be bluffing. Either way, Emily's not about to give away her best card, even though she has an almost irresistible urge to tell this wild woman everything. Emily has already opened up more than she's wanted to. Silver knows about her job, her abandoned love of searching for historic secrets, her way-too-quiet Ohio life.

Even though she's disappointed, Emily realizes her evening with reluctant Silver is part of some new beginning. She will have to be patient. They part amiably but at a slight impasse, with lots of unanswered questions and Emily's laughing promise to stop by in the next day or two to borrow a cup of sugar.

Buoyed by the fact that unseen good forces, and not just the evil ones, are now watching her, Emily convinces herself that she doesn't mind the dark drive back to her cabin. She's almost back to the lodge before she discovers that one of Silver's dogs has jumped into her car through the open window and is dead asleep in the back seat.

"What in the world?" she says when she hits a bump. The dog yelps, jumps out of the back seat, and then snuggles into her lap like it's been there a hundred times before. The dog looks like a cross between a large poodle, a beagle, and a basset hound. She's a wild ball of warm fluff and when Emily looks into her huge brown eyes she can see why Silver couldn't resist her either. And the thought of having a barking dog in the car is more of a comfort than she'd admit to anyone. The unlit roads are absolutely black and even though she would never call herself afraid of the unknown, Emily is actually far from comfortable given everything that's happened.

She turns around, drives back to Silver's house, not entirely thrilled about backtracking, until the dog begins licking her forearm and she starts to giggle. This is the same moment when Emily sees that a valley of blossoming stars are starting to hang themselves in a long swooping pattern across the sky. She's so besotted by the bright twinkling planets dancing against the dark sky that she almost goes off the highway.

When she turns back into Silver's long drive, there's not one light on in the house. She's only been gone fifteen minutes and Emily is befuddled. Silver either took off for parts unknown or is sitting alone in the dark.

The dog hops out of the window before she can even stop the car and barks twice as if to announce its homecoming. When Emily swings her car in a large circle without stopping and heads back to the lodge, she doesn't notice Silver lying in the front yard, arms spread like a scarecrow, watching the very same stars brighten the November sky.

When she pulls back onto the highway, the bright sky fades for a moment as a rush of clouds passes overhead. Emily instinctively rolls up her windows and locks all the car doors. When she glances into her rearview mirror, she notices the sudden appearance of a vehicle behind her and her stomach twists into a huge knot. Without realizing it at first, she begins to accelerate, which is terribly dangerous on a dark, unfamiliar highway. But the car behind her also accelerates, as if it's trying to catch up.

Emily thinks about making a fast U-turn and driving back to Silver's. But Silver might not even be there. Then what? She slows the car and the car behind her, which has narrowed the distance to less than a few blocks, slows as well.

"Shit!" Emily goes faster and tries to reason with herself, but gets absolutely nowhere. When she finally sees the turn-off for Happy Hollow, she's so relieved she almost runs the car off the road.

She drives quickly toward the cabins, and the car behind her races past on the side of the road, raising dust and making it impossible for Emily to see if the car following her was a red SUV.

# 5

*"I opened my eyes and there was nothing but early morning light and when I looked up there was a trail, a path barely visible, and I did not hesitate but moved forward and oh what a journey I had started! What a journey!"*
—*Lost Hearts in the Swamp of Life* - MKR - 1963

Emily's tormented night ends abruptly when she wakes suddenly to nothing but silence. It takes her a few moments to remember where she is, what day it is, and why she feels as if she's been drugged, and needs to shake her head back and forth to wake up her mind.

She lies absolutely still, and then remembers popping open the window above her bed after reading for several hours and eventually falling asleep while mentally wrestling with herself for what seemed like forever. She desperately wanted to feel some air coming in through the window, but she was also terrified someone had seriously been following her. She finally rummaged through the drawers in the cabin and found a fork and butter knife that she kept in one hand while she continued to read. She decided, at the very least, she could maim someone, and the feeling of having at least one thing to defend herself with might have looked ridiculous, but it made her feel better.

She remembers that sleep, when it came, was interrupted by occasional panic and by recalling what she had been reading. Halfway through the alleged Rawlings manuscript, Emily had to admit that whoever had written it was beyond an average writer. The book was set in rural Florida and centered on a woman in the late 1950s coming to grips with her own unhappiness while living in a place where women were expected to be tough, strong, and yet still follow the unwritten rules that ordered a patriarchal society. The protagonist was a woman torn by the way she had been brought up, always lived, and half-heartedly raised her own four daughters, yet she was slowly creeping toward the changes that so many other women faced in the late fifties and early sixties.

Emily had started making notes in the margin while she read: "amazingly perceptive"; "realistic characterization of rural life"; "characters perhaps based on living models". She felt as if she were back in school, researching, as she turned page after page and realized she was getting lost in a story that totally transported her back in time and to a place-perhaps this very place.

Alone, lost in her reading and, admittedly, in her own life, Emily started to talk herself out of whatever in the world she was doing. Anyone could have written this book. There was no magical wind or supernatural or mystic force guiding her through these palm tree-lined back roads. Dessie was just a lodge owner, cook, and sweet woman who was starved for female conversation. Silver was obviously a flashy old lonely hippie who couldn't give it up. Leslie Kincade was just an eccentric writer who got kicked out of her own literary world. Mr. Small Penis in the red car simply had a neck that matched the color of his vehicle. Marjorie Kinnan Rawlings most likely really did die in 1953 and Emily Weaver was simply a fifty-seven-year-old nutcase who needed to go home, take a yoga class, get some therapy, and stay the hell out of Florida.

These thoughts paraded back and forth through her mind for hours. Emily lay prone on the single bed with the manuscript pages lying around her, her hands resting on her chest, eyes on the ceiling and her mind jumping like one of Silver's frisky dogs. She fell asleep that way, with one utensil in each hand, and struggled to make a decision, uncertain about where she would even stay if she decided to keep doing... what? Looking for remnants of a dead woman? Getting answers to questions that didn't have answers? Yet she had the time. She had the boxes. She had a set of clues that were pulling her in as if she were a hunk of loose metal being yanked by a magnet that had some kind of great power.

The early morning's absolute silence, folded against the darkness, startles Emily almost as much as the gunshots she heard the day before when she abruptly wakes up. She's surprised to see that she's lying in the same prone position she was in when she must have finally fallen asleep, and there's a fork in her hair and a knife lying under her left arm. She's relieved to be alive. There are manuscript pages all over the floor. It almost looks as if someone had crept into the room, pulled them off her chest one by one, and made a twisting path throughout her room.

Did they fall while she was sleeping? Emily seriously wonders if someone has been in her room to lay out a secret paper trail. She sits up, bunches the remaining pages that are all over the bed and her chest, and sets them to the side. Then she swings her legs out of bed, and follows the trail to the door. She's barefoot, wearing the old nightgown, and when she pulls open the door and steps outside, the world remains absolutely silent. She hesitates and then turns back, fishes the knife and fork out of the bed, and does something she did when she was a little girl.

Emily looks in the bathroom, under the bed, in the tiny closet and all around her fairly small cabin to make certain she is alone. Her little-girl-bogeyman routine has been replaced by a grown-woman routine that has her feeling absolutely paranoid. She's telling herself she has every right to feel this way, considering the events of the past few days. Emily's mystified by how suddenly wide-awake she is, and her rising desire to follow the paper trail that leads to the door of the cabin.

She has no idea what time it is. Near dawn? Emily walks back outside and stands absolutely still for a moment, then she crosses her arms even though it's not cold and is careful to hold onto her utensils-turned-weapons. In Ohio she'd be wearing a down coat, snow pants, and winter boots. She rocks back and forth for a few seconds and spontaneously decides to follow the small rock path that leads away from the lodge.

Emily realizes she could be putting herself in danger and she's uneasy as she starts to walk. Driving in the middle of nowhere is one thing, but no one knows she's about to take a walk in the dark. It's stupid, she realizes, considering the building sense of danger she's felt when she thinks about the man in the car showing up at this very lodge, Bob's encounter, and the strange car last night. Emily convinces herself that this is no time to be a coward, even as a cold shiver runs up her spine and makes her shake like a wet dog.

There are no lights but she can see the white stones that form the path, tiny specks of light in the far off distance, and she inches along until her eyes totally adjust to the outside darkness. She keeps walking and is surprised that she doesn't hear animals crunching old leaves, twigs breaking from tiny claws, wind in the trees. It must be that silent hour before the world begins to stir. The silence is comforting and even though one part of her wants to run screaming back to the cabin, another part of her feels totally compelled to move forward. She's focused on watching for movement, listening for the sound of footsteps, and realizes that she's clutching the fork and knife so forcefully her arms are beginning to cramp.

The path is very straight and she follows it past several peeling wooden benches, a huge birdhouse, Dessie's garden brush pile and ever-thickening patches of shrubs. Emily wonders what the names of the trees, bushes and flowers are as she creeps on her tiptoes, farther and farther away from her cabin, as if she's the one stalking.

Even though Emily realizes she's walking away from the security of being near Dessie, who could probably hear her scream, and a mess of hunters with guns and real knives, there's no going back in her mind now. Maybe her imagination has gotten the best of her and Silver is right. Women do need to always be on guard, and the jerk in the red car has probably moved on. Powered by this thought, she starts walking with her entire foot and not just her toes after a while, stepping easier, striding faster, curious now to see where the trail ends up.

The path narrows and Emily drops her arms and stifles a scream when she feels the shrubs brushing against her. It's just the bushes, she tells herself, stopping to catch her breath. Surely there must also be bugs and spiders and who knows what hiding on the branches. Emily takes a moment to look around before she moves forward, and imagines the world that surrounds her could be filled with hundreds of watching eyes. What in God's name is she doing walking through the dark jungle in her nightgown with a fork in her hand? She brings her arms back up as if she's protecting her face with the silverware and questions her own sanity, while a group of white moths suddenly arrive, begin circling her, and nearly make her faint with surprise.

Emily wonders too how is it that until the last few days she's been so afraid-afraid of the dark, of moving forward, of taking a path that has no road signs or directions. Right now it seems to her that one day she was a cocky teenager, smoking joints with her best friend behind her garage and talking about all the worlds there were to conquer, and the next she was rolled up in a tiny ball in a condo she disliked immensely, watching reality shows on the weekend.

How does that happen? How does a life slip away? How do the Leslie Kincades of the world or the Emily Weavers turn into a Dessie or a Silver, who appear to live just as they damn well please?

Emily shakes off her questions, shoos away the moths and inches forward. She has no idea how far she is walking. It's as if she's back in the car just two days ago, watching those trees dance and thinking that an hour has gone by when it's only been a few minutes. She walks on and feels as if she's getting close to water. Because of the darkness, Emily's senses are heightened-she actually smells water, or perhaps it's the duck hunter's lake, or the river or creek running into it. She almost turns around and runs back to the cabin. How easy would it be to push some strange woman into the water, drown her, and then drag her off to the swamps so the alligators could feed on her?

Emily slaps her imagination back down and continues. The path is now damp and the stones taper until they disappear and Emily is walking on cool, thick, dark earth. There's a moment of sweet relief because her feet feel glorious! Imagine not wearing shoes outside in November! Emily walks faster now, the soft earth has given her confidence and she's hoping to see morning light before she has to walk back through the menacing jungle.

Finally, she sees where she's going. There's a small clearing that looks like it was chopped out of the bush a long time ago and what appears to be an old wooden pier where the hunters have tied their skiffs. She can't be sure, but it looks like a creek that fans out and most likely leads into the lake, which apparently has fabulous duck hunting.

Emily gingerly walks onto the pier, taking one small step at a time to make certain it will hold her weight, walks to the end, and sits down with such great relief she almost feels like crying. She sets down her weapons, shakes her hands and is absolutely stunned by the calm and quiet. There isn't the sound of a freeway, car horns, the buzzing of electric wires, people talking. She hears the quiet.

Then she closes her eyes for a moment, tips back her head, and feels as if she's taking a bath in the lack of sound. Emily realizes that might be ridiculous to anyone she tried to explain this moment to, but somehow she feels as if something is slipping away, perhaps years of unwanted noise, and something else is moving closer.

Before she has a chance to think more about her profound pre-dawn adventure, she hears a sound and throws her head up, grasps for the fork and knife, and stops breathing. It's the rustling of something moving behind her in the scrub and she swears she can hear soft footsteps-one, two, three, four. The clear thought that someone could indeed have been following her and that she is now alone on this pier takes her breath away. Emily feels absolutely vulnerable and city-stupid as she sits frozen on the pier. How absolutely insane it is to be posing as a sitting duck herself! Before she can decide what to do, she hears more footsteps, this time just two, and the unmistakable sound of something touching water. She feels as if she may be ill. Emily doesn't want to turn but there's a soft sucking sound, and she can't help it-she turns slowly and the animal, not a man, notices her, and looks directly into her eyes.

It's a deer. Emily takes in a much-needed breath as the graceful animal pauses and a waterfall of relief cascades through her entire body. She thought someone had been following her. All she can think about now is *The Yearling,* which made Marjorie famous and won her the Pulitzer Prize. Emily pushes way back and recalls it's a story about a deer and a boy moving from the emotional oasis of childhood to the realities of life as a young man. Maybe the book was about this deer's great-grandfather, she muses, as she drops her hands in utter relief.

"Are you related?" Emily whispers, not sure if she's serious or intoxicated by the adventure and the cascading feeling of the adrenaline that's rushing through her entire body.

The deer's ears twitch. Emily will later swear to anyone who will listen without laughing that the animal then nodded its head up and down twice, and gently leapt back where it came from.

Emily's own startled laugh echoes across the creek and out into the scrub and she wonders if people back in Ohio can hear her. She throws back her head, sucks in some sweet morning air and knows now that she no longer has a choice, no matter who might be following her. She feels as if this Florida world has complete control over her. Perhaps it was even her own ready-for-a-change inner self who laid a path of manuscript pages to her cabin door. She has got to go find a library, she has got to go through all those boxes, she has got to-first of all-go get dressed, and a bit of caution when venturing out might not be a bad idea either. Just because she never saw anyone on the trail does not mean there wasn't someone there.

Halfway back to her cabin she meets a herd of duck hunters led by Dessie. They all scream when they see a woman dressed in a flowing nightgown moving towards them with silverware in her hands, and Emily laughs again.

"What in the hell are you doing?" Dessie asks, throwing her hands to her chest in an exaggerated show of fear.

"I woke up and took a walk."

"Lovely hiking gear," she snorts, pointing to the silverware and then to the nightgown. The duck hunters are lined up behind Dessie and look like school kids on a field trip.

"When you get the urge, sometimes you just have to follow it," Emily says with a shrug, totally lying about how terrified she was just moments ago.

"There's coffee in the lodge, Ohio, and you don't have to bring your own fork," Dessie tells her, waving the men forward. "Don't mind her. She's here as part of a special program."

Emily laughs all the way back to her cabin, where she finds a note taped to the outside of her door.

"Now what," she says, yanking it off and ripping it open.

*Ohio,*

*Thanks for bringing my dog home. Sometimes she drives me to town. Come stay with me when Dessie kicks your sorry ass out of there today. I've got room and, besides that, you need to borrow some sugar and we have some business to discuss. A girl can't be too careful, either. I may eventually even be bold enough to talk about the loneliness issue you saw me avoid last night. That's a big maybe.*

    *Later Alligator*

    *Silver*

Emily doesn't even bother to wonder why Silver was driving past the lodge before sunrise. She takes a shower, gets dressed, packs up her few possessions and her boxes of literary treasures, and decides to have another whopping big Florida breakfast before she finds the closest library. After that, who knows what will happen. Emily's almost certain an animal, a strange woman, or a messenger dressed in white will tell her what to do and where to go.

Little Juniper Lake looks like it's half-abandoned. Dessie said the nearest library is small but they have flush toilets and computers and the one and only librarian, Shirley, will be glad to help her as long as she doesn't hog the computer.

    Emily is so full of bacon and eggs and homemade blueberry waffles that she wants to lie down in her car and hibernate. But she's also had six cups of coffee that were so strong she wonders if it doesn't double as car oil in case of an emergency out here. She could lie down on her car seats, but she'd just levitate.

    The library is nestled behind what must have once been a bustling train station. When Emily pulls into the small gravel parking lot, she is all but mesmerized by the old building. Its tin roof is rusty but still guarding a long, elegant brick structure that must have seen the faces of generations of travelers. Could there still be treasures locked inside? Does the train still go through here? Did Rawlings drive over here to catch the train to New York City? Does anyone but her know the literary history of this region could be on the verge of exploding once again?

Closing her eyes, Emily imagines a world not so far gone from this one. Dusty streets, horse hooves pounding night and day, a farmers' market around the corner. A place where life was always slower, more cordial, perhaps even kinder, in spite of the sometimes unforgiving sun, than living in a place where you might not even know your own neighbors.

The pull of the past has always excited Emily. When most of her friends were trying out for school plays or sports teams, she was usually reading history books, begging her parents to take her to museums, or watching old movies. Even before that, when she was a little girl, her parents were concerned because she was constantly dragging home rusty objects she found when she was out playing. She littered their small garage with tin cans, keys, an old wagon, rocks she thought were Indian artifacts-absolutely anything she could find that might be older than she was.

In college, when she was torn between history, library science, historical documentation, archeology and anthropology, she messed around so long taking a variety of classes it took her almost six years to get an undergraduate degree.

Even now, the decisions she'd made after that are still painful. She took a job at the city library and thought about applying to graduate schools that had historical and documentation degrees. Emily thought about a lot of things, but never really did anything. She passed up a chance to go on an archeological dig to Greece with an old professor. When her friends started to marry, she started to panic. An old college roommate invited her to move to New York City with her, but Emily was afraid to give up her job.

Remembering it all now, Emily thinks that she must have lived in fear most of her life. She married because she was afraid no one else would ever ask her. Convinced she loved the smiling banker who was absolutely the most boring male in Ohio, she took a library job at the university that was at least close to what she thought she wanted to do, had a son, divorced, and then drove her aunt to Florida. The thrills one might expect to have out of life have been totally non-existent.

"You're a piece of work, Emily," she mutters, slamming the car door in disgust, turning her back on the stately train station, and heading into the library.

The library is really the old post office. Before Emily walks in through the door, she can see the lettering on the windows that hasn't quite faded from the pounding Florida sun. This excites her almost as much as the train station. She immediately begins imagining who came to mail and retrieve letters, and lost in thought, almost trips on the last step.

"Excuse me?" An extremely thin woman, with small black glasses hanging on the tip of her nose, strands of grey hair sticking up as if they belong to a spider's web, and fingering a triple strand of neck pearls, is sitting behind the front desk.

Emily can't take her eyes off the pearls. Who wears pearls, except to a wedding? "I'm sorry. I was mumbling."

"Well, dear, we're one of those old-fashioned libraries where we like to keep everything nice and quiet so people can think. Isn't that something unusual?" The woman has risen to her feet, and she's as short as she is thin. Emily considers her five feet five inches average and this woman is at least four or five inches shorter.

"I work in a library that's quiet too," Emily whispers, putting out her hand. "Emily Weaver."

"Lovely, that's just lovely. You can call me Shirley, because that's my name! And thank heavens you know what a library is and how to use one," the librarian says, pursing her lips. "I'm sick of people coming in here and expecting me to hold their hands."

Emily decides every single person she has met thus far in this corner of the world is a unique character, as she asks about using the computer. She does admit that she's doing some research about Rawlings as long as she's in the area, and Shirley lights up as if she's just been plugged into a wall socket. The librarian grabs her by the hand, walks her into the library, past several rows of books and when they get to the very back-which isn't far at all because the library is tiny-there's a literal shrine to Rawlings. There are books and photographs, an entire bulletin board filled with old photocopied newspaper clippings all about Rawlings, and Emily feels as if she has just won the lottery.

"It must be national Marjorie Rawlings week or something because you are the second stranger this week to come in here asking about her," Shirley shares. "Why do people who aren't even interested in literature bother to come into a library and pepper us with questions?"

"What do you mean?" Emily can't believe what she is hearing.

"A snot-nosed young man came by wanting to know if Marjorie, he didn't even pronounce her last name correctly, had any living relatives in this area. He didn't care about her books or her life here or the remarkable things she did for the people and for literature. Can you imagine?"

Emily can pretty much imagine anything right now. "Did he say anything about why he wanted to know or where he was from or anything?"

Shirley looks at her sternly. "Are you a police officer?"

Emily assures her she is not an officer of the law, but that she also finds it odd that the young man would come here asking questions like that. She hesitates to let the librarian know that she's a Rawlings semi-illiterate herself, but decides to let it pass. But the idea that there really is someone snooping around makes her head start to pound. She dares to ask what the man looked like.

"He was tall. Thin. Looked like he needed a haircut. Now don't take me wrong here, I don't usually judge people, but he seemed, well, ignorant." Shirley is looking away as she speaks. "I'm no psychologist, but people tell a story about themselves very quickly. You, for example, are nice, smart, and you know how to act in a library."

Emily smiles and agrees with Shirley. "He wasn't nice?"

Shirley shakes her head back and forth. "He was demanding, and he actually pushed a chair over when I wasn't forthcoming with information about people who might have known her personally. I finally told him to read a book about her or leave the library."

"I don't suppose you knew Marjorie?" Emily asks, leaning in for a quick glimpse of the bulletin board before turning back to Shirley and trying hard not to look as apprehensive as she feels.

"I'm only sixty-three, dear," Shirley says, with a hint of disgust in her voice. "Marjorie knew a lot of people and her mark is all over this area. If that insipid young man had half a brain he could find out for himself."

Emily can't help herself. "Did you by any chance see what he was driving?"

Shirley hesitates, grits her teeth, blinks twice and simply points to the lone computer. "I am a librarian. Not a private detective." Then she turns and leaves the flabbergasted Emily standing by herself.

Emily sets her purse down by the computer and tries to shake off everything she has just heard. Why would that man be asking about Marjorie? She leans in to look at the photographs on the wall. Marjorie looks stern in almost all of the photos. She's attractive, has dark hair that's curled around her face, round, almost puffy cheeks and a faraway look that Emily immediately thinks is wistful. Without a doubt, it's a face of longing. All of the photos are in black and white but it appears as if Marjorie has dark eyes, lovely white skin, thin lips and she looks like she left the refrigerator door open or forgot to close the bedroom window. She's definitely got the "I'm thinking about something else" look.

In the past, Emily would often look at old photographs like this and make up a story about the person she was looking at, almost like the car game she played with her siblings. "He was a sailor who had five wives, drank like a fish, and then one day all the wives found out and beat him to death," or, "This woman was a spy, she often dressed as a man, crossed enemy lines, and then fell in love with a German soldier who betrayed her and was a member of the firing squad that killed her."

Marjorie Rawlings almost looks sad to her. In every photo she has a half-smile, or really no smile at all, as if she were posing and saying under her breath, "Get me the hell out of here as fast as you can." Emily can understand being in one place and so wanting to be in another, even if you aren't sure where that place might be.

"Who were you?" Emily has leaned in so close to the photo on the bottom of the display that it looks as if she's kissing it. "Talk to me, Marjorie. I think you had a really big secret."

Rather than waste precious computer time reading what's on the wall, Emily decides to start some serious research. She backs away and settles in front of the ancient machine that reminds her of the huge, very first computer she bought back in the 1980s. This antiquated library gem has a loud mechanical sound, a kind of thumping hum that makes her wonder if there aren't mice inside of it making the damn thing work. She pushes a key; there's a slight flicker of light, the humming accelerates, and there's the library home page.

Emily almost shouts, she's so happy, but at the last minute she remembers that Shirley could be lurking. Thankful it's not a dial-up connection, Emily simply types in Rawlings' name and is immediately overwhelmed by pages of information.

Clicking through the sources, she's thrilled to discover there's something called The Marjorie Kinnan Rawlings Society. That means there must be some diehard fans and supporters of the writer's work. She pulls up a biography and reads the first paragraph.

*Marjorie Kinnan Rawlins was born in 1896 and died in 1953. She was born on August 8 in Washington D.C., attended the University of Wisconsin-Madison, where she received a degree in English in 1918, and married Charles Rawlings, a fellow student and also a writer.*

Emily is about to continue reading when the computer starts sounding as if it's grinding its own teeth; the screen flickers and then goes black. She looks up and notices that the lights in the library have also gone out and even though it's late morning, she's sitting in almost total darkness. Then she hears the lovely shrill voice of Shirley.

"Don't panic!"

"I'm fine," she lies, wondering what has just happened as she tries to resist the urge to run screaming from the library and head directly back to safe Ohio.

"I'm coming!"

Shirley quickly arrives in the dark backside of the library with a small flashlight and some very bad news. "This happens a lot, and I'm so sorry."

"What happened?" Emily hasn't moved and is looking at the dead computer.

"There's some kind of a glitch in the county power system and unfortunately we're at the end of the line and it takes them forever to get here when the power zaps out like this," Shirley explains, hovering by Emily's left ear with her light.

"How long is forever?"

"Well, isn't that a great question!" Shirley is chuckling. "Last week it was six hours. I usually grab a book and some coffee and go outside."

"Six hours?" Emily is trying not to cry. Six hours drinking coffee with Shirley might push her over the edge. "Can I take some books? Do you have any of Miss Rawlings' books?"

Shirley snorts. "Of course we have her books. She lived in this very county. She's also my personal heroine. Do you have a county library card?"

Some preconceived notions about librarians are absolutely true. In Miss Shirley's case, the notion about always following the rules, being strict and a bit uptight totally describe Shirley, the mistress of the Little Juniper Lake library. Mistress Shirley doesn't give a rat's ass that Emily works at one of the largest university libraries in the country. In fact, Emily could be Marjorie herself and there's no way in hell she's checking out a book or copying reference materials, or taking photographs of the Rawlings display without the proper credentials.

Emily doesn't bother to argue. "I guess I'll just drive over to Silver's and wait out the outage."

"Silver?" Shirley almost looks excited now. "You know Silver?"

"Well, yes." Emily is afraid to say why or how or that she really isn't sure where she is going after her library research.

"Why didn't you say so?" Shirley is already grabbing books off the shelf as she speaks. "I'll give you a couple of books, although I know Silver has all of the Rawlings books, and we'll just put them under her card. It will be our little secret. Then you can come back when we're up and running here again. "

Emily is sitting in her car with three Marjorie Kinnan Rawlings books before she knows what's happened. She does know she's going directly to Silver's house and that Rawlings must have been one hell of a person to live here with the likes of women like Shirley, the bespeckled librarian who runs her literary kingdom like a dictatorial queen.

And even though Emily's excited to begin reading Rawlings words and totally immersing herself in the writer's life, she can't help but wonder about the man who preceded her, searching for his own set of clues into the increasingly more fascinating life of the author of *The Yearling,* and perhaps *Lost Hearts in the Swamp of Life* too.

# 6

*"My own laugh startled me. It crept up like something vaguely familiar, an old friend, a lost shoe that once fit perfectly, and when I recognized it—my own voice, vibrant and clear, I could not stop the sound and it went on and on..."*
—*Lost Hearts in the Swamp of Life* - MKR - 1963

Sitting in her car with her elbows on her knees, watching yellow and blue butterflies tiptoeing across the flowers in front of the train station, Emily is trying hard to remember the last time she had been spontaneous. She's been struggling to come up with one thing for the past fifteen minutes. Even though she understands routines, because that's what consumes most of her life-and everyone else's, she assumes-she's disgusted at what she now realizes is a life that has slipped across an unseen line and into predictable boredom.

The fact that she could even take time off work to drive her persnickety aunt to Florida is predictable. She imagines her cousins and everyone else in the family waiting for her to volunteer for the long drive this year because they know she doesn't go anywhere, have a companion, or anything pressing in her life besides punching the time clock in the basement of the library every morning at 9:00 am.

*Why have I not bothered to think about this?* Becoming a creature of habit, someone who doesn't bother to step out of the box but who instead walks all of the straight lines inside of the box over and over again, feels like a death sentence punctuated by everything predictable in her life.

Monday mornings, she stops on the way to work to buy yogurt and vegetables for a week's worth of lunch; after work, she gets groceries for dinner; then she cooks something that she can eat three days in a row. Tuesday mornings, she gets up a little early and does a thirty-minute workout video, eats lunch with her friend Sarah, who's a professor in the humanities department, and then, Tuesday night, she watches television and reads the newspaper. Emily doesn't even want to go through the rest of her weekly routines; she's making herself nauseous. Spontaneous is apparently a word that has been erased from her vocabulary.

She decides that a weekend with Sarah at the beach, another weekend trip to Denver to see her son, Michael, who is a fifth-grade geography teacher and terribly happy, a dinner for one at the new restaurant just off campus, and the night she almost signed up on a computer dating site don't really qualify.

Emily now believes she's borderline boring, as she drops her arms and legs at the same time and tries hard to forget about the pre-Florida-trip part of her life. Maybe she can create a new psychiatric diagnosis, Borderline Boring Disorder-after all people can now claim sexual addiction and computer overuse as illnesses. Imagine what the hearty men and women who settled this region of the country would think of that?

She's also already beginning to compare her life to Marjorie Rawlings. Simply reading the backside of her books in the library parking lot has made Emily feel like a slug. Marjorie always seemed to be ahead of her time, graduating from the University of Wisconsin and then flinging herself into a marriage with another writer, Charles Rawlings, a college sweetheart, while she worked as a reporter in Kentucky and New York in the early 1920s. Emily could barely get past the idea of Rawlings in her long skirts, throwing herself into what was then a total man's world as a newspaper reporter.

How hard and challenging those years must have been as she wrote her poetry for the women's pages and most likely had to plow through a smoke-filled newsroom to get to a desk that was probably in the back corner. And that husband, Charles, was he her competition or a true partner? Emily sits with the books on her lap and thinks about her own fairly easy walk from the university into a library job that is sometimes fascinating but surely not filled with the unique challenges Rawlings had to face while working in a profession that was very slowly opening its doors to women.

Before she starts to drive, she has the bright idea to call Bev and ask her nonchalantly if she had ever read any of Marjorie's books. She knows Bev is an avid reader and has a particular love for literature that has gone out of print. But when she leans over to fish her cell phone out of the glove box, where she thinks she has thrown it, the phone isn't there. Then she spends ten solid minutes rummaging through the car and trying to remember if she really put the phone in the glove compartment. Maybe she threw it under the seat like she sometimes does when she is driving in Ohio, talking on the phone, and a police car pulls up next to her.

Emily knows she looked like a crazy woman, bent over as she stands outside of the car to look under the seats, flinging her car mats aside, and pawing through her trunk like she has lost her mind. She finally gives up and decides that she must have put it inside of one of the boxes or perhaps her suitcase. "Menopause," she convinces herself, as she finally starts up her car and takes off.

Emily's drive from the library back to Silver's house in daylight is an amazement to her. Last night, driving in the dusk and then back to the lodge at dark, she was so frightened by the car behind her that the beauty of the ride was all but erased. Daylight reveals an entirely different world; a land punctuated by fields of orange groves, old wooden fences, a glimpse of isolated houses set back against the river or inside of towering stands of huge trees that look like oaks to her.

When she pulls into Silver's, hops from her car, and discovers that Silver isn't home, Emily sits on the steps and has tries to connect what she thinks are the unremarkable dots of her own life. She immediately decides that being fifty-seven doesn't quite qualify her as a midlife-crisis candidate. Her divorce pretty much swallowed up that excuse, as did her move to the outdated but affordable condo, when she gave up the house in the suburbs and started over.

Now she wonders if she really started over or if she just moved over; simply trading in married life and a loveless marriage for new walls, not one ounce of spontaneity and a lifestyle that was disgustingly predictable. But is that really so bad?

Emily thinks about some of her friends who didn't step from one life to another, but flew into it. Her oldest and dearest friend, Cynthia, moved to the Florida Keys the very same day her youngest daughter started college and has been happily tending bar at a tiki hut with a mess of twenty-year-olds for ten years. The talk of the old neighborhood was her carpooling neighbor, Char, who ran off with the second-grade teacher, an absolutely gorgeous blonde swimmer who just happened to be a woman. At least three friends went back to graduate school, two colleagues quit and moved into a trailer park in Arkansas, of all places, and a male friend, leftover from her unmarried days, recently left his day job to develop apps for a start-up company and is making a fortune.

It's ridiculous, Emily knows, to compare herself to anyone but herself. Silver's front porch would be really crowded right now if everyone was the same; but what about really, seriously thinking about whether or not you are happy? She certainly knew she was unhappy the last few years of her marriage; when her mother died; when she was in the throes of menopause; when Michael was a shit in high school; and to this very day, every time she thinks about the excuses she's made for thirty years about why she can't move to New York.

And happiness? The mere idea makes Emily laugh, again, and then she realizes she's been laughing a lot the last few days, in spite of the bizarre appearance of the unnamed man in the red car everywhere she looks.

"I'm happy now," she murmurs, following a flock of medium-sized white birds with curved orange beaks, as they pump their wings and then glide in the sky. She believes that it's borderline enchanting everywhere she looks. And she feels a resurgence of excitement every time she thinks about piecing together the papers in the boxes, discovering Marjorie Rawlings' life, and piercing the secret worlds of Silver and Leslie. It's almost as if she's fallen backwards in time herself, and has ignited her own long-ago-extinguished fires.

Emily decides to stroll to the back of Silver's house while she waits, and as she contemplates the notion of happiness. When she rises, butterflies resting in the flowers scatter and move so quickly there's a blur of color in front of her that looks like someone is actually painting the air with yellow dots, and as she turns to walk around the house, the idea of happiness dissolves when she begins to think about Silver.

Who is she, and why does the mere mention of her name evoke such interesting responses from people, like strict librarians who start handing out books without proper identification? If this isn't spontaneous, Emily doesn't know the meaning of the word. She's about to step into yet another person's world without so much as a blink of the eye.

Silver's a half-recluse with some kind of secret, who knows at least a few locals and who's been living here long enough to know the unwritten rules of social etiquette. Emily can't wait to find out her story, and she's certain there's more than one reason why Silver is being so generous—and why she isn't thinking twice about accepting lodging from a half-stranger. Perhaps there is something magical in the air here that connects people, both past and present!

Struggling not to make up something ridiculous about Silver and her life, Emily stops in mid-stride when she comes around the side of the house and sees a huge garden that she doesn't remember from the night before. It loops around the left side of the house and stretches back for a good half-acre before it hits the edge of the shrubs and trees along the river. It makes sense that she couldn't see it from where she was standing in the kitchen last night and now the sheer size of the garden takes her breath away.

Emily bends down and then drops to her knees in front of a row of ripening green beans. The soil is warm, a wave of heat that almost feels like a gentle hand moves into her knees, and she picks one almost ripe bean, starts to eat it and can't even imagine how much work tending the garden must be. Maybe Silver doesn't live alone after all.

And there she is, kneeling in front of the beans, when Silver drives in and stops her truck very close to where Emily is kneeling.

"Are you praying to the beans, sister?" Silver asks, jumping from the truck and walking towards her.

Silver is a vision. She's a truck-driving goddess, dressed in a rainbow-colored checked skirt, a purple turban that can't contain her humongous dreads, a strapless top that all but displays her ample bosom. A cotton gauze shawl is covering her shoulders, she's got on what must be her requisite bracelets, and a pair of silver hoop earrings that could double as handcuffs hang almost to her shoulders.

Emily wonders if she isn't dreaming. Silver is also adorned with a pair of Whoopie-Goldbergish-looking granny-style gold-rimmed sunglasses and, because she's looking directly into the sun, she's shielding her eyes with her left arm and hand.

"You look like a mirage," Emily admits, still kneeling and chewing slowly on the bean. "What a sight you are!"

"Arise and your sins shall be forgiven." Silver is now waving her right hand up and down as if she's giving Emily a blessing.

Emily obeys, brushes off her knees, and walks toward Silver with her arms straight out in front of her as if she's in a trance. "Do with me what you will."

Silver has a smile that could knock out a passing satellite. She's exquisite, beautiful, and alive with a vibrant force of energy that can't be seen but can surely be felt, and Emily is absolutely dying to know what in the world she is doing living out here, dressed like a goddess, and driving around in a four-wheel diesel drive pick-up truck that's half the size of her Ohio condo. She looks genuinely happy to see Emily.

"Ohio, are you taking me up on my offer or are you just here to eat raw beans?"

"I'm thinking," Emily jokes, closing her eyes and rocking back and forth on her heels.

Silver sighs, holds onto her smile, and motions for Emily to follow her. Emily thinks they already look like the odd couple. Statuesque Silver doesn't so much walk as glide, and her colorful clothes swaying everywhere are not unlike watching a solo parade. Emily feels as if she's always been kind of a shuffler, trying to blend in, and today, with her chalky white legs, her hair caught up in a tiny knob on top of her head with a rubber band, her old T-shirt looking duller by the moment, she looks like a refugee from the Midwest.

Inside, Silver decides they must have coffee and sit and talk before they can do another thing. Emily catches her looking into her car as they step inside, and figures she's checking to make certain she's brought along the boxes. She has, and they are visible in the back seat.

Emily decides not to say anything, but to let Silver lead her into the house and into whatever phase of this very interesting week is about to happen next. And she's feeling calm, happy, and excited until she notices a subtle change in the air-the gentle but very real push of wind against her back, and that same unmistakable feeling that something or someone is pushing her into new and absolutely uncharted territory.

Silver has changed into a basic white cotton T-shirt, not unlike Emily's only much cleaner, some baggy shorts and a pair of flip-flops by the time Emily has carried her belongings, including the boxes, into the guest room. She's been ordered to settle in while Silver makes some business calls.

*Business calls?* Emily has to force herself not to tiptoe down the hall and listen to the phone conversations. *What business?*

Emily sizes up the guestroom and imagines that someone like Silver could be involved with everything from drug running to vegetable farming. The two women have just had a continuation of their previous night's discussion over coffee, absolutely non-revealing and bland, in the kitchen while the dogs jumped and barked outside the window at invisible enemies, just as they had the night before.

In spite of Silver's outward appearance, which Emily thought was a big "Come on in!" label, she could tell that she was still being evaluated. Silver asked her a few questions, mainly about her work and research, and tap-danced around anything Emily wanted to know. She decided it was best to be polite, to let Silver be in charge, and to wait her out lest she end up sleeping in her car in the library parking lot.

What a strange predicament she has gotten herself into because she has dared to go down an unmarked highway! When Silver leaves for a few moments to make certain the dogs have water and to ask them to please keep it down a bit, she thinks about people she knew who would never do what she is doing. One woman in her office had a three-day rule for staying with anyone, even her own mother, because she said after that people started to hate each in ways that could never be erased. "Adults become creatures of habit," she explained. "I never, ever speak before I have my first cup of coffee and there's my mother rattling on and the *Today* show blaring and my father snorting in the bathroom. The three-day rule or the hotel. It's what big girls do."

Emily does not feel like a big girl sitting at Silver's table, but she decides it is the right thing to do. She will be polite, wait for Silver to reveal whatever she wants to reveal in her own time, and in the meantime she has the manuscript, all those other papers, and this small opening of light that seems to be offering her new and old insights into her own life.

After a discussion about Florida weather, the garden, and how Silver thinks her dogs must be reincarnated truck drivers, because they absolutely love to be in the back of her pick-up, Silver jumps up and says, "Let me take care of some business while you bring in your things."

Emily is now discovering that her room is just as charming as the rest of the house, with its Florida-orange walls, a colorful bedspread, and a beautiful polished wood floor that looks fairly new. Actually, when she wanders round the room, she discovers a spacious bathroom that surely must have been added during the past few years, and a door she didn't notice before that leads onto the side of the front porch.

She didn't expect a suite with a private entrance but it's just as charming and inviting as the rest of the house. While she pushes the boxes against the wall and puts her lone suitcase on the dresser, Emily decides to leave the bag of clothes and the old newspapers from the Kincade house in her car. The boxes and Silver should be enough for starters. Then Emily remembers that she took the shopping list off the wall of Leslie's house. The note is thankfully intact even though it has been riding in her back pocket for two days. She unfolds it carefully and can't help but smile when she reads what's on the list. *Vinegar. Three pounds of butter. Gin. Toilet paper. Guest beer. Two rat traps. Typing paper. Red wine x three. Green thread.*

Whoever Leslie Kincade was, she must have been a lot of fun to be around. Knowing the importance of preserving last objects, Emily sets the paper on top of her bed and then wonders how long the note had actually been pinned to the door. The paper looks yellowed. She lifts it to her nose and is wheeled back to the moment when she walked into the kitchen and could almost feel the spirit of the woman who had labored there. She's thinking that if the list is older, and it appears to be, that there's even more weight and power in keeping it. It's such a simple thing, but to someone who knew Leslie, a simple note with her handwriting might be priceless.

In the middle of her second sniff, Emily is summoned back to the front of the house. "Ohio!" Silver calls, "It's safe to come out."

"You're lying!" Emily shouts back and immediately hears Silver start to laugh.

Before she leaves the room, Emily looks again for her cell phone. It's not in any of her bags or pockets and now she's wondering if she bothered to lock the car door when she all but ran into the library. The thought of someone stealing her phone makes her clench her hands in anger and she stops and tries to re-trace her steps. With everything going on, she quickly decides it's impossible for her to remember if she locked the car. She was excited about the train station, about finding something out about Marjorie, and the last thing she was worried about was being safe. She feels stupid and too trusting and tries without success to calm down.

Silver finds her a few minutes later on her hands and knees, looking under the bed.

"What are you doing?"

Emily jerks her head up and pushes back so she can sit down. "I'm going crazy trying to find my cell phone."

"When did you last have it?"

"At the library. Maybe I'm being paranoid. I'm imagining all kinds of things, but for good reason." Emily suddenly feels as if she's going to cry.

"Girl, get up," Silver orders, clearly taken aback by Emily's show of emotion over a lost phone.

Silver walks over, extends her hand, and helps Emily get to her feet. She notices that there are tears welled up in her eyes and Emily is the next one taken aback when Silver gives her a huge bear hug.

"I'm sorry," she half-whimpers into Silver's shoulder, reluctant to tell her all the reasons why she's so worried. "It's just a phone. I'm sure it will turn up."

Silver pulls away and looks at Emily as if she's examining a patient. "Sometimes it's the little things in life that slap us down. Sit down. You look through the room and I'll go check the car."

Emily feels totally foolish. The last thing she wants is for Silver to think she's lost her marbles and kick her out, although she could probably find another lodge or even drive back to Ocala and get a hotel. But then everything would change and she might never discover why Silver wanted Leslie's furniture and why she's so interested in the boxes. Emily forces herself to get control of her emotions and takes one more look around the room. The cell phone is nowhere.

Silver comes back empty-handed and tells her they can call the library, or head over there if she wants, but she has some work to do first.

"Don't worry about it," Emily says, wondering what kind of work Silver is talking about. "I have some reading to do. Shirley lent me some books and I'm dying to tear into them."

Silver is suddenly interested in what she's checked out of the library. Emily shows her the Rawlings books and Silver looks puzzled. Emily takes this as a sign that she really doesn't know what's in the boxes and as much as she wants to tell Silver, she holds back.

"Marjorie?"

"A local legend."

"So much more than that." Silver is holding Marjorie's book *Cross Creek* in her hand. "Start with this. Rawlings was... well, I'm not even sure how to describe her. She wasn't just a literary warrior, but a female warrior in every sense of the word."

"You're an expert, I take it?" Emily does not want this conversation to end.

Silver hesitates and then smiles. Emily gets the feeling that she's still being tested and so she continues to talk. She's determined to win over this woman, to flip the lid off her life and its secrets, and to perhaps reveal what's under the lid of the boxes as well. So before Silver has a chance to say one word, Emily launches into a detailed monologue about her work at the library and how important place can be and how sometimes little details like a grocery list on a wall can tell an entire story.

"This was Rawlings territory and as long as I'm here for a while I thought I might as well get to know her and her world," Emily half-lies again. "I've already found out a little bit about Leslie, and then there are those boxes and—"

"Enough, super spy," Silver interrupts. "You know your stuff, and proved several of your points."

Emily is so close to telling her what's in the box she starts to cough to stop herself from speaking. She's promised herself she's not going to give away her secrets until she finds out a few of Silver's. But she has one thing to share.

She leans over and grabs the grocery list off the dresser where she's placed it like someone would place a treasured photo or jewelry box. She gently places it in Silver's hands and tells her to read it.

Silver reads through the list, smiles, and then passes it back to Emily. "This was Leslie's wasn't it?"

Emily shakes her head up and down. "Would you like it?"

"It's yours, just like those mysterious boxes. But thanks. You earned it. Just seeing her handwriting is a gift right now."

Emily has the feeling that Silver wants to hug her again but instead she tells her to read and that she'll be back after some work to talk about Marjorie. Then Silver taps her on the arm, winks, and closes the door as she leaves the room.

Perplexed, Emily grabs Marjorie's non-fiction book *Cross Creek*, flops on the bed and is immediately mesmerized by a photograph on the inside of the book. Marjorie Kinnan Rawlings is standing with her right hand on her hip cradling a shotgun; her left hand is tucked behind her back in a military-like pose, her left leg is cocked forward, and her dark eyes are half covered by a short-brimmed fedora. She's wearing a collared hunting jacket, calf-high leather hunting boots with jodhpurs pushed inside of them and she looks as if she could bite a bear.

Standing guard just to her right is a very tired-looking black-spotted spaniel who is wearing a studded leather collar. Marjorie's obviously been working him hard, because his tongue is hanging halfway down his neck.

Emily is captivated by the photograph of Rawlings. This particular photo, she believes, tells a story all on its own.

Rawlings is tough, sporty, outdoorsy, unafraid, wild, and the commander of her immediate surroundings. Behind her are stands of scrub oaks, a darkening sky, a tiny sliver of white that runs parallel to the ground and must be the edge of a lake or river. She looks as if she could part the water, walk through it, grab a couple of fish and then reach up and pluck the ducks she was probably hunting right out of the sky.

And there's something haunting and elegant about her, even as she stands like a hunter goddess ready to shoot, kill, cook and then eat.

Emily begins to read and doesn't remember falling asleep. Exhausted from her early morning walk, and all but an emotional breakdown, she slips into sleep and she wakes up hours later with a jolt, as if she is falling. Terrified, it takes her a few moments to remember where she is.

It's dark outside and quiet in the house when she gets out of bed, walks to the bedroom door, opens it and finds a note lying by her feet.

*Ohio -*

*You were passed out. Shirley called. She found your phone in the restroom. Went to fetch it and do some other work. Food in fridge.*

*Silver*

Emily knows she did not use the restroom at the library. But before she gets herself all worked up, she imagines someone found it, left it there, and then forgot to turn it in. That's what she would do if she found a lost phone, she tries to convince herself, as she feels her heart accelerate.

Either that, or someone really did take it out of her glove compartment. Emily chooses not to go with that option, even as she begins to wonder if it's safe to be in Silver's house alone, and if Silver's spontaneous show of affection means she's ready to open up more than just her arms to a wayward stranger.

**7**

*"The mysteries of the unspoken, of what isn't seen, the pieces that hide in between the cracks of life, are sometimes easier to see than the crooked veins in the fingers of our own lives."*
—Lost Hearts in the Swamp of Life - MKR - 1963

When Emily finds herself back on the road to Shirley and the library in the morning, without having talked to Silver, she wonders if Silver isn't just a ghost who has taken to simply writing notes to communicate. Emily had rummaged through the refrigerator, made herself a sandwich, and then sat in the living room reading until past midnight. She hadn't heard Silver come home or leave again.

Instead of her lost cell phone, and what she had hoped would be an open and lively conversation with her new housemate, she had discovered yet another note. In the note, Silver said she had to run back to town and was going to call her on the house phone. *Pick up the phone this time when it rings!* Silver also had written. Emily didn't recall hearing a phone ring but she was also woozy from her nap and half scared to death being in Silver's house alone. Her recent bold moves during the past few days have all but been erased.

The sun is beaming through the kitchen windows and Emily can see the dogs chasing gophers in the backyard when she goes to make coffee. The pot is still on and hot, which means Silver must have been there not so long ago.

Emily walks through the back door and stands on the deck. Her mind is buzzing with the idea of creating a new Nancy Drew mystery called *The Case of the Missing Cell Phone*, and more importantly, with all of the things she's learned from reading *Cross Creek*. She has written down notes, just like the old days, as she's read. The book is to her an amazement of true grit, survival, and wonderment.

Looking out across Silver's gardens and over the treetops and into the bright blue morning sky, Emily can understand the draw a former newspaper woman who longed for seclusion might have to this remote part of the country. Perhaps that is also what brought Silver here, because it is a place to be alone, and maybe to grow lonely if you aren't careful.

Emily sets down her coffee on a small table when the dogs notice her and come running. They bounce around her and she bends down, petting them one at a time, and then goes back in to get her copy of *Cross Creek*. The stories she has read about how Rawlings carved a life for herself here, so far removed from New York, Wisconsin, Louisville-the places she had come from-are still swinging through her mind.

Grabbing her coffee and sitting on the back step, Emily opens the book and re-reads the first paragraph, which she finds just as enchanting the second time. "*Cross Creek is a bend in a country road, by land, and the flowing of Lochloosa Lake into Orange Lake, by water. We are four miles west of the small village of Island Grove, nine miles east of a turpentine still and on the other sides we do not count distance at* all, for the two lakes and the broad marshes create an infinite space between us and the horizon."

Emily now remembers where she left off after several hours of reading. She flips to Page 101. "*In late spring I sailed comfortably from off an intractable horse and broke my neck and fractured my skull. I rode the horse back to the stables and dismissed the incident.*" This is when Emily didn't just get hooked, but addicted to the work of Marjorie Rawlings. When she forced herself to turn off the light and climb into bed, she's now remembering her dreams were a tangled mass of thick vines, wild women riding through the brush on horseback, and back-country men, women, and children who rejoice if they are lucky enough to have a simple glass of cold water.

She's about to continue reading when she hears the phone ring. Emily jumps up, runs inside, and is delighted to hear Silver's voice.

"What in the world is going on?"

"I'm sorry I missed you last night and this morning, but you were clearly tapped out, Ohio."

"Did you get my phone?"

"It's strange, but no."

Emily's not sure what to say.

Silver explains that Shirley had it. It was in the bathroom, a lady turned it in, and she set it on her desk-and then it disappeared again.

"I wasn't in the bathroom."

"Maybe you dropped it."

Emily is beginning to think she's been drugged but she decides not to argue. Silver tells her that Shirley has gathered up some more Rawlings materials for her and she needs to drive in and get them.

"Can't you bring them here? I'm sort of getting addicted to your house and yard."

Silver chuckles with pleasure and tells Emily she's someplace else doing some business. Emily can hear voices in the background. It sounds like she's in some kind of office.

"Fine," Emily agrees. "Silver, thanks for trying, and helping with Shirley, and coffee, and the bed—"

"Stop! I'm sorry I've left you alone so much. You're easy to be nice to, Emily from Ohio. You could be the real deal."

Before Emily can say another word Silver hangs up and Emily puts down the phone and claps. That was progress, even without the phone!

She dresses, forgets about eating, and calls herself the real deal all the way to the library.


"Well, isn't this special," Shirley says in greeting, still adorned with her pearls, and absolutely serious about being glad to see Emily.

"Silver has been just wonderful," Emily says, still taken aback by what she is discovering must be regional generosity and hospitality. "My research is consuming me and I just got here."

Shirley throws back her head and laughs in a way that seems totally out of character, or so Emily thinks. It's a brassy, deep-throated sound that makes Emily wonder if Miss Shirley isn't a smoker or a great lover of the local moonshine.

"Well, Miss Rawlings is legend here, absolutely legend, and I think the world needs to get re-acquainted with her," Shirley eagerly suggests, jumping to her feet, and motioning for Emily to follow her. "You could spend years investigating that woman's life and work, and who knows what you might find!"

Then Shirley stops in mid-stride, turns to look Emily in the eye, and winks.

Emily feels her heart flutter and wonders what the wink is supposed to mean as Shirley hoists a box of materials onto her shoulder as if she's a longshoreman. Emily follows her out the door as Shirley reminds her what a great favor this is and to please not mess up any of the materials.

"And dear, I'm sorry about your phone," Shirley says, setting the box on the hood of Emily's car. "It's the strangest thing. The phone was right there on my desk and then it disappeared."

"What does Silver think about all of this?"

"Haven't you talked with her yet?"

"No. She called and said she's doing something. Why?"

Shirley hesitates, then dismisses whatever she might have been thinking by shaking her head. "I don't really know. She just flew out of here. I'm sure the phone will turn up. Most of the people around here are not the kind to steal anything. We don't even lock our doors, for crying out loud. Perhaps it was someone who doesn't live around here."

Emily is now thinking about the man who was in the library just before her who was rude and demanding. Could he somehow have taken her phone? She's also wondering if she should have said something to Silver about being followed the other night. Her fears seem to be escalating unreasonably fast. Emily forces herself to try and stay positive.

"Everyone's certainly been nice to me," she says, smiling as she opens her car door. "But I know not everyone is as kind as you have been."

Then before she can add a thank you, Shirley gives her even more advice. "You know, sweetheart, you will have to go to Cross Creek, and you should drive into Gainesville and see what they have at the university library, and then you could head over to St. Augustine and see Crescent Beach..."

Shirley can tell Emily is bewildered. She shakes her head from side to side, apologizes, and says, "Start with those few things, and then I'm sure the trail will become more visible."

What Emily really wants is someone to hand her a detailed map of the area with a huge red X marking the spot where Marjorie Kinnan Rawlings lived in hiding following her faked 1953 death.

What she gets instead is an amazing box filled with slices of information about a woman who even by today's standards would be an example of brave fortitude, living the dream, wild adventure, feminism, social adaptability and probably fifty-five other attributes that Emily has yet to discover.

Emily drives back so fast to Silver's that she almost goes over on two wheels when she turns into the long driveway. She feels like a little girl about to walk into her own birthday party. The box of materials, and the research involved in what has obviously turned into a major project, have made her giddy.

She races in through the front door, just as unlocked as every other door in the area, and sets her box down on a table in front of Silver's extra-long couch, and the rest of the world quickly vanishes.

Besides copies of most of her books, Shirley has managed to unearth some old black and white photocopies, book reviews, a few biographies and copies of some of Marjorie's short stories. Emily's never been a woman who is a slave to modern technology, but she'd give her eye teeth to be able to sit down and simply read article after article on a computer.

This fact makes her ponder Silver's ability to survive in what is seriously the middle of nowhere, without what most people consider the basic tools of the trade. Silver told her she prefers not to have cable or Internet access and that sometimes cell phone reception is sketchy, and that's why she needs a land line phone connection. There are no neighbors to be seen through the front window, the town is at least a twenty- to thirty-minute drive away, and that's if you know where you're going, the summers down here are notoriously sweltering, there's the garden, the house upkeep, sending off packages and mail and... It's simply not easy to live in the middle of nowhere in the 21st century. Imagining what it was like when Rawlings lived here is almost impossible.

Emily plops on the floor, surrounds herself with her research, and doesn't bother to stop and eat. She could care less about the weather, her cramped knees and legs from rotating in a circle, or what in the world she might find in Cross Creek or when she reads the next Marjorie Kinnan Rawlings book. What she's discovering is fascinating to her, not just as a professional, but also as a woman who, up until a few days ago, considered going out to eat alone a great adventure.

Rawlings was born in Washington D.C. on August 8, 1896. Her father worked in the U.S. Patent office, but according to articles written by Rawlings, he was really a farmer at heart, who shared his love of the land with his children on his farm in Maryland. Marjorie had a double dose of nature and life on the land, because her mother's family farmed in southern Michigan and Rawlings spent her summer's there, learning the importance of nature, hard work, and the inherent risks of making your living from the very ground you stand on.

Marjorie was always interested in writing and started on her lifelong career path when she was just a young girl writing short stories, essays, and poetry. She was published by the time she was fourteen and, when her father died in 1913 and the family moved to Wisconsin, a new chapter in her own life began.

Within a few minutes, and without realizing it, Emily begins to take notes and is not reading for pleasure but for purpose. She's looking for names, people, places and trying to establish a chronology that may lead her to the biggest treasure of all. Emily also begins compiling a list of names—relatives, friends, business associates, absolutely anyone mentioned in any of the newspaper clips or articles she is reading.

It's no surprise to her that Marjorie loved college and was an active part of its academic and social communities. She appeared in plays, wrote for the *Wisconsin Literary Magazine*, fell in love with a fellow writer, and promised to marry him during her senior year.

Emily finds this portion of Rawlings' life fascinating. She can't recall ever hearing about a writer or author named Charles Rawlings and given Marjorie's success, he was either a grand husband or a jealous rival, who contemplated throwing himself off a bridge when his wife became famous.

Marjorie graduated with honors from the university, moved to New York City, where she took a job as a publicist for the YWCA, married her Mr. Rawlings and moved with him to his hometown of Rochester, New York. The couple then moved to Louisville, Kentucky, where Marjorie worked as a feature writer for the *Louisville Courier-Journal*. Emily snorts out loud when she reads that Marjorie wrote a column called *Live Women in Louisville.*

Emily makes a note to try and find some of those articles as she wonders what Charles was writing about at the same time. And how many female reporters were there in 1920?

Emily doubts that Rawlings had her oiled shotgun back then when she still lived in the city but it's so easy for her to imagine what challenges she must have faced, being a woman in a profession that was totally dominated by men. When she pauses in her reading, closes her eyes, and puts her head back against the couch for a few moments, she can see Marjorie Rawlings in her long skirt, a tiny veil-covered hat tipped to one side of her head, walking through an old newsroom where there was a haze of smoke, typewriters clanking, men with hats rushing out the door to cover a train wreck, and all the pretty ladies writing about sewing, floor polish, where to buy stockings and what time to have dinner ready when the husband arrives home.

The dichotomy of Rawlings' life is puzzling. How in the world did this woman get from the newsroom and a somewhat traditional marriage to the swamps of central Florida? "To hell with fiction," she murmurs, starting to read again, "this woman's life should be made into a series of movies."

Emily puts down her papers for moment and picks up *Cross Creek.* She thumbs through the first few pages and finds the bibliography. She is stunned to see how many books Rawlings had written besides the three she has from the library. *When the Whippoorwill, Golden Apples, South Moon Under, Jacob's Ladder, The Sojourner* and so many short stories and more books. Emily can't recall ever reading anything Rawlings wrote but *The Yearling* and she now wonders why.

Literary shadows often fade fast, she knows, but from what she is discovering, Rawlings was incredibly popular, and prolific as well.

She sets down the book, pushes out her arms to stretch and uncurls her feet. Her list of names is growing-Rawlings, Perkins, Dunlin, Smith, Mitchell. Emily's already filled up several pages with notes and is wondering about all the places Rawlings lived. Surely, one place was closest to her heart. It would make sense for that to be Cross Creek from what she's read so far and from what she can see out her window it would be the easiest place to hide.

Emily has totally forgotten about everything but her work. Missing cell phones, red cars, manuscripts from dead authors, and her Ohio life have all disappeared. Right now there is nothing but a slight pounding at the back of her head, urging her to finish what she used to call the basics. The facts of a life. The spicy details will hopefully come later. She throws her hands back on the table and is determined to finish her makeshift timeline.

Mr. and Mrs. Rawlings didn't last too long in Kentucky. They moved back to Rochester and she started writing for the *Rochester Evening Journal*. Emily now realizes she really doesn't care too much about Mr. Rawlings; while he was probably covering downtown corruption and back alley murders, his wife was composing poems for a series called *Songs of a Housewife*, and in-between that and trying to figure out exactly what song and dance a housewife might do, Marjorie managed to write a novel called *Blood of My Blood*. The book must have been kept in the bottom of her traveling trunk, because it wasn't published until 2002, after her death.

She pauses again and can almost feel the tension in the Rawlings household when Marjorie retired to the back room, and typed out her novel, while Charles fiddled with a radio in the living room and contemplated the mess he had gotten himself into by marrying not just a confident, headstrong woman, but also the competition.

Emily realizes she's now making up portions of Marjorie's life, but she knows she might be right on target. Surely there were progressive men back in that era, men who didn't care if their wives stayed home, had babies, cooked meat, potatoes and gravy every night and ironed the sheets, or if they had a professional life. What that must have been like, though, is very hard to imagine. Even now, when relationships are supposed to be open and free and equal, there's so much carping going on with couples that it doesn't seem worth it to Emily to even consider getting involved with someone-not that it's even likely. It's too damn much work. He measures what she does; she measures what he does; the people next door measure both of them; then the in-laws start measuring. It's difficult at best to be in any kind of relationship, but back in the 1920s, when two university graduates who were journalists and budding authors lived under the same roof, that must have been beyond a grand adventure.

And it's not a big shock that Mrs. Rawlings, who admitted a great love of the land, would grow restless writing poetry about housewives. She loved the outdoors and the challenges of hard work not just with her brains, but with her back as well. So when Charles and Marjorie took a trip to Florida in 1928, it's a good guess that they were looking for more than oranges-at least, Marjorie was.

When the couple stumbled upon an abandoned 72-acre farm near a middle-of-nowhere place called Cross Creek, Marjorie really fell in love. Charles should not have bothered to unpack, but for a short time he acted like he loved the rural wilderness too. "She totally fell in love with the place," Emily, whispers, understanding its importance not just for the heart of the person who loves, but also for her own world of research.

When she reads a paragraph about Marjorie's love of "her" place, she has to hold her hand over her heart.

*"Any grove or any wood is a fine thing to see. But the magic here, strangely, is not apparent from the road. It is necessary to leave the impersonal highway, to step inside the rusty gate and close it behind. By this, an act of faith is committed, through which one accepts blindly the communion cup of beauty. One is now inside the grove, out of one world and in the mysterious heart of another. Enchantment lies in different things for each of us. For me, it is in this: to step out of the bright sunlight into the shade of orange trees; to walk under the arched canopy of their jadelike leaves; to see the long aisles of lichened trunks stretch ahead in a geometric rhythm; to feel the mystery of seclusion that yet has shafts of light striking through it. This is the essence of an ancient and secret magic."*

Emily is struck not just by the beautiful prose, but also by the way Rawlings so captured her love of the land. And she's struck by the realization that this has never happened to her. Surely she's gasped when she's seen beautiful sunsets, the mountains on her trips to visit her son, the ocean, the color of fall floating across her own Ohio horizon. But Emily has never had a place capture her like Cross Creek and Central Florida captured Rawlings.

The pull of a place when you come, when you go, when it appears in your dreams, your writing, the very way that you think-none of that has ever happened to Emily. Reading just a few paragraphs of Marjorie's powerful writing has already left Emily with a physical ache, a longing for a place she has yet to feel or know.

Silver's house is totally quiet as Emily sorts through her library treasures. When she occasionally pauses to look up or stretch, she almost expects Marjorie Kinnan Rawlings to be sitting across from her. How wonderful it would be if that were true! Emily already feels as if she has a million questions that she would love Marjorie to answer.

Emily thinks it totally makes sense that once Rawlings found her paradise, she wasn't about to leave. Charles stayed for a short while, but they parted ways and because she had purchased the farm with money from an inheritance from her mother, she kept it, and Charles headed back to the northern cities. What must that have been like? The parting of two writers, a breakup where all ties were severed, the beginning and the end. Was there shouting? Did they stay in touch? How in God's name could Rawlings work a farm, write, do what she did all by herself?

Emily has now started to jot down all her questions as she reads and she knows that research like this always brings up more questions; it's as if the work is feeding on itself. Some researchers that she has worked with at the library get so caught up in the research they never end up writing what they started out to study. It's like some kind of intellectual disease where you think one more page, one more fact, one more clue will spin you into a place that has never been discovered.

A car door slams and Silver's dogs bark, but Emily is so engrossed in her reading she doesn't hear a thing. She's moved on to the next phase of Marjorie's life and is astonished by what she is reading.

Her new home and the surrounding farmland sound as if they are all being held together by a thin piece of thread. There is no indoor plumbing, and the nearest store is miles and miles away. Neighbors are few and far between and sound as if they are from a different planet. There was land to be cleared, rattlesnakes to be shot, dinner to be cooked, water hauled. Emily, who has fallen in love with her own microwave, state-of-the-art coffee maker and her computer, now believes that the neighbors probably thought Rawlings was nuts, and perhaps she was a little bit crazy. What was that Rawlings city-slicker doing out here?

Emily has barely started diving into the Cross Creek phase of Marjorie's life when she hears the front door slam. Totally startled by the sound, a line of fear races up her back and she screams as if she's been shot, rolls over so whoever is coming in can't see her, and watches as some very large feet approach the living room where she's working.

# 8

*"Sometimes being so alone made me disappear. Days would pass and I had not uttered one simple word. Occasionally, when I remembered, I would walk fifty paces from the cabin, scream at the top of my lungs and listen as the world around me screeched back as if everything was laughing at the silly woman who had forgotten how to speak."*
—*Lost Hearts in the Swamp of Life* - MKR - 1963

It takes all of five seconds for Emily to feel like a complete fool. Whoever's feet are approaching has stopped moving and is laughing. Emily pushes herself back up, covers her face in half-fright and half-embarrassment, and then dares to look up.

There's a woman standing in the doorway of the living room, still laughing, her arms loaded with grocery bags, and she's resting her foot on a box of food.

"Well that was one sweet scream," the woman says. "I haven't had a welcome like that in years."

Emily closes her eyes for a moment as relief floods over her; then, she springs into action.

"Oh my gosh, let me help you!" Emily is on her feet and has her hands on the box before the woman can say another word. "You scared the heck out of me, and I was so engrossed in what I was doing I kind of freaked out." She dares not mention all the other reasons why she might be on edge.

"You're Emily, or Ohio to some people," the woman says as she continues to walk. "The wayward traveler who is researching Miss Rawlings."

Emily sets the box of food on the kitchen counter and looks at the latest character who has stepped into her life. This woman is almost as wide as she is tall, but Emily would never call her heavy or fat. She's solid and she's oozing confidence, which seems to be a local trait, and she has the most flawless, white skin and shining green eyes Emily can ever remember seeing.

"That's me," Emily affirms, "It's a pleasure to meet you."

"Pardon my manners. I'm Auggie, which is short for August, and yes, my brothers and sisters-all eight of them-are named after months, and I've been grateful my entire life I wasn't born in October or February," she says, hoisting her hands onto her hips and smiling so widely that she reveals perfect white teeth. "My parents were not the brightest bulbs in the pack but we were loved and fed and I had one hell of a childhood."

"It seems as if every person I meet has a life story that's fascinating," Emily says, unable to keep herself from smiling. This woman is so likeable it's almost ridiculous.

Auggie is wearing a pair of fashionable jeans, her blonde hair is cut into short wisps that tangle amongst themselves and circle her face as if each one has been pinned into place, and she's wearing a subtle hint of make-up. Her cotton v-neck t-shirt has a hand-painted palm tree on the front, her Birkenstocks are so new Emily doesn't recognize the style, and Ms.

Auggie has a diamond the size of three Milk Duds on her left ring finger.

"Please don't tell me you're here to spy on me," Emily begs, feigning despair by raising her left hand to her forehead. "Some strange things have been happening to me."

"Hell no," Auggie says, with a soft laugh. "I'm a doctor. Silver and I are pals. She lets me buy her groceries and come over to cook and keep her ass on the straight and narrow when I have five free minutes. I once wrestled an alligator and there's not one brother who could out-shoot me, so Silver is a piece of cake for me."

"None of this surprises me," Emily says, throwing up her hands and then letting them drop so they dangle near her knees. "I swear to God, I have never been to a place like this before, or met people who were so interesting."

"Honey, I'm not that interesting. I'm a frigging dermatologist, but I could tell you stories about life around here, and the people who settled here that would make you wonder if I'm a crack addict."

Emily has to bite her tongue to keep from asking if she knew Marjorie. At this point, it's possible they may even have been next-door neighbors. Emily feels so comfortable with Auggie. Standing in the kitchen and talking while Auggie explains how she's going to eventually cook salmon, new potatoes, and some kind of salad that sounds like it's right out of a gourmet restaurant, she temporarily forgets about the mess she left in the living room.

Emily watches Auggie put away groceries and then dares to ask her if she knows where Silver might be.

"She didn't tell you where she went or what she does?" Emily's not sure if Auggie looks angry or perplexed.

Emily shakes her head and explains about the missing cell phone and almost launches into everything else, but decides it's best to keep quiet.

"That woman is going to drive me insane," Auggie huffs. "She lets you into her house and life, clearly trusts you, I'm sure she's done a damn background check, and she can't open up and tell you who she is? I'm going to slap her upside the head when she gets here."

Emily gulps for air and mouths the words *background check*, while Auggie shakes her head back and forth.

"I'm going to go call her, and you are going to go do what you were doing in there," Auggie explains. "By the way, what were you doing that had you so engrossed you freaked out?"

Auggie is no dummy. Emily explains about her recent obsession with Marjorie Rawlings and Auggie immediately wants to know if it has something to do with the boxes Silver told her she found over at Leslie's. Of course Auggie knows about the boxes and the cell phone, and probably what color underwear she has on. Of course everyone knows what everyone else is doing pretty much all of the time around here. Of course it's possible that Silver and Auggie know what's inside the boxes.

Emily hesitates. She feels a sudden burst of loyalty to Silver even though it's impossible not to trust the swaying and totally open dermatologist who is standing in front of her. She makes a deal with Auggie. Let her talk with Silver first and then she'll explain everything, if Silver agrees.

"Well, aren't you the negotiator?" Auggie grins. "I'm thinking it's time for everyone, especially Silver, to lay her cards on the table. You know she gets so damn lonely sometimes for conversation with someone who wants to discuss something beside hog dressing, hurricane season, and the price of gas, that she actually considers getting the Internet in here."

Before Emily can ask about that, Auggie raises her hand like a stop sign and tells her that she's busy and doesn't have a lot of free time to keep Silver company 24/7. When she does have free time, like today, they cook and talk and try to act as normal as possible, which isn't easy considering their personalities. The social implications of the Internet and Silver's work will apparently have to come out of Silver's own mouth.

"I'm going to go call her and tell her to get home and talk to you," Auggie says.

But before she turns to go outside and use her cell phone, Auggie tells her that she's going to have to eventually fold up her paper-based research and get over to Cross Creek as soon as possible, if she really wants to see who Marjorie Rawlings was and how she lived and loved.

"Cross Creek? You mean the village or whatever it was where Marjorie settled?" Emily asks.

"No darling," Auggie explains. "You probably haven't gotten that far yet but her farm, her house, the barn, the land-it's all still standing and it's a state historic site, and before you read all of that, you just need to get over there and see it for yourself."

"How far is it from here? I had no idea," Emily feels a bit foolish but realizes there's been no reason before this trip to dip herself into rural Florida history or the life of an apparently-forgotten brilliant author.

"Local people could walk there, but you'd better take the car," Auggie quips. "It's about eight miles straight through the back of the house but you, my dear, should take the road. I'm guessing you didn't pack a gun for rattlers and gators."

Emily doesn't laugh because she knows that Auggie is totally serious. "I don't even have a blow dryer, clean underwear, or the sense to get the hell out of here."

Auggie's laugh is so absolutely genuine, Emily can't help but laugh herself. She reaches out and touches Auggie on the arm for a second to stop her from leaving and tries to explain herself.

She realizes that Auggie probably already knows everything she's telling her but she proceeds anyway, describing her drive, the alligator, finding the boxes and how she realizes Silver has gone out on a limb to welcome her into her house. Emily explains that she's not certain what she's doing, but every time she questions the fact that she's here and exploring and meeting people like Auggie and Silver and even the quirky librarian, she's compelled to keep going.

"I'm working like I haven't worked in a long time, and I would never cross boundaries or hurt anyone," she continues, looking down because she's embarrassed and surprised she's being so open and honest. "I know Silver has secrets. Someone like her doesn't move to a place like this simply for the scenery."

Emily raises her eyes and tells Auggie that she only has one secret, and she's been waiting to trade hers for Silver's.

"She has good reason to be so closed off, but sometimes she's her own worst enemy," Auggie says softly. "You'd better prepare yourself because when she does tell you, you are not going to believe it, and I'm guessing you may scream again."

Emily's not sure if she should laugh or cry. Her emotions have been flapping in the wind so much the past few days she almost feels as if she's stepped back into puberty. While Auggie leaves to make her call, Emily forgoes returning to what she can't believe she's taken to calling her "work", and walks out the kitchen door to stand on the back porch.

The dogs return the second the door opens and all three of them are carrying beat-up tennis balls in their mouths. Emily correctly guesses that they want to play fetch and she commences throwing one ball after another until her arm is about to fall off. She fills their water bowls and then sits on the last step where the dogs plop at her feet, panting, and for some insane reason she feels as if she's exactly where she's supposed to be.

Then she can't help but wonder what secret Silver is hopefully about to reveal to her that can match the manuscript sitting on her bedroom floor.


Silver's arrival coincides with the dogs going absolutely crazy when they hear her truck pulling in front of the house. They get up so quickly all Emily can see is a quick flash of fur as their rear ends go around the corner of the house.

It's been a long time since she's had a pet. When her son was growing up, she would often joke that he was her pet, and in a way he was. The feeding and caring of a child is very similar to raising an animal and as much as Emily wanted a dog, it was impossible to work, raise a child, and think about taking care of an animal. But sitting on the steps and simply knowing the dogs are around the yard and are so affectionate has made her see how they can fill a void in a person's life. She imagines that Silver sits in the exact same spot a lot, talking to the dogs, perhaps even anxious to hear the sound of her own voice while she's talking to them.

Emily leans back against the steps and waits. She can hear the front door bang and the dogs return just as fast as they left, and it looks as if they are almost smiling when they lay against her legs again. The muffled voices of Silver and Auggie slip under the door and mingle so that it sounds like a quiet rumble by the time the sound reaches Emily.

It doesn't take long for Silver to come out the door, walk down the steps and plop next to Emily as if she's a fourth dog.

"I guess I can't leave you two alone for a minute," she says, gesturing with her hand back toward the house. "Apparently we have a lot to talk about."

Emily sits up and scoots over a few inches so she can look Silver in the eyes. It's obvious that opening up is not her strong suit. It looks as if she's been through the wringer.

"Auggie is delightful," Emily says, unsure of which direction she must go with the conversation. "If I'm ever in a big fight, I'm going to call her first."

"Smart thinking. She is true blue, loyal, and has a heart almost as big as her feet."

"So..." Emily says, letting out a bit of tension, and not certain what to say next or where to begin.

Silver throws up both hands and says before they start unwrapping each other's secrets, they had better talk about the cell phone. Emily stops her and admits that she's been afraid to tell her everything because she didn't want Silver to think she was an over-reacting city girl. Then she explains about the man in the red car who gave Bob trouble, Shirley's encounter at the library, the guy who showed up at Happy Hollow, and the car that she is almost certain followed her home from Silver's house.

"It's too much of a coincidence," Emily shares. "It's just weird. Something is going on."

"Don't be angry, but I already know everything you just told me," Silver confesses. "Shirley didn't tell you everything because I asked her not to. The same guy who came in looking for information about Marjorie was in the library when your phone disappeared the second time. I feel like a fool for not opening up to you sooner so that you could open up to me, but I have my reasons."

Emily's not sure if she should be relieved or scream again. "You think this is all related?"

"I have no idea, and no one saw him take the phone. Everything is random, which is why we have to be together on this."

"Look, I'm no fool, but I'm almost certain I put the phone in my glove compartment, and I'm so excited about what's in those boxes I can't remember if I locked the car door," Emily admits. "And just so you know, it's okay not to spill your guts to a woman who shows up out of nowhere. I get it."

Silver gives her a half smile and waves her right hand. "The guy in the red car is a common thread to all of this," Silver says, standing with her hands on her hips and frowning. "You should go into the kitchen and call someone you know to see if anyone has used the phone, and perhaps we should discuss what's in those boxes. Something is definitely going on around here, Ms. Ohio."

Emily and Silver go back into the house. Emily quickly calls Bev, who picks up immediately and is so relieved when she hears Emily's voice that she almost starts to cry. "Someone called here using your phone," she explains without giving Emily a chance to say a word. "He was so stupid he didn't realize your number would show up on my cell phone and he kept asking me questions about who you were, while doing a horrid job of acting like a telemarketer. He wanted to know if you were a relative of the author, Marjorie Rawlings."

"Oh, God..."

"Where in the hell are you, and what in the hell is going on?"

"I'm safe and staying with a new friend," Emily shares, wondering how much of her story to reveal. "It's just... Rawlings is from this area, and I thought it would be fun, as long as I have the time, to do a little research."

"Who is this idiot who has your phone?" Bev is apparently buying Emily's spontaneous research excuse, which is actually true.

"Just some local bad boy. Don't worry about me. I've been adopted by a gang of Floridians who are very wonderful people."

Bev wonders if Emily has fallen and hit her head. She tells Emily she even sounds different.

"It's just nice to be away and to have time to think and see that there's more to the world than Ohio," she shares. "My mind is spinning, and at the same time I feel light and clear."

"Are you drinking that rot gut whiskey they make, or smoking corn stalks?"

Emily surprises Bev again by telling her how much she means to her. "Thanks for keeping tabs on me. You know I love you."

Bev is thankfully speechless and Emily finally promises to check in occasionally, to try and pick up a replacement phone, and she adds, only half jokingly, to sleep with a knife, sawed off shotgun, and an ice pick.

Back outside, she shares the news with Silver, who promises to call the sheriff-who is, of course, a friend-and let him know what's going on.

"We'll figure this out," Silver assures her. "You're safe here and believe me, no slimy cell phone ignoramus is going to mess with me."

"It's frightening," Emily says, unable now to shake off something that feels like a short blast of nausea. "He was on the road. He was at the house where I found the boxes, which I'm sure you've guessed have something to do with Marjorie Rawlings. The cell phone. The library. I'm trying not to be crazy, but someone really followed me home from your house last night."

"Trust me. Seriously, Ohio, take a breath. Let's forget about that jackass for a while, and just you and I talk. Okay?"

Emily nods her head in agreement then asks for a fifteen minute break so she can use the restroom. Auggie shouts to her that she's going to cook while they talk as she walks down the hall.

In the bathroom, Emily glances into the mirror, looks into her eyes, and tries without success to imagine the secret that is about to shift from Silver's life into her own. She washes her face and hands, walks past the six boxes that are lying on her bedroom floor, and in her wildest dreams would never be able to imagine the story that is waiting for her.

**9**

*"There is a sense of lightness and freedom that comes from the truth. It is a force of life that can carry you to places that some only dream of. My secrets were buried under the low and lovely bush that sat beneath my kitchen window. When I finally had the courage to dig it up, transplant it to a place of light and love, the blossoms multiplied and everything changed—absolutely everything "*
—*Lost Hearts in the Swamp of Life* - MKR - 1963


Emily peeks around the corner and sees Silver waiting for her down the hall. Silver sees her eyes and nose around the corner, and her laugh is like a whip that reaches out and grabs whoever might be standing nearby. Emily's never thought of the actual sound of laughter before, but it seems to be a major part of her new life roadmap. She can't help but laugh when she hears Silver.

Before she follows Silver out onto the porch, where there are two Adirondack-style rocking chairs backed up against the house and separated by a small table, Emily slips into the kitchen where Auggie has food spread out on every surface, and says, "Thank you."

Auggie shoos her away and she joins Silver on the porch. Emily feels as if she's got a decade's worth of questions backed up inside of her, but she waits as Silver settles back into her chair.

"You are one colorful woman," Emily finally offers, pointing to the bright blue chair Silver is sitting on. Emily is struggling not to worry but somehow, simply being close to Silver makes her feel safe and absolutely comfortable.

"Honey, you don't know the half of it." Silver has let out a huge sigh and is looking out into the garden. Then she turns, smiles and reaches over to pat Emily on the arm. "Here it comes, are you ready?"

"Probably not," Emily admits.

Silver laughs yet again, and tells Emily that she's checked her out.

"Meaning you looked at my rear end, or what?"

"I called people. That's where I was half the morning. I made sure you are who you say you are and that you stumbled here magically and didn't know about Leslie Kincade or the real identity of yours truly."

Emily braces herself by gripping the armrests. She's been checked out? "Really?"

"Ohio, would you just let anyone waltz into your life like this? Open the doors? Drop down the gates to your secrets?"

Emily shakes her head back and forth, even though she really doesn't have a gate or any secrets except what's in the boxes. There's not a waiting room at the entrance to her life. "It makes sense," she finally admits. "My prison record has been expunged, so you're pretty safe."

"You are trusting, that's for sure," Silver tells her, shaking her own head back and forth. "I could be the axe murderer here."

"But you aren't, are you?"

Silver purses her lips, closes her eyes, and whispers, "No, Ohio. But I'm going to tell you who I am, and who Leslie was, because I think you are one of us and for reasons I could never explain, I have finally decided to trust you."

She begins to rock in her chair as she speaks. Emily is unable to move and will wonder, three hours later when they finally finish talking, if she was even breathing the entire time Silver was telling her the most incredible tale she has ever heard.

Silver starts with Leslie's story, and Leslie was indeed an author who slowly rose to prominence beginning in the late 1950s, by writing novels about immigrant women in the early 1900s that were a revelation of reality. Her novels, at first, were widely received, and, as she gained notoriety and prominence, Leslie started to speak out about the mischaracterization of women in fiction. She was especially harsh when asked about editors, mostly all men at the time, who often demanded a specific kind of portrayal about the women in the novels they helped produce.

Even though Leslie had meticulously researched her books, often spending years interviewing, reading diaries, talking with the sons and daughters of the women she was writing about, the negative publicity started to take a toll on her career.

Leslie, who was married and had three children, walked cautiously into the 1960s and the women's movement, all but devastated by the way the literary world treated her. She had tried to be realistic, to blend fact and fiction in a way that offered the world a vision, albeit it fictitiously, of real women's voices, and she had all but been shut down.

After her husband died suddenly, and when no one would publish her fourth book, and when she was told to conform to her editor's rules-rules that she was told were the rules of the rest of the world too-she decided enough was enough.

Leslie had been enchanted by Marjorie Rawlings' work and life, and decided to walk away from a world she had once loved and embraced. She moved to that yellow house where Emily discovered the boxes and started a kind of literary retreat for like-minded writers. She became a muse to many, many writers, male and female, who had admired her work and who had also struggled with the often-ridiculous trends, narcissism, and the unwritten rules of the literary world; rules that more and more leapt onto trends and genres as if they were the last train out of town; rules that often ignored quality writing and promise, for what was the hot ticket that week; rules that Leslie often joked would make the Eudora Weltys and Willa Cathers of the world roll over in their graves.

"She never locked her door and there were always authors and writers coming and going; some patrons built houses close to her and there was also an unwritten rule," Silver explains, continuing to rock as she speaks in what Emily assumes is almost an unnaturally quiet way. "You couldn't talk about her, or where she lived, or what she was writing herself. It was secret, and every single person who came, and there were many, never said a word."

Emily can feel her heart brace against her chest as if it has become stuck. Her head is spinning. *A secret world of writers!*

Silver hesitates for a moment and turns to look at Emily, who is staring at her with her mouth open a good inch. "I'm just beginning to know you, Ohio, but you would have loved her. Absolutely."

"I can just imagine," Emily says, finally lifting her mouth into a sweet smile. "And I bet she loved you."

"Sometimes," Silver chuckles. "Like most people, she also thought I was a pain in the ass part of the time too, but she taught me to get over myself. If it wasn't for her, you'd be back in Ohio now and I'd never be telling you this."

"Why?"

"She made me a better person, a better writer, more open and eager to hang onto my own passion and not let someone else take away my power."

Emily remains silent. Silver turns away and continues her story as more pieces of this wild puzzle fall into place for Emily.

Silver tells Emily that she is really Jenka Armador, a once famous, rising literary star, who disappeared in the early 1990s after a blazingly horrid review in the *New York Times Book Review*. The article, written by someone no one else thought was a very good writer, was devastating to Jenka's career. When other media reviewers, back when there were real newspapers and magazines, mimicked the *Times* review, Jenka sent out a nasty response that was all but a call to arms for reviewers to agree to a debate about what is good literature and what isn't.

Jenka, with what she called her useless creative writing master's degree, had already written five books, and was an outspoken critic about the book publishing process, the good-old-boys editor's club, and the unrealistic world many publishing house employees had built for themselves.

"I was a bit ruthless and over the top," Silver recalls. "There were tons of good editors and many great authors and books but still, it's such a cruel, unfair world that was turning into a Hollywood-like scene where a literary star would be hatched by some money hungry editor, while the real writers starved to death."

Emily is remembering the controversy surrounding the challenge Jenka threw out. At the same moment she is in awe of the woman who is sitting next to her.

"So many people felt the same way," Emily tells her. "You know that, don't you?"

"Of course, but no one wanted to risk losing what they had-their jobs, their contracts, their chance to appear on *Oprah*," Silver tells her. "People would call or write me and say, 'Way to go,' but in the end I was left standing alone. So I left."

By the time of the huge controversy, Silver had already been in contact with Leslie, and within three days she had packed up her apartment, severed all ties with her publisher, turned her back on the literary world as she knew it, and headed to Florida.

Silver tells Emily that like many other authors, she stayed for a short time with Leslie until she went into what they all called Creative Recovery. For Silver, Creative Recovery really started when an editor, who was also friends with Leslie, contacted her and convinced her she could help her. Thus Jenka Armador disappeared and two new women took her place. One part of her became Silver and the other part of her became Grace Novell.

Emily bends at the waist to keep from fainting, and Silver starts to laugh yet again.

"Easy girl," Silver says, asking her if she needs a glass of water.

"Whiskey," Emily half jokes. "You're Grace Novell?"

Silver nods. "In case you haven't noticed, the bios in those novels are very short and there's never been a photo in one of them."

"You have been on the *New York Times* bestseller list for, like, ten years!"

"Yes, I have."

"Which totally proves your point."

"Yes, it does."

"I'm serious about the whiskey now," Emily says, finally sitting back up. "It's what? After three? I really need a drink."

Silver doesn't hesitate and within minutes they are sipping whiskey on the rocks in the middle of the day, while Auggie rattles pans in the kitchen, and Emily peppers her with questions. She quickly discovers even more details about the secret central Florida society of lost and misplaced writers and the people who cover for them. No one tattles; people come here for many reasons, the least of them being their need to be private and live their lives the way they want to live, and not the way someone else tells them to.

There are other Leslies who have come and gone and some who still remain, and the secrets carried between houses and around the orange groves and into the brush country are as sacred as any thought, feeling, or place anywhere else in the world.

Emily totally understands, even as she is riding out the last portion of her shock. Grace Novell's novels are immensely popular and have been printed in so many counties Silver tells her she's lost track. And yes, she picked Novell as her last name as a kind of joke, and people who don't know-not many around here-think she's just a rich black woman whose daddy was a doctor.

"Was he?"

Silver snorts right into her own whiskey glass. "He was a steel worker, and my mother was a first-grade teacher in New Jersey."

"What's real and what isn't?" Emily says this out loud as a kind of personal question, then quickly adds, "Why me?"

"What does that mean?"

"I stumbled across Leslie's house and now you're telling me these secrets, and there's obviously something important in those boxes sitting on my bedroom floor."

Silver smiles.

"So?" Emily asks. "Why me?"

"As Leslie got older, she got a bit superstitious and rather mystical, and she kept saying that when she died she was still going to be a force around here," Silver tries to explain. "I don't know what in the hell that means, but with or without magic, I always say there's a reason for bringing a person to a place."

Emily keeps thinking about the alligator, the leaf in her backseat, the wind and the trail of papers in her cabin and the banging door. Now that she knows Silver is really three different women, she's ready to believe anything.

She decides, after Silver's stunning confession, to tell her what she's discovered so far in those sought-after boxes. While she tells Silver about the manuscript, the other boxes with papers and who knows what else, Silver doesn't act surprised.

"So is it possible that Marjorie Kinnan Rawlings didn't die in 1953, and kept writing?"

Silver gets up slowly and doesn't say anything. She walks into the house and comes back in five seconds with the entire bottle of whiskey.

"You know Marjorie loved whiskey," she says, refilling Emily's glass.

"You are driving me crazy," Emily squeaks, as her ice rattles. "How do you know she liked whiskey?"

Silver sits down, starts rocking, and looks out into her garden again. The flock of white birds with the orange beaks circles just then, a whirling trail of white against the brilliant blue sky that captures the attention of both of them. The birds are silent and as their wings filter the air, Emily feels a shiver that starts in her toes and runs all the way through her body.

"Ohio, I think you need to go see if you can find Marjorie Kinnan Rawlings. I think that might be part of the reason why you are here, and why you have those boxes in my guest room-which, by the way, I am absolutely dying to dig into, whenever you let me. "

"Go find her?" Emily is perplexed.

"Dead or alive or whatever you find, she was worth knowing. You know her life was so much harder, so much more challenging then my own life, and she was so much more daring and alive."

Emily finds it hard to believe that anyone could be more daring and bold than the colorful woman with myriad identities who sits beside her. She looks to her right, way beyond the garden, and sees that the white birds have landed and are now picking at the earth, hunting for something, totally dauntless as they step one inch at a time, looking everywhere for something to eat. When she looks at Silver, Silver is staring at her, unmoving. She wonders how much this kind woman really knows about what she found on the porch inside those boxes and about Marjorie.

"Go find Miss Rawlings, Ohio," Silver whispers. "I think you're up for the challenge. You can share what's in your boxes when you're ready. I think I just proved my sincerity. And by the way, just being a living writer near Cross Creek and exposing myself to what's here has made me a bit of a Rawlings expert myself."

When Emily brings her glass to her lips and inhales, she doesn't smell the burnt, earthy whiskey. Instead, the unmistakable scent of perfume-sweet and flowery-fills her nose. All of this news, and the mysterious call Bev received, have made her unsteady. She closes her eyes to calm her heart and is not at all surprised when a sudden gust of wind blows across the yard and all the white birds take to the air at once.

When she looks up the birds look like cheerleaders with their wings flapping and their long orange legs dangling as they gain altitude. Emily blinks twice and swears they are all trying to form the initials MKR in the sky.

The dogs, who have been lying in the front yard in the sun, suddenly start to bark. Emily points to the birds as an excuse for the barking and then she points out the initials to Silver, who starts to chuckle as she agrees. "Marjorie Kinnan Rawlings," they both say at the same time.

Dinner ends up to be a glorious affair, which includes not just a meal to die for, but also letting Auggie know about the papers in the boxes. Storm clouds begin forming from the south as the dinner discussion lurches between Emily's onslaught of questions about the secret world of writers, and the possibility that Marjorie Kinnan Rawlings could have faked her death the very year Emily was born.

Emily tells them she had started reading the Rawlings manuscript that she had found sitting on the very top of the first box she opened, *Lost Hearts*, and Silver immediately agrees that the mere title absolutely would have been something Rawlings dreamed up.

Given what she knows about Silver and Leslie, Auggie is only half-skeptical about the entire idea of a famous writer, even back in the days prior to *CSI*, faking her death and then disappearing for decades.

"Don't you think it would have been impossible to pull that off?" Emily asks, while the dogs bark at the approaching clouds and the increasing wind.

"Absolutely not," Silver disagrees, closing her eyes and waving her left hand in the air as if she were dismissing the mere idea. "You are going to find out how smart Marjorie was and when you get into it, well, you'll see. Besides that, look at my life, for God's sake. I disappeared too, and here I am."

"All this mystery! I could just take those boxes right to some expert and we'd know in a second."

Silver drops her fork and leans across the table. "But you won't do that, and that's precisely why you're here. If you are half the woman I think you are, you'll do your homework, find out who Marjorie really was and then... well, then you might just find Marjorie."

"The damn Florida bush code of honor," Emily pouts.

"You think we know something we really don't," Auggie interjects. "I agree that it's more than possible for her to have faked her own death and that she would have to have had help and that this is the perfect place for that to happen. People keep secrets. We don't share what isn't ours to share. There is a code of honor here and you've just been brought into the fold. Now you have a duty to find out the truth, and to keep your mouth shut about Silver."

Emily doesn't know what to say. One day she's an aging librarian from Ohio and the next she's been initiated into a secret world where hidden treasure and buried lives are popping up all over the place. She's thrilled and terrified at the same time.

"You know you're excited about this," Silver says. "You seem to be fond of research and I'll help when I can."

Emily isn't so sure searching for Marjorie Kinnan Rawlings out in the boondocks with crazy men in red cars in hot pursuit is the wisest way to spend the last few days of her extended vacation. But Silver reassures her again that she's safe and that the possibilities of what might be in the boxes are just too damn exciting to pass up.

"I'm on high alert now, I promise," Silver says, reaching over to put her hand on Emily's arm. "I have guns. I have friends. We'll listen to those fierce watchdogs. Don't worry. That's my job."

Emily wants to believe her, but the lost cell phone and the call Bev has received still have her feeling more than unsettled, even as the day's revelations have her floating. If it wasn't for the soothing arms of the whiskey, and Silver's confidence, she realizes she might become a hysterical disaster.

The three women are talking so much they almost forget to eat until Auggie reminds them she's been slaving over the stove and she'd appreciate some culinary feedback. Silver and Emily oblige by finishing dinner and asking for seconds of everything. When they finally push away their plates the conversation begins again as it gently starts to rain and the dogs jump onto the far side of the back porch, where Silver keeps their dog beds.

Emily is curious about the lack of Internet, which is going to make her own research difficult. Silver explains that having a portal to the universe ruins her concentration, and she loves going to the library. The two rooms at the back of the house are her office and bedroom and before she can say anything else, Emily tells her she would never go into a drawer, a room, anything, unless she was invited.

"I get that about you," Silver says, smiling. "You probably don't realize how nice you are. I hope you can understand now why it took me so long to tell you about the trio of personalities I carry around."

"Are you kidding?" Emily tells Silver she's honored and grateful.

Auggie wants to know if Emily is aware of the fact that half the county already knows who she is.

"I do now."

Auggie quickly adds that only a select few know Silver's real identity, and absolutely no one will know about the manuscripts unless Emily tells them or is ready to talk about it with someone else.

That she has landed on a whole new planet is definitely not lost on Emily. She orders Silver and Auggie out of the kitchen so she can clean up and do the dishes and they don't argue. The two women head back out onto the porch. The rain is now pounding against the windows and Emily watches as the women push the chairs against the side of the house so they can stay dry.

Emily quickly cleans off the table and stacks all the dishes inside of the dishwasher. She notices that Auggie has drawn her a map to Cross Creek on a piece of paper towel that she must have yanked off the kitchen wall. Emily is now totally excited about seeing the real places she has been reading when she hears Silver and Auggie shouting.

She walks to the door and sees that both Silver and Auggie have abandoned the kitchen and are standing at the edge of the deck. Water is splashing off the roof and the two women are taking turns dipping their heads in and out of the water as if they are participating in some kind of seasonal ritual.

"Join us, Ohio!" Silver shrieks.

"What are you two doing?" Emily wonders if they've taken the whiskey bottle outside with them.

"If you get wet during a sweet storm like this you become a virgin again," Auggie tells her, as she prepares to stick her face into the rain.

Emily explodes with laughter. Then she spontaneously walks off the porch, lifts her hands into the air, opens her mouth to catch some rain, turns to face her astounded new friends and shouts, "This should get me through the next ten years, the way my luck has been running."

Then Silver and Auggie leap off the deck and join her. The three women dance like young girls, their laughter mingling with the soft raindrops until Silver shouts, "This is exactly something your Miss Rawlings would have done!" as if she's just spoken to her.

"How do you know?" Emily asks her, still dazed by her brazen water dancing.

"You'll find out soon enough, Ohio!" Silver says, waving her hands with abandon and glee.

Then there's a huge clap of thunder, all three women scream, and while they all stand dripping on the deck, Emily can't help but smile and feel like a young virgin.

What the thunder, bright bursts of lightening, and screams disguise is the clicking whirl of a hidden camera. Someone is smart enough to take photographs of Silver's house, the cars, and the dancing shadows of three wild women, but not smart enough to realize that the sandy soil surrounding the house and yard refuses to relinquish footprints and tire marks after a hard Florida rain.

# 10

*"How was I to know what changed me? Was it the stark land-scape of my life that camouflaged my once dark soul? The reflection of my dreams staring me in the face and then whispering to me in a dance of seduction that could no longer be ignored? Or was it the sealing of this place in my heart, the grand gestures of nature that continue to leave me spell-bound, even now when I have grown so old?"*
 —*Lost Hearts in the Swamp of Life* - MKR - 1963

Emily's first vision, when she's awakened by noise coming from the front of the house and she looks out of her bedroom window, is jaw-dropping. Silver is standing next to a police car wearing a flowing purple satin robe and a tall, gorgeous man is bent over her, and they are kissing so passionately Emily looks away.

She steps away from the long window, counts to twenty, and then looks again. Thank God, the kiss is over. Silver is now leaning against the car and the man, dressed in requisite tan and brown sheriff's department clothing, is obviously the kind of person who talks with his hands. It looks as if he's either got a great story or he's chasing flies.

Emily quickly takes her nightgown off, throws on a pair of baggy shorts and a T-shirt, and makes as much noise as possible walking onto the front porch from her private bed-room entrance.

"Emily, get over here." Silver is motioning to her, and Emily can see from her half-exposed breasts that she's naked under the lovely gown.

She steps off the porch and can't take her eyes off the man. The patch over his pocket says Sheriff Gettleman, but it's hard to focus on anything beyond that because he is one of the most beautiful male specimens Emily has ever seen. Apparently, Silver has a stud for a lover. Even though the sun hasn't yet risen above the trees, Emily puts her arm across her forehead. She's afraid when he starts speaking and she looks into his eyes she may go blind. He's tall, blonde, blue-eyed, and it looks as if he could tip over his own car with one hand.

"Emily, meet Sheriff Jim Gettleman. Sheriff Jim Gettle-man, meet Emily, a.k.a. Ohio, who has brought a whole pack of trouble into this here territory," Silver says, laughing at her own joke. "And Emily, before you move, look down and to your far left for a second."

Emily obeys without question and sees a pattern of obvi-ous footprints, tire tracks, and a circle of cigarette butts. She looks up without moving, her eyes wide, and asks, "What's this?"

"We've had uninvited company," Silver explains. "It looks like someone was watching us and the house last night, and whomever came is such a dumbass he left evidence every-where. The cigarettes. The tire tracks. His shoe size. My friend here-Getts, as the locals call him, because yes, he always gets his man-is going to gather up some evidence and see what's happening."

And one more thing. It's Emily's cell phone. Silver pushes out her arm, opens her hand, and Emily throws her hands against her mouth and stifles a scream.

"It was on the top step leading into the house," Silver explains, reaching out to steady Emily. "It's dry and still working, which means it wasn't in the rain."

"I know I didn't leave it on the porch," Emily says with her voice shaking. "What is going on?"

"I'm going to try and find that out," the sheriff says, moving to shake Emily's hand.

Just looking at this man seems to calm Emily down. She isn't sure who's luckier, Getts or Silver. Silver could probably run the tests on the evidence by herself, for crying out loud. The sheriff looks like a movie star, and he must be Silver's connection for things like checking up on women from Ohio.

"You are in great hands with Silver," he tells her. "I know this is unsettling, and I promise I'm going to personally make certain we find out who was here, and who took your phone from the library and used it to call your friend."

Emily looks at Silver, and Silver explains that she's told him everything.

"So I'm not crazy?"

Silver smiles. "I'm pretty sure you are crazy but that's part of your charm. It's obvious, to us at least, that someone took your phone."

Relieved, but still shaken, Emily wonders what will happen next. The sheriff then politely asks both women to go inside to make coffee while he does a bit of work. Emily is all over Silver the second they get into the kitchen and the coffee is brewing.

"Well, he's a secret that can't be too hard to keep around here!" Silver is starting to make omelets and turns around slowly and Emily can't believe she is blushing. "Your Getts doesn't just get his man, sister, but his woman too."

"Is it that obvious?" Silver is smiling as if she's just won the lottery. She's also glad Emily has something else to focus on instead of all the bad news.

"I saw him climbing down your throat when I heard noise out front. I'm just praying that he has a brother. Sweet hell, woman, he's already melted my toenails and all he did was touch my hand."

"You have no idea, sugar," Silver says, tossing back her head and closing her eyes.

While Silver shares the story of her not-so-secret love, the love is outside measuring tire tracks, making phone calls, and putting cigarette butts into small plastic evidence bags. By the time he has walked around the back yard, checked windows, made certain there are no more foot-prints, and had a little chat with the dogs about not being quite so friendly, Emily mistakenly thinks she has learned all about the sheriff, his undying love for Silver, and a rela-tionship that is like the frosting on the cake for someone whose dating prospects in rural Florida have not been front page news.

Getts, as he prefers to be called, stays for breakfast, which obviously happens quite a lot, and then excuses himself to make phone calls. When he comes back twenty minutes later, he explains that he checked to see if there was a tracking device in Emily's phone and he found none. He tells them that he's certain the tracks in the front yard are from an SUV but unfortunately tire tracks don't reveal the color of the vehicle.

Without getting caught up in details, Getts tells them he's going to try and get prints off the cigarettes, and start a file on everything that's happened. He pauses, looks first at Silver, then Emily, and says that unfortunately with the phone back where it belongs, it's hard to press forward.

"It's obvious he's after something," Emily protests. "I know you think I'm safe with Silver but this is frightening."

"We have some of our own rules down here and I can promise you that if he makes one wrong move... well, as they say on TV, his ass is grass."

"Do you think all of these things are tied together?" Silver asks. "It seems to me as if the red car man is after something."

"Could he be dangerous?" Emily asks before Getts has a chance to answer Silver's question.

Getts lets out a big sigh as if he's already been through this before. "You know that I believe everyone is dangerous or potentially dangerous-even you, Ms. Silver. I wish I had some notion about what he might be doing around here."

Silver raises her eyebrows and looks at Emily. Emily knows it's up to her to tell Getts about the manuscript and the boxes, and she's half-waiting for permission from Silver to plunge ahead.

"You didn't tell him?

Silver looks almost stricken. She shakes her head back and forth and says, "No. I told you the boxes are yours and that your secret is as safe with me as I know mine is with you. And before you ask, he knows who I really am."

The sheriff has reached over and is holding Silver's hand. Emily looks at Silver and then Getts, and realizes it would be ridiculous not to tell him. So she does, and then she waits for him to laugh or ask her if she's fallen and hit her head.

But he doesn't think that at all. After she tells him about the manuscript, Marjorie, her crazy idea that Rawlings faked her own death and lived to write again, and the unseen forces that she feels may be guiding her to uncover a long-held mystery, he simply points to Silver and shrugs. Then he proves why he's the sheriff by telling them something they haven't bothered to figure out themselves.

"Even if she didn't write the manuscript, or anything else in the box, and Leslie Kincade wrote it, those papers could be worth a few dollars because Leslie, as we all know, has recently passed away." Getts isn't just gorgeous, he's smart.

Silver and Emily look at each other and both agree without saying a word that they are about as dumb as the idiot who called Bev with Emily's phone for not thinking about this sooner.

"Have you looked at anything in the boxes yet, Silver?" Getts asks, while Emily quickly realizes the stakes in her quest to find Marjorie Kinnan Rawlings have suddenly risen much higher.

Silver shakes her head, and Getts looks at Emily.

"We were just getting to that," Emily says with a smile. "I'm hoping to go to Cross Creek today and I was thinking Silver could read the manuscript a bit. She's obviously the expert here."

"I thought you'd never ask," Silver all but shouts, acting as if she's just received a long-awaited marriage proposal.

The three of them talk over coffee for the next ninety minutes, discussing the possibilities of faking one's death in the 1950s, and, more importantly for Emily, the real necessity of being cautious, no matter where she is or what she's doing.

As he prepares to leave, Getts hands Emily her phone back, and she's almost afraid to touch it as she thinks about where it has been and who might have been using it.

"Charge up the phone before you go anywhere, and you two should keep track of each other," he advises. "I'm going to spend some time later today asking around about the red SUV and I'm going to try and talk with Bob and Shirley myself, to see if this is the same person. It sounds like it might be."

Gets pauses then and turns to Silver. "You be careful too," he says softly. "Lock the damn doors and don't be acting like you're a cowgirl. This is serious stuff. Someone was out there last night and even though I want to be, I can't be with you 24/7."

Emily slips out of the kitchen while they are still talking to give them some privacy, and heads to her room to change and plug in what she thinks is now her tainted cell phone.

While it charges, she decides to look over the notes she was writing as she read through *Cross Creek*. Emily can hear Silver and her man talking through her closed door but the moment she begins to run her finger down the pages of notes, the rest of the world disappears and it's 1942. When her phone starts flashing twenty minutes later, Emily is quickly brought back to reality.

She's decided that even though she's headed to Cross Creek it may be totally possible to spy a name on a mailbox that still matches a name from Marjorie's book. Why not? It's more likely than not that descendants of some of the people who were tangled up in Rawlings' world still lived in the area. Emily knows that her co-workers often drive through neighborhoods when they are researching, hang out at local coffee shops to ask questions, and literally act like investigative reporters.

Emily loves listening to the stories of the professors and researchers she works with during sessions where they discuss project progress. When her university worked with the Jewish Relief Fund to help track down survivors of concentration camps and their descendants, the entire staff was involved in the project. Even though Emily hadn't been selected to work with the outreach team, the group that actually tried to physically locate survivors once information had been gathered, she was mesmerized by the stories they brought back with them.

And some of them had done just what she was preparing to do-drive through neighborhoods to look for names on mailboxes. It was a seemingly simple way to find people, especially in rural areas, and Emily is suddenly so excited about this new idea that she almost forgets to be frightened.

But when she finally leaves for Cross Creek, she's riding with a baseball bat that has a huge metal hook on the end-a gaff hook for hauling in large fish, Silver explained as she put it in her car-a charged cell phone, and a wad of uneasiness rolling through her stomach that feels like a lead ball.


Amazons. The word finally barges into the correct position in Emily's mind and she immediately wonders if she's going crazy. Menopause is one thing-actually it's been one thing after another-but this forgetting major details trend is sometimes frightening. First the period went, and wasn't that cause for celebrating? Then the boobs fell, then the chin, then the knees started aching, her back went out, tiny veins started rising like red rivers not just on her face but on her legs and then the forgetfulness began manifesting itself in ways that sometimes seemed cruel, and occasionally hilarious.

Forgetting where you park the car wasn't that bad but Emily always freaked out when she couldn't remember why she had gotten up to go into the kitchen, if she had turned off the stove, or brushed her teeth after the last cup of coffee. All her friends told her this was normal but she still had a running argument with Bev over the fact that she was simply getting older and not a candidate for assisted living.

"You are way too active physically and mentally to worry about this stuff," Bev warned her during their last conversation about the demise of her intellectual capacity.

"Don't you think a brain sort of fills up and then after a certain number of years the stuff that comes in the front pushes older stuff out the back?" Emily had suggested during their last go-around during a long evening at Emily's house.

"Oh for God's sake, Emily! How many times do we have to go over this? Some of the most brilliant people in the world are still functioning at a very high level and working and contributing. Yesterday some old fart was on the *Today* show and he's 102 and still drives."

"Yes, but can he remember where he parked the car?"

"Look," Bev sighed, totally exasperated, "you go to the doctor for checkups, you're as healthy as big horse, no one in your family that we know of has lost his or her marbles, you have a job that semi-stimulates you at least a few days a week when you aren't caught up in the mundane bullshit they make you do because you never got the damn graduate degree, and you remembered I'm now drinking cabernet and not merlot."

"But it makes me crazy when I forget simple things and then I start to worry—"

"Do you want me to be honest?" Bev, sick of her rambling, has cut her off.

"Yes," Emily was half-lying because Bev's honesty is often like a slap in the face, and usually spot on.

"If you had more of a life than you've allowed yourself, and you didn't sit around here worrying about useless shit that you have no control over, well, you wouldn't think twice about not remembering things."

Today, even if it took her ten minutes to remember the word Amazon, she'd love to tell Bev what she's been doing. Emily wishes she could be sitting in the same room with her friend as she tells her about the events of the last four days. If Bev saw the gaff hook riding shotgun next to her right leg she might sense something has definitely changed in her best friend.

Emily's driving like a snail toward Cross Creek and decides in mid-thought that Bev would have her committed if she told her everything else, even though she's certain she's not losing her mind this time.

"To hell with Bev, anyone could have forgotten the word Amazon," she shouts out the window as she glances at the crude map to Cross Creek Auggie had drawn for her on a paper towel that is already half-shredded. "It's not like it's a common everyday name for a woman from Ohio."

Emily had been thinking that this part of the world either created Amazonian women or demanded them. So far every woman she has met has been strong, wild, fun, engaging and seemingly capable of anything life and her current surroundings throws her way. Even though she's barely tiptoed into this scrub-country semi-wilderness, Emily can see the harshness of what life here must really be like. There has to be a ton of sacrifice and hardship hiding behind the lush carpet of green that is spread over everything she sees.

There are broken-down fences, house trailers backed up against small stands of old pines that do not appear to be hooked up to any electric lines, miles of dense jungle-like stretches of land that must have hidden trails and secrets of survival that she could only guess are exacting and more demanding then anyone used to city life can handle.

There's absolutely a quiet kind of rustic beauty everywhere she looks too, as she steers her car toward Marjorie's homestead, but it's November now and the temperatures are mild compared to the scorching hot humidity-filled days of spring, summer, and fall.

The word "hard" does come to her mind easily. Living here must have been terribly difficult back in the 1930s. It doesn't look so easy now either, she decides, pulling off the road to look at her paper towel map.

Emily has been driving with all four of the windows down and with one hand so that she can turn and read names on mailboxes, signposts, or anywhere. She's got a list of names from *Cross Creek* in her other hand and she's at once grateful there are no stoplights and beeping horns, and also not-so-grateful to be alone.

There is absolutely no traffic at 10:00 am, and as Emily bravely nestles her car into a small open space next to the highway, she fishes under her seat for her Florida map to see where she might be in relation to the rest of the state. Before she folds out the map, Emily puts her hand around the bat shaped weapon that is apparently going to be her new best friend. She's been glancing at it every five seconds, and now she's wondering if she could actually whack someone with it if she were being threatened.

The gaff doesn't look like the can of mace or the car key she used in self-defense class about thirty-plus years ago. She twists her right hand a bit and sees a long thin white scar that runs from her wrist several inches up her arm and recalls how the woman who was her sparring partner had forgotten to trim her nails, and gouged her so severely she had to leave class and elevate her arm to stop the blood flow. But even that wasn't like a real attack.

While the sun beats through her open windows, Emily convinces herself that even if she's been down more than up lately her life is absolutely worth protecting. She also knows that adrenaline, and the basic instincts of survival kick in very fast when humans, no matter how sad and sorry, are faced with their own demise. She decides that if she had to, she could take her gaff hook, and beat the living hell out of someone. Marjorie probably did it more than once to beast and human.

Relieved, it then takes her almost five minutes to find Cross Creek on her map. She's east of St. Augustine, south of Gainesville, north of Ocala, and quickly realizes that none of the roads she's been traveling for the past few days are even on the map. She does find Marjorie's two lakes, Orange and Lochloosa, and is surprised they are so large. They are spots of ragged blue set against the modern roads marked by parallel red and black lines that look as if they are protecting the water. There are tiny dots representing other communities; Island Grove, Rochelle, Grove Park, Citra, Reddick, Johnson, Bay Lake, all small dots east of I-75, the big modern monster that runs through the heart of the entire state. Just to the east a bit and south lays a huge chunk of green, Ocala National Forest, which Emily correctly guesses is one of the largest inland jungles in the United States.

Bending her head, she puts her finger to the right of Cross Creek on the map and draws a small circle, envisioning this as Rawlings territory. What little she does know of Marjorie leads her to be almost certain that the brash woman would be commander of this area within a matter of months. Emily's certain not all the major highways were in place back in the 1920s when the young journalist from "the north" headed this way with her husband, never intending to fall so deeply in love with her destination.

Or did she? Emily knows that Rawlings and her then-husband Charles came to Florida for a semi-vacation, but they also seemed restless. Even back in the 1920s and 30s, when newspapers were such a huge part of the country's daily life, it must not have been easy to keep a job-especially if you were a woman. Competition was always keen, and by the time the young couple headed to Florida, they had already worked for two separate newspapers.

Emily can't help but think Marjorie Rawlings was already pining for some kind of rural retreat to call her own. Did she know before she left the north that her marriage wouldn't survive? Emily remembers the very moment she realized that her own marriage, lackluster at best from the beginning, was destined to perish. It wasn't a huge fight, or an affair, or just one horrid thing that pushed her over the edge. Her husband was talking on the phone, and she didn't know he had come home. Their son was at a friend's house and Emily felt a kind of joyous peace because she was alone, there was no tension, and everything unspoken had left with her husband earlier that afternoon.

Emily had actually been studying because she was thinking of taking her graduate school entrance exams. Her husband had been shockingly silent about that decision and she had already reached the point in what was left of their relationship not to expect support or encouragement. In need of a break and another cup of coffee, she got up from her desk, stretched, and walked toward the kitchen.

Lost in her own thoughts, she was startled when she saw him leaning against the counter and talking on the phone. Something inside of her flipped in a circle, her heart started to pound, and she had to force herself to be quiet and not yell at him, because she had gotten very good at yelling. It was as if several years of unhappiness was trying to roll out of her at once. She quickly backed up, closed her office door, and realized it was time to move on. Emily also knew her husband wasn't totally to blame and she shouldered the agonizing decision to leave with as much grace and dignity as she could muster.

Perhaps for Marjorie, the trip to Florida simply settled not just the direction of her life, but of her marriage as well. If her husband Charles wasn't as much in love with the land as she was there would have been approaching storms right from the beginning of the Cross Creek adventure. Is that what happened? And what would he do? People back in those days didn't commute, and if he were a tried-and-true newspaperman, where would he work? Could he go from the lively pressure of daily deadlines, meetings, and interviewing exciting people to watering trees, chasing gophers and chopping wood?

Emily realizes that she gets a ton of new unanswered questions about Rawlings every hour. She's hoping that she will eventually get more answers than questions about both Mr. and Mrs. Rawlings as she folds up the map and begins driving even more slowly than before.

More than a few times while she's looking at mailboxes, she almost goes into the ditch but she continues her somewhat perilous one-handed journey with as much abandon as she can muster, considering the circumstances. Getts and Silver are strong people but they aren't with her now. The cell phone is tucked in her pocket and she gingerly touches it as she rounds a corner and passes an old wooden fence that looks as if it's been patched every few feet.

It's obviously old and weathered and she slows even more and is barely moving when she notices a small sign just past what could be a dirt driveway. She pulls up as close to the edge of the highway as possible and tries to read the sign, which is just as weathered as the rest of the fence. She can make out the letter D and then without thinking, puts the car in park, flings open the car door and races through the ditch to the sign.

*Dunlin.*

Emily's heart thumps just as she realizes she's standing in the ditch without her weapon. She races back to the car, turns off the engine, and paws through the files she is carrying to find her notes. She's both ecstatic and horrified when she finds the list of notes, discovers a Dunlin, and then realizes all she wrote down was a name. There's no association, no way she can remember who the last name belongs to, and what the person's relationship might have been to Rawlings.

She clearly needs an investigator's refresher course. Emily turns her head and sees what surely must be the driveway. She puts the car in reverse and backs up so she can look down the dirt road, but twenty feet in, the road disappears behind a sea of green bushes. Her researcher's heart suddenly overpowers every other ounce of her body: the part of her brain that is screaming, "Are you nuts?" and the rawness she feels when she simply brushes her elbow across the pocket where her phone is resting, and the wild thump at the back of her head when she imagines an attacker might hit her are all in second place as she turns down the driveway.

Emily drives past the bushes blocking the road and the view opens up. She's in a huge field that was totally blocked by the bushes behind the fence and the land is obviously a farm. There are cows grazing on both sides of the road and she can see what might possibly be a house straight ahead. She glances at her list again and is startled when she looks up and sees a man on a horse in front of her car. She instinctively reaches for her gaff hook and wants to whack herself for being so damn stupid. The last time she pulled over like this she almost got killed for God's sake.

Ordering herself not to panic, she cautiously sticks her head out of the open window and she's almost surprised not to see an alligator in the road. "Hello!" she says as cheerfully as possible, aware that a strange man on a horse probably couldn't outrun her and her car. She gently locks the door with her left hand, just as a precaution.

The horse is a small black and white, spotted, skinny-looking thing, and if animals are supposed to look like their owners, it's very true in this case. The man is black, he has absolutely pure white hair tied in a knot that flows down his back, he's wearing a light cotton shirt, a wide brimmed straw hat and even though he's sitting on a brown saddle, he's barefoot. Emily is almost embarrassed for being frightened because the man is beyond elderly. He must be at least eighty, if not more. Emily is praying that he's nice, and that he's a Dunlin.

He reins his horse over to the side of the car and bends down to look at Emily. "Hi," he says quietly with an enormous southern twang. "I came out of the brush and saw you headin' down my driveway. Can I help you? Are you lost?"

Emily has the ridiculous notion again that she's either been transported back in time or she's become trapped in some kind of rural never-never land. This man could have ridden his horse right out of 1934.

"Not really," she tells him. "I just wanted to get my bearings. Lots of the roads here aren't marked very well. I'm headed over to Cross Creek." She can't very well tell him the truth.

The man smiles, tips his hat with his left hand and says, "I'm Tag Dunlin. Are you going to see Miz Rawlings' place?"

Emily feels as if she's just been resurrected.

"Yes I am. I'm Emily. It's beautiful here. I can see why she loved it."

Tag hesitates, squints, and looks into her eyes as if he's lost something and might find it there. "You either love it or hate it. She loved it. This scrub country rode itself right into her heart and she became herself, if y'all know what I mean."

Emily nods her head even though she's not certain. *She became herself?* Tag is still staring at her. There's no wind and with her head half out the window, Emily can feel heat already rising from the earth. The sweet Florida cowboy looks so peaceful sitting on his horse in the sun that Emily has a sudden urge to hop up behind him and see where he's headed.

"Where did you come from?" she asks, wondering if she should get out of the car.

"Born here. Never left. Love it," he answers and Emily gets the feeling she's supposed to ask something else.

She smiles and asks him were he came from just now and where he's going. He points to Emily's right, and Emily can see a faint opening in the fence line that must mean there's a way to get into the field. He tells her he lives several miles back in the woods, behind the house she can see up ahead, and that he's on is way to check on some cattle he keeps on the other side of the highway.

Tag's face is weather beaten from what must have been years and years in the Florida sun. He shifts in his saddle, his horse throws back his head, and before she has a chance to ask him her next question, he answers it as if he knew exactly what Emily was thinking.

"I knew her, Miss Emily, and my mother worked for her," he says, closing his eyes as if he's now trying to remember something. "It was a while ago, and people keep coming to try and find Miz Rawlings, but not like before, not like after her house first opened up. People now, they forget. They read books on those computer things and they just don't know what it was like for her. They don't know."

Emily feels as if she's just won the lottery. She glances at herself for a quick moment in the rearview mirror to make certain she's alive. The chances that a man riding a horse would pop out of the woods and tell her he knew Marjorie Rawlings seem ridiculously low to her. But then again, she sought him out, and there must be others who knew her as well.

Emily looks back at Tag, almost afraid he'll disappear like the alligator did a few days ago when she looked away. "You really knew her?"

Tag laughs and nods his head up and down. "Of course. Out here, anyone within a twenty-mile radius is a neighbor. My mama helped her with cookin' sometimes when she had them big parties."

Emily is astonished. She's remembering the passage from *Cross Creek* where Rawlings talked about a woman helping her cook for large parties. And if Rawlings hadn't died in 1953, surely the people in this area would know if she stayed close by. But wouldn't people recognize her? She remembers Silver's lesson on Florida bush etiquette, and decides there could be a thousand people hiding out in this area and no one would say a word.

And Tag's knowing her, having a memory of what he thought of her is such a priceless piece of information for a historian, someone like Emily who relishes verbal and written snapshots of the past, that she has to stop herself from jumping out of the car and throwing her arms around him.

She proceeds cautiously, like one of the snakes in the bushes beyond her car that she doesn't see. "Can you tell me what she was like?"

Tag purses his lips, takes in a breath, and it looks as if he's reaching down deep to remember. "You don't forget a woman like that, Miss Emily. I was a little boy, but I remember some things, and when my mama came home from helpin' over there, well, she was full of stories."

Ever so slowly, Emma sticks her head out of the window as far as it can go without the rest of her body falling after it, and gently tells him she would love to know what he thought. She adds that she has recently fallen under Miss Rawlings' spell herself and that it would mean a great deal to her if he could share some memories.

Tag smiles and leans back in his brown saddle. He says there were other people around who had memories of, "that writer woman from the north," as he calls her. No one, he shares, had ever met anyone like her. She wasn't a native but she dug right in, "dipping her hands right into the very heart of this here Cross Creek world."

Emily pauses and waits for his memories to rise. Although she isn't involved in oral research now, and she desperately wants to be, she knows what to do. People love to talk about their lives and how they have intersected with someone or something another person might want to know about. She studied interviewing in college and often talked to the researchers in her department about how they were able to help pry stories loose, incidents, old memories from people who either didn't want to remember them or simply forgot.

Some researchers had to feign interest and others were patient, peppering their subjects with short questions, quiet, perhaps a soft touch on the arm, or something personal from their own lives to let them know that what they had to say was of great interest and in fact, could help people.

Emily correctly assumes that someone like Tag relishes the quiet and spends good parts of his day alone, listening to the elements and the creatures who prance through this wild country where the sound of a single car is a huge distraction. She's a foreigner, but she's quickly learned some of the rules of this land, a land that appears to be harsh and wild but that also thrives on the manners it has demanded. After all, this is the south and she is a city girl from the north. And in the north people get upset if their lattes are too hot or not hot enough. They beep their horns and rob each other. They flip out if someone isn't driving fast enough and then they try to run them off the road. They interrupt when someone else is speaking and their manners would make a million mothers roll over in their graves.

Of course part of that is a misconception, just as Emily and some of her northerners might assume that everyone in Florida raises pigs, votes conservatively, and has high cholesterol from eating butter, grits, bacon, and fried everything. She's already seen an organic garden and has discovered a literary world that would make every bestselling author who thinks he or she has it made head to Cross Creek.

So she's patient as Tag sorts through memories that either span before 1953 or after.

"My mama used ta come home with her hands a-wavin' and say that the Good Lord created something one-of-a-kind when he made up that Miz Marjorie," Tag recalls, speaking with his eyes closed, his head still tipped back. "She had parties, and called my mama to work at them and once or twice I went along, although that was a long, long time ago and I'm older than purty much anything you can see for a hundred miles."

"How old are you?"

"That's a secret my mama took to her grave, but near as I can figure I'm at least ninety."

"Ninety!" Emily throws back her own head and whistles in astonishment and appreciation. "Look at you!"

"I try not to, Miss Emily," he says, laughing. "I don't even think there's a mirror left in the cabin."

She asks him if he remembers being at Marjorie's house, the same house she is about to try and find.

And Tag says yes. He remembers sitting on a tall stool near a window and Miz Rawlings rushing in and out while the women tried to cook. He said his mama kept saying, "Leave us be woman!" when Miz Rawlings came fluttering into the kitchen. But then he got to eat the food and it wasn't like anything he had ever tasted. It was rich and creamy and there were pies and cakes and someone famous was coming that had Miz Rawlings all excited.

Well, of course Marjorie would have visitors. Emily hasn't thought about this but at her peak she must have known the other great writers of her time. Who could have been there? Her mind is spinning, and the sun isn't even past the tree line yet.

"Do you remember who might have been coming to visit?" Emily has some vague ideas about prominent authors back in the twenties, thirties and forties. Hemingway? Virginia Wolf? Her mind is going blank again.

"My mama told me later that I snuck into the room, sat behind the door, and listened when the man spoke," he shares, shifting his weight forward in the saddle. "It was poetry I think. But that was so long ago. So very long..."

Tag trails off as if he's gotten lost inside of his own mind and Emily can't imagine what he has seen, felt, and experienced for nearly a hundred years. So many changes have occurred in the world but here, a mile from a lone highway, where men still ride horses barefoot, perhaps time has stood still. Not remembering the name of a poet can hardly be a fault.

Emily so wants to keep him talking. She asks him what people generally thought about Rawlings. Does he remember what people said?

Tag laughs and says people here have never stopped talking. It's the outside world that has forgotten about who Miz Rawlings was, how she lived, and what she brought to this mostly forgotten part of the world. He speaks slowly, as if he's standing right in front of the resurrected Miz Rawlings and says how she was stubborn, and feisty, and smart and how she always had to have the last word. But everyone loved her, and she helped so many people.

"But something happened to her here too, something that turned her heart inside out," Tag has dropped his head so low in a gesture of sadness that his hat is covering his entire face.

Before Emily can say anything else, the horse throws back his head and begins backing up. Tag quickly controls him, calming the animal with his low voice, and then walks the horse close to the car.

"This little girl is my time clock," he tells her, tipping his hat as he reins the horse towards the other side of the road. "You go on now to Cross Creek. Ya'll find what you are lookin' for if you look hard enough."

Emily doesn't want him to go. "Can I talk to you again, Tag?" she shouts after him as the horse pulls up from the shallow ditch.

"If you can find me, ma'am," Tag hollers as he heads into a stand of towering oaks.

For a moment Emily can see the last half of the horse sauntering, Tag Dunlin's head moving back and forth with his trusty companion, his bare feet dangling and ignoring the stirrups as the sun slithers through the trees. She almost expects a band to drop out of the sky and start playing an old country western song.

But there's only the soft rustle of animals scurrying through the bushes, the sound of her heart cascading from her chest to her ears, and the whisper of someone who can only be Marjorie Kinnan Rawlins saying, "Cross Creek, Cross Creek, Cross Creek."

Emily starts her car, pushes aside her gaff, turns the car around, doesn't bother to look for oncoming traffic, throws Tag a kiss out the window, and as she accelerates, the wind picks up and it feels as if someone has brushed the side of her face with a hand as soft as silk.

Then for a few terribly brief moments, Emily is exhilarated because she has not only found Tag, but temporarily banished all thoughts of evil as she forces herself to imagine that she's safe.

It is an illusion that she will later remember disappeared as quickly as Tag and his trusty four-legged companion.

# 11

*"I stood there, my hands straight as arrows against my thighs, my eyes closed and in the darkness, in the deep world behind my own eyes, I saw something so pure and right that from that moment on, nothing, absolutely nothing would ever be the same again."*
— *Lost Hearts in the Swamp of Life* - MKR - 1963

County Highway 325 that meanders toward Cross Creek from Silver's house is thankfully a paved road that has an almost constant canopy of moss-laden trees swaying on both of its sides. Palm fronds and bright flowered bushes announce an occasional opening in the thick underbrush that reveals a driveway or a long gravel road that disappears just a few feet from the edge of the highway. Birds seem to be everywhere-white, black, pink, small, big-and the sound of a flock of wild parrots squawking as if they are having a massive debate lingers for a good mile after Emily has passed them.

She is still driving so slowly she could actually get out and run alongside of her own car, but Emily's afraid she's going to miss something if she drives too fast. Maybe she will find another Tag, or someone who matches the list she of names she has crumpled up in her right hand. She can't ever remember being this enthralled by a place since her college research days when she was constantly traipsing through musty libraries. She absolutely doesn't want to miss the turn off to what her map has told her is Marjorie Kinnan Rawlings Historic State Park.

The locals like Tag, Silver, and Auggue-doesn't anyone here have a real name in this state? call the once-famous writer's homestead Cross Creek, but the tiny dot on her map next to Cross Creek is directing her to a state park. Someone in Florida must have recognized the importance of this woman's life, even if the rest of the world has seemingly forgotten who she is.

Emily's thinking about that as she meanders down the almost deserted highway, occasionally being passed by a truck or car whose occupants always smile and wave at her as if they might know who she is or where she's going. But the sound of an approaching car still makes her stomach lurch, and she's relieved each time a car approaches and it isn't red. She shakes her head to try and stay away from negative thoughts, but the reality of what's going on and what could happen at any moment is hard to ignore.

Emily is torn about her emotions. One part of her is jubilant about the work she's doing, how she managed to discover Tag all on her own, and the potential for the shattering of history that would happen if she can prove that the papers she discovered are real. The other part is totally on edge and feels almost as helpless as Marjorie must have felt the first months she lived in Cross Creek.

Yet Emily can't bring herself to retreat. This day, everything that has happened, and everything that might happen is still a broad gift. That's how she convinces herself to keep going with the simple notion that- *she will survive.*

Empowered by Marjorie's own life, Emily uses that as her personal fuel.

Someone like Rawlings, who she's embarrassed to acknowledge she remembers very little about from her long-ago English classes, must still have a cadre of fans and followers who trek to the historic site, and perhaps devour anything written about her or by her. Emily will find out soon enough.

Emily likes to think she knows a few things about the world beyond her office and the expansive library where she prowls through boxes, shelves, and the lives of people who no longer exist. There are always lively discussions about the world and often, because so many university workers and professors are obsessed with publishing, they talk about the literary world. Popular modern writers seem to come and go like the latest fashions she notices in the student union. Trends in literature have been fascinating to her, not just because she's an avid reader herself, but because she agrees that anything that gets people reading, and then talking about it, is good.

But she's also seen the demise of so many writers and authors, many at her own university, who fall victim to the whims of fickle reviewers and the even more fickle world beyond. And she's always felt that writers should be allowed to stretch and grow like athletes who decide one day to put down their balls and clubs and switch careers.

But so often, if a popular writer's second or third book veers from some type of expected path, they are tossed aside by the reading pubic, who often demand the same story but with new characters and a different cover. And over the years, when the writers from Marjorie's own generation died off, the literary world, it seems, has become more and more about the bottom line, and less about literary merit.

Emily now sees a small cluster of homes and an increase of road signs and wonders if she's getting close to Cross Creek. A peacock is standing by the side of the road sunning itself with it's tail fanned out as if a show is about to start, when Emily remembers a recent discussion with an English professor who was researching this very topic.

He told her that the economic downturn and the rise of computer readers had not just hacked off publishing house employees, bookstores, and profits but many talented authors as well. His contention was that the decades of nurturing great potential authors like Hemingway, Fitzgerald-and, Emily now realizes, the Marjorie Kinnan Rawlings of the world-had all but come to an end. "The bottom line in publishing has switched from developing great talent, or even recognizing it, to which book is going to make the most money," the professor had told her.

Emily argued with him. She said there had to be true hearts and souls left in publishing who wept when they read a beautiful sentence, would fight to get something magical published, and who were in it for more than just a weekly paycheck. Now, she knew she could prove it to him-if only Silver's story were hers for the sharing.

Emily forcefully shook her head from side to side to banish any notions of what she might actually do if she proves her manuscripts are real. If Leslie wrote them then the decision about what to do would be much easier, because Leslie's Florida retreat wasn't a huge secret. Marjorie Rawlings faking her death and then going into hiding for dozens of years would offer an entirely new set of choices.

Then there is the mysterious man in the red car, whoever in the world he may be. The mere thought of him sneaking around makes Emily's skin crawl. Just like the sheriff and Silver, she understands enough about human beings to know that when people are desperate, their behavior often escalates until they do something that crosses the invisible line society has drawn that defines what is acceptable and what is not.

When she glances down and looks at the beat up gaff, which is now resting against the passenger door, she wishes the damn thing would fit in her purse. If this jerk who drove to the house last night knows more than she does, and is already making mistakes, who's to say what he might do next? There has to be some connection. He must know something. Emily has always thought of herself as someone who puts together the puzzle pieces of other's lives. She uses a long lost letter, a handkerchief with initials carefully stitched onto the hem, fading photographs, a frayed marriage certificate, whatever clues land on her desk to put together life story after life story. This search for Marjorie Rawlings is perhaps no different than that. People often leave clues on purpose. She's discovered letters tucked inside of vases and once she found a gold ring with initials hand-carved in the side that she traced back to Eleanor Roosevelt. The boxes might be part of an elaborate and carefully planned scavenger hunt. Emily also knows that people often plan ahead because they know who has the mind, the talent, and the desire to find the pieces of the puzzle.

There are missing pieces to the story she is now trying to piece together, she realizes, and the man clearly following her, or so she thinks, might have some of the biggest pieces. Emily is determined now in ways she has not been determined since she drove off that major highway. She's also beginning to think there is more at stake then she or Silver might realize, and she almost wishes the gaff were a machine gun.

Emily almost goes off the road when she reaches down to grab the frightening-looking weapon and tucks it against her leg. She also makes an instant promise to herself that when and if she gets back to Ohio, she's going to take a self-defense refresher course and do everything she can to prepare herself for battle. For now her backup team of Silver, Auggie, Mr. Beautiful and whatever weapons they have stockpiled will have to do.

Emily suddenly realizes she's started to drive across a bridge. She tickles her brakes and the car glides to a stop in the middle of the concrete structure. She motions the car behind her forward and a lovely couple with straw hats on waves as she looks to her left and sees a faded green sign that says Cross Creek. The sides of the low creek are shaded by massive brown and green trees and although the dark water shimmers in the sun, Emily can't help but feel that something ominous could be lurking around the next bend.

The world feels like church beyond the brown sign announcing entrance to Marjorie Kinnan Rawlings Historic State Park. Emily has convinced herself that the searing feeling of approaching doom has something do with the continued quiet. When she pulls off the highway and her tires once again hit gravel, there isn't another car in sight.

The entrance to the park and historic site is apparently also an entrance to many things. Emily parks in the small lot to the right, not far from the entrance, and can see picnic tables scattered in a dozen places. It looks as if there's also an established boat launch, a small pavilion, and restrooms. But for now, all Emily cares about is seeing where Marjorie lived.

Before she gets out of the car, she dutifully calls Silver, who assured her cell phones work on that end of the county, to check in, but Silver suddenly doesn't seem interested in knowing if Emily has been hacked to death. "I'm here and safe," she announces.

"Okay," Silver mumbles.

Emily is about to step out of her car and stops. She's already thinking like the sheriff. It's not like Silver to say only one word. Maybe she's being held at gunpoint.

"Are you okay?" Before she gives Silver a chance to respond, Emily keeps talking. "If someone is there and you can't speak, say the word…" Emily is looking around to think of a word, "…*trespass*."

Silver snorts. "What the hell is wrong with you?"

"Does this mean you are not being held at gunpoint?"

"Well, trespass is not something I would say if someone had tape around my ankles and there was a .38 special pointed at my head."

"My imagination was running wild, I guess, and I just pulled into Cross Creek and that's the first thing I saw, a 'No Trespassing' sign next door." Emily is sitting with her legs out of the car, her rear on the seat, and her head in her hands.

"Honey, it's probably a good idea considering some whack job is out there watching us walk around the house. I've been reading the manuscript since you left, and I'm a bit distracted."

"What do you think?" Emily sits up, and totally forgets about the safe word.

Silver does not. "The safe word will now be *excellent*. Do you get that?"

"Yes. I won't even say it now because I don't need to. But the reading?"

"All I'm going to say now is *holy shit*. Go see Cross Creek. Be careful. I mean, really be careful now that I'm reading this. If this is what I think it is... holy shit!"

Silver clicks off and Emily, invigorated by all things not *excellent*, leaves the rest of the world, and her weapon behind her, as she slowly walks into the world one once inhabited by MKR. She thinks about taking the gaff but decides, even in this part of the country, it would look ridiculous for her to carry it around the park. Seriously, she tells herself, it's a historic site, a park, a place to fish, even as her heart thumps a bit and she looks around before she shuts her car door to verify that she is still alone.

There is a well-worn path extending from the parking lot to her right and Emily eagerly follows it past a fence overgrown with a tangle of vines and flowers. Then she's immediately disappointed. "Damn!" she shouts. The sign lists the tour schedule and there isn't one for another hour. But she quickly discovers that she can still walk through the grounds. Emily pauses at a metal gate, places her hand over her heart and realizes she's about to walk into a world that has been frozen in time.

The metal gate hangs a bit crookedly and she gingerly pushes it open and starts to walk up the path. She's immediately greeted on the right by a large brown sign with carved white lettering:

*It is necessary to leave the impersonal highway, to step inside the rusty gate and close it behind. One is now inside the orange grove, out of the world and in the mysterious heart of another. And after long years of spiritual homelessness, of nostalgia, here is that mystic loveliness of childhood again. Here is home. Marjorie Kinnan Rawlings, Cross Creek, 1942.*

Emily turns to her left, and now notices that she is standing in what once must have been Marjorie's orange grove. The air is totally still as she walks forward and thinks about what she has just read. Marjorie must have felt as if she had truly come home the moment she stepped out of her car and onto the hot, sandy soil here. The old metal gate with the curved top was apparently her entryway into a world that she had dreamed about finding most of her life.

It's hard for Emily to feel the pull of place that Rawlings must have felt. She realizes she's been seduced by the glorious wild surroundings that she's immersed herself in for the past five days, but to live so remotely, all those years ago, must have been like stepping into a third-world country. There's a mild flutter of longing that sweeps through her chest as she bends to pick up a half rotted orange from a tree just to the side of the path. Emily realizes that perhaps she's jealous. She's avoided her own search for place for such a long time it feels almost as if she's intruding.

Obviously this is a public park, but surely Marjorie came here not just for the wildness but because she craved solitude. That has to be a huge part of why she followed her heart to Florida and then to Cross Creek. Anxious now to fill in the blanks of a story she has only been guessing about, Emily walks forward and comes to a seating area attached to a barn. There are benches lined up where visitors must begin the tour. She bends in to read a notice that invites visitors to look around until the tour starts.

Emily steps out of the seating area, glances into the attached barn and then sees the white-sided house where Rawlings must have lived. She's torn between running full speed ahead to look in the windows or to continue exploring and waiting for the proper tour. She decides to turn around, walk through the rest of the park, and wait patiently for the tour to begin.

Just then her cell phone buzzes to announce that she's received a text message, and she freezes in place. The grand sights she is looking at can't override the constant reminder that she needs to be alert and stay focused. Emily catches her breath, gingerly removes the cell phone from her pocket, and flips it open. Even though she all but sterilized the phone before she used it, simply touching it makes her shiver as if she's just stepped into a freezer.

The message is thankfully from Silver, reminding her not to be stupid and to remain cautious. Emily shuts the phone and realizes how easy it is to be seduced by her surroundings. She is going to have to try and stay focused, already something that is not easily accomplished.

Back at the gate, Emily grabs a park brochure out of a box attached to the entrance sign and decides to walk toward the water, which according to the brochure is Lochloosa Lake. Obviously the huge section of land that is now a park had to have been Rawlings' backyard.

She starts to walk, quickly forgetting as she is swept away by her own imagination and the glorious morning, that less than an hour ago she was thinking about machine guns and self-defense. The park fans out toward what looks like an ever-widening creek-Cross Creek, perhaps-and she walks to the edge of the water and is startled to see three huge herons, white, with light blue beards and chests lined with off-white feathers, stepping through the water as if they are walking on glass.

The birds are hunting for food, and an occasional slurping sound as they dip their beaks into the water is all that she hears as she stands watching them for a very long time. Suddenly, there is the faint sound of a boat motor. Emily moves down to the water and away from the birds, and walks toward a pier that is on the far side of the park that she hasn't noticed before. There are several trucks parked next to the ramp with empty trailers.

She hops off the riverbank just as a small silver boat turns the corner and heads toward her. The man running the boat motor sees her, smiles and waves, and asks over the soft whirl of the boat motor, if she can help him bring the boat in.

"I'll try," she says, smiling back and dropping to her knees.

The grey-haired man has a weathered tan face that tells its own story. His cheeks are lined with cascading crevices that must have been beaten into place during decades of sun drenched days on the lakes. His old blue cap is resting on his knee and he wheels the boat against the side of the dock with absolute perfection as if he is steering a small car.

"Just grab the line, if you don't mind," he suggests, shifting in his seat. "I can do this myself but I have to admit, it gets a little harder every day."

Emily grabs the rope, steadies the boat and then without further instruction, wraps it around a post as the man steps out and onto the dock.

He struggles to his feet and then sticks out his hand and says, "I'm Jimmy Carlton, and I thank you very much."

"Emily Weaver, and the pleasure is all mine," Emily takes his hand and then, totally enamored by his bright blue eyes and sweet smile, can't help herself and clasps both her hands around his. She also trying to remember if she's seen the name Carlton in *Cross Creek* or any of the magazine articles she has read.

Enchanted, Emily asks him about fishing, and the lake and so many things all at once he puts up his hands and laughs. "Slow down girl! You sound like you're writing a term paper."

"Sorry," Emily apologizes. "I'm doing some research and... well, this Rawlings country has sort of captured me like it must have captured her."

"It did indeed," he agrees. "I grew up around the corner from her. My father took her fishing and hunting and I suppose you could say we were in some way part of the family she created here."

Emily has to force herself to keep breathing. She can't believe this is the second person in a row she's met who actually knew Marjorie Rawlings. "You knew her?"

"More than knew her," he says, smiling happily. "I slept in her house, she cooked for me, and she inspired me to go to college, and maybe we were kindred spirits because I couldn't stay away from Cross Creek either."

"This is unbelievable," she admits. "I met someone else who knew her a while ago."

"It's only unbelievable if you don't live here. There are only a few hundred people in this area. If you look closely, you'll see there hasn't been any new homes built in years and the people like me who either stayed or came back, well, we all know each other."

Emily agrees that makes sense and Jimmy tells her that it's likely every other person she meets either had a relative who knew her, knew her personally, or knew someone who was touched in some way by Rawlings' life. "But us old farts are dying off so the Rawlings legend is dying off too, which is kind of sad," he adds quietly. "Maybe someone like you can keep it all alive."

Stunned, Emily peppers him with more questions about life in Cross Creek after she identifies herself, only half lying once again, as a historical librarian from the university. She wants to know if the park is true to Marjorie's life.

"Very true," he says. "Haven't you been on the tour?"

"I'm going on the next one."

"You better hurry then, it's starting in a few minutes."

Emily's been swept away by their conversation and has forgotten the time. She's torn. Emily could talk to this man all day.

She looks back toward the park entrance and hesitates. "I don't suppose you'd ever consider taking a city girl out fishing on that lake, would you?"

Jimmy chuckles and bends down to grab the stringer of fish that's dangling off the side of the boat. "I bet you'd talk my ears off."

"Yes, I would but you have a lot to say-don't you?"

"I've been meaning to write a book."

"There's been a lot of that going on around here. There's no reason for it not to keep happening." Emily is crossing her fingers that she can snag a day on the lake with this man.

Jimmy puts his cap back on his head, sighs, and tells her that he fishes every single day of the year. It could rain or be cold or even miraculously snow, and he still fishes.

"You want to fish and talk, Miss Emily, then you come down here any morning at 6:00 am, and I'll take you fishing," he agrees. "Now hurry on up there, because your tour is starting."

Emily literally jumps for joy, which makes him laugh out loud, and then she turns and runs like a little girl back through the metal gate, totally forgetting to look into the parking lot where a big red SUV has parked on the very far side of the park entrance.

# 12

*"The feeling came over me gradually, like the fluttering of tiny wings at first. Then the wings grew larger, day-by-day, until I became the very birds I had been watching. It was a powerful thing to know that I could fly, leave, stay or go and that I had a choice. I finally knew I had a choice."*
—*Lost Hearts in the Swamp of Life* - MKR - 1963

Emily is breathless as she all but falls into the seating area next to the barn. When she skids to a halt near the back row a small cloud of dust announces her arrival and the more than two dozen people who had been paying attention to the docent turn and look at her with disgust.

"Sorry," she says cheerfully, waving to everyone.

Embarrassed, she tries to melt into the back of the crowd as everyone refocuses and the docent, dressed in a 1940s long skirt, apron, and with her hair tied up in a flower-patterned scarf continues talking. It takes Emily a few moments to focus. She surprised so many people have shown up for the tour. Maybe the Rawlings legacy isn't as diminished as she thought.

"So, where were we?" The docent begins again, looking directly at Emily. "For those of you who just arrived, I'm Betsy

Gimbel and I work for the park, but my family has lived in Cross Creek for three generations. This is what someone might have worn when Miss Rawlings lived here. Before I continue, I'd like to know how many of you have been here before."

Betsy is obviously another connection to Rawlings. Jimmy must be right. Even if Marjorie died in 1953, stories of encounters with the famous writer would have been passed down from one generation to the next. Emily wonders who Rawlings trusted the most and if she would have dared to tell someone in Cross Creek if she had decided to disappear.

Emily can't see around the entire circle or along the back of where they are sitting but she's amazed when she sees at least ten hands go up following Betsy's question.

"This doesn't surprise me," Betsy says, clapping her hands in delight. "I think the record for someone coming back is close to fifty visits now. Cross Creek inspires many people, the least of all being Marjorie Kinnan Rawlings."

Betsy quickly gives some brief background about Marjorie's early life and mentions her younger brother Arthur, her parents, and her years at the University of Wisconsin. By the time she came to Florida with her then-husband Charles, Betsy tells the crowd that Marjorie was eager for a new place to grow her stories and anxious for solitude. She fell in love with Florida and the rural trappings of Cross Creek and the challenges the land brought to her were a seductive force for the young writer.

The seventy-four acre farm that Rawlings purchased for $14,500 in 1928 with money from her mother's estate was originally a hodgepodge of buildings and land that had become abandoned by a succession of tired families. Betsy explained that when Rawlings took on the Cross Creek challenge she had her work cut out for her. First of all, she was an outsider and that meant she was stepping into an unfamiliar world where new faces were not necessarily welcomed and accepted. Also the farm was in great disrepair and needed much work to get it back into working order.

"And the living conditions were normal for this area but primitive for someone who had been living in the city," she told the group. "Marjorie Rawlings was up for the challenge but her husband Charles was not. Marjorie wanted to be an author and was obviously inspired by the surroundings here, but Charles didn't fall in love with Cross Creek and the marriage did not last."

Emily finds it remarkable that it was Charles and not Marjorie who fled from the wilderness. It's usually the woman who wants a flush toilet and not an outhouse and who packs up and heads north at the first sign of hardship. Rawlings must have been a piece of work.

She is so focused on the short lecture she hasn't bothered to see who else is in attendance. While Betsy has been speaking, Emily's fished in her purse, located an old notebook, and has been writing furiously. She doesn't want to miss a thing and is already hoping that Betsy will be able to answer questions when the tour is finished. Emily is also beside herself with excitement. It's one thing to read history and to imagine what it was like where a person lived, what they saw when they looked out the window, what the chair was like they sat in every day, how far they had to walk to the highway or a hundred other details that fill in the blanks of a life well-lived. But to actually see those details makes her squirm as Betsy talks about orange groves, and how Marjorie slowly worked her way into the hearts and lives of her neighbors.

"Here was a woman who had a college degree and had already worked for big city newspapers and traveled," Betsy says with such enthusiasm Emily thinks she could be saying these things for the very first time. "Not everyone warmed up right away, but Miss Rawlings quickly became known as a woman who would help anyone, at any time, and she fell into life here as if she had been born down the road and lived here her entire life."

There's a bit of noise at the far side of the group and Emily glances up to see a woman frantically waving her hand. Betsy stops for a moment and says there will be plenty of time at the end of the tour to ask questions. Emily has been focusing so hard on the talk that she's tensed up the muscles in her neck. She leans forward, stretches, and turns her head. When she opens her eyes she sees that a man is staring at her.

She shakes her head, thinks nothing of it, and Betsy has now launched into what she calls "the golden years" when Marjorie was inspired to write novels and short stories, worked the farm, and fell into the rhythms of every aspect of Florida Cracker life. That life included hunting, fishing, camping and managing a small farm and its workers.

"Then," Betsy says wistfully, "she met Norton. Norton Baskin. He was a handsome, smart, young businessman and Marjorie fell in love, only this time it wasn't with a place, it was with a man."

Several women start clapping, someone whistles, and Emily stops writing and senses that someone has moved in behind her. She leans forward and notices that the man who had been staring at her is not there. Now, she tries to remember, without acting crazy, what he looked like. Tall-ish, light hair, thin, and too damn young to be sitting in this crowd listening to a woman in a long skirt talk about a dead author.

Emily tries to calm down and at the very same time she's wanting to stand up and scream *excellent* so loudly that Silver will hear her all those miles away. She forces herself to stay calm and listen, and she can't bring herself to turn around and see if it's the man who was staring at her who has come to stand behind her.

Emily's head starts to pound. The man who was staring at her totally fits the description of the man Bob saw, and the man who was nothing but trouble at the library. She slowly moves her right hand down to touch her cell phone and wishes she would have learned how to text without looking, like everyone in the world under the age of twenty-five.

Even though her concentration is shot, Emily forces herself to listen. She inches forward on the bench as far as she can without falling off and stops taking notes. While Betsy tells of the wild parties and the famous visitors and the parade of hired hands that came and went, Emily is wondering if she could use her pen to attack someone. This is not how she thought her Cross Creek visit would go. Emily knows she could be overreacting. Maybe the young man is a budding English professor, or someone like herself who's doing research for a graduate course, or simply because he's interested in history.

But probably not. Emily's thinking he may have been following her all day and immediately worries about Tag and now Jimmy too. And now he's standing right behind her. She hates herself for being so stupid. She should have looked in the parking lot instead of booking a fishing expedition. Forcing herself to be logical, Emily tries hard to relax. She's with other people. She's landed at Marjorie's Mecca and how dare he bother her, if that's his intention. She's obviously safer sitting in this group than out driving around the country roads and running around in the rain with two wild women.

Emily's almost angry when she pushes back on her seat and starts to write while Betsy talks about Marjorie's marriage to Norton and how writing *The Yearling* drastically changed her life. But now it's almost impossible for her to even hold her pen steady and she clenches it in her hand so tightly her knuckles turn white.

"She became an international celebrity after she won the Pulitzer Prize for *The Yearling*," Betsy says proudly, as if she were talking about her own great aunt. "People came from everywhere just to see her and it wasn't uncommon to find her out in the front yard, handing out oranges and signing copies of her book for strangers."

While Emily sits immobile, Betsy explains that *The Yearling* and the Hollywood movie that was made based on the book were nothing compared to what happened when Marjorie dared to write the book *Cross Creek*, a first person account of her life and struggles and the people who were her neighbors. Rawlings, Betsy said, opened up rural Florida in ways that no one else ever had. Through humor, insight, and honesty Rawlings' portrayal of life in the central Florida, or scrub country, opened up this part of the world in ways that changed many hearts and minds.

"Those of us who live here know what it's like, but the rest of the world saw us as nothing but backwoods fools most of the time." Betsy now has her hands on her hips as if she's trying to prove a point. "Her memoir proved we were hard-working, loyal, kind, generous people who had so much determination and grit we wouldn't let something like a hurricane, hundred-degree temperatures, or runaway pigs stop us from living here."

The crowd laughs and the impatient woman who raised her hand earlier can't seem to stop herself. "But not everyone who lived here liked her or what she wrote in *Cross Creek*. Her friend Zelma ended up hating her guts."

Emily is certain that Betsy would love to dismiss the loud mouth visitor or give her a time out like teachers do in first grade. She's also glad for a bit of comic relief, even if she still won't turn around to see who's standing behind her. Maybe he'll disappear if she ignores him.

"Someone's been doing their research," Betsy says tactfully. "I plan to talk about Zelma and her famous lawsuit a bit later, if that's all right with you."

The woman gets the point and nods in agreement. Betsy pauses to grab some brochures off the table next to her and then asks that they be passed around before they go look at Marjorie's house and the other buildings at the park. When the papers are passed to her, Emily suddenly realizes that she needs to pass them to whoever is standing behind her.

She takes in a breath, turns to confront the man, or at the very least look him in the eye, and there's no one behind her. She jumps up and frantically starts looking around oblivious to the fact that she looks absolutely crazy.

"Are you okay back there?" Betsy asks, leaning to one side to see what in the world is going on.

"I... I thought someone was behind me, that's all," Emily stammers, wondering if she's not suddenly suffering from heat stroke.

"Someone was back there but it appears as if he left, so just pass those back this way," Betsy orders, unfazed, it seems, by pretty much anything. "He should have stuck around because I haven't gotten to the good part yet. The good part being the parties and the whiskey and the cigarettes and the grand celebrations when the indoor toilet was christened."

Emily is relieved and confused. She sits down, tries to focus on the brochures, which detail the interior of the house they are about to see, and wonders if she shouldn't call Silver.

And suddenly she feels as if she has taken a huge step backwards. Here she is about to tour the home of a woman who was obviously ahead of her time and she's acting like a nutcase, but for good reason. There is so much she still needs to learn about Rawlings, who without question wasn't afraid of a challenge, or a new life, or digging through the tangled vines of this primitive place. Emily sits quietly, gazing at the hand drawn photos in the brochure of the very rooms where Marjorie lived and loved and she has a revelation about history and memory that surely others have had before her.

*No one really knows.*

Absolutely no one knows what was really in Marjorie's heart the day she stepped out of that car and saw this place. No one knows, even if she wrote about it, what it was exactly like to leave a marriage back then, live alone, marry again and then literally carve a new life out of the swamps and brush and bush where people looked at you funny if you were not one of them. No one knows if she cried herself to sleep or sat behind this very barn wishing for someone to come carry her away on the hardest days.

The days when something else broke, or the heat rendered her faint, or the water stopped, or whatever in the hell animals live on the other side of the fence broke though. The nights when she wondered if she had been right to claim

Cross Creek and watch as Charles turned with his suitcase and walked away forever. The weeks and months and years when the struggle for survival, for simply living, bashed up against the creative veins in her soul like waves in the middle of a wild storm. The months when the stories didn't sell and the fence needed to be fixed and a frost might be less than a mile away.

Emily has her head in her hands and is thinking about how people always second guess and assume. She does it herself. People in the department next door make more money. Her sister hates her. The son she adores really isn't busy but she somehow offended him on her last visit. On this very trip, for example, she discovered that the aunt she always thought was a spinster had actually been married once for five years to a lovely Hispanic man who treated her like a queen until the day he died in a car accident.

It had to be like that for brave Marjorie too. Back then, when women were secretaries, teachers, or nuns-there was Marjorie Kinnan Rawlings, running through life with a machete in one hand, a typewriter in the other, and some of those nylons she was obviously wearing in those wall photos she saw at Shirley's library.

When Emily laughs she doesn't realize that it's absolutely quiet and everyone is looking at the brochures while Betty scurries ahead to open up the house.

"Pretty funny brochure, is it?" This of course, from the big-mouth who kept raising her hand.

Emily doesn't respond at first but thinks, even though she acknowledges she really doesn't yet know Marjorie, that Rawlings might tell this woman to kiss her ass. All the unspoken thoughts and words in her life seem to be merging and she's straining not to jump up and slap this woman. Instead she struggles to control herself, looks up, smiles, and instead of saying something to embarrass the woman, Emily decides to remain silent. Her arms are shaking with nervousness, and she's definitely no Marjorie Rawlings.

Just then Betty comes back into view clapping her hands and singing, "Are we excited?"

Emily is anxious to get the spotlight off of herself and so buoyed by the fact that human beings are still excited to walk backwards into history that she all but leaps like a ballet dancer to her feet. She's not quite at the rear of the pack when they amble just a few feet and Betty explains that the barn is a replica, but built from photographs to look exactly like the barn that was in the same place when Marjorie was alive.

The group shuffles along and, like Emily, they are not too excited about a fake barn. She glances inside and sees a few tools placed here and there. A rake, a bale of hay, some old milk cans and through the open back door she has a glimpse of the highway that runs directly in front of the property. Emily lingers for a moment while everyone passes her. It's likely that some of the tools actually were Marjorie's. Emily can feel herself falling into the "I can't believe I'm really here" zone.

Years ago, when she visited the Thomas Edison museum on the other side of Florida, she recalls walking through the laboratory where Edison worked as if she were about to touch Jesus. The museum had been kept in the exact same condition as it had been the day Edison died. Tubes and vials and pencils and paper, and perhaps here and there the fingerprints, too, of one of the greatest inventors of all time. Emily doesn't know the entire story yet, but she's hoping Marjorie's house is the real deal.

She's thinking about Edison and all the great people of the past when she hears Betty clap her hands as if she's calling all the cows to the barn. She starts to turn when she sees something or someone move very fast past the open back barn door. Emily stops, focuses on the open door, and waits. Nothing happens, and no one is coming out from in back of the barn. Convinced she's seeing things, and totally on edge, she turns away, and hurries to catch up with the group.

Betty is standing on top of three steps leading into the house. Emily wishes she'd had more time or even access to a computer, God forbid, to do a bit more research. The white-sided house looks as if it has a fairly new shake shingle roof and the screened porch they are about to enter is framed in forest green wood trim. Everything looks new and well kept. The crowd is surging a bit as if they are at a rock concert and close to the stage.

"People, relax," Betty admonishes. "You will all get in here. No photographs, please, or I'll throw your camera into Cross Creek with the other five thousand that I've put there. We've worked very hard to make this exactly the way it was when Marjorie lived here and besides simply being rude, the flash is horrid. Focus on what's here. Now..."

"Is this her stuff?" The big-mouth obviously can't help herself. She's standing on her tiptoes and pushing against the woman standing in front of her. Emily is now certain Rawlings would have thrown her off the property by now.

Betty is really starting to lose her patience. She's glaring at big mouth as if she could eat her for breakfast. Instead of answering her question she simply keeps talking. Someone like this woman is probably visiting here every day.

"What I see constantly is that people are so busy taking photographs that they don't even see what they are looking at," Betty, clearly in control, explains. "The woman who lived in this house was amazing. The house she made and the life she lived here are also amazing. Please think about that. Focus on every little thing you see and then think about it later using the photographs in your mind because that's exactly what she would have done."

No one is moving now and even big-mouth has gotten the hint. Betty continues and tells them Marjorie donated the house to the University of Florida, and for a while young authors were allowed to live in the home and work. The university eventually gave it to the state of Florida park system and the people running the show were smart enough to realize the significance of restoring the home and grounds.

"Marjorie Kinnan Rawlings wasn't just one of the greatest American female authors of all times, but she was an environmentalist, a feminist, someone who seriously changed the way the world viewed the people who lived here, and also how the world viewed and interacted with African Americans," Betty shares, clearly a Rawlings scholar and fan. "She was not a conformist but a woman who lived her life with the very same kind of poetry that she wrote."

Emily is as captivated by Betty's speech as is the rest of the group. Clearly there is much, much more to Miss Rawlings than the books she wrote and the awards she won. Rawlings, Emily now realizes, was like so many other women of her era. The world had certain standards, and you were expected to live by those standards. She now realizes that Rawlings' life was a passionate swim upstream. It's one thing to take on and survive in the literary world, but another altogether to do that by living an unconventional life. Emily is thinking about how the hard parts of her own life pale in comparison to what Rawlings must have gone though.

"Lastly, before we go in, I have to tell you that the furnishings in this house, down to the old packages of cigarettes, were Marjorie's." Betty is pausing for an expected reaction and it comes immediately.

Everyone gasps and Betty smiles.

"Norton, who was absolutely smitten with her, removed everything from the home after his wife died, boxed it up and put it into storage." Betty is now rocking from heel to toe as she touches finger to finger like a preacher or schoolteacher. "It's remarkable that he had the foresight to know the importance of preserving her things, and this place as well."

With that said, Betty sweeps her hand in front of her, turns and invites the crowd into the front porch. It is without question a jaw-dropping room of amazement.

Emily is transfixed while Betty stands behind the round weather-beaten oak table that was Marjorie's desk and reveals that this is where she sat and wrote *The Yearling*. The table is surrounded by three ladder-back leather chairs, and the chair Marjorie obviously sat in, directly in front of the typewriter, has worn wooden arm rests. Emily can't help herself. She slides past three women and runs her fingers across the back of the chair as she closes her eyes. Three inches from her hand on the table are Marjorie's typewriter, her ashtray, a stack of yellowed papers, two pens, a china saucer, a yellow-bottom paperweight, paper clips and a box of staples.

Emily does not need a camera to remember what she is looking at, touching, and feeling. Her eyes well up and she struggles to compose herself. Behind her the other men and women are bumping each other and looking around and she actually sees someone slip out a camera and take a photo of the typewriter when Betty turns to point out the couch and the worn wooden porch floor.

The emotion rising up inside of Emily seems absolutely natural to her, as if she's discovered something she's lost, or caught the eye of someone she loves. *She loves this.* Emily has to force herself to stay in the moment least she start hating herself for all the years she spent in the library with her head in a box. She knows this is what she's supposed to be doing.

"When we get inside we'll talk more about all the entertaining that went on here but it's safe to say, without ever having met her of course, that this is the spot she loved the best," Betty says, sliding close to the door leading into the house from the porch. "She loved to sit out here and work and she was absolutely strict with the people who worked for her so that when she was working, the world around her, except for the birds of course, must remain quiet."

People mumble that she was a writer, of course she needed quiet, as they shuffle through a narrow door that leads into what looks like a formal living room. Mesmerized by the writing table, Emily finds it hard to move forward, but she really doesn't have a choice. She shuffles along with everyone else and is suddenly standing in Marjorie's living room.

Much later, after she has come back to the house for a private tour, she will absolutely memorize every detail of this room. The black stained brick fireplace, the yellow, blue and green patterned sofa and matching side chair, the large white lamp, elegant paintings, the long white drapes and especially the bar that has been carved out of a closet, because as she will soon find out, Marjorie was more than just a one-a-day drinker. Eventually, Emily will have her time in this room. She will be allowed to pick books off the shelf that have been signed with the names Ernest Hemingway, Robert Frost, and Margaret Mitchell. Betty will talk with her for four solid hours and they will share their own glass of after-hours whiskey in the park. But that won't happen for quite a while.

Emily is gazing at the couch where Marjorie must have sat with her legs on the maple coffee table, sipping her rye or whiskey, when she glances to the left and sees the man who was standing behind her when she was sitting in the barn. She has no idea where he came from or how he managed to slip back into the crowd but that doesn't surprise her considering she's been in a trance since she walked into the house. Her heart rate accelerates so quickly that she almost loses her balance.

The man is trapped next to big-mouth and her pathetic husband, and as she struggles to control her rising sense of panic, Emily walks backwards, moves onto the porch, runs down the steps and has absolutely no idea where to go or what to do next.

She races toward the barn and when she looks back she sees the group moving through the living room and down a small hall. Emily steps into the barn and drops down behind an old wooden box. Struggling to stay quiet, Emily fishes her cell phone out of her pocket, flips open the top and sends a text message to Silver.

*"Excellent. Hurry. In barn at MKR's."*

Then, like a trapped rat, she sits and waits.

# 13

*"It was never easy to admit my failures. Often, I would be so close to recapturing everything I had given away and then I would slip and fall and with great effort and remorse struggle back to my feet and start all over again. Maybe this is the way for so many of us women. Perhaps though, years from now, someone will see my footsteps one day and it will ease their own journey."*
—*Lost Hearts in the Swamp of Life* - MKR - 1963

Cardiovascular activity is obviously Silver's Achilles heel. When Emily hears her laboring up the short trail she manages to jump to her feet and come out from behind the barrel where she has been chastising herself for being such a damn baby. When Silver storms into the barn, Emily drops her head and struggles to keep from crying.

"I'm sorry," she half-whimpers.

"Oh for crying out loud, don't be sorry. Something must have happened. Sweet hell, woman, what is going on?"

Silver has stepped next to Emily and throws her arm around her shoulder. She can feel Emily shaking and there's no way in hell to fake that kind of fear.

"He was here. He is here."

"Who?" Silver asks, turning Emily so she can look into her eyes.

Emily lifts up her head. "The guy in the red car."

"Well, shit, girl! Let's scoot out the back and go sit someplace. Did you see his truck?" Silver is trying hard not to show her own uneasiness.

Emily shakes her head back and forth. "I was so excited about the tour I pretty much let down my guard, and then he was there in the barn and then he disappeared and then he came back again."

"Slow down. Let's go sit where no one can see us. Come on."

Emily glances back at the house and can see that everyone has disappeared into the side rooms. She keeps apologizing as Silver steers her back down the trail and across the open lawn to a picnic table that is totally hidden from view. She reassures Emily that there's no reason to apologize. The guy stalking her is a dirt ball and, after all, she's been reading the manuscripts all morning.

"And...?" Emily wants some reassurance that she's not losing her mind.

Silver smiles and then throws both hands into the air as if she's in the middle of a revival. "It's brilliant stuff. I'm dying to get to what else is in the box."

"Do you think Marjorie wrote it?"

"I know a lot about her style but there would have to be some work by experts to know for sure. Right now, to me anyway, that really doesn't matter as much as why this guy is following you around and what he knows that we don't."

Silver orders Emily to stay where she is, and says she's going to see if there's a red truck in the parking lot. She doesn't appear to be frightened of anything. Whoever he is, he obviously knows who she is by now, knows where she lives, knows Emily is staying there, and possibly even knows about the boxes.

Emily is thinking about this as Silver strolls back to the parking lot. Was it just as much of a coincidence for him as it was for her to stop at Leslie's house, or did he already know about the boxes? Emily is certain now that he is following her. She gets up and starts pacing in front of the picnic table, oblivious to the glorious roseate spoonbills that are standing less than ten feet from her near the water. It's one thing to be thinking about the possibility that Rawlings faked her own death and kept on writing but something else to be running around in fear of her own life.

Everything seems ludicrous to Emily right now. Her grand moments of personal empowerment and professional re-awakening seem to have disappeared as fast as one of Marjorie's whiskey drinks.

Silver comes back shaking her head. "It's a red SUV, but seriously, so what?"

"What does that mean?" Emily is starting to feel totally foolish.

"The problem with him is he's a sneaky SOB. He's not doing anything wrong by being here, and let's get real. Why don't we just ask him what in the hell he's doing snooping around here? We can't prove he's done anything wrong and honestly, I hate it when some guy thinks he's got something on me. I do not like to be pushed around by any man."

"So you want to confront him?" Emily isn't quite incredulous but with each sentence she feels more and more like a scared city girl. But Silver's presence surely gives her courage. The woman is like an army of one.

"Why not? The sheriff will kill me, but honey, hiding in a barn is kinda stupid."

It takes all but three seconds for Emily to start laughing and then Silver starts laughing and then the spoonbills are so frightened by the noise they start flapping their wings and take off and the sight of their pink and white bodies lifting into the air against the blue sky paralyzes both women for a few moments.

They are both standing with their backs to the parking lot, their hands over their eyes as if they are watching an air show, and they miss the man they were about to confront walking swiftly out the gate, into the parking lot, and then disappearing around the backside of the park.

The women wait until the birds have vanished and then turn to walk toward the house. Emily tells Silver that she was so enchanted by the first part of the tour, in spite of the woman with the big mouth, that she's sad she missed the rest of it. That's when they see everyone coming down the dirt path leading to the house.

"It must be over," Silver says, holding Emily back. "Let's see if Superman passes by. We can have a little chat with his sorry self."

They wait as one couple after another leaves the park and there's no bad man anywhere. Dauntless, Silver strides to the parking lot only to discover that the red SUV has disappeared, along with the man driving it.

"Foiled again, Miss Ohio," Silver laments. "You know I'm putting on a good front here. Guys like that can flip out at any moment."

Now it's Emily's turn to try to be brave. "I'm pretty sure he wasn't that interested in the tour. Maybe we're both wrong and he's harmless, in spite of his fast car and undercover work."

Part of Emily remains shaken and yet she is longing to go back and look at the house and see the rest of Marjorie's Cross Creek life.

Silver, who looks about as normal as someone like her must get, is wearing a pair of black shorts, a T-shirt that has a huge pair of red lips on it, and a rainbow-colored gauze scarf wrapped around her head to hold back her massive tangles of gorgeous black hair. She's almost as colorful as one of the birds they just saw and Emily smiles because she's positive Silver would never quite make it as an undercover detective.

It's just after noon, and before either one of them can stop her to ask about the next tour, Betsy approaches, smiles and then without hesitation lifts up her long skirt and pulls it up past her knees. "I have no clue how those women did it," she sighs, fanning herself with her free hand.

"No air conditioning or ice machines either," Silver chimes in.

Betsy stops and turns around. "Aren't you Silver?"

"Yes I am."

"Please tell me you aren't here for a tour. You probably know more about Marjorie than I do."

Emily should have known this might happen. Who doesn't know this woman? It's the other two women inside of her that no one knows about.

Before Silver can say anything, Betsy looks at Emily and asks her why she left the tour. "You seemed as if you were in Rawlings heaven back there. What happened?"

Emily and Silver exchange a glance, Silver winks, and Emily who is getting really good at lying says she didn't feel well. "There were so many people and that woman who kept interrupting you was ruining it for me."

"That was nothing," Betsy says, fanning her legs with her skirt. "In high season here people wait hours for a tour. That woman was a pain, but sometimes we have to bring in extra help just to make sure people don't misbehave. Last year one man who claimed to be a huge Rawlings fan was actually caught trying to take a piece of the barn to his car. And yes, don't ask, he knew the barn was fake."

Emily wants to know about the next tour and Betsy says she's sorry, but the park has a special group coming in for the entire afternoon. It's a literary society from Atlanta and they've donated $10,000 to the park.

"Money is our God these days, so we're having a lemonade and pie social and I wish I could invite you, but you'll just have to come back some other time," Betsy looks tired just talking about the afternoon reception. "Silver probably can walk you around outside. She knows more than most of the guides here, for gosh sake. Go ahead and look in the windows."

Silver looks as if she's getting ready to try and charm Betsy. Emily's starting to know what to watch for with this woman.

"Betsy, can't we just go in and look around? You know me. You've had beer with me in my backyard, for God's sake."

Betsy looks as if she might cry. "Oh Silver, of course I know you, and I trust you with my life, but things have changed so much here." Betsy shrugs as if she doesn't even believe it her-self. "We're barely staying open and it's as if the big boys are always looking for one small thing to shut us down. My heart is in this place, you know that. They make us serve cookies to fat rich women, pardon me for saying it, but for the love of God, Marjorie would have a stroke all over again if she knew some of this stuff."

Silver walks over and puts her arms on Betsy's shoulders. Emily correctly guesses that there's more bones and skin under those clothes than fat and gristle. Betsy was all on when she was giving the tour, but now she looks exhausted.

"Not many people know how hard you and the other docents work," Silver says gently. "I know what Marjorie did for the families around here, and I also know how important it is to keep this place going. Remember, as soon as my ship comes in, sister, I'm giving the park a bundle and we'll have our own picnic, but there sure as hell won't be lemonade."

Betsy drops her skirts and gives Silver a warm hug. She shoos them toward the house and scurries down the trail. And for a moment, when Emily turns to watch her leave with her dress flying, her apron draped over her shoulder, and her head hanging, Emily decides Miss Betsy could be living right inside a Marjorie Rawlings novel.


An hour later, while both their stomachs gurgle from lack of food, Silver and Emily are sitting on Marjorie Rawlings' back porch, dangling their feet down the steps and talking. Emily is giddy not from just that simple fact but being able to look into Rawlings' bedroom, kitchen, dining room and even her bathroom have her reeling with joy.

Silver is lying back on her elbows and watching a mess of insects dance around the garden that lines the entire backside of the yard.

They have imagined what it must have been like when Rawlings first arrived. Silver explained that the house was more or less in shambles and over the years Rawlings added rooms and furnishings that turned the place into a country showpiece.

Emily could see the glimmering pine floors through the windows and was immediately surprised by how much more elegant and modern the house appeared. She thought, for some insane reason, that there would be dirt floors, or mice running wild throughout the entire place. Instead what she saw through the gleaming windows was lovely furniture, a well-stocked kitchen, a formal dining room and a well-planned yard and orchard.

"This just didn't happen," Silver explained as they walked around the outside of the house. "She used the outhouse for a long time and in her lean years, before *The Yearling* made her some money, she was often worried about buying basic necessities."

Obviously it was a big deal when she was able to put in the first indoor plumbing in Cross Creek. The brochure Emily carried around said that she had a party in the bathroom to celebrate, and put ice in the bathtub and roses inside of the toilet.

"She liked to have a good time I take it?" Emily still couldn't get over the liquor cabinet she had seen in the living room that had been built inside of a closet with the door cut in half and a serving tray built into it.

"Girl, she was something from the stories I've heard," Silver had shared, bending down to look in the windows with her. "I often think how grand it would have been to be one of her friends; one of her trusted friends. You know, not someone who just wanted to be around some fancy-pants writer. But Marjorie apparently wasn't like that."

"I've only seen a few photos of her but she's always dressed up," Emily said. "I suppose she wasn't always like that."

"You've got that right. Before I shed my Jenka Armador skin and turned into the mysterious Grace Novell and Silver No-Last-Name, I knew first hand what that posing-for-photos writer's life was like," Silver told her, standing back up after they'd looked into the guest room. "People expect things out of you that you don't even expect yourself."

"But isn't that part of the deal? I mean if you're famous and in the public eye that's part of the trade-off, it seems."

"Oh of course it is, but that doesn't mean it's easy," Silver admitted, walking around the side of the house to the long back porch. "It can also interfere with your writing and the process that many people like myself try to develop to keep the creative river alive and flowing, you know?"

Emily argued that it made sense that it would have been easier to escape from those kinds of pressures back when Marjorie was famous. There were no damn blogs or Facebook or the Internet to drive you absolutely crazy.

"True," Silver agreed, "but the same expectations that drove me to become three people instead of just one have always been there. The next book, the grand magazine article, an editor who suddenly feels his or her talent is wiser or stronger than the author. It's not an easy world now and it wasn't easy then," she said, almost as if she were trying to forget what had made her world so difficult.

The two women had walked all around the outside of the house and when they got to the kitchen window Emily could see that Silver was smiling. "That woman loved to cook," Silver chuckled. "I think she drove half her hired help crazy with her pickiness—and that reminds me, you need to look at her cook book, *Cross Creek Cookery*. If she really did die, it's because her arteries were clogged with so much butter, cream and booze that she committed suicide."

"Everyone ate like that back then though," Emily said, defending her new heroine. "I think when I was born, half of my blood was gin from my mother's martinis and the other half was filled with smoke from her Salem cigarettes, a little beer, and lots of meat, potatoes, and gravy. I swear to God I hate potatoes now."

The old cast iron stove, what looked like a long pantry through the window, a small wooden table and a sink made the kitchen seem workable and practical. Silver explained how weather played a huge part in everything that happened, especially in the kitchen, because if it wasn't hot it was most likely going to get hot at any minute.

The placement of windows and a long interior porch helped keep the kitchen cool but often, especially in summer, cooking was a serious labor of love because of the heat. Silver was definitely in the know about this house and its former occupants. She said winters, on the other hand, because Cross Creek was more north than south, could sometimes be very cold. There was occasional frost, no central heating beyond what the stove or the fireplaces allowed, and obviously, living this way out in the country there were wild pigs and deer and snakes and bears.

"Sounds so relaxing," Emily jokes, as they sat down to rest where they are now sitting.

Silver wants to know what it is about this place, or perhaps any place like this, that so fascinates Emily. "Before you stumbled into my life, and I mean that with great affection, you barely knew who Marjorie Rawlings was-or is, pardon me. What is it about all of this that makes you so happy?"

"Oh Silver, you know the answer to that! It's so easy."

"It is?"

"It's all about storytelling. Looking at where she placed her dresser and then bending down, because she was obviously shorter then we are, to see what she saw standing there when she combed her hair. It's the elegant floral pattern on the couch and chair and the shelf in the living room to hold her booze bottles, and the space on the porch looking out across the highway where she chose to write."

Emily is obviously on a roll here, and Silver is smiling as she listens.

She talks about the braided rug and the beautiful tablecloth and the story in the brochure that explained how she always sat at a certain spot when she had guests, facing the outhouse so that they didn't have to look at it. A birdbath and even the chickens say something about the person who lived here.

"Okay then," Silver challenges her as she drops her elbows and lies on the porch. "Tell me who she was, trying to focus on just what you see here."

Emily loves this game. It's almost as much fun as making up the lives of the people game she played when she was young.

Marjorie Kinnan Rawlings, Emily begins, was a woman who was torn. She obviously loved the solitude and quiet, or she would never have fallen so hard for this place but she also loved people. She loved to cook for them and make sure they were comfortable, and it was important to her that they felt as if they were always welcome.

"I can just see her sitting out there smoking and working when a car pulls around the corner and stops in her driveway," Emily, has her eyes closed as she talks. "I wonder if she swore."

"Like a lumberjack," Silver tells her.

"Well, then she would have said, 'Shit, Goddamn it! Can't a woman write in peace around here?'"

Maybe, Emily guesses, she'd swear and then kick the door and then go into the yard and act as if she had been waiting all day for Jack or Jill to show up. All the while, of course, she'd be hoping they'd want a drink right away so that she could have one and then get them the hell out of there as fast as she could.

Silver is now laughing. "You should write a play about this."

"How am I doing?"

"As Marjorie would say, 'Pretty damn good.'"

Emily thinks she may have been lonely, especially before Norton came courting, but that was part of her angst. To work she had to be alone, and yet she was social. "It was hard for her," Emily almost whispers.

"You're good at this, you know." Silver isn't at all surprised.

"Well, it's what I do really, all of the time, except I mostly use scraps of paper. I like this so much more."

"Are you done yet?"

This time Emily laughs. "Are you kidding me?"

Silver doesn't bother to move but motions with her hand in the air for her to continue.

"I think she was afraid too, because of some of those things you told me about writers, and I realize that's cheating but that's a clue I need," Emily admits. "She thought about Charles. I think she loved him for a long time, but wasn't willing to sacrifice this place and her need to write those stories, and she wondered about him and I think there was pressure from that too, from not just wanting but needing to succeed, to show him up and to survive financially. I mean, seriously, living here could not have been easy. The pressures must have been huge all the way around."

Emily is talking now as if something's burning inside of her and both women are secretly relieved they have temporarily forgotten about what brought them both together this afternoon. She said even with her moments of hesitation, Marjorie had made up her mind, Emily continues. Maybe she was stubborn. There really was no going back with her tail between her legs. Obviously she was strong and somewhat fearless, when she wasn't terrified, or she couldn't be out here like this.

"Oh, that reminds me," Silver interrupts. "Tomorrow we are going to have a shooting lesson in my backyard."

"What?"

"A shooting lesson, as in guns, and tin cans and stuff."

"Are you crazy?"

"Well, yes. But so are you, honey."

Emily slaps Silver lightly on tip of her head and waits for her to explain this latest bright idea.

Silver is quiet. Her eyes are now closed and Emily can see she's squeezing her eyes as if she's trying not to cry.

"Hey, are you okay?"

"Oh, Lord. I wasn't going to get into this but at this point it's not like you don't already know half my secrets," Silver says, covering her eyes with both hands. "Can you keep talking for a while and let me tell you the whole story later?"

"Okay."

"Just remember there's a whack job out there running around. I know we keep trying to think he's harmless but it's been my experience that what we think and what is the truth isn't always the same thing."

"So we should be prepared. Just like the Girl Scouts and just like Marjorie... right?"

Silver nods, and Emily takes the hint and tries hard to make up more stories about Marjorie, but she's lost the edge. She invents something whimsical about gardening and canning vegetables and killing chickens until Silver regains her composure and tells her that now she's obviously talking out the side of her left ear, and Emily stops talking.

They finally walk around the backside of the house and see a restored tenant home, which holds absolutely no interest for either of them, and then they see a bus pull up and a parade of bouncing red hats emerge as they quickly duck into the woods and discover a trail that leads away from Marjorie's house.

They circle through the woods behind her house and come out on the highway about a quarter of a mile from the parking lot. Emily thinks it's hilarious to be hiding from the lunch ladies but she's having fun, considering how the afternoon started.

Silver, ever cautious, walks around Emily's car and her own, to make certain the tires haven't been slashed, there's no one hiding in the backseat or there's not a hand grenade under the floor mat. Then she offers to buy them lunch at the restaurant down the street. It's called The Yearling.

"You have got to be kidding me?" Emily thinks the day has already been strange enough but apparently there's no end to this Cross Creek madness and Marjorie worship.

"It's fabulous and authentic and I think as good a place as any for us to have our own whiskey so I can tell you how I met the sheriff and why we are going to teach you how to shoot a gun tomorrow," Silver explains, pointing with her thumb in the direction of the restaurant. "It's not all loveliness and good neighbors down here. You need to hear this."

Even though Silver's story about the Sheriff obviously has a happy ending, Emily's suddenly certain it didn't start out that way and now she's worried all over again, not just about the red SUV, but about everything else she doesn't yet know about Cross Creek.

# 14

*"There were times then, so horrible, that I have tucked them into a black space in the back of my mind. Sometimes, in the midst of it all, the saving hand that held me up was the simple sight of white whirling clouds spiraling against the ocean blue sky. That was my heaven. It was often all I had."*
—*Lost Hearts in the Swamp of Life* - MKR - 1963

Emily is certain that if she remains in Florida much longer she may have to go into a detox facility. Whiskey on the back porch, wine in the kitchen, and now more whiskey for a late lunch as Silver prepares to tell her a story that must obviously be resurrecting a painful memory.

Silver has slipped off to use the restroom and Emily is gazing around the back room of The Yearling in astonishment. Time has definitely stood still in this place. Its rustic ambience is totally charming and reminds her, once again, that this part of the world is indeed a special place.

When she realizes the restaurant is so close to Rawlings' farm, she is surprised she hadn't seen it earlier when she drove right by it on her way to the park. But a second glance tells her why. The building is shingled from head to toe; there is some kind of generator or machine sticking out of the front of the building, and a cage for propane that should have been used for chickens. Emily mistakenly thinks it is someone's home.

Silver sets her straight immediately by telling her people came from all over not just the state, but the world, to eat here. The restaurant opened in 1950 when Rawlings mania was at its peak. People came driving through just to get a glimpse of her and her house and orchards and a smart restaurateur decided it was a terrific place to give people a taste of Cross Creek. Marjorie was obviously giving them another kind of taste with her novels, and the restaurant was an immediate and lasting hit.

Even though Emily is ravenous, she knows better than to hurry Silver when she is in the middle of a history lesson. Silver says because food and entertaining are so important to Rawlings, The Yearling has high standards to uphold, and they do that just fine. Just like Marjorie's own popularity, the restaurant floundered and then closed in 1992, but a man who had eaten there when he was a boy could never forget the adventure of driving to the restaurant and thinking about how his favorite book had been written down the road from where he was eating his pork chops.

They lean against Silver's car as she tells Emily how the new owner has basically restored the entire building. He even hired the son of the woman who had cooked for Marjorie, and now it's back where it was all those years ago when people from literally everywhere, who love the books Marjorie wrote, also wanted a taste of her Cross Creek world.

"Oh," Silver added, just before they walk into the restaurant, "just so you know, the people around here always call her Miz Rawlings."

Emily is poring over the menu when Silver comes back to the table. Her mouth is open as wide as the rim of her whiskey glass.

"Have you seen this menu?

Silver smiles and says, "It's amazing, isn't it?

"Deep fried frog legs? Quail? Grits? Hush Puppies?"

"It's marvelous. Absolute perfection."

"I have no idea if it's marvelous," Emily says seriously. "All I know is that I get frightened about every twenty minutes around here and now this menu appears to be written in a foreign language."

Silver dismisses her with a wave of her hand and orders a mess of food, because she says she is starving, but she also wants Emily to experience regional cooking at its best. "This is the stuff people have eaten around here for generations. Consider it part of your research, wherever that's taking you."

Emily knows Silver is working up to tell her a personal story. Even though it is warm outside there is a small fire burning in the fireplace and Silver points out a drawing of a young boy that is hanging behind her. "That's Jody, the young boy in *The Yearling*," she says, sipping her drink. "There's about ten grown men who once lived here who all think their Miz Rawlings modeled Jody after them."

The two women are sitting in the back of the restaurant at pine tables. Emily has a sweet view of the creek and through the open window she can actually hear frogs chirping. She gulps when she thinks of the frog legs they have ordered but decides that she's been enough of a baby for one day.

Silver orders another drink for both of them and is about halfway through it when she begins her story. Emily sets down her glass and prepares herself for what's coming. Silver is always open and gracious and fun, and Emily can't help but already be grateful for what she is giving her, for a place to stay, but especially for trusting her.

She reaches across the table and touches Silver's hand. "I suspect you are about to tell me something hard and horrible. You have already given me so much Silver."

Silver brushes her hand in front of her face. "Emily, you are trusting and kind yourself, and the part of you that is frightened is frightened for good reason. The world is full of bad men, good ones too, but I honestly think we need to be even more cautious."

"So I wasn't an idiot to be hiding in the barn?"

Silver smiles. "Well, sort of, but not really. Let me tell you what happened to me and I hope that will explain my fondness for guns, men in police uniforms, and the reason why from now on, you are not going anywhere without me."

Emily almost chokes as she's taking a drink, puts her hands up and moves her fingers back and forth toward herself as if to say, "Bring it on." And very quickly she realizes why they needed to have a drink.

First, the history lesson continues. Silver knows there's no place in the world like the South, and even though the Cross Creek country has been populated by a eclectic and wonderful mix of humanity-African Americans, the original Crackers, so named for the cracking of the whips the Spaniards used to drive cattle through the region, a mess of white folks, and everyone in-between. "I think you need to see how Marjorie bridged the gap down here, reluctantly at first, between the blacks and everyone else, because it's an important part of who she was and what she did," Silver explains. "But even as the years passed and the role of the blacks here changed, not everyone considered us equal."

"Is that why I still see Confederate flags here and there?" Emily can't believe how many she has seen, not just in the area, but everywhere in Florida.

"That's part of the reason but also, as I'm about to tell you, not everything changed when the Civil War ended."

Silver tells her that when she relocated to this area and fell in with the Creative Recovery process Leslie had started, she was the first black woman to do so. None of the writers thought it was a big deal but apparently some of the good old boys didn't see it that way. It didn't help that Silver had money and purchased the home she now lives in and immediately started to hire local men, most of them not black, to help with some of her remodeling.

Silver says she could have been the Queen of England or a famous country-western singer, someone the workers generally worshiped, but some of them simply didn't like the idea of a black woman who had money and who was telling them that she still wanted another three-eights of an inch shaved off the bottom of the bathroom doors.

It didn't matter that she was kind and generous. It didn't matter that she was paying them fair wages and cooking for them and making certain they had enough time off with their families. What mattered was that she was black *and* she was a woman *and* she had money.

Silver swishes her glass and admits that she had been naive. Leslie and the other people she had been introduced to had been absolutely kind to her and she recklessly assumed that everyone in the area was the same way.

"I learned the hard way that many of the people who live here don't like their ways or their lifestyles or their anything tampered with, and I was doing that by simply being myself," she shares, talking quietly and making certain no one else is listening. "Later, as I came to study Marjorie's life and what she had lived through and how she had changed her own ways of thinking, there were so many parallel things in my own life, except one thing that I hope she never had to go through."

Oblivious to the seeds of jealousy that several of the men on her work crew had planted, Silver had no idea that she was in danger. The men were all drinkers and that never bothered her, in fact she often gave them beer after work. Now, she knows that the three men who attacked her had been planning it for a long time.

They knew her schedule of comings and goings because they had been working on her house for several months. She went to Leslie's one day, to the grocery store another, and she let them know what nights she had meetings in town or at Leslie's, so they had her life memorized down to the minute.

"There is a strain of evil in some people that I have struggled with accepting ever since," Silver has gotten more and more quiet as her story has unfolded. "When I asked you that question back at the park, about why you love that place so much, I already understood so much about it myself. Some of us blame place and circumstance for our behavior. We both know we all have choices but there are people here, and everywhere, who use that as an excuse to do things that are not right."

It was the end of her second year in Florida and six months after she had purchased her house, and was almost finished adding the guest room and remodeling, when it happened. Driving home late on a Thursday night from the library, because don't you know Shirley could only keep the library open late one night a week, three men ran Silver off the highway.

"It was the most terrifying night of my life," she recalls, holding up her hand to stop the waitress from coming over to the table. "They wore white hoods, like the damn Ku Klux Klan, and they pulled me out of the car and threw me on the ground."

Silver's ordeal lasted almost an hour. The men had followed her up to her long driveway and knew that no other cars would be turning down the road that late at night. They blindfolded her and took turns cutting off her jeans, and then her blouse, her bra and underwear, until she was lying on the ground naked. They spit on her, kicked her, and cut her arms and legs with a knife. She was certain they were going to rape her but the men made a point of telling her over and over again that white men don't screw dirty black animals.

Emily hasn't moved since Silver started telling her this part of the story. Her own heart has stopped and without realizing it, tears are running down her face. Silver reaches over and gently puts her fingers under both of Emily's eyes to wipe away her tears.

"Honey, don't cry, because I'm getting to the good part where I meet the sheriff."

"Oh God, Silver, this is absolutely horrible! I'm sad and totally pissed off at the same time."

"I think you'll like the ending of the story."

"Please," Emily begs.

The men threw her car keys into the weeds and, weak from fear, bruised and battered, Silver crawled on her hands and knees to her house.

Emily interrupts. "That's like half a mile for God's sake!"

"Yes it is," Silver agrees, "And I can tell you what every inch of the road feels like when your knees and hands are moving across gravel."

She called the Sheriff's Department, wrapped herself in a blanket and laid on the kitchen floor shaking and praying that a woman would show up to help her and not some dumbass redneck sheriff. But, thank Jesus it was Sheriff Gettleman.

"I saw him leap up the front steps and glide through the door and at first I thought I had fallen into a coma," she recalls, closing her eyes for a second to recapture the moment. "But then he dropped down beside me, put his hand gently on the side of my face where most of the blood had pooled, and I could see that he was crying."

Jim Gettleman, it turns out, was also a registered nurse, a firefighter, a closet poet and the most gentle, loving, beautiful man Silver had ever met in her life. He stabilized her, ushered in the ambulance crew, made someone else drive his car, and didn't leave her side until the following morning when he all but hopped on his white horse and went to find the men who had assaulted her.

Emily is glad she has set her glass down because she's positive that she would have dropped it on the floor by now. "This sounds like a novel, for God's sake," she stutters, totally realizing the irony of what she has said.

"People think those of us who write novels make this shit up, but I'm here to tell you most of us just look around, or move to Cross Creek," Silver says, totally serious, and obviously glad she's done with the hard part of the story.

"What happened to the bad guys?"

"I wish I could have seen their faces when Getts showed up. He's local, his family ran one of the fishing camps for years and after jobs in Miami, then Tampa, he'd had enough and came home. No one messes with the Gettleman family. He was not the sheriff when this happened but a patrol officer. What he did was pretty much clean up the entire county, and he started with those three men."

Silver has motioned for the waitress to bring their salads. Emily looks down and sees fresh watercress, some mysterious greens, and a pile of vegetables that look as if they were picked five minutes ago.

The suspense is killing her and Emily wants to know exactly what happened when Getts found the men.

"There's always been a bad bunch running around here and scaring the living hell out of the rest of us," she says, holding a fork full of salad close to her mouth. "I call them adult bullies and the men who attacked me were part of that group."

Silver chews for a moment and then explains that the bullies would steal and beat people up and start fights at the drop of a hat. If anything went missing, or someone's calf disappeared, or the new motor clogged when someone who couldn't afford one poured sugar down it, everyone pretty much knew who had done it.

Getts put a stop to it all, Silver says. It was easy to find out who had attacked her and he had the men in custody in less than a day. Silver says she honestly doesn't know exactly what he did, but the men did get jail time and then they disappeared and so did the rest of the gang.

"But that's what I want to talk to you about, Emily," Silver continues, putting down her fork, and grabbing Emily's hand. "Now don't freak out when I tell you this, okay?"

Emily can't imagine what Silver could possibly say now that would shock her or make her start screaming.

"Please tell me what they say about your sex change operation isn't true!" Emily has clasped her hands to her chest and leaned forward against the table.

Silver snorts and then starts coughing. "Do not do that when I have lettuce in my mouth!"

Silver wants Emily to know that she carries a gun. This time Emily almost chokes on her food. Before she can say a word, Silver explains that after what happened to her Getts told her she'd be foolish not to get a permit to carry a concealed weapon, which is apparently all the rage in Florida and half the country anyway. She shares some of the region's unique gun laws, including a "stand and defend" law that allows a person to shoot someone if they are being threatened on their property.

Emily's eyes are open as wide as they can possibly get. "It sounds like the Wild West down here, for the love of God! Are you serious? Do you have the gun with you right now? Where is it?"

Silver holds up her hand like a stop sign. "Here comes the alligator and possum meat, wait a minute."

The bleach blonde waitress sets a platter in the middle of the table that looks as if it's holding one of everything on the menu. Silver is not lying about the alligator and possum meat. There's also fresh bass, oysters, and that's absolutely all Emily can identify.

"Please help me, oh gunslinger to the clueless," Emily begs.

"Venison. Fried Green Tomatoes. Turnip Greens. Cheese Grits." Silver has pointed out everything on the plate.

"If Marjorie really did die," Emily says, still big-eyed. "This is what killed her."

The women forget about guns for almost thirty minutes as they eat and Emily realizes that she may have missed out on yet another one of life's glorious attributes by not eating this kind of food sooner. In a blaze of gluttony they forget for a short while about bad men and dark roads and hiding in barns. They forget about yellowed manuscripts and new and old lives and the lost dreams of men and women everywhere. There is only room for crisp skin, soft meat, and tomatoes so juicy that they both start to moan.

When Emily glances around, she notices that the same thing is going on at every table. People are eating with their fingers, and wiping each other's chins and drinking one beer after another. A couple with two small children has given up on the idea of using plates for the babes. A little girl and boy are greedily licking their fingers and reaching out for more French fries and the woman laughs and says, "Honey, no, first eat your pie!"

Emily can't remember the last time she saw people enjoy food like this. Not one to worry about what she eats, mostly because it's not important to her, she's also missed eating with abandonment, even if she's eating something that the Surgeon General is worried about. When she looks across the table, Silver is chewing a piece of meat with her eyes closed.

Emily feels a sweet slice of emotion run right from the center of her chest, down her arms, and into her fingertips. It's been such a long time since she's felt close to anyone, except of course Bev. Silver has suddenly become her best friend, her confidante, someone that she loves as if she's known her for a very long time. What a life she has had, and is having! Emily feels a swell of compassion too for what Silver must have gone through the night she was attacked. It's a swirl of anger and sorrow that she knows will have to be channeled into a new form of strength and energy.

She's had friends who have been assaulted and raped, and she's had her own share of close calls, but nothing like what happened to Silver. It's already difficult for her to put it out of her mind and almost impossible for her to imagine how Silver can.

"What are you staring at, woman?" Silver wipes her mouth with the back of her hand and then dives in again.

"I'm looking at one remarkable woman."

"Oh, get out of here!" Silver is now not even bothering to cover her mouth when she chews.

"Let's see, you're not just one, but three famous authors. You've bravely carved out a new life for yourself. You've held fast to your principals. You are kind and generous…"

"And a little piggy!" Silver cuts her off and then tells her to stop it. "If you admire anyone, admire that Miz Rawlings who got you here. You have only started to touch on her life. You need to find out about the lawsuit and Zora and Norton and New York…"

This time Emily cuts Silver off. "Enough! Can we finish about the guns first? What's up with the guns?"

Before Silver will continue, she orders dessert, which almost makes Emily faint, and coffee for both of them. The plates are cleared and the waitress says she's proud because this is her first table of the day where she doesn't have to provide a doggie bag.

Emily would normally be embarrassed but she surprises herself by high fiving Silver instead. She actually thought about licking the grease off the plate before the waitress removed it. This type of living could turn her into a whole new woman in many, many ways.

"We're not done talking about the food, just so you know, but let's not forget about the guns because tomorrow is going to be a big day for you," Silver says, as the waitress sets down their coffee and then quickly comes back with blueberry pie and some kind of orange torte that Emily is thinking about dropping her face into. "Marjorie had a corner on the food around her. No one did it like she did—but first, as they say in Florida, the guns."

Emily sips her coffee, splits up the desserts, and then listens as Silver launches into her reasoning for self-protection, being prepared, and never ever letting a man or woman or beast harm her, or anyone she cares about, again. She tells Emily that it's absolutely ridiculous now for her to be driving around snooping into past and present lives, hiding in barns, discovering lost treasure and trying to out-smart this guy who has become a dark shadow in their lives.

"I'm not saying there's danger around every corner, but, Emily, I can't in good conscience lead you on and let you think it's Never-Never Land and that everyone is like me or some of my friends," she says with absolute seriousness. "Getts did not chase every bad guy out of the woods down here and there are some people who hate me, relatives of some of the men in jail, who didn't leave. I would never be able to forgive myself if something happened to you and neither would Getts."

"Are you saying I'm in danger?"

"Hell, every woman alive is in danger. Are you kidding me? It's dangerous to ride a public bus and drive on the freeway and cruise around in the middle of nowhere in places where alligators stop traffic. Be reasonable, here. You've discovered something that may be of great value. We both think this guy knows something and, just between us, so does Getts. I can't send you home because I've watched you blossom the past few days and I think you may be on to something huge. I swear your skin is even turning a new shade of white now that you are doing something you love."

Silver stops to take a breath and Emily can feel the possum, fish, venison and clams starting to tango inside of her stomach. "Silver, I…"

"No, you listen here, sister," Silver says, moving her pointer finger and down as if she's in the middle of a lecture. "There is no turning back now, and there is no way in hell I'm going to let that little asshole hurt you, or me. Period. End of story."

Before Emily can move her brain to form a word, Silver's phone rings and she fishes it out of her pocket and has it to her ear by the second ring. "Hi, honey," she says, all smiles.

Emily's pretty sure she knows who's calling. Silver's happy greeting and smile are soon replaced by a serious looking face and lots of *oh no*s.

"We're just finishing up at The Yearling. Yeah, he showed up at the park today. No. I don't think so, but she was upset when I first got there. Okay. No! You'd better tell her. We'll see you at the house in about half an hour. Bye for now, and thank you."

Emily is asking, "What?" by simply raising her eyebrows.

"It was Getts. Today is his day off and he-how should I say this?-he was doing some special investigating for us."

"What does that mean?"

Silver leans in and whispers, "Something kind of illegal that has to do with Mr. What's-his-name."

"The suspense is killing me. What is it?"

Silver leans forward again. "He found out where the mystery man is staying, and sort of broke into his cabin when he was gone."

Emily goes pale and Silver says Getts is going to meet them at the house. They finish quickly and exit the restaurant and then form a two-woman caravan back to Silver's house. But just before they get home, Getts calls Silver and says he's been called out on an emergency. Once they get inside, Silver tells Emily what's happened and shares that an emergency usually means a bad accident or domestic violence, and he would definitely have told her if the emergency has anything to do with what he's discovered.

"It also means he probably won't be here until tomorrow morning," she warns Emily. "You may as well settle in. Good news or bad news, it can wait until tomorrow. I for one am exhausted."

Thirty minutes later, Emily's in the bathroom back at Silver's, fishing around for Rolaids, when she realizes Silver never told her where she keeps her gun. The tail end of their conversation at the restaurant has left her with an aching stomach that has just as much to do with the reality of eating fried foods as it does with realizing that this part of the world isn't necessarily the fairy-tale land she has been imagining.

Silver has already gone into her room when Emily sticks her head of her bedroom door, hoping for some reassurance before she tries to sleep. But all she sees is a mostly dark house and the soft glow of a rising moon drifting like a dim light throughout the house.

Emily walks into the kitchen and then pauses by the sink to watch the clouds dancing around the moon. When she drops her eyes there are darting shadows everywhere and within seconds her heart is racing. The shadows could be animals, bending branches, her own imagination, or the slinking form of a man darting in and out of the trees.

Emily closes her eyes, just like she did when she was a little girl and something frightened her. She would pinch her eyes so tight that her face would ache and then she would count to fifty. It almost always worked. When she opened her eyes the bogyman would be gone, the dark shadows would have disappeared, and she could fall asleep without worry.

This time when she opens her eyes, nothing has changed except the night seems to have gotten darker as the moon has all but disappeared. Emily tries without success to convince herself everything is okay and that she's overreacting. After all, Silver's just down the hall, hopefully sleeping like a baby, with her gun tucked under her pillow or resting on the bedside table. The sheriff can't be that far away and the house phone and the cell phones are all in working order. Their stalker, clearly brazen, could not be slinking around in the bushes-or could he?

Emily closes her eyes again and begins to count one more time. Now, instead of utter darkness, what she sees is Silver, bruised and battered crawling up her own driveway as three laughing men roll down the highway in their jacked up truck. Then there's Silver lying on the floor and sobbing into her own bloody hands. This time Emily doesn't make it to fifty. When she moves her hand off her face she realizes she's perspiring as if she's standing in the oven and when she looks up there are now even more shadows.

Strangely, she thinks of Marjorie next. There's Miz Rawlings, standing on her own porch with her shotgun resting against her left knee as she oils the barrel and looks off into the distance towards the small opening beyond her orange trees that offer her a view of blue shimmering water. There's a white and black spotted dog lying at her feet, the sound of someone banging pans in the kitchen, and a hungry look in the author's eye because there is so much work yet to be done. Emily thinks that survival, on any level, takes courage and more than a dash of foolishness. She turns away from the sink, makes certain the front door is locked, double checks the back door locks as well, grabs a huge carving knife out of the kitchen, tiptoes to her room, and starts counting off the hours until daybreak.

# 15

*"My first glance of morning light always seems to bring with it a tiny bit of hope. There was a morning, so long ago now that I could never remember the day, but I remember how I stretched my hand through the open kitchen window and how the light danced through my fingers as if we were lovers in mid tango. After that I went to the same window every morning, as I still do, to reach out my hand and touch the day. Even now the morning light feels as if it is giving me a dose of hope, strength, and happiness every blessed morning."*
—*Lost Hearts in the Swamp of Life* - MKR - 1963

Somewhere between 10:00pm when she started reading, and 3:30am when she fell asleep, Emily Weaver slowly felt as if she was stepping across some kind of secret doorway and into a world that was so real she actually got out of bed three times to look out the window and make certain she was in Silver's guest room, and not floating through the universe.

Terrified by what might be lurking outside her bedroom window, Emily could not fall asleep and picked up *Cross Creek*, then *Cross Creek Cookery*, then switched them back and forth because she loved them both. She spent the next five hours floating between one book and the next and was so amused, amazed, and entertained that time was non-existent and she only stopped reading because she accidentally saw the bedside clock.

Emily realized as she was spiraling off into sleep that her search for Marjorie Rawlings, dead or alive, was beginning to pay off. She was discovering a writer so gifted that she could make the send off of pet ducks a powerful and hilarious tale of warmth and love. It didn't matter if she was writing about the succession of men and women who worked for her, her various hunting and fishing companions, the red-birds sitting in her backyard sun or mustard greens, rattlesnakes, or her broken fireplace—Rawlings was a truly born to write. At one point, when Rawlings was writing about an encounter she and her friend Dessie had with a skunk, Emily laughed so hard she was afraid she was going to wake Silver. "*I called Dessie and she came from her room with her revolver. We went together to the coop.*"

Emily rolled over, pulled the blankets tight around her shoulders, and could envision Silver barging from her room with her own revolver, or whatever kind of weapon she had, and chasing not just skunks but all the bad guys too. In many ways, Marjorie's world and the one inhabited by Silver were perhaps not so different. Of course, Silver had modern conveniences, the most important one being air conditioning as far as she was concerned, but after the partial tour of Marjorie's house and the surrounding orchard and trails, many things have seriously not changed.

There wasn't a new house under construction anywhere on the journey to Cross Creek and she was wondering, as she struggled to shut off her brain, what people did for a living here besides hunt and fish. Back in Marjorie's day, a family could live off the land, albeit at the level of poverty. But with living off the land-and that included a massive garden, and what was apparently a thriving moonshine business, according to what she was picking up in her reading-it might have been possible to live that way for a very long time. And equally as possible for anyone to live quietly and without notice on a back road, or nestled along the river miles from town, or another human being, or the adoring eyes of millions of fans.

Silver has managed to keep her two previous identities secret from all but her inner circle of close friends and that gorgeous sheriff, who would apparently hang anyone who messed with his girl. But could it really happen? Could someone like Marjorie Rawlings seriously fake her death and continue to live happily ever after in a place she truly loved?

Even though Silver is proof that such a thing is possible, Emily wonders if she should try and prove Marjorie died-and not that she didn't-in 1953. That might be safer than what is happening now, what with some maniac following her like he's one of Marjorie's hunting dogs.

The notion of disappearing is so appealing to Emily that she's smiling as she shifts again, kicks off the covers for the tenth time, and then realizes she's already been participating in this missing person scavenger hunt for almost a week. It doesn't seem possible, because there's so much going on, but activity has a way of doing that to a person. Emily knows she only has one week left before she has to be back in Ohio for work, and then starts imagining what it would be like if she disappeared. The idea is so intoxicating she's suddenly wide-awake again.

If someone doesn't kill her, and she didn't have to go back to work or Ohio or the dingy walls of the condo that have needed new paint for the past five years, what would she do? Two weeks ago the answer might have been easy. Go to some gorgeous island where it doesn't snow, flirt with all the cabana boys, and perhaps let one sneak into her room for a pity-bout of sexual activity. Develop a taste for rum on the rocks and read sixteen books in a row. Turn off her cell phone and send hate letters to the three idiots who run the front desk at the library, and let them know it's a front desk and not Central Command. Then what? Maybe boldly apply to graduate school, go off on some kind of volunteer archeological dig, move to Manhattan and act as if she's twenty-seven and not fifty-seven, look up the guy from high school who pops in and out of her dreams every other month?

Even lying alone in her bed and flailing around like a restless baby, Emily is embarrassed that she's having a difficult time dreaming about what she could do if only... Only what? It's not like the world is depending on her for a meal every evening or a warm bed, or if anyone besides Bev has even missed her, for God's sake. The library wouldn't close, and to be honest about it they'd probably hire someone in five seconds who's a master's graduate and who will work for lots less than she does, because she's been there so long.

By now Emily is so angry with herself her covers are on the floor and she's lying as stiff as a board in the center of the extremely large, and very firm, full-sized bed. This is a fine time to be thinking about the lost days and nights of a life that has, to the best of her poor knowledge, been lived on less than a full tank. Emily's hated herself like this before, and it's very easy to slip back and remember all the times she felt like a failure. Instead, saturated with Marjorie's tales of rabid dogs, the end of September storms, and how Orange Lake often smelled like jessamine that had been spilled from a perfume flask on the stars, she can only think of that bold author.

Emily knows she's only beginning to discover who Rawlings was and she's so hungry to know more she excitedly rises out of bed, as if she's just been resurrected from the dead. She's wearing the same-and now slightly disgusting-nightgown that she pulled out of one of the bags she salvaged from Leslie's house, and she starts pacing like a manic crazy woman who has just gone off her medication. What she would do if she were to run away, and allowed herself to think about it for more than five seconds, is to become a literary archeologist. If there weren't such a thing, she would invent it and then do it.

Holy shit! That's what Marjorie would say, without a doubt. On her second lunge through her bedroom Emily thinks about sliding back into the kitchen and getting herself a glass of whiskey and she has a sudden urge for a Lucky Strike that makes her stop and then laugh. Her mind is whirling like a top and she's thinking about what it might be like to be out on Orange Lake with Jimmy when the sun comes up and the stars shake and throw off the scent of famous authors.

Time evaporates again and Emily is wondering how much money she has amassed in her university pension fund and in that one account she inherited when her father died that just keeps reinvesting itself. Then something new and wonderful waltzes right into her mind.

She finally realizes that she's becoming a literary archaeologist! She's remembering the hundreds and hundreds of hours of research she has done and all the yellowed pages, boxed up in attics and trucks and backyard storage bins, that she's touched through thin white gloves. She knows that the world is littered with written treasures that are sometimes disposed of by the great-granddaughters, and lost cousins of great people who are the only ones left when the house has to be sold.

The risks, not of finding something remarkable or throwing new light on an old written treasure, don't halt her in mid-step; but the loss of security, of familiarity and comfortableness bring her to a complete halt in front of the tall dresser. Emily turns and, when she does, the faint glow of her night-light illuminates a small mirror on top of the dresser. She cannot bear to look into her own eyes and instead turns toward the window, still dark, a haunting reminder of who and what might be out there.

Emily strains to go back to 1928. There's a woman on a porch, listening as her husband storms through a house that is falling down more then it's standing up. This woman's hands are clenched in fists at her side and she turns while he rages and walks into the black shadows of trees she does not yet know the name of, but she can tell by their long, slender trunks that their roots run deep and true and that the storms of life will not harm them.

The woman hides. She weaves herself inside of the skinny limbs and becomes a shadow herself. It is perhaps November, and she will always remember the chilly night and all those to follow as nothing but lovely. She can hear something dropping-*plop, plop, plop*-when her husband becomes thankfully still, and in the morning she will find pecans all over the yard. The air is sweet and when she closes her eyes and the wind picks up, ever so slightly, she begins to sway as if she is part of the tree, as if she has always been there.

Eventually the woman must come out of her secret forest but when she emerges she is not the same woman as the one who slid out of view from an angry man. This woman is already possessed by a desire that has been haunting her for a very long time. It is as if the night and all its smells brought with them the scent of passion and freedom.

Already, when she heard the distant echo of a howling dog and then the answering moan of the next dog and the wail of the dog after that this woman was writing a story that would one day become a book that would change not only her life but the lives of everyone who read it.

"Marjorie."

Emily turns from the dresser and whispers the name of her newfound muse into her own hands. It is a kind of prayer, of asking for inspiration, and perhaps the courage to live a life the way Emily once thought a life should be lived. Bold and remarkable women are remembered not just for what they do or how they create but also for how they live while doing it.

Emily finally sits but she can't be still. For the next hour she writes. She thinks about the life of a literary archeologist, what it would be like, how it might happen, what she would need to make it work. When she stops to think she glances at the boxes and has to stop herself from getting up and kissing them, and she is thankful for the grand day when she got lost in this wonderful Florida world.

Finally, afraid to glance at her clock for fear it's almost time for breakfast, she gets up, drops her notes on the floor and steps to the window. When she peels back the dark curtains, she's almost certain she sees morning light peaking across the sky. There's a tiny orange slice so far away it seems like forever, but it's there, and she raises her hand to the window and sees a hint of light waving across her right hand.

But it's what she doesn't see that is even more important.

# 16

*"The strong winds started at midnight, almost as if the storm had been orchestrated to start at a specific time. You think you are ready for this kind of madness, for outsmarting the forces around you, but sometimes it takes the kindness of strangers to get you through the eye of the storm."*
—*Lost Hearts in the Swamp of Life* - MKR - 1963

It sounds as if there's a party going on somewhere in the house when Emily rolls over, opens one eye and sees that it's almost noon. The last thing she remembers is falling into bed with dreams of her newly created literary archaeologist business dancing through her head as if she'd just discovered gold. She'd even designed a logo. It will be simple. An old black typewriter, just like the one Marjorie used, with yellowed paper coming out of the top and surrounded by stacks of notes, pencils, and maybe even an antique ashtray. Her motto would be *Bringing History Alive* but then she kept making up more, *One Step From the Past*, or *Reaching Past Time,* and finally she must have collapsed into an exhausted heap and now half the day has passed. And something is going on out there without her.

Emily struggles to her feet, and, woozy from lack of sleep, heads to the shower to try and wake up and make herself presentable. The shower partially revives her and she's in good spirits, buoyed by her crazy and more than half-serious idea to start her own business. Even with the light of day filtering in through the bathroom curtains, Emily thinks she just may be onto something. She's drying her hair with a towel and already deciding that she might have to hire a detective to help her, which is something that might come in handy right now.

She steps forward and pushes back the small bathroom curtain to look out the window and sees that both the sheriff and Auggie's cars are parked in the front yard. There's the source of the party. She's obviously missed something by staying up until dawn.

Throwing down the towel she quickly walks into the kitchen where she finds anything but a party. All three of them are bent over at the waist, and looking at something that's in the middle of the table. Emily is puzzled and suddenly her euphoria is replaced by what is starting to be a constant stomachache.

"Good morning," she says gingerly, reaching for the coffee pot.

They all look up but no one is smiling. "We were about to send in the dogs to see if you were dead or alive," Silver says, resting on her elbows. "Are you all right?"

"Just tired," Emily says, walking to the table, where she sees they are all looking at a map. "I was up until dawn reading and trying to reinvent myself."

The sheriff looks up as if someone has jerked his head from behind. "Were you by any chance looking out the window? Did you see anything? What time did you fall asleep? Did you have the window open?"

"Honey, easy," Silver says, putting her hand on his arm to slow him down. "One question at a time."

Emily's uneasiness is now making her woozy. She pulls out the chair on the end, takes a long sip of coffee, then she looks around the table and sees nothing but worry and concern. The caffeine always does the trick for her and after one simple sip, she at least feels as if she won't fall over.

"What in the world is going on?"

"We think the intruder came back last night," Silver explains, keeping her hand on Getts' arm to keep him calm. "Getts came by this morning to talk about what happened yesterday and then we called Auggie and well..."

"How do you know he was here?" Emily is trying to remember the shapes of the shadows she saw from the kitchen window and later out of her bedroom window. "I was in the kitchen late and there were shadows everywhere and, to be totally honest with you people because you'd find out anyway, I was scared. I took a knife to bed with me. It was spooky, and after what happened yesterday at Cross Creek, I was frightened."

Auggie reaches over and puts her hand over the top of Emily's and says she has knives and baseball bats all over her house. She's waiting to learn how to shoot a gun too, but so far, she says with a half-smile, there are not a lot of men stumbling over themselves to get into the house.

The sheriff, who is wearing his uniform, explains that when he pulled up to the house he saw another pile of cigarette butts, the same tire tracks, and this time footsteps that went around the entire house. "Either this guy is brazen or a complete fool."

Emily drops her head into her hands and wishes she could say for certain that she saw someone moving around the house. The only thing she knows for sure is that something frightened her. It could have been nothing or a newly-developing sixth sense, or one of the shadows might have been him slinking around.

Silver and Emily look at each other and Emily feels totally responsible for what she interprets as a serious look of sadness on Silver's face. She probably needs this like she needs to be exposed to a mess of reporters who discover her true identity.

"I'm so sorry, everyone," Emily can't believe this is happening and that she may have put these people in danger. "This is my fault. All you have done, all three of you, is be kind to me, and now some nutcase is stalking me and who knows what's going to happen."

"Oh for God's sake," Silver says, almost shouting, the sad look suddenly evaporating. "This is the most exciting thing that's happened around here in a year. We were just saying how glad we are that you found those boxes and not him or some idiot from Miami or Tampa who might think the old cardboard box is worth more than the contents."

Silver drifts off as if she's either trying to remember something, or getting up the courage to finish her sentence.

"Silver," Auggie says, slapping the table with both hands, "tell her, so we can get on with this. She deserves to know, and I'm guessing your dreamboat there doesn't have all day to spend with this great mystery."

Emily can only imagine with her own mouth hanging open what is going to come out of Silver's mouth next. There's a dramatic pause when Silver takes in a breath and even Getts, who must know what she's going to say, turns to look at her.

Silver begins by apologizing for what she is about to tell Emily, but adding quickly that it will all make sense, hopefully, when she's finished and when they all figure out how the man came to find them, and exactly who he might be.

"I was looking for those manuscripts the day you found them and that's why I was such a crank-box when I met you the first time," she explains. "This is sort of a long story, but give me a chance to try and string it all together because, as you know, I do not have all the pieces of this bizarre puzzle."

"How did you know?" Emily has moved to the edge of her chair and is now leaning halfway across the table.

"I didn't know for sure, but let me tell you what happened and why I've been half-heartedly looking for those damn boxes for several years," Silver continues, taking a breath so large that half her body seems to flutter across the table. "And you must know that I trust you with everything, or you wouldn't even be sitting here right now. When we say we checked you out, we *really* checked you out."

Emily is not sure at all how to take that. She believes that Silver cares for her or she wouldn't be sitting in her kitchen with her lover and her best friend. She knows it's never too late to say goodbye or start over or get in the car and leave, and she knows she doesn't want to do any of those things right now, which is as amazing as the fact that she's been looking for a dead woman.

Before she continues, Getts looks at her, taps his wrist-watch, and smiles.

"The short version now," she continues, holding up her hand in a surrender pose. "Our chief consultant here has to get back to his other clients very soon, or people might think he's sleeping with me. He also needs to tell you what he found yesterday."

Everyone, including the sheriff himself, smiles and Silver elaborates as quickly as possible. Leslie, it seems, may have been harboring more than just disgust for the literary world and a few disgruntled writers. Many of the men and women who came to stay only did so for a short time, or for semi-extended periods that meant they were not putting down roots in Florida like Leslie did. When Silver arrived she had what everyone called a "Marjorie Moment". She loved the heat and the sky and the feel of nothing but hot air blowing on her. She felt as if this place, the people who were gathered at that particular moment, would also hold on to her.

Silver explains that she was just as devastated about her work and life when she came here as Leslie had been, and, as she was soon to find out, as Marjorie Rawlings had been as well. Prior to coming to Florida, Silver says her writing was based on the rollercoaster of life. Emotional ups and downs were her bread and butter and because she had never experienced anything like this remarkable place, she had been unable to write about it.

But Leslie and Florida set her free, and gave her back her life. She was clearly gifted with the ability to be a successful writer and she totally needed the space and place and the support of people who knew that. So Silver was the one who stayed. The cottages built adjacent to Leslie's house were never lived in full time and, as Leslie aged, she needed someone close to become her confidante, her caretaker, the keeper of her dying flame.

And, of course, that was Silver.

"She had children but their lives, like so many children's lives, were centered in different places and Leslie needed me, she needed someone who understood about her periods of silence, her quirky rules, the way she had secrets that I didn't even know about," Silver explains, talking now with her hands. "She was eccentric, and it takes someone who understands that to handle what comes with it all."

Auggie is smiling and raising her hands up and down as if she's at a revival. The sheriff is smiling too, and obviously trying hard not to shake his head up and down in agreement. Silver, to her credit, ignores them both.

"I had been working with Leslie for the past five years on her biography," Silver reveals. "There is so much material-and talk about a life lived on your own terms-but there were also secrets that she was sharing with me, and I believe that you stumbled onto the biggest one of them all." Emily has not moved since Silver started to talk. It's impossible for her to even imagine being upset because Silver has waited this long to give her this part of the missing puzzle. She wishes she could fast forward Silver right now but she's also thinking about the importance of details. More. Faster. Quicker. She must be patient, even as she's wiggling in her seat.

Leslie had taken care of Silver and Silver was taking care of Leslie. Clearly, it was a friendship based on great love and respect. Silver continues haltingly, stopping occasionally to compose herself, and speaking with such great affection that it's impossible not to see how much she cared for her friend.

Silver met with her regularly during the past five years, amassing notes and photographs, and discovering an even deeper and more secretive world than she had at first known existed. Leslie had lovers, and they were not your run-of-the-mill lovers. There were movie stars and politicians and great literary figures that stopped for a visit and stayed much longer. There were Leslie's writings from decades of work, many unpublished, that fell under Silver's care. There was also the hint of something much, much bigger that they were about to address when Leslie became ill.

"She had breast cancer, and no one knew," Silver says as quietly as Emily has ever heard her speak. "She wanted to protect her children and grandchildren, and I protested, but in the end she wanted them to remember the woman she had always been and not the one that got so ill, so fast, and wasted away so quickly."

Leslie died only four weeks after her diagnosis and Silver suspects there was much more to her physical demise but Leslie didn't want an autopsy and in the last few weeks of her life, as she slipped in and out of consciousness, she started talking about Marjorie.

"She was lucid quite a lot, but she started talking all of the time about Marjorie as if she had known her, and I kept taking notes and soon I believed her." Silver shakes her head quickly, either to dislodge a memory, or to bury one. "I thought I was going crazy because she knew so much about her, and was saying things about the time she had dinner at her house, and they went over some of their work... it was almost maddening because she could not have known her before she moved down here, and then I started to be firm and ask questions."

And Leslie answered them, and said there was a big secret somewhere in the house and that she had promised Marjorie she would keep quiet about it until she died. Silver says she was beside herself with not just excitement but with worry as well. She didn't have one slice of proof that Rawlings had faked her own death and lived in hiding and only the word of a woman half crazed with pain, who in the end was attached to a morphine drip and begging for fresh honey, red wine, and for Silver to read to her almost constantly.

"I'm in charge of the literary end of the estate. Her children came and took very few things and I wanted that bedroom because I have this idea to do a small museum some day-yes, just like Cross Creek-and I swear those boxes must have been thrown on the porch by Bob after I left," Silver is talking as if she's trying to figure out where they were stored. "I bet they were in the attic. I never looked in the attic. I didn't even know she had an attic."

Emily is beginning to understand why Marjorie drank so much whiskey. All the blood in her head feels as if it's rushed to her feet. She opens her mouth to ask all the questions that are jammed up in her mind when the sheriff raises both hands into the air and says, "Stop, please!"

Everyone obeys.

"I need to leave and I also need to tell you quickly what I found in your stalker's cabin, which of course none of you will ever repeat because I was never really there." The sheriff now, in spite of his blazing blue eyes and cheekbones that should be outlawed on a human, especially a man, is looking first at Silver, then Auggie, then Emily for a nod of the head. "You can finish this story after I leave, but for now, give me five minutes and I'm out of here."

Everyone pauses and sits at attention. Silver even manages to fold her hands as if she is sitting in church. Emily now believes she may be living inside of a novel right this moment. Even though everything seems to be making more sense now that she knows about Leslie's last conversations, life at this moment still feels a bit surreal.

The sheriff, who speaks slowly and yet with such great authority Emily totally understands why he's called Getts, says that the first thing he found were photographs taken the night it rained. And yes, he was watching them.

"Who the hell are we talking about?" Auggie is clearly agitated by this news.

"I'm working on that," Getts explains. "He registered at the cabin under the name of Brian Smith. There is no Brian Smith-well, I'm sure there is, but he is not Brian Smith. I'm looking for the red SUV, which may be rented. I haven't had a chance to do that yet."

"This is not comforting," Auggie tells him.

"How did you find where he was staying?" Silver asks as Auggie closes her eyes and shakes her head.

"People talk and apparently he's been driving all over the place. It wasn't hard for me to make a few calls and find out where someone in a red SUV who is not local was staying."

And there's more. Somehow Getts believes the man must know about the manuscripts. He's not just following Emily, and now Silver around, he's also been beating them to the places they have been visiting. Leslie's house, the library, Cross Creek and from what the sheriff discovered in the man's cabin, he's already been to St. Augustine and also a tiny village twenty-five miles south called Big Cotton Hollow.

Emily screams, and she doesn't even realize it. The sheriff jumps up and Auggie is right behind him, but Silver is looking at Emily with astonishment. "How do you know this?" Emily manages to ask, while Auggie and the sheriff sit back down.

"Why?" he asks.

"Please tell us, and then I will explain."

Silver lightly touches the sheriff's shoulder, nods her head, and he takes in a breath to calm himself and says, "I watched him leave his cabin and then I simply walked in the unlocked back door. This man, or boy as I prefer to call him, is clearly an amateur. An unlocked door? The place was a mess, and there was a map spread out on the kitchen table with all these spots circled."

"What does this mean?" Auggie asks.

"He's looking for something, knows something, wants something and probably needs something very badly too."

Getts says he didn't find anything else that could be useful but the guy clearly is settled in for a while. The refrigerator was stocked with beer, there were a mess of microwave meals in the freezer, and the sheriff hesitates and then turns to look at Silver.

"Tell us Mr. Sheriff," Silver commands.

"There was a pile of tools. Rope. A huge locker-sized metal box with a lock on it that was not locked, a drill, and a big pile of dirty dishes and clothes. So the good is that he obviously can't take care of himself, and the bad is he's looking for something." The sheriff turns to Emily and says, "Now, it's your turn."

Clearly Auggie is now part of this Rawlings hunting team, so Emily tells them that the manuscript she and Silver have been reading seems to have been written in a place called Big Cotton Hollow. The initials MKR are typed in the manuscript, along with the date, 1963, and the words Big Cotton Hollow.

The sheriff chuckles. He tells them that Big Cotton Hollow is hardly a turn in the road and that the tiny gas station and convenience store that was there closed last year. There are a few cottages along the river but he seriously says that it's more a name on the map then anything else. He can't recall ever making a police visit in the area, doesn't know anyone who lives there, and says it seems unlikely that anything exciting ever happened within a ten mile radius of the place.

The three women start a rambling discourse on every possibility they can imagine. Marjorie dyed her hair and stayed in Cross Creek. She did move to Big Cotton Hollow, but became a recluse. Why not? If Getts doesn't even know anyone there, there's every possibility in the world that not just Marjorie but a mess of mobsters, and maybe even Amelia Earhart, could be there too. Leslie discovered her and they became fast friends. They start talking over each other and finally the sheriff jumps to his feet and says he must leave.

"But what should we do?" Silver asks this with such sincerity that the sheriff, who is clearly trying to hold back a huge laugh, sits back down for a moment.

"I've been waiting for you to say that since the day I met you, sweetheart."

Everyone breaks into a much-needed laugh, especially Silver, and the release eases the tension. Getts tells them he has some ideas and a semi-plan but in order to keep his job he must go serve the rest of the public.

"Auggie, it's your day off, right?" he asks.

Auggie nods.

"Good, good. Can the three of you broads stay here today? Don't leave or go driving off to Big Cotton Hollow and knocking on doors. I'll be back at dinnertime and we will figure this out. Yes?"

They all nod in agreement and then sit dumbfounded as the sheriff drives off and they are now alone and staring at each other.

Silver wiggles and then so does Auggie, and Emily starts to laugh again. They are all trying to restrain themselves from running out the door, jumping into a car, and driving as fast as possible to Big Cotton Hollow.

"We can't, can we?" This from Auggie, who is nervously moving her legs back and forth under the table.

Silver is silent. She's pursed her lips and is thinking. When she finally speaks, it's not what Emily and Auggie want to hear.

"I think Getts has a plan, and that we might blow it if we go driving around like Charlie's Angels and asking stupid questions. I think we need to be smart about this, too. There's nothing I'd like better than to drive over there as fast as possible and do a door-to-door search but remember, someone has been watching us, and he's already been there too."

"I hate it when you're practical," Auggie moans, dropping her head onto the table.

Emily is lost in thought while her friends pout. This mysterious search would offer her a perfect chance to launch her new business, and perhaps that's what she's already doing. But Silver's right, the element of danger that has risen up surrounding the boxes and the man isn't worth risking the treasure they might have discovered. She'd like nothing more than to be halfway to Big Cotton Hollow herself-or even in St. Augustine or anywhere else their stalker has already been. But she also remembers what it felt like to look into that man's eyes at Cross Creek and how quickly she dissolved into a frightened heap. She hates to admit it, but the sheriff and Silver are right.

All three of them look as if they are teenage girls who've just been told they can't go to the mall on Friday night. The clock is ticking and they are sitting absolutely still when the dogs start to bark. Silver jumps up to look out the window and see what's going on. She watches the tail end of a deer fly across the far side of the field adjacent to her house and sits down with relief.

"A deer," she explains.

It's quiet again and then Emily leans forward, plops her elbows on the table, rests her head in her hands and asks, "What would Marjorie do?"

The quiet doesn't last much longer. Auggie pushes herself from behind the table, jumps up, and claps her hands.

"Oh my God, she'd cook, and drink, and probably open up the back door and fire off a few rounds from her shotgun if she had a free day." Auggie looks as if she's just won the lottery. "I bet that's what she'd do!"

"Cooking now?" Silver looks disgusted.

"She loved to cook, you know that. From what I've learned about her I think it was almost-almost being a key word here- as important as writing. She wrote a cookbook, for God's sake. You're the one who showed it to me. Her parties were famous and I kind of feel the same way about being in the kitchen. You know that, that's why I shop and cook for you. Get a grip, honey!"

Silver, clearly not a "love it all the time" kitchen or cooking aficionado, even with her fabulous kitchen, drops her head and moans. "The same way, meaning you want a martini, or to throw yourself off the roof the minute someone sets down a bowl and asks you to help them prepare a meal?"

"I know this is not always your cup of tea, little Miss Can't-We-Eat-Out, but trust me on this. Cooking is a release and maybe, just maybe, there's a secret hidden away in Marjorie's cookbook that will give us another clue. Besides, you sometimes love doing this, or you'd never have made this kitchen the way you did. Stop pretending."

Silver sighs, smiles, and throws up her hands in surrender, while Auggie starts to clear away the coffee cups. Cooking it is, even though she'd rather be plotting the demise of the guy who seems to be one step ahead of all of them.

Emily is already up and running to her bedroom. When she comes back a few moments later, *Cross Creek Cookery* is in her hands. "I spent half the night reading this, and it's amazing."

The dogs stop barking the second Emily drops the cookbook on the table and the three would-be detectives momentarily forget about secrets, a coiled rope on the cabin floor, and the dusty footprints that surround the very kitchen where they hope to recreate a feast designed by their literary and life heroine.

If only for a very little while.

**17**

*"The brightest days, so seldom it seemed, were carefree of the normal worries and filled with the juicy expectations of what I might create in the kitchen. How I loved the smells of roasting meat and bubbling sauces mingling with my own laughter. The joy would be doubled if there was company, a double gift, to share such special time. It was as if the heavy weight on my heart and soul lifted, if only for as long as it took for the sweet bread to rise."*
—*Lost Hearts in the Swamp of Life* - MKR - 1963

Emily and reluctant Silver are almost happily bumping rear ends in Silver's kitchen and working hard to forget about the dangers of discovering secret boxes. The counter is littered with pots and pans and spoons and knives. Auggie has accepted the task of reader, ingredient announcer, and modern-day interrupter of *Cross Creek Cookery* before they start filling up the mixing bowls. Silver has already given them a once-over-lightly history of the creation of the book, with the caveat that she does not know everything and Emily, at least, must get herself over to the University of Florida library soon to learn more.

Silver explained that the unbridled success of the book *Cross Creek* all but demanded that Marjorie pull some of her personal recipes and write a cookbook. *Cross Creek*, which is non-fiction, is full of cooking adventures and tales of Marjorie going off to hunt and fish so she could put food on the table. And just as the world fell in love with that book, and the scrub country way of life, their mouths were also watering for the food that she described throughout.

The women have decided only three things so far. First of all, they are going to try not to drink until after the pots are simmering. Silver's already pretty sure that's not going to happen. They have all agreed on what they are going to cook, which was totally based on what Silver had in the house so they could keep their promise to Getts, and thirdly, they are going to work really hard at not driving themselves crazy about Big Cotton Hollow, the man, or Leslie's big secret. The plan works for almost fifteen minutes.

Emily is bent over at the waist and running her fingers down the page of ingredients from the list Auggie has made. They've decided on Crab a la Newburg, Cross Creek style, Aunt Luella's Boiled Salad Dressing, Beet and Cabbage Salad and Black Bottom Pie. Emily is trying to keep herself from drooling on the counter when Auggie shouts, "Who the hell was Dora again?"

Silver bursts out laughing and shouts back, "Marjorie's cow."

"What?"

Emily has turned to look at Auggie and can't wait for the rest of this conversation.

"Dora was her cow," Silver says, still shouting as if Auggie is deaf. "She apparently loved to name her animals and Dora's high octane milk made delicious cream. Maybe we should forget about this and drive around and look for a place where someone kept a mess of animals. Rawlings had every-thing from ducks and chickens to that cow and who knows what else."

"Why are you shouting?" Auggie answers.

"Because you were shouting."

"Can we drink now?" Auggie shouts one more time as she also starts to laugh.

Silver turns to look at Emily the same moment Emily turns to look at her, and Emily decides she'd better throw on another pot of coffee. They have selected recipes that need more than a small bit of concentration and this is no time to be forgetting an ingredient. Auggie remains buried in the cookbook while Silver sorts through her cupboards for dishes and ingredients. She's now crossed over to the happy side of cooking and baking, and has agreed that this adventure might end up being a great idea.

It's a gorgeous day outside and Silver has opened all the windows and a slight breeze is floating into the house from behind the kitchen. The smell is sweet. Emily guesses the wind is sweeping past the flowers Silver has planted outside the windows. She also realizes how hard Silver must have worked to create her own slice of heaven as far from civiliza-tion as Marjorie's Cross Creek.

When she turns to ask about that, she sees Silver bent over Auggie, one of her hands is resting gently on Auggie's shoulder, and the other is on her hip. She wonders how they met and when she asks, the both look up as if they've touched a live wire.

Auggie reaches up and pats Silver's hand and then ends up holding it while she speaks. "I happened to be checking on a patient at the Ocala hospital the night the sheriff brought Silver in," she says quietly, holding Silver's hand even tighter.

"There were no female doctors on duty and the damn hospital still didn't have any kind of rape or assault policy in place yet. I'm the one who took care of Silver. She requested a woman, for good reason. Then she actually came and stayed with me for awhile, and unless she screws up any of these recipes, it's been one of the greatest friendships of my life."

Silver squeezes Auggie's hand and Emily feels a slight pang of guilt for not having called Bev or checking emails or anything she might have done, or would be doing, if she had hurried back to her normal life. She wonders if she's been a good friend-obviously not, for the past week or so-and tries to imagine what life must *really* be like, living like this.

Both Silver and Auggie see that Emily's gone off somewhere inside of her own mind and for a few seconds the kitchen is about as quiet as it's going to get with these three women inside of it. When Emily lowers her eyes and sees them staring at her, she tells her what she's been thinking about without them having to ask.

Loneliness, it seems, has been an important if ignored issue with her, and Silver admits that her habits are more hermit-like than Auggie's. Auggie is with people all of the time and most of them drive her crazy, she shares without hesitation. But at the end of the day she ends up helping more people than not and that makes the struggle worth it. Silver assures her that when she's not running around looking for Marjorie, she's mostly holed up in her office writing or working in her beloved gardens.

She knows enough people, she says, and of course, now that Mr. Lovely is her man there's not much time to be bothered with wondering what her life might have been like if she had not disappeared and become someone new. And, most importantly, she craves the quiet because of her work, but opening up like she has with Auggie and Emily, well, that's something she can't do very often for reasons that are now out in the open.

Emily wants to know so much more about that and about Marjorie and her obvious desire to live remotely but yet entertain as if she were living in the middle of Manhattan. Silver is thinking as Auggie gets up, pushes past her, and pours all of them a cup of coffee.

"I think many people like me, and Marjorie for sure, struggle with that balance," Silver says, leaning against the side of the table. "People talk about the life of the artist or the life of the author as if we are different from the rest of the world but when you think about it, I mean *really* think about it, I believe we are all inspired by similar things. Marjorie loved Cross Creek and everything about it from what I can see, even when things were hard. It's the same for all of us. Getts has a brother who's an engineer and you couldn't get him out of Kansas if you tried. He loves it. But that doesn't mean once a month he doesn't call his brother and pine away for a day on the lake behind the house where he grew up down here. "

Emily understands the point Silver is trying to make. Cooking has now taken a back seat to a philosophical discussion that could last a decade or two. Emily acts as if she's shooing away a fly but she's trying to refocus on the cooking project. Her mind is jumping around from thought to thought so fast she's having a hard time thinking about anything but Marjorie out at Cross Creek, probably sleeping with the windows open and listening to the wolves or coyotes or whatever wild animals roamed near her house and who howled the moment it got dark.

Auggie breaks the spell by reading from the cookbook as if she's in the middle of some kind of theatrical production. "Ah-hum, ladies, listen up. Maybe we should make Minorcan Gopher Stew. Listen to this. Wash the decapitated gopher. Cut the shell away from the meat. Scald the feet until the skin and claws can be removed. Discard Entrails. Cut meat in two-inch pieces. Simmer until thoroughly tender in two cups water to every cup meat, adding one-half teaspoon salt and a dash of pepper to every cup of meat."

It's one thing to read it but another to listen to it being read aloud. Emily looks as if she's just had a taste of this dish. Auggie looks up, smiles, and then continues. "Blah, blah, blah… oh here we go. When gopher is tender, turn the sauce into the gopher pot. There should be enough liquid to make plenty of gravy. Thicken by mashing the yolks of hardboiled eggs, two eggs to every cup of meat, and stirring into the stew. Good Lord, who knew?"

"Is that last sentence part of the recipe?" Emily asks, at the exact moment both Silver and Auggie burst out laughing.

So far the idea to stop thinking about the sheriff's plan and what might happen next is working. The women finish their coffee and thumb through the cookbook for another twenty minutes, talking about skinning coots, cooking rabbit that has just been shot out the back door, or how delicious Sweet Potatoes in Orange Baskets might taste on a hot summer night. They almost forget to cook their own meal when Silver's phone buzzes and she picks it up and starts talking before the phone even gets to her mouth.

"Yes, sir, we have not left the building."

Emily and Auggie roll their eyes as Silver waves and walks out of the kitchen for a second. Auggie whispers that it's not just a match made in heaven, if there is such a place, but an example of true love if she's ever seen one. Emily takes the opportunity to ask Auggie if she's ever married and Auggie says yes, she went through the obligatory first marriage and the subsequent divorce before she realized she's perfectly happy to be single and remain that way forever. The diamond she wears is just a decoration and it helps her keep away potential unwanted dates.

It's quiet for a moment and both women can hear Silver talking in the living room. Emily lets her mind drift, looks out the window, thinks about the footprints that Getts discovered, and in the time it takes for Silver to end her conversation and walk back into the kitchen, the notion of not thinking or talking about the stalker and the manuscripts is over.

Silver tells them Getts is excited about coming over for dinner, and if it's not too late and it's still light out, he wants to do a handgun seminar in the backyard. Emily can't even imagine touching a gun, let alone firing one; she's decided to rely on Silver and Auggie for protection if she can convince them that it's more likely she'd shoot one of them and not the bad guy.

The bad guy and Marjorie's whereabouts have leapt back into her mind full force and it's impossible now for her to focus on what Silver is saying about Getts or cooking.

"Earth to Ohio," Silver starts saying over and over again as she waves her hand in front of Emily's face.

"I'm sorry, it's just, I can't stop thinking about this guy and what he might know and the chances that Marjorie might have lived much longer than 1953 and those manuscripts…" Emily trails off and clearly consumed, jumps up and starts pacing in the kitchen.

Silver and Auggie look at each other and smile. The cooking extravaganza has suddenly been put on pause.

Emily starts talking about their stalker and about the boxes she discovered and about how they need to be thinking like detectives, and not just like... well, police officers or bodyguards, or clueless women. "Don't take that wrong," she shares, stopping to hold up her hands. "I think we need to slow down today and think about this, well, differently."

Without discussing her literary archeologist revelation, Emily talks about clues and where to look for them and spends a good thirty minutes pumping Silver for answers to questions about what a person has to do if they decide they are going to disappear. It would have to be planned, Silver suggests, because of legal documents and Social Security numbers and the paper trail of life that follows everyone till the day they die.

Silver explains that her departure from her first two lives was made much easier because she had an editor who did, and continues to do everything for her. Her finances and legal documents are all set up in a secret account that is monitored constantly by her editor and Silver says she trusts the woman who holds the key to her many secrets with her life. There have been no slip-ups and at this point in her life if someone did discover her, it wouldn't even matter, in fact it would probably boost her already huge book sales.

Auggie has found a notebook and pen and is starting to take notes. Silver can clearly see that Emily is in some kind of zone and she's making yet another pot of coffee and resisting the temptation to get out some Irish Cream when she starts to think about Emily's job and how she pieces together the slivers of people's lives-a note, a shoe, a fragment of hair, a wedding ring-until she can see who they were, how they lived, what became of them. She almost drops the coffee beans when she realizes what Emily has been trying to tell her.

"I get it now," she says loudly, half scaring both Emily and Auggie. "The clues. There must be more of them, and maybe that's what that jackass is looking for. If we already have the prize, which would be the manuscripts, he might still be looking for the clues. But he doesn't realize that he'd also have to prove Marjorie didn't die in 1953."

Emily claps her hands and breaths a long sigh of relief. "Yes!"

Auggie isn't clapping. She's now also deep in thought. "My sister's kids use to make me watch this show called *Where in the World is Carmen Sandiego?*" she begins, totally confusing Silver and Emily. Auggie looks up and says, "Stay with me here."

The show was all about geography but it was also like a treasure hunt and it was addicting. From what she remembers there would be clues about products, famous people, landmarks, great events and it was like putting a puzzle together and the kids loved it, so did she, because it was fast and fun.

Emily and Silver are waiting for this to make sense. Auggie knows she sounds crazy but this is how her brain works. She goes on to talk about medical school and trying to diagnose problems and illnesses with only a few symptoms. Now her point is beginning to come into focus.

"Eventually everything comes together and that's what this is like, and forgive me for taking so long to get to the point," she says, exhaling. "Marjorie had to leave clues. She was human and a drinker and a writer like Silver so we know she was at least a little crazy."

Emily says "yes" again and Silver turns without saying a word and puts the milk, butter, crabmeat and eggs they were going to use back in the refrigerator. Emily is still pacing. Then, just like she does when she's in the basement of the university library, she has Auggie start to write down what they do know, what they have, what they might need to fit everything together. It doesn't take long to get to the boxes on the porch, Leslie's house, and the guy they have now decided to call Mr. Asshole. Emily keeps thinking. Silver gets up, grabs the Irish Cream and says as she pours some into each one of their coffee cups, "It's the least we can do for Marjorie."

Auggie gets up too, stretches, and then abruptly looks at Silver. "Well, duh," she says pointing at her. "We are missing one big clue. Someone helped her just like someone helped you. Do you remember how she supposedly died?"

Silver sets down her cup, holds up one finger, and disappears. When she comes back just a few moments later she's carrying a file folder. She sets it down and fishes out an old obituary. Auggie and Emily huddle around her and Auggie takes it upon herself to read out loud.

*Marjorie Kinnan Rawlings, the author whose story about a backwoods boy living in Florida's scrub country won the Pulitzer Prize, died yesterday of a cerebral hemorrhage after suddenly becoming ill. She was at her Crescent Beach, Florida home when she became ill and was rushed to Flagler Hospital in St. Augustine.*

Before Auggie can continue, Silver is already talking about how remote Crescent Beach is and how back in 1953 there were hardly any homes. "She could have been whisked away in a heartbeat. Norton, if I remember correctly, knew everyone. "

"Wait a second," Emily says. "I think we are still ahead of ourselves here. We aren't in St. Augustine now; we are here, close to Big Cotton Hollow and close to Leslie's house. Obviously, we have a few field trips on the horizon, but let's start here. Think for a minute."

Dr. Auggie is now the one who is pacing. She has a nervous habit, or a thinking habit, of knocking her knuckles together when she's clicking through her mind and in deep thought. Right now it sounds like bone hitting bone when her hands are moving. "Do you know how easy it would be for her to have done this? I mean, seriously, I know you want us to focus here but people disappear, like we said before, all of the time. Three years ago my friend who works in the emergency room had a woman beg him to say she had died so she could run away. It would have been really easy for him to do that. I'm guessing it was even easier back when Marjorie was alive so first of all, yes, she could have done it."

Auggie looks up and apologizes. "Local clues", she says, bowing as she asks for forgiveness. Then she sits back down, picks up the pen, and waits for Emily to verbalize what she is thinking, but it's Silver who starts to talk.

She knew something was in the house and why she thought it was in Leslie's bedroom is beyond her. Leslie led her on, when she was able to think clearly, and yet she never said what Silver might find. Leslie herself could have written the manuscript and then there are all the other boxes of writings that they have yet to examine closely. What else do they have?

Emily wants to know about Marjorie's relatives. There was Norton and the first husband, what about the brother?

"His name was Arthur. He was kind of a wild card, he's also dead, and he had a son who has not had that great of a life but that's part of the reason why you need to go to Gainesville and the university," Silver explains. "Marjorie's papers, original manuscripts, and letters are all there."

"Could Arthur have had another child, or could there be a relative who we don't know about?" Emily knows she's jumping ahead herself but her mind is spinning.

"Well, good Lord, at this point don't you think anything is possible?" Silver has dropped her hands to her side and left them dangle as if she's given up. "This is one of those few moments when I wish I had Internet so we can see if there are still relatives, some kind of connection, or really anything."

"There are so many sophisticated ways of getting information now it's almost ridiculous," Emily agrees. "The genealogy libraries and search engines we use where I work could find an ant in Chicago and your sheriff can find things quick, too, but maybe that's already part of his plan."

The dogs start barking again and all three women run to the window. They're more jumpy than they realize and when they see another deer running for its life they shake it off and all agree they are done with the coffee. Auggie mentions how the thought of someone sneaking around has changed how she feels about everything she does. Knowing someone could be watching you, she admits, is more frightening than she might have imagined.

That reminds Emily to ask Silver where she keeps her gun or pistol or whatever she calls it. Silver says it's in her purse, where all respectable southern women keep their weapons, except the ones who have ankle, hip, or arm holsters.

"Clues, girls," Auggie starts clapping. "Think."

"Maybe we should haul out the boxes and look at each page," Emily suggests. "I have to say though, what I'd really like to do is go back to Leslie's house and see if we missed anything."

This perks up both Silver and Auggie. Did Getts say not to go to Big Cotton Hollow or did he say stay home all day? Silver is obviously conflicted about the answer to that question. She knows she could call Bob and he'd let her back into Leslie's home in a heartbeat. But Getts would not be a happy man if that happened.

Emily is trying to justify racing over to Leslie's when she remembers something else, something she should have thought of an hour ago or three days ago. This detective business is not that easy.

"Silver, you know that spare bedroom at Leslie's toward the front of the house?"

Silver nods.

"Who slept in that room?"

"It was for very special guests and visitors," she tells Emily, looking puzzled by the question. "I mean there are those other houses, so she kept that room for really special visitors and I found out, just before she died, how special. I had no idea she was such a naughty girl."

"So if Marjorie really didn't die in 1953 and visited Leslie, she would have stayed in that room, and maybe the things that were in the drawers might have been hers." Emily is guessing but she's getting a feeling now, like she sometimes does at work, when she finds a missing link. It's a flush of excitement that makes her stomach dance and her head spin a bit faster then it normally does.

She tells them that she took all the clothes from the dresser that was in that extra bedroom, and the box of newspapers, all dated from January of 1973. Silver and Auggie are looking at her as if to say, "So what?" Then she explains how sometimes clothes are donated where she works that are very old. She's found money, watches, and most importantly, documents and notes in the pockets. It's definitely a few steps beyond finding a mess of quarters in the bottom of the washing machine.

"I may have been wearing Marjorie Kinnan Rawlings' nightgown all week," she says, crossing her hands in adoration over her chest and closing her eyes. Before she has time to open them, Silver and Auggie are rushing down the hall and grabbing the bags as if they've just discovered the biggest clue of all. Emily can hear them struggling against each other to get though her door first.

"Go on in," she jokingly hollers down the hall. "I don't mind at all if you go in there!"


Two hours later, Silver's living room is littered with clothes. It looks as if someone has gone berserk at a rummage sale or had a bipolar episode. The women first divided the clothes into three piles and then Emily gave them a five minute in-service about how to feel along the seams for bumps, adding that she once found a small ring that way. Hems that look as if they have been hand stitched need to be opened because that's a perfect place for small notes to be stored. Buttons can tell a story also. The larger buttons with the metal backing that are removable are great hiding places and it's not unusual to actually find that someone has written right on the clothing.

Silver and Auggie look at Emily with admiration as she talks about clothing treasure hunting. They know she is so much more than just a research and historical librarian but they also know she's a bit hard on herself. They watch as she smoothes a blouse, checks the label to see if it is a modern or antiquated clothing manufacturer or something handmade. They all work with great abandon, totally forgetting about time, or the dinner they are supposed to be making for themselves and the sheriff.

Emily asks Silver if Marjorie was the kind of woman who might have hidden something, given them a clue, laughed at the world before, and after, her death.

Silver, claiming once again not to be an expert, says that all you have to do is read *Cross Creek* or some of the letters she wrote to know that she had a wicked sense of humor. She laughed at the world and with the world and she also laughed at herself. But, Silver admonishes for about the tenth time, the archivist at the University of Florida, who can talk about Marjorie as if she had just been over to her house for dinner.

The word dinner makes their stomachs growl and they all laugh as they pull apart seams and joke about the luxury of calling out to have a pizza delivered. Emily thinks that some of the clothing, a pair of beige peddle pushers, a floral house-dress, a long jacket that has blood stains on the collar and could have been used for hunting, are prime suspects.

But after two hours, all they have discovered is lint and one piece of paper that had obviously gone through the washing machine. It is amazing that it has taken them so long to go through three garbage bags of clothing. But when they think they are done, Emily laughs like a witch and says, "Oh, no, no, no! Now I go through the pile Silver went through, Silver goes through my pile, and I go through Auggie's."

"You're kidding, right?" Silver says, leaning back against the couch from her position on the floor.

"Guess again, my little intern," Emily replies. "After this round there's one more."

They finally all agree it is time for some sustenance. Silver jumps up, grabs two boxes of crackers, some cheese, and a bottle of ice cold Pinot Grigio and suddenly the tasks are much easier to complete. They rip more hems, destroy a pile of buttons, and all they find is more lint.

"Shit," Auggie finally says when it is closing in on five o'clock. "This reminds me of medical school boot camp, minus the wine, of course. We look like a bunch of fools."

"Yes we do," Emily agrees, "but now we know there isn't anything hidden in these new rags. We do know that some of them come from what I guess are the 1960s, so that's at least something."

Silver fake cries and says they could be eating crab and pie now. Then she looks a bit like the devil and adds, "Or going through Leslie's house with Emily, our human Geiger counter."

Emily lifts her shoulders and hands in a fake apology and she's also thinking about how grand it would be to be over at the house or in Gainesville or maybe even sitting on Marjorie's back porch right this second.

"This is it?" Auggie asks, getting off the floor and stretching. "What about those newspapers? I hate to bring it up. Maybe there's a reason why they are all from one year. Who the heck would save them?"

"You're right," Emily agrees. "But before we do that, I think we should do some research and find out what happened on that date. It makes more sense than going through every paper at this point."

Emily gets up next and looks down at the mess they've made. Her excitement has faded but she believes they are headed in the right direction. She is trying to remember what the bedroom at Leslie's looked like and what she might have overlooked when she remembers something terribly important, screams, and runs down the hall.

Silver and Auggie can hear her galloping like a pony into her bedroom. They hear a wild screech, then the door slams shut, and Emily is back standing in front of them and holding out her hands as if she's a priest offering them something extremely holy. She's holding a light brown box the size of a hardcover book and her smile is so wide her lips are almost back to her ears.

"I forgot I found this jewelry box in the top drawer," she tells them. "Believe me; this will be easier than looking under buttons."

Silver and Auggie descend on her as if she's the resurrected Marjorie Rawlings herself. They kick aside the clothes, which makes the living room look even worse, and painstakingly lay out the necklaces, rings, and bracelets, which are a tangled mess.

Several of the necklaces have lockets and they open one after the other and don't find so much as a scratch. Silver stands up, walks into the kitchen and gets another bottle of wine out of the refrigerator. She fills up their glasses again and makes everyone take a sip before they start in on the rings and bracelets.

Emily loves this kind of research more than anything. She can already tell that most of the jewelry is old, some of it is solid gold, and three tarnished silver pieces will be beautiful when they are polished. She doesn't care about the potential monetary value. She's imagining the fingers of the women who wore the rings, the graceful way the necklaces dangled just to the top of someone's breast, the look of awe when the woman who owned it looked into the mirror and saw how beautiful the piece of jewelry looked against her skin.

Silver and Auggie are taking a much-needed break and sitting in the chairs next to the couch when Emily makes an astounding discovery. There is a matching necklace, ring and bracelet, all in gold, and she gently places them next to each other before she dares to look for any identifying marks. They are exquisite pieces, hand carved with swirls and diamonds. She lifts the ring, then the necklace, and then the bracelet and when she sets them down her hands are shaking, as is her voice, when she speaks.

"Silver," she says, barely able to speak. "What was Marjorie's second husband's name again?"

Silver sits upright and almost shouts, "Norton Baskin." Then she waits.

Emily gets off the floor and when she walks over to Silver she has the three pieces of jewelry laid out in her hand. Silver looks but doesn't touch. Then she raises her eyes to look at Emily.

Emily feels as if she's going to fall over. "All three of these pieces match and all three of these pieces have the initials, MKR and NB carved on them."

Auggie screams, just as the sheriff walks in the door, draws his gun and goes into what Emily always thinks of as the NYPD stance.

"What the holy hell?" he shouts.

Silver jumps up, runs to him and says, "We found something!"

Getts re-holsters his pistol, exhales, grabs Silver in a huge bear hug and says, "So did I. One of my deputies arrested the guy in the red SUV early this afternoon."

# 18

*"Some weeks the only news I had came on the wings of the migrating birds. Their comings and goings would announce the change of yet another season, and how I often wished they could pick me up, carry me over the tops of the trees, and show me all of the places I thought I might never see. How I longed to fly free!"*
—*Lost Hearts in the Swamp of Life* - MKR - 1963

The story behind all the news takes momentary second place as Getts realizes his girls haven't cooked the meal he has been dreaming about all day. He's thinking about not sharing details about the arrest of the man the three women have taken to calling Mr. Asshole until he eats, but one long and very mean look from Silver is all it takes, and he throws up his hands and quickly explains that their man has been arrested for driving under the influence.

One of the department deputies had seen him weaving over the center line near the town of Micanopy where he had apparently enjoyed a long and very liquid lunch at a diner on the edge of town. Getts was called immediately because he had alerted everyone in the department to watch out for him.

Silver, Auggie and Emily stand around him in the kitchen with their own growling stomachs, and with more than one eye on the gold-initialed jewelry that Emily has set on top of a white dishtowel on the kitchen counter. Getts is dying to look at the gold pieces but they have him surrounded and won't show him anything until he gives them every last detail of his own story.

Mr. Stalker was a feisty drunk, he begins, and it's even more clear now that he is a young man with quite a temper. There is a long dramatic pause when Getts simply looks at Silver and they have an entire conversation without saying a word. "Feisty," Emily assumes, means potentially danger-ous, and she swallows hard and inches a tiny bit sideways, so she can feel the comforting touch of Auggie's shoulder. Emily's world isn't terribly large but the last time she saw a feisty drunk at a small pub near her house, two men left with bloody faces and there were three broken chairs.

"Who is he?" Auggie impatiently asks.

"I'm getting there, Dr. Auggie," Getts says with a sigh.

Getts says he didn't interrogate the man, he thought it best to simply observe and listen. The deputy who booked him was a veteran woman who looked as if she ate nails for breakfast and possibly lunch. The guy appeared to sober up fast when he realized he was going to have to spend the after-noon and possibly the night in jail, and even though he blew well over Florida's legal limit for a DUI, he acted almost sober when he was thrown into a cell.

"We now have his photograph and we know he's a loose canon," Getts shares as he is shifting a piece of paper back and forth in his hands. "When I left, he was pacing like a caged animal and to be honest, I can't believe he doesn't have more of a record. Some people just look like criminals, which I know sounds horrible, but…"

Silver interrupts and says he might be frustrated, that's why he was drinking at lunch. "Maybe he's getting desperate. We really don't know how long he's been around here looking for something."

"Or he could just be a drunk," Emily suggests.

Getts is the one now impatiently waiting to finish. This three-to-one routine is overpowering. "Well, I know your jewelry find is huge, but I was just about to get to two other major developments in this... whatever you are calling it," he continued. "It's sort of a case, or an investigation or..."

"Getts," Auggie says, cutting him off, "get to it, will you please? What did you find, and who the hell is he?"

Patience is not Auggie's strong suit and the sheriff is smart enough to proceed as fast as possible. He tells them that during the intake his deputy asked Mr. Ass so many questions so fast that she threw him off balance. She wanted to know where he lived, what he was doing here because his license was from New Jersey, and why he was in the small town so very close to Cross Creek, which is still in the middle of nowhere. The man was agitated and at first said he was fishing. Then he said, no, he was hunting, but he had taken the day off. The deputy quickly ran an out-of-state license check from the Fish and Game Division and no licenses had been issued in his name.

"She's good," Auggie says, clearly impressed. "What did she find out?"

The sheriff sighs again and Auggie makes believe she is zippering her mouth shut.

"I think he finally told the truth. He said that he was looking for someone, a relative, who probably wasn't alive any longer but he'd discovered something about her and wanted to see if anyone had known her, and where she might have lived."

Emily's heart quickens at the mention of the word relative but she remains silent.

Finally, to the great relief of the sheriff, no one else is saying a word either. He lets the news sink in and then continues.

"At that point he started to shut down," Getts says, wishing with all his heart something was bubbling on the stove. "I think the beer and the arrest and chasing after you three women finally got to him. He mumbled something about his grandfather, and then he slumped on the cot and the last I heard he was sulking with his back toward the cell door. "

The women are so engrossed in what Getts is saying they haven't bothered to ask him what he is holding. He remains patient while Silver asks if the man is still in jail, and how long they can keep him. He tells them that he has to post bail and because it's a first offense, and after all this is Florida and he was arrested in the heart of moonshine country, he'll probably be released sometime tomorrow morning.

"We can't really keep him even through I'd like nothing better," he admits. "One part of me wants simply to go in there and ask him what in the hell is going on, but I also want to see where he leads us. Does that make sense?"

The women agree that if he does know more than they do about Marjorie—dead, alive or in-between—it does make sense to let everything play out, even with the risk.

"Do you think he seriously knows more, or he's just following some hunch, or he's chasing after some long-held family treasure-hunting story because he's broke?" Auggie wants to go smack the living hell out of him and make him tell her everything.

"He knows something, because his name is Brett Kinnan."

"What?" Emily has to lean against Silver when she hears his name. "Kinnan?"

"Brett Kinnan from New Jersey," Getts says again. "I almost fainted when I heard the name too. It could be a coincidence, but I also found something else."

That's when the sheriff holds out the piece of paper he has been shifting from hand to hand. "While he was being processed I went out and looked through his SUV. Besides a mess of beer cans, I found this letter in the glove box. It was tucked on the backside of the passenger's visor and, to be honest, this is the real reason I didn't go in and scare the crap out of him."

Silver, who is standing in the middle, takes the piece of paper and holds it out so they can all read at once. It is typewritten, obviously not from a computer because all the Is and periods are terribly uneven. The paper is off white, perhaps faded, and the edges are even dimmer, as if someone has been handling it a lot with dirty fingers.

*Dear Francis,*

*I despair that it has taken me so long to write. You know after all these years, twenty, if you can imagine, I still worry with every posting. Yet you have somehow managed to keep our secret. If I were the praying type I would build a tower with them so that I might live forever. Damn if we should not have thought of this sooner! Yes. I am fine and healthy and the view from the deck stops me every single morning when I glance at the beautiful, and terribly secluded, backyard. Back in Cross Creek this would have been a porch. Modern words for modern times mean that I now own a deck. But I cannot imagine ever using one of the new computers I hear about on the radio. When I work as I do I love the feel of the pen in my hand or these old keys under my fingers.*

*Last week I was able to spend a lovely day at the beach where I now blend in quite perfectly with every old lady who stumbles in the sand. Do you remember when I told you about the time I walked four miles on the sand bare-footed and developed a blister that crippled me like an old goat? I thought about that and so many other fine times and remain grateful that you have been faithful to me all these years. This part of my life has given me much, much joy and my heart and health have healed in ways I never imagined.*

*So let us get to the point. If you could please transfer for the next six months, or until a bird flies past and tells you I have croaked, the usual funds I would be beyond grateful. Remember to tear this letter into small pieces or I will send up one of the wild pigs I see constantly to nibble off your toes. Oh, and if you care to visit on the next go-around with your business I can arrange everything. Neither one of us is a spring chicken. I'm thinking we are late fall chicks at best.*

*Love,*

*Marjorie*

Emily finishes reading and realizes she has been holding her breath. She breathes, gulping air with her mouth open, and gently takes the letter out of Silver's hand. The paper is definitely old, and the letter was typed. She turns it over to see that several of the letters have punched out through the back. She's guessing it was a later-1960s model typewriter that was used. She's analyzing the letter and keeping her thoughts to herself when she looks up and sees that everyone is staring at her.

"Was it in an envelope?" She's looking at the sheriff who moves his head back and forth.

Then she asks Silver to comment on the signature. "Does it look like hers? Would you know it?" The word Marjorie is signed in black ink. The M almost looks like an exaggerated W, the A has a small loop at the top, the R almost disappears into a very long J that is dotted half an inch beyond the end of the R and the O, R, I and E all run together, and are almost undecipherable. There is a bold black line under the entire word.

"I'm no expert," Silver admits, "but it looks like her signature from the few documents I've seen. The only way to really know is to go over to Gainesville and compare it with what they have in the archives."

"But it could also be forged, right?" Auggie is skeptical. "Why wouldn't this letter be destroyed? Let's talk about this."

Which is exactly what they do for another thirty minutes, because Getts says if he doesn't eat he is going to faint. Auggie pushes past them, opens the refrigerator and begins whipping up a mess of eggs, meat, and potatoes and they all sit at the table eating breakfast for dinner and discuss what they think is every conceivable possibility surrounding the discovery of the letter and the jewelry.

Perhaps the letter was real and Brett discovered it, and decided to see if there was more treasure, which would obviously be worth a fortune. Someone faked the letter and Brett is an idiot. Maybe Francis is a friend or a relative who helped Marjorie disappear and then survive in some new life and location. He could be the illegitimate son of her brother Arthur, or perhaps some obscure relative or a distant cousin. If Brett has one letter there could possibly be more. The jewelry is obviously real but the initials could also be fake, or could have been engraved in the pieces to create some kind of confusion or even as a joke, because MKR was always after a good joke. It might be possible to go through old photographs of Marjorie at the university library and see if she is wearing any of the discovered pieces. And yes, even with a death certificate and obituary notices, and everything else that happened when Marjorie supposedly died in 1953, it's more than possible she could have faked everything. She was brilliant, talented, and a woman who can survive in the backcountry can pretty much do anything she damn well pleases.

They also talk about why she would want to disappear and Silver takes the lead in that portion of the discussion. Literary forces, bad reviews, the pressure of performance and her increasing notoriety would have all been reason enough for her to disappear. And perhaps her heart had been broken.

"By Norton?" Emily is confused.

"No, by her best friend, Zelma Cason," Silver says, bending her head and trying to remember details of the long-ago incident. "We have to find out about it in more detail because all I remember is that it had something to do with *Cross Creek*, the book, and it was precedent-setting, and when it was all over, well, people say she changed and her heart had been broken and she turned away from Cross Creek."

This is big news to Emily. But she knows lawsuits can definitely break hearts. Hers was split in half during her own divorce, which was relatively simple compared to some of the stories she has heard. Simply sitting in a courtroom, with her soon-to-be-ex-husband staring at her as if she had just stabbed him was painful enough. When some of her friends shared details about their custody battles and alimony payments and cross-examinations, she knew her divorce proceedings had been a walk in the park.

Everyone is picking at his or her eggs, heads bowed, trying to string together everything that has been happening when Emily remembers something Tag said to her.

"Remember when I told you I met Tag on the road on my way to Cross Creek?" she asks, raising her head and dropping her fork. "He said something that didn't make sense to me then but maybe this is what he was talking about. He said, 'Something turned her heart,' and I wondered about it, and he seemed so sad when he told me."

The sheriff looks astounded. He's stopped eating, and considering he's been asking for everyone's extra sausage and toast, this means he's really astounded.

"You met Tag?"

Emily explains how he appeared out of the bushes when she was looking for him or for someone who had the same last name. "I saw his last name in some of her writing and when I drove to Cross Creek I was actually doing research, trying to see if any of the names I had written down were on mailboxes."

Everyone is impressed. Auggie asks the sheriff if Tag really knew Marjorie.

Getts smiles and nods. "He's kind of a local folk hero not just for that but because he's so old and he still rides around on a horse and acts like he's a Florida cowboy. People from the county check on him now and then, and I'm pretty sure someone from the university has been out there to do some oral recordings with him."

Getts looks puzzled. He tips his head and then leans across the table. "He's kind of a recluse though, and to be honest, I can't believe he even talked to you. He loves solitude, never married, survives on very little and he's been known to hide if he sees someone coming. Maybe Marjorie or her spirit did send him out to meet you."

Auggie slaps her left hand on the table. "So now something cosmic and otherworldly is also involved in this mess?"

"Well, why not?" Silver has turned to her and looks astonished at her skepticism. "You are the last person I would expect to be skeptical about messages from the other side."

"I'm just saying that this is getting to be beyond odd now. You know me better than to question my belief in miracles. I see them every day. It has taken all my will power not to drive over to Big Cotton Hollow and account for every last house and human. And you know damn well I think that life, the universe, angels-whatever in the hell you want to believe in, speak to us all of the time. But most of us are so busy listening to ourselves we don't bother to hear what's being whispered in our own ears or handed to us."

Emily gulps and doesn't say yes, things like leaves in the back seat and the smell of something sweet and the fact that she feels as if she's been led by something or someone unseen to this place to find those boxes.

Silver and Auggie are in the middle of a stare-down, and the sheriff can't wait to see what happens next. But Silver just smiles, raises her hand to Auggie's face, and says, "You are probably a reincarnated donkey, sweet girl. And there's just one more reason to love you."

"Dang!" Getts shouts, throwing back his head. "Here I was hoping for a big fight, and it ends up being a love-fest. I hate it when that happens."

Emily has been watching the three of them with delight and a bit of jealousy. They have formed an interesting life balance that is clearly based on a great deal of love. Throw in fun, respect, forgiveness and understanding and there you have the basis for not just great relationships, but a true sense of community. This is what Marjorie must have felt here as well, as she slowly-but not so successfully, apparently-began to blend in with her surroundings. She clearly loved it so much she never left, wrote a book based here, then another, then another... and then, "something turned her heart."

Getts has gotten up from the table to make some phone calls, and Silver and Auggie have looped the discussion back to Brett and lost relatives. Emily is watching them as she feels a yearning for something familiar. She excuses herself for a moment, walks to her room, and picks up the phone to call first her son and then Bev. Her son, like always, doesn't answer, but she leaves him a simple message: "Hey, you. It's just Mom. I wanted to let you know I was thinking about you and that I love you." Disappointed, but happy at least that she could hear his recorded voice, Emily tries Bev next and gets the same thing. "I'm fine. Just checking in and..." She hesitates. Has she ever told Bev how much she cares about her? "And thanks for keeping tabs on me. You know I love you, right?" She hangs up quickly and walks back into the kitchen where she is greeted with three smiling faces. Apparently there's good news.

Getts tells them that Brett is spending the night in jail. The preliminary reports run through the system show that he's not really much of a hardened criminal and he's only been arrested for disorderly conduct and has several hundred dollars in overdue parking tickets. He's obviously in some kind of financial trouble, too. He's so broke, which also means he must be so desperate, that he couldn't make bail and they won't release him because he's been drinking and he has no one to call.

"That should give us all one good night of sleep," he assures them. "I'm pretty sure we won't find footprints around the house tomorrow morning. I'm going to find someone in New Jersey to talk to as soon as I get a chance. There has to be information on him, or his family, that will help us."

After a very long discussion about who each of them would call for bail money if they were in jail, how necessary it is to get to the university archives in Gainesville, and a four-way pledge to keep their mouths shut and keep looking, Auggie heads home and Silver and Getts head down the hall with a long wink.

Emily shuts off the lights, fishes in refrigerator for a glass of bedtime wine, and then turns to go down the hall to her bedroom where she intends to read without worry until morning. When she starts walking, her eye catches on a calendar hanging near the kitchen that she's never noticed. She leans in, begins to read, and almost drops her wine. The large photo on the calendar is a picture of Charles and Marjorie Rawlings from 1928. Even in the half-darkness, she can see that he was handsome. A short man with a receding hairline, dressed in a dark sport coat, a collared shirt and white pants. Marjorie is holding their cat, Jib, smiling, and dressed in a flowered dress and a hat that looks like a pan with the edges turned out. It looks as if they are standing near a grove of orange trees and for the moment, at least, are happy. The caption reads, "When I came to the Creek, and knew the old grove and farmhouse as home, there was some terror, such as one feels in the first recognition of a human love, for the joining of person to place, as of person to person, is a commitment to shared sorrow, even as to shared joy." *Cross Creek.*

Emily leans into the photo as close as possible and whispers, "Oh Marjorie! What did you do?" Then she tiptoes into her bedroom, picks up her borrowed copy of Cross Creek, and is not at all surprised when the book flips open to the very same passage she has just read on the calendar.

She can only wonder, with growing excitement, what she will find tomorrow when she and Silver go back to take another look at Leslie's house. That excitement is multiplied when she thinks about Brett Kinnan and the possible link he may possess to the mystery she is trying to solve. A sense of danger be damned, she naively tries to convince herself, even as she reaches under her pillow to make certain the carving knife is still within reach.

# 19

*"Surviving in a place where loss is part of every-day living does not lessen any of the blows. All those years, before I left, I would make an invisible notch on my heart when something or someone I loved disappeared. Then, when it was my turn, when so many of the scars had healed, I could finally see that some part of loss can be a beginning."*
—*Lost Hearts in the Swamp of Life* - MKR - 1963

Emily has never had a sheriff's escort before. She's riding shotgun in Silver's big truck, following Getts, who's leading them to Leslie's to unlock the door, with Bob's permission, before he heads off to what he jokingly calls his part-time-job as sheriff. His full-time job being that of Silver's assistant, he said with all seriousness, as they were slamming down coffee so he wouldn't be late for his first meeting.

Silver, of course, had emerged from her bedroom like the goddess she is, dressed in lime green pedal pushers, a pink sleeveless top, and glowing from whatever had happened behind the closed doors all night. Emily was beginning to think that she needed to go to finishing school in order to keep up. Her shabby shorts and the few t-shirts she has been wearing didn't seem to do much for her image, not that Silver cared.

The plan was to go through the house, and depending on how long that took, eventually head to Gainesville and the university library where Silver will arrange for access to all of the Rawlings collection, which is beyond extensive. The mere thought of going through the archives made Emily's entire body tingle.

Silver was in good spirits as Getts fed the dogs, made certain the house was locked up-which drove Silver crazy because she hated doing that even as she understood how important it was now-and they caravanned toward Leslie's. Emily couldn't believe that it had been ten days since she had last been to Leslie's. It seemed like fifty, or maybe even forever. She had grown comfortable, not just with her surroundings, but with the people who inhabited it as well.

Getts pulls to the side of the road as they get to Leslie's, and admonishes them one more time to be careful, stay in touch, and not do anything more stupid than they already have. He also promises to let them know when and if Brett has been released. Silver bends in to kiss him and in a gesture that Emily can only explain as being "Marjorie-like" she leans in after her and does the same thing.

"Two women!" Getts hollers out his door as he speeds away, leaving Silver laughing as they walk toward the house.

"Good one, honey," Silver says, verbally applauding Emily. "Something is definitely happening to you, girl."

"No kidding," Emily agrees. "I also know how to cook grits and skin a coon, thanks to *Cross Creek Cookery*, and I've never done either."

They both laugh as they stand at the bottom of the very steps where Emily had met Bob. Emily feels as if twelve years have passed and it's only been days. It's quiet and the cloudless sky is already a deep shade of blue unlike any blue Emily is used to seeing in Ohio. The light and what it does to color the world here almost make Emily feel as if someone gets up very early to paint the sky. Perhaps it's because there are no factories and thousands of cars and all the waste that comes from hordes of people living so close to each other.

When she turns to walk up the steps Emily notices that Silver isn't moving. She's standing with one hand on the rail and looking at the front door as if she's waiting for someone to come out. Emily pauses so Silver can move first or say something.

It takes several minutes for Silver to compose herself. Then she keeps her eyes on the front door and says, "You know I loved her very much, and I owe so much of who I am, who I became, to her."

Emily says she understands by simply touching Silver's shoulder as they slowly walk up the steps.

When they get inside, Silver stops again. She tells Emily that it was easier to walk inside the house when Leslie's things were still there. Her smell was everywhere and it was as if her spirit were still alive. Silver says she doesn't think Leslie was quite ready to go because everything happened so fast and before the funeral-and after, when she helped her children sort through some of her things-there was still a presence in the house.

"Maybe it was you who wasn't ready to let go," Emily gently suggests.

Silver shuts the door and stands in what was once the living room. The old hardwood floors have dark marks where furniture rested and there's already a thin layer of dust everywhere.

"I was so angry at first because I think I had started to take her and our relationship for granted," Silver admits. "Getts had come into my life and even though she was happy for me I wasn't thinking about the time I used to spend with her and she was lonely, and then when she died, I was lonely."

"Oh Silver! I'm sure she understood, and you were there for her at the end. Is this too hard? Do you want me to go through the house?"

Silver shakes her head back and forth and apologizes with a smile. Leslie would love what they are doing and she tells Emily that she wouldn't be surprised if she forged the manuscripts and everything else in those damn boxes just to get back at her.

Emily has seriously wondered if that's possible anyway. They walk toward the kitchen as they talk about that. Silver reassures her that Leslie wouldn't have even known Marjorie in 1963. But Emily says with the right kind of equipment, say an old typewriter for starters, anything might be possible.

"I just don't think she'd do it," Silver says as they walk into the empty kitchen. "It's true that everyone has secrets, Leslie had some real dandies, but she wouldn't mess with us like this because it has to do with writing. It was sacred to her."

Emily believes her. The boxes and the paper grade used to type the manuscript, its condition, and now Mr. Asshole all confirm Silver's thoughts. Emily thinks it makes more sense that Marjorie would have done it to thumb her nose at the world. Leslie had no need for that. She'd already told the world to go to hell by moving to this very house. Maybe Marjorie was just writing because she had to write. Perhaps when Marjorie really did die, she had made arrangements for the boxes to go to Leslie and Leslie was simply keeping them until she either died herself, or could trust someone enough to share what she had.

"This is frustrating," Silver admits, leaning against the old sink. "It's possible we may never know the truth about anything."

Emily is the one who is now smiling. "That's correct, but think of the fun people like me have trying to find out what is real and what isn't. And hey," she says pushing Silver gently on the side of her face, "women like us, who focus, we can *feel* the truth."

Silver lifts up the corner of her mouth, smirks at Emily, and has to agree.

Both women are now leaning against the sink as Emily tells her it's unlikely they're going to find anything new in the house but sometimes a fresh pair of eyes and new intentions can result in something spectacular.

Silver winces. She's not sure she wants to find anything more spectacular then what they've already found. But Emily, who didn't want to rush past Silver's emotions, can hardly wait to begin. She suggests they work together in case Silver finds something, or she does, and they can help each other discern what it might be or mean.

They start right where they are, and Emily walks Silver though the kitchen and shows her the yellowed sink, the marks on the wall, the way the light from the back windows has permanently faded some of the woodwork. Silver, Emily discovers quickly, loves to touch. She may not be much of a rush-to-hug kind of gal, but her hands are all over the kitchen. Silver's instincts are also perfect. While they paw through the empty kitchen, Emily is recalling some of the Grace Novell books she's read. Those stories were riddled with fine details, both physical and emotional, and Emily correctly assumes she's found the perfect literary archaeologist assistant and partner.

The kitchen holds no new secrets and neither does the living room, which Silver reveals was the least-used room in the house. Visitors gathered on the back porch, in the kitchen, or inside Leslie's writing shed when Leslie was having a good day and didn't mind being interrupted.

"What writing shed?" Emily is already racing to the back of the house and the porch where she found the boxes to look for a shed.

Silver is on her heels and doesn't say a word as they step through the porch, out the door, and are in the backyard in three seconds. Emily is looking around, throws her hands into the air, and then turns just in time to see Silver slip through a large stand of bamboo at the side of the house.

She follows her, and is momentarily disorientated because she feels as if she's stepped into a new country. There's a grass-covered path-the thick southern grass so unlike what she is used to in Ohio-and as she walks, presumably following Silver, the path narrows until she can barely fit through the trees. Emily stops for a second and runs her hands along the thin tall branches of the trees and then looks up. The trees are well over twenty-five feet high and the sun is dancing through them so that shadows are swaying everywhere she looks. It's absolutely lovely. Leslie must have felt as if she were walking into a very special place when she crossed through here, which was probably the reason why she did it.

Emily starts walking again and can see a small wooden building ahead of her partially engulfed in white flowers. She takes a whiff and the perfume almost makes her dizzy. The flowers have huge green leaves exactly like the leaf that blew into Emily's car the day she discovered this house.

Silver is standing with one hand on a small door and apologizing. "I don't know why I never thought to show you this, or talk about it. Maybe I was subconsciously trying to keep it to myself, or I'm still battling with her loss more than I realized."

Silver pushes open the door and Emily steps inside first. There is only one room and it extends back about twenty-five or thirty feet. There are windows along both sides, there's no back door, and the room is totally empty.

"Tell me what it was like in here and then I'll have a look around, but it seems like it would be impossible to have anything hidden here," Emily says, stepping to the right wall and walking back so she can see if there are any marks, writing, messages—anything at all.

Silver says the room was always very simple. Leslie had a desk facing the east window, sets of file cabinets, a small refrigerator and about five thousand books and shelves. There was a couch and some stuffed chairs towards the front, she used an outhouse out back, and she always typed on an old typewriter.

"A typewriter?"

"She was old-school about that, and for some odd reason the week before she died she made me bring the typewriter into her bedroom..."

"Please don't say you destroyed it!" Emily almost feels as if she might cry.

"She wanted me to smash it in front of her, and we argued about it," Silver explains. "I had already told her I was going to keep her things and some day make a small museum or something, like Cross Creek. Actually, now that we're in here I think I might just move this whole damn building onto my property. I don't know why I didn't think about this sooner."

"The typewriter?"

"There are actually three of them because she kept extras and was terrified that she'd never be able to get parts again, and they are all in my storage shed with the rest of her things from the bedroom. She wanted the one in this building smashed and I couldn't understand why, except that maybe she knew she was done writing forever and it was some grand gesture, but I'm thinking you have a new idea about that."

The new idea had everything to do with the note Getts had found in Brett's glove compartment, and that's what the two women discuss as they walk around Leslie's unique office. Emily wants to see if the typewriter letters worked the same as the letters on the note found in Brett's car. Silver also tells Emily that Leslie had devised a unique way of letting people know she wanted, or didn't want, to be disturbed back here. She left a box and notepad on her back porch and if she was open for company she would simply write yes on the top page. Visitors would leave her messages if there was a no but a yes meant come on in and they would sometimes sit for hours reading or talking or listening to what Leslie might be working on if she was in the mood to share.

Excited about the big news concerning the typewriters, Emily has to force herself to make certain they didn't overlook anything. There's nothing to discover in the writing space, but simply being inside of it makes Emily curious about Silver's own writing process and need for space and quiet while she works.

Silver promises to show Emily where she works, which is a huge room that is nothing but windows on one side so she can watch the sky and whatever might be happening out there when she's writing. Silver gently shuts the door to the cabin and they head back to the house, and Silver tells Emily that she prefers the quiet and works without music or any noise. In the winter, when it's not so hot, she loves to open all the windows and will often sit on the back side of the house with her laptop so she can feel the wind and sun. Every writer is different, she explains. Some love to work in crowded coffee shops or on the top of a high-rise. The Marjories and Leslies of the world obviously preferred seclusion, and she doesn't know any successful authors who don't struggle with a desire to run and hide, even as they sometimes enjoy the notoriety that comes with success-and is necessary for it, as well.

They're just about to go through Leslie's bedroom and bathroom when Emily stops, puts her hands on her hips and asks Silver if she ever thinks about revealing her real identity.

"Funny you should ask," Silver says, stopping directly in front of Emily. "I thought I was all set for the next fifty years until you showed up."

"Me?"

"Yes, you. There's always that small part of me that wonders what life would have been like if things had been different and sometimes, not very often, I've thought about the world I left behind and many of the people in it. This whole Marjorie business has stirred up lots of feelings, the least of all being what would happen, not just to me, but to everyone around here if those really are Marjorie's manuscripts."

"I'm sorry," Emily whispers.

"There's nothing to be sorry about, Ohio. One thing I know for sure is that we can't control everything and that when something like this happens, if we ignore it, or walk away from it, we're bound to fall over or run into it again. The best thing to do is walk right into it with your arms open and see what in the hell happens."

"I'm not unaware of what might happen to you and everyone I've met in the past week," Emily admits, pausing to think for a few moments. "I've ignored and walked away from lots of things, and I guess I'm sick of being scared. I would never do anything to jeopardize your life, and to be honest, I have no clue what's going to happen or what we might find."

Silver smiles. She tells Emily that what they are doing is not at all unlike writing a novel. Emily's had the big opening, lots of drama, interesting characters, a bit of confusion, life changing thoughts, a few good meals and now it's time to try and figure out the ending. She also reassures Emily that she's not seriously worried about how the story is going to end. "A good story keeps you involved, and I'd say there's quite a few of us really involved."

Emily can't disagree and they refocus on their search. The bedroom and bathroom yield no clues and even walking back through the guestroom, which they jokingly call the Marjorie Kinnan Rawlings bedroom, there doesn't seem to be anything to discover. They walk around the living room again and Emily runs a hand under all the windowsills and wishes she had a ladder so she could look on top of the doorways as well. Silver walks through the entire house while Emily checks the kitchen one more time, and reports that there is no attic.

Emily asks Silver to call Bob and ask him where the boxes came from without letting on about what they've found. Silver steps outside to sit on the front steps and Emily twirls in the living room trying to think if there's anything they may have missed. She can hear Silver's muffled voice through the half-open front door and she walks down the hall, past Marjorie's room, into Leslie's bedroom and back out onto the porch.

She turns to look in the corner where she found the boxes and wishes she would have been paying more attention when she knelt in front of them for the first time. *Attention.* There's a word that's become terribly important. She moves next to the screen and notices the dental floss that she's guessing Leslie must have used to mend the screens. Emily lifts her hand to touch the off-white pieces of floss and runs two fingers back and forth across the longest piece that is almost at eye level. How odd that she didn't see the floss before-but then again, she was more than a bit distracted.

Emily turns to look behind her where she sat on the stool and where the wine bottles had been lined up. She hears the front door slam, and then Silver's footsteps coming toward her.

"Under the bed", Silver says, looking at the spot on the screen where Emily's hand is resting. "The boxes were under the bed. They've probably been under there for years and Bob said we may as well stop looking, even though I didn't tell him what we're looking for. He said he's done everything but rip up the floorboards. He told me he goes through every house about a dozen times and there's nothing left here but memories."

Emily is half-listening. Silver asks her what she's thinking about.

"Mr. Asshole," Emily tells her. "He's the one who has the answers, and we may as well get it over with and go talk to him."

"Are you serious?"

"Think about it. We have the biggest prize already and he knew to come here. I no longer believe it was a coincidence. He's in jail. What do we have to lose?"

Silver could list many things but she can tell by the serious look on Emily's face that it probably won't matter what she says.

"So we just get in the car and drive to the jail and ask him what?"

"Whatever we want if he'll see us."

"I'm not sure we can get in. I just tried to call Getts and he's out."

"Do you have that gun in your purse?" Emily is serious and Silver bursts out laughing.

"I'm serious about that too." Emily can't imagine what a man in jail could do to hurt them.

Silver throws up her hands and can't quite agree that it's necessary at this particular moment to go talk to Brett Kinnan. She's certain Getts has a plan, some kind of an idea at the very least, about following him or trapping him. Yet here's another part of her that would love to drive like hell to the country jail and find out the answers to all of their questions. The sheriff would probably have a stroke if they showed up. He's the one who helped Silver find out if Emily was a nutcase who was driving around and looking for dead authors but showing up at the jail to verbally assault an inmate might be a bit much. She also realizes that Emily has gotten fairly cocky since she found her hiding in Marjorie's old barn.

Suddenly, Silver gets an idea that pushes everything else to the backside of her fast-spinning brain. Her entire face has opened up, her eyes are glowing and Emily can tell by simply looking at her that she's gone away.

"What's going on over there?"

Silver holds up her hand like a stop sign and realizes she's forgotten to bring along a notebook or something to write on.

When she gets an idea that might later turn into something she can use in one of her novels, she always writes down everything that is parading through her mind. There have been so many times when a great book title, an opening sentence, a new character or some wild scene has popped into her mind and she's lost the thought. Auggie has told her it's because her brain is full of so much bullshit that there's not room for anything else. She's also showed her vivid pictures of what an aging brain looks like and Silver knows that it's impossible to retain everything, even without the bullshit.

She asks Emily if she's got anything to write on and when Emily says no, she decides that Emily will have to be her human tablet. The two women walk through the screen door and sit on the back step. Emily correctly guesses that they are not immediately going to drive over to see Brett Kinnan.

What Silver shares for the next thirty minutes is the cosmic notion that they may be living inside of a novel themselves. Emily understands that. She's met enough authors during her library years who all say the same thing. All you have to do is pick up a newspaper, turn on the television or fish around the Internet, and the craziness of reality is all over the place. A man in Colorado tries to fool the world into thinking his son was carried off in a balloon. Lindsay Lohan steals another necklace and then celebrates by going on a bender. A man in Wisconsin rides his lawn mower all the way to Florida because he doesn't have a driver's license. Donald Trump doesn't believe President Obama was born in the United States. The intersection of fiction and non-fiction is a blur of reality tinted with a few wonderful adjectives.

This is why Silver thinks that if they are never able to prove anything, or if what they do discover is so life-changing people might get hurt, there's a story to be told anyway. Maybe, she adds quickly, as a pack of clouds temporarily cover up the sky surrounding them so that it looks like dusk, that's the whole point of this.

"What?" Emily is starting to wonder if Silver's blood-sugar levels have suddenly dropped.

"Maybe we're being set up."

"Who would set us up? I don't get it."

This is when one more secret pops out of Silver's mouth. She drops her head back so that's it's touching the top of her back and she's looking directly into the dark sky. Then she rocks forward, rests her hands on her knees and tells Emily that for the past year she's been suffering with the first and only case of writer's block that she's ever had in her life. Leslie knew about it because until she got sick that's pretty much all they talked about. Leslie was trying to convince her to ease up and take a break. She suggested something insane like a vacation with the sheriff, or maybe just a total break where she didn't worry about writing and just relaxed.

"I was a little over-the-top nuts," Silver admits. "This block came out of nowhere and even though I have tons of ideas and characters it was like running into a big wall every single time I at down to work."

"So you're not writing at all now?" Emily still has no clue what this has to do with anything.

"I try. I go in there and I start something and then I walk out the back door and throw tennis balls for the dogs and then you showed up and the distraction has been wonderful."

Emily laughs. "Sure, some nutcase has taken photos of us dancing in the rain, he's stalking me, and he's apparently dangerous. This is just a blast."

Silver sits back up and turns to face her. She looks as if she's afraid to keep talking. Emily is learning how to be patient in ways she never expected. Motherhood was one thing, but it's no secret to the people who know her well that her gentle exterior is often hiding an urge to roll down the window and scream at the slow-moving world around her. She waits while Silver tries to figure out how to explain the unexplainable. It doesn't take long, because Silver quickly realizes everything is seemingly ridiculous lately, so it won't really matter what she says to Ohio.

"Maybe I'm the one who was supposed to find the boxes and use them for inspiration," Silver says. "I was standing out there and it just struck me that what we are doing, what might be in the boxes, everything that's happening would be an amazing novel."

Silver hesitates and Emily is still being patient, but she has to sit on her hands to stay that way.

"So just now, standing in the house, I had this feeling, and I can only describe it as that-*a feeling*-and suddenly this whole idea came to me, and I had to fight an urge to go jump into the car and rush back to my office and start to write," Silver is now talking very fast and explains how she hasn't felt like this in a long time. "It's almost like a story within a story where this woman finds this box, and it won't be the story that we are living right now, but all these faces and ideas were like a sudden Rose Bowl parade in my mind."

There's no way Emily is going to burst her bubble by asking what they are supposed to do if the manuscripts are real. If inspiration is the whole point of this then perhaps their jobs are done. Silver certainly isn't done talking.

"You know, I've never set a novel in Florida, and I think it's because I've been scared that someone would connect all the dots eventually and find out who I am, but now I really don't give a damn."

Perhaps Silver's just answered Emily's unasked question. This bold woman sitting next to her is absolutely glowing. Something's going on inside of her unplugged head, that's for sure, and Emily leans back and lets her continue.

Silver starts to wave her hands and she's talking with her eyes closed about what she sees in her mind's eye. There's a man who wears a smelly Fedora hat in a old beat-up 1950 Dodge truck, three kids who are trying to convince their mother to leave their father, a missing writer and a small town where people have been known to shoot each other over the last beer or a missing dog.

Emily has never seen anything like this. This truly is magic and Silver is writing an entire novel without using a pen, or pencil, or a typewriter that has some off-balance keys. This is also how she felt the night in her room, when she realized that she's becoming a literary archeologist.

Silver stops to catch her breath, opens her eyes, and then tells Emily it's her job to remember every single word she's saying. Emily snorts and reminds Silver that she can't even keep track of her cell phone. If she expects her to remember a 400-page novel she's going to be in a lot of trouble.

"You must think I'm crazy now," Silver exclaims, slapping her own thighs.

Emily shakes her head and says, "I already know you're crazy, and it's exciting to watch this process. I have no idea what's going on, Silver. Maybe this is a literary set-up for more than one reason. Maybe it's a coincidence. Maybe Brett's just a nutcase. But I'm in for any and all answers. For sure, there's no way I can stop."

During the next hour Silver manages not only to convince Emily that a trip to the county jail could mean the end of her relationship with Getts, but to try and help her come up with an ending for the novel that doesn't even have a beginning.

The women end up walking though the house one more time and finding nothing they can touch, but a world of memories, passion, and possibility that lingers as Silver locks the front door and they drive back to her house totally unaware of what the good sheriff has discovered.

# 20

*"Someone told me once that life was an adventure. They failed to mention that sometimes the adventure is such a risk of time, life, and limb that you might not want to sign on the dotted line if you don't have a sense of humor. "*
— *Lost Hearts in the Swamp of Life* - MKR - 1963

Emily has never driven a big truck before, but the moment she gets behind the wheel of Silver's pickup she feels a surge of power that charges up both legs and makes her feel as if she can take on the world. Silver was so lost in thought when they left Leslie's house she was worried that she might drive them into the ditch so she threw Emily the keys and pointed to the driver's side of the truck.

"You are the only women left on this side of the Mississippi who knows how to drive a manual transmission besides me," Silver said as she jumped into the passenger seat and immediately started looking for something to write on.

Emily shifted the truck into reverse without hesitation and told Silver about her first driving lesson. She was sixteen and working at a summer day camp when her father showed up driving their old Ford truck with a beat-up camper shell on the back. He told her to get in the truck and drive it. Up until that moment Emily was quite fond of her father. He was an electrician who worked hard and always made certain his family had food and knew that they were loved. He did not, however, know a thing about how to handle teenage girls.

"Dad, I don't know how to drive. The whole point of driving lessons is that you teach me what to do."

Emily's father had slapped both hands on the dashboard and told her that learning how to drive was just the same as swimming. He had learned how to swim when his father had rowed an old boat out into the middle of the lake and thrown him in. What this had to do with learning how to drive was beyond Emily, then and now.

"I don't even know how to start the car," she told him, thinking about how all her girlfriends were calmly driving around in little sedans with automatic transmissions.

Emily now knows her lack of patience was inherited from her driving instructor. "Just turn the damn key, honey."

Emily turned the key and nothing happened. "Clutch," he yelled, gripping the backrest.

"A clutch?" she asked him, then quickly added, "that's a purse dad."

Things went downhill after that. Emily eventually started the truck that had a totally obstructed rear view and chugged out onto the highway. The truck was so old it still had a column shift. "Down, up, down, up," her dad was yelling as the truck hit fifty.

But then within minutes there was a sharp curve and Emily didn't know about downshifting. She took the corner going forty-five and the truck went over on two wheels as her father screamed obscenities out the window.

Emily doesn't realize that Silver is writing down every word she is saying. Silver can see the big-ass truck on two wheels, and her father yelling, and Emily panicking.

"I eventually stopped the truck, took the keys out of the ignition, threw them at my father and called him an asshole," Emily tells Silver, as she shifts into fourth gear and wishes they could drive forever. "My dad slapped me, because back then parents always hit their children when they didn't know what else to do, and I didn't ride with him again for the next five years."

"Who taught you how to drive?" Silver is still writing as Emily slides the truck into its fifth gear and beams with delight.

"My mother. We had an old beat-up Dodge, I think it was, that had a stick shift and my quiet, sane mother taught me. I think I took out a few mailboxes and lots of grass before it was all over."

Silver laughs and tells her the driving story will end up in one of her novels some day. Maybe even the one they are both working on. Emily chastises her for stealing from other people, but Silver keeps writing anyway. She tells her that almost every author she knows is an occasional good listener. Marjorie Rawlings, for example, actually moved in with a family who was living so remotely they rarely saw another human being. It was total research and that's what made her books so realistic and memorable.

Silver explains how Rawlings is credited with opening up the world of the people who live in the scrub country to outsiders. And she was able to do that because she herself lived in it, accepted the people for who they were, and was an eager participant in every aspect of their lives.

"We're talking totally-remote, hauling-water, shooting-and-cleaning-animals-for-dinner kind of research," Silver shares as they bump off the main highway and approach Silver's long driveway. "I think a part of her was always a journalist. She loved trying things, feeling things, and making certain that what she wrote about was real and true."

Emily looks out the window just then and notices something what looks like a dog running along the side of the fence. She quickly stops the truck and points to it. "What is that thing?" she asks Silver.

When she finds out it's a wild pig Emily shrieks. "Are they dangerous?"

"Yes and no. They're omnivores, so they eat plants and animals and they call them pigs for a reason. They eat everything, including pets and ducks and whatever else is in their way, and if they get mad, watch out. They get huge, some over two-hundred pounds, and they have tusks."

They both watch as the feral hog runs along the fence and then suddenly there are three more pigs. This is when Emily realizes that they have been talking so much and focusing on their search that they haven't been terrified or afraid for hours. She tells Silver it's nice knowing Brett's in jail even if they have decided, or one of them has decided, it would be stupid to go see him. Their brief interlude while they were temporarily divorced from their fear has suddenly evaporated.

Emily throws the truck into first gear and slowly pulls away from her pig-viewing position, and very quickly she's back on task and asking about where the typewriter from Leslie is stored. She knows it might not mean anything but she has to check out the keys to see if they match the letter they found in Brett's truck. They both agree that at this point they need to research every possible angle.

Talking about Brett is not as much fun as talking about wild pigs. Silver is still grateful and relieved they didn't go to talk with Brett. Getts is right about waiting it out and making certain Brett knows more than they do before they rush in and blindside him. They both agree that even though they are smart, fun and good-looking, there's a chance Sheriff Gettleman might know a thing or two more about this kind of thing then they do.

They are both laughing at their own ridiculous remarks when Emily turns into the driveway and the first thing they see is Getts leaning against his car and talking on his phone. The women look at each other, don't say a word, but both lean forward at the same time as if that might help them get the truck there sooner.

Getts waves to them as Emily parks the truck and Silver jumps out before the car even stops. Then she impatiently hops in place at a polite distance while Getts finishes his phone conversation. He motions for Emily to join them as he turns off his phone. The dogs are already going crazy. Silver claps her hands and orders them up on the porch so the tires of all of the vehicles don't get any more urine-stained then they already are, and so they can focus on whatever might happen next.

"Girls," he says in greeting. "Did we unearth any dead bodies or treasures?" Then before Silver can open her mouth to say one word he walks over, puts one hand on each shoulder, and squats down to look into her eyes. "Something's happened. Your eyes are sparkling. What do you to do?"

Emily is amazed, and a bit jealous. Getts and Silver are clearly so much in touch with each other's feelings he can sense that something is going on. It's been so long since she's even bothered to imagine what that might be like that the entire scene almost takes her breath away. Emily was never the kind of young girl who sat around pining away for the cutest boy in class, or dreaming about some guy like Getts showing up on a horse or even driving a big old truck to whisk her away. Most of the time, if she had a choice, she'd pick a good book over a mediocre date. Along the way there have been a few men who made her heart flip in circles and she'd had a horrid crush for twenty years on her friend's uncle. He was terribly handsome, smoked a pipe, and always seemed to be totally engrossed in whatever anyone was saying to him. The year her friend told her that object of her affection had a storage shed filled with pornography-not the legal kind-and was more or less a pervert waiting to get caught was also the year Emily decided to settle and marry.

Right now, watching Getts and Silver dance into each other's eyes, she also feels stricken by a sense of loss. There were surely men who could have loved her the way these two obviously love each other. Emily knows she often sent out mixed signals and that there are plenty of decent, kind, wonderful men in the world. Who knew most of them lived in Florida? Not a big fan of male-bashing-her complaints have usually been more like self-bashing. Emily can understand how a partner, a real partner, can make all the difference in the world if both people are seriously in love.

Silver is going on about her new source of inspiration and Emily now wonders what her life might have been like if someone had been able to look into her eyes and know what she was feeling. Her husband should have been able to see how much she wanted one more degree, a chance to be the person she just might be turning into now, a life that was beyond the structure of nine-to-five and the faked emotions they had become.

And she knows that it was partially her fault too. Emily has always held back. She never raised her hand first, said "I love you" enough, was able to let go and embrace whatever spontaneous feelings rose to the surface and for all of that, she realizes now more than ever, she's paid a price for her emotional restraint.

Silver has stopped talking and snaps her fingers when she sees Emily staring off into space. "Ohio, focus," she orders.

Getts tells them he's glad they behaved because he was terrified they might show up at the jail. Silver and Emily exchange a quick glance that they hope he doesn't see. Maybe the sheriff is starting to read Emily's mind as well.

When Silver tells him they didn't find anything physical, but that she's decided to try and move Leslie's writing shack to her property, Getts looks as if he might cry for a moment. This means *he* will be moving the old building to her property.

Silver, who is finally able to focus, wants to know what in the world Getts is doing at the house. Emily takes one look at his face and can tell something big is coming.

"I can't stay long because I'm on my way to Ocala to talk to someone, but I was driving past and thought I may as well stop and tell you the latest," he begins. "We got back a bit of information about the man you two have taken to calling *Mr. Asshole*-which, by the way, I almost did today during our status meeting. I almost bit a hole in my tongue. Please help me call him *Brett*."

"Out with it," Silver orders.

Emily is now smart enough to wait. She feels as if she's getting better at it every day.

Getts tells them he received a brief report from someone he refuses to name in New Jersey who pulled some records for him and did a bit of snooping. Before the sheriff continues, he warns them not to get their hopes up because there's not much to tell. Brett lives in a sub-let apartment above a small restaurant in Somerville, a semi-hip town that is filled with restored buildings and boutiques. He worked at a small engineering firm for a while, running errands and interning, until the company found out that he lied about being a junior in college. He never went to college and from his work record, haphazard at best, he's been trying to find himself and be somebody with his lackluster high school education since the day he graduated. He owes back rent, his car payments are late, and he's clearly in need of an infusion of cash.

Both Emily and Silver are thinking, and waiting for more information. Brett obviously needs money, which makes his actions of late understandable. One can only guess how much money unpublished manuscripts from a deceased author of greatness might fetch.

"I pulled his birth certificate myself and it appears that your Mr. Asshole-and I swear to God, I just said that for the last time-was adopted or changed his name"

This is semi-startling news. Before either of the women can start shouting out questions, Getts, in his usual calm manner, simply keeps talking. There is no father listed on his certificate. The mother was not some high school girl but a thirty year-old woman whose last name was not Kinnan, but that could mean she gave him up for adoption, and there are no records available about the adoption.

"Isn't all that stuff sealed anyway?" Silver asks. "There wasn't such a thing as open adoption twenty-eight years ago, when he was born."

"If you are a law enforcement officer with connections, pretty much anything is possible." Getts explains that his contact assured him that Brett was not adopted.

Everyone is quiet for a moment. Emily was hoping for more than this, but it's better than nothing-and yet, it opens up an entire world of new questions and possibilities.

"Not the same last name?" Silver is trying to understand all of this.

"It could be anything," the sheriff advises. "The kid found out who his real dad was, maybe he was adopted, maybe he is just enamored of Rawlings. It could be many things. But it's been my experience-limited at best with this kind of thing, whatever this kind of thing is turning out to be-that when lots of children reach a certain age they want answers to questions, like 'Who was my father?'"

Emily was thinking the exact same thing. When her son was in high school, his best friend, a sweet girl named Allie, had discovered that her mother had been lying to her about her father. The man she thought was her father was actually her stepfather, who married her mother when she was a baby. Allie became obsessed with two things-finding her real father, and hating her mother for lying to her. The girl all but moved into Emily's living room for weeks on end, until her mother showed up one day looking as if she had been dragged cross-country behind a truck. She asked to speak to Emily alone and then Emily, after she had regained her composure from what the mother had told her, facilitated a meeting between mother and daughter.

The mother had been raped. Even now, so many years later, Emily feels a line of pain run right through her remembering what that day was like. Allie at first was inconsolable and there was much screaming and so many tears Emily ran out of tissue and had to start passing out paper towels. Gradually Allie, who to this day still contacts Emily on Mother's Day to say thank you, came to realize what the ordeal must have been like for her mother. The rapist had never been caught and Allie's mother said over and over how she had loved Allie every second of her entire life. There was family counseling after that, a brief period when Allie came back, and then the gradual realization that family and love and true fatherhood has nothing to do about the creation and everything to do about what happens after it.

It's absolutely possible, Emily believes, that Brett could have found out something about his real father and perhaps made some kind of discovery that led him to change his name.

"What's going on in your head over there, Ohio?" Silver asks.

"Did your contact try and locate his mother?" Emily has so many ideas running through her mind she almost feels dizzy.

"I didn't want to push my friend and besides that, I don't know where this is going. Do we know where this is going, ladies?"

Silver and Emily are now staring at each other. Emily's not certain where they are going next but she's sure they are going someplace, and Brett and their search for Marjorie are going to go right along with them. She has another week before she needs to be back at work and at the rate things are happening, she can't even think about that right now. Silver looks eager; she's not ready to stop either.

Getts has put his hands on his hips and he's looking back and forth between them, and he's clearly feeling outnumbered.

"My gut tells me that Brett's last name, Kinnan, is significant for more than just one reason," Emily finally says. "Silver, you mentioned something a while back about Marjorie's brother Arthur being somewhat of a wild card, yes?

"He was always broke and Marjorie took care of him and was at times, if I remember correctly, almost obsessed with him and his son because Arthur's marriage was a bit of a mess." Silver is trying hard to remember details and she's struggling. "There's more to this, but it's been a long time since I researched her, but…"

Silver trails off and Getts can see that she's already decided where they are going to go next. Emily knows too.

"Apparently we're going to go to Gainesville next." Silver is nodding her head up and down. "What's the name of the institution, Silver?"

"The University of Florida Department of Special and Area Studies Collections at the George A. Smathers Libraries."

The mere sound of it makes Emily quiver with excitement and makes Getts roll his eyes. He orders them to lock the house before they leave and to let him know what's happening, and what their plans are. "You must remain cautious!"

"Isn't Brett still in jail?" Silver frowns and realizes he could be released at any time. They've been so busy talking they haven't even asked Getts about Mr. Asshole's status.

"He's still there, and from the look of things might be for quite some time," Getts tells them. "He's made a few phone calls but apparently he doesn't have many friends. I would say it's because he's an asshole but I'm not going to use that word ever again."

The sheriff tells them that the deputies on duty have orders to keep him apprised of Brett's status, and he's going to keep an eye on the cabin where he's been staying if and when he's released. Before he has a chance to say anything else Silver throws him a kiss and says she's going to go call the archivist who handles the Rawlings collection to set up a visit. Then she runs up to the porch, pets each one of the dogs, and disappears into the house.

Getts takes a step toward Emily and puts his right hand on her shoulder. The sun is directly behind him and yet Emily can see waving trees and a line of clouds that look as if they had just been sent to the sky from a cotton-ball factory. Emily is still amazed by the brilliant colors in Florida and when she stops for a moment like this to think about what she is seeing the appeal of the land is magnified. How strange, and wonderful too, that a place that at first seemed almost odd to her has come to rest right against her heart-just like Silver and Getts.

Perhaps Marjorie felt just like this, with the sky blinding her with its beauty even on the hottest and hardest days. Emily is also amazed at how often she thinks about the author. It's as if Rawlings has somehow managed to invade her psyche, or perhaps she's channeling her so that she can find out when she really did die. So much of this part of the world has not changed and Emily sees it much the same way as Marjorie must have seen it. It's been a kind of harbor for her and it must have been a relief for Rawlings to finally feel as if she had found a home, her place, a way to inspire and nurture all those ideas and stories and characters that had been waiting patiently to be released.

Not unlike me, Emily thinks, smiling as Getts is apparently thinking about what to say to her. Well, Marjorie found her Norton Baskin down here and Silver found her Getts, and Emily so far is finding herself, which is pretty damn good, all things considered. Still, she can't imagine herself being as brave and reckless as Rawlings. Even as Emily feels more sure of herself and her direction every day, she has a hard time imaging what it might have been like if she had felt this way her entire life.

Her ability to put together the pieces of other people's lives has never extended into her own life; at least, she hasn't allowed that to happen. When she's focused on a project Emily has rarely compared it to her own world; she's held herself apart and always worked diligently to keep everything she's working on at arms length lest she become too close-that closeness, she always thought, can be blinding.

But now, standing in Silver's front yard, totally mesmerized by her surroundings-Getts included-she realizes the missing emotional component to her work and world has been resurrected, if not recently born, since she's discovered the boxes. It's as if she's discovered the missing link in her own life.

Emily spontaneously laughs so loud that three birds who have been hiding on the far side of the house rise up, and pass so close over-head that Emily could touch their wings if she lifted up her hand.

Getts is startled by the sound and drops his hand. He looks into her eyes and then smiles. "You too!"

Emily looks at him with a question in her eyes as she regains control of her own voice.

"Something's happened to you, too! Did you get into the evidence locker where we keep confiscated drugs?"

Emily laughs again, much softer, and tells this sweet man that she's just happy, in spite of Mr. Asshole.

Getts looks serious then and tells her that's what he was going to talk about. "Silver has clearly turned a corner since

---

you've been here, and I'm grateful, but I'm also worried. She told me that she told you everything and I'm sure there's no way she could have shared how absolutely horrible the attack really was and how it's affected her."

This time Emily is the one who raises a hand and places it on Getts' arm. "I do understand," she says, trying to reassure him.

"Please be careful when you go to Gainesville. Make sure she has the gun in her purse, and I wish I had time to show you how to use it."

Emily's elation has now totally been replaced by a wave of solid fear. She can feel sweat start to drip down the center of her back as she imagines having to pull out the gun herself and use it.

"Do you seriously think he could do something?"

Getts hesitates for a moment and then decides to tell the truth. "I try and protect her, you know that, and I don't want her to stop working with you because she's clearly gotten a new lease on life. She needs to work again, it's her salvation. But when I add up everything Mr. Asshole-and he really is an asshole-has done or might be capable of doing, especially now that we know he's broke, yes, he could do something. He's started a pattern and he's a bit stupid, but he's also desperate."

Emily swallows and feels as if she may choke. She promises to try and be alert and lets Getts know how much she cares about Silver now too. "At least he's in jail for the time being, and that's something."

Getts shakes his head back and forth and reminds Emily that Brett could get out at any moment. That's part of the reason why he's glad they're leaving. There won't be any way for Brett to know where they are or what they are doing.

"This is a good thing, leaving for a while," he suggests. "I'm also going to see what, if anything else, I can find out about him. I have to be careful too, you know. I ran all the cowboys out of this territory and I have to make certain I don't turn into one myself."

When his phone starts buzzing, Emily squeezes his arm, mouths "thank you" and then watches as he climbs into his car and leaves in a cloud of dust as if it's the end of a Law and Order television show.

Before she goes into the house Emily does the obligatory dog petting and then stands on the steps for a moment to see what happened to the cotton balls. They have all moved and formed one huge ball and the enormous puffy cloud has filled up half of the sky. Emily turns a bit and sees a long stretch behind the cloud that is dark and slowly descending as if it's going to swallow all of the whiteness.

It appears as if a storm is approaching and the ominous scene looks like it fell right out of one of Marjorie's own novels. Emily wishes she was Marjorie Kinnan Rawlings right this second-a brave, brash, bring-it-on kinda gal who would laugh at the dark clouds and someone like Brett Kinnan, even if he may be a descendent.

Emily, however, can't bring herself to laugh as she turns to walk inside, where the first thing she intends to do is to make certain Silver packs her pistol.

## 21

*"Familiar was a word I latched onto and held close as if it would keep me safe, a life raft in my sea of perpetual doubt. I took great comfort in what I had known, what I had always seen, heard and felt. But there was a day in late summer when I took one step in a new direction and then looked around. Soon everything there was familiar and I kept walking, every day a little further, until it became almost impossible to stop."*
—*Lost Hearts in the Swamp of Life* - MKR - 1963

Silver is on the phone forever with Crawford Langley, the archivist at the university library, who apparently is the queen of all things Marjorie. She is wandering around in the kitchen, talking with her hands, and Emily finally retreats to her bedroom, unsure of what the plan is going to be if and when Silver ever gets off the phone.

It is early afternoon, and Emily correctly assumes it might not be worth it to head to Gainesville until the following morning, but Silver has other plans. By the time she gets off the phone, Emily is already sitting on the floor of her room going through some of the other boxes that she has yet to look at, from when she brought them in from her car. By the time Silver barges into the room, beaming, she's uncovered piles of random typewritten pages that look as if they'd been thrown into the box without any thought or purpose. Emily is trying to put them into stacks but that doesn't work either because there doesn't seem to be much of a connection between any of the pages.

Silver starts talking with her hands and says that Crawford Langley is going to spend the afternoon pulling Rawlings documents for them and she'll have everything ready in the morning.

"Crawford Langley?" Emily says incredulously. "That's a real person's name? And I suppose this woman has a nickname like everyone else around here."

"We call her Mary," Silver says in all seriousness.

"Mary." Emily snorts as she says it.

Silver says Mary's real name actually is Crawford Langley and when she was getting her PhD she added an M in front of her name when she was about to go through her interviews because it was still a man's world and she didn't want to be a victim of gender discrimination. She was hoping everyone would think she was a man. When she showed up for the interviews the very first person she talked to, and who could have cared less if she was a man or woman, asked her what the M stood for, and Crawford had stammered and said the first thing that came to her mind.

"That's what she says anyway, but who knows what the real story is," Silver tells her, dropping down to sit next to her. "Mary makes even you look as if you don't care about old documents. She's brilliant, and I see her as a kind of literary knight because she will do anything to protect and acquire documents-especially if they have anything to do with Marjorie."

Emily certainly understands that kind of passion and its necessity. Interestingly enough, at her own library, where they expected a decrease in the number of people coming in to look at collections because of Internet accessibility, there has been an increase. People still love to touch the past, run their fingers over signatures of great men and women, and breathe in anything they can from years gone by. The Internet is fantastic, but Emily can't imagine a world without real books and papers and pens and ink. And after hearing Silver go on about Mary, she can't wait to meet her.

The fatal move is Silver settling in next to her on the floor. There are six boxes in all and Emily has barely tapped into two of them. What she really wants to do is go look for the typewriter, but once Silver sits down there is no stopping her, and within an hour the floor is littered with stacks of papers and Emily has started to wonder if and when they are leaving for Gainesville.

"Later," Silver keeps saying for another hour as the piles grow even more spread out and Emily falls into the project as well.

They both agree that nothing makes much sense. Some of the papers look as if they have come from a teacher. There are marks and notations on the sides of many of the pages, and letter-grades here and there also. Silver is making up all kinds of stories as she digs through the boxes. Emily looks at her at first as if she's lost her mind. She is dying to get into every box but something tells her that they have already found the biggest treasure, and are not supposed to be trying to find out if and when Marjorie died.

Emily tries in vain to convince Silver that one of them should finish the *Lost Hearts* manuscript while the other goes through all the boxes. Emily is also getting possessive and wants to think about how to proceed in a professional, librarian-like manner, before all hell breaks lose. But it is too late.

When Silver isn't looking, Emily, who has already determined that there is no rhyme or reason to how papers have been placed in the boxes, ignores Silver, crosses her feet, leans against the far wall and happily reads *Lost Hearts*. Silver is humming as she picks up one piece of paper after another, and the two women sit like that for a very long time until Silver's cell phone rings and startles them both back to reality.

It is the sheriff, checking to see how the trip to Gainesville, short as it is, has been.

"We're still at the house," Silver tells him, while Emily gets up, stretches and looks down at Silver. "We saw something shiny and got distracted, but we're going to get ready right now, swear to God."

There is a flurry of activity after that, with Silver deciding they should pack for at least one night if not more. Emily is all for going in the morning but Silver, clearly excited, says they won't want to waste a moment of crucial library time. They feed the dogs, call Auggie to come house-sit, check to make sure the pistol is still in Silver's purse and then it is seriously time to leave. Emily begs to take the truck and when they pull out, her little car with the Ohio license plates is being carefully guarded by three barking dogs.

The truly fatal mistake is stopping at The Yearling for an early dinner. "We owe it to Marjorie," Silver whines as they hit the road and both their stomachs growl.

Emily doesn't argue and they have another feast, minus the whiskey, and then hop on I-75 and are in Gainesville in less than an hour, with stomachs filled to the brim with fried catfish, cornbread, and a mess of butter-dipped greens.

Now, lying on their matching double beds at the downtown Gainesville Holiday Inn and looking like twin scarecrows, both women are groaning in post-food-orgy pleasure, and discussing tomorrow's plan of action.

"Do we tell Mary anything?" Emily's afraid she may fall under the woman's spell and spill the beans.

"I told her who you are and that you are thinking of going back to school to get another degree, and that you want to use something about Marjorie as your next thesis." Silver is so full and so tired she can only move her lips.

Emily can't believe what she has just heard. She rises up on her elbows and looks at Silver who could be posing for a funeral home poster. "You told her that?" Silver moves her head very slowly up and down. "What were you thinking?"

"Did you want me to say that you found a box with a manuscript in it that we think was written by Marjorie after she had died?"

"No," Emily says softly, dropping back onto the bed.

"Maybe I wasn't even lying."

Emily rises up again, grabs the pillow from the top of the bed, and throws it on Silver's face. "One step at a time, little Miss Life Coach," she says with fake anger.

Later, even though Emily is exhausted, it takes her forever to get to the edge of sleep. Silver drops off immediately and Emily turns on her side and watches her friend breathing deeply, completely relaxed, and looking totally peaceful. Emily feels a sense of gratitude for her connection to Silver, and for the trust both women have developed for each other. She also has a renewed sense of duty following her conversation with

Getts, and she's worried that she might let him or Silver down in some way.

If something happens to Silver because of her and what they are doing, Emily knows she'll never be able to forgive herself. She's gone over Brett's obsession with tracking her, the way he's frightened half of Central Florida, and his trying to find relatives of Rawlings dozens of times, and even though he's temporarily out of commission Emily's heart starts to thump with fear whenever she thinks about him.

When she finally falls asleep, she has a restless night that's packed with vivid dreams that leave her tangled in her sheets and running from a menacing dark figure that always seems to be one step ahead of her.

The small restaurant across the street from the Holiday Inn is about the size of Emily's bathroom and the two women have tried unsuccessfully to have a private conversation about what's about to happen at the library. Gainesville is not a very large city and apparently everyone in it either attends the university, works at the university, or is related to someone who works at the university. The eavesdropping inside the twenty-seat cafe could set a new record.

The first time Emily says the words Crawford Langley the woman three seats over lean back and say, "You mean Mary, don't you?"

Emily smiles politely and says, "Yes," and then looks at Silver as if an elephant has flown out of her ear. She lowers her voice and then a man in the last seat says, "Oh, the library is chock-full of Marjorie Kinnan Rawlings documents. Are you doing research?"

Silver nods her head up and down and motions to Emily to eat faster and they whisper through the eating of whole wheat toast about small cities, and caring people, and then simply about the weather.

Outside, they walk quickly towards the university, which is just across the street, while Emily rants about privacy and almost belts Silver in the chops when she laughs at her. Silver throws up her hands and says that even though Gainesville is a university town, it's small and not unlike the area around Cross Creek where everyone seems to know everyone else's business. She says it is caring, and not nosiness, that drives all the big ears.

Emily finds the first available bench and makes them both sit down. She wants to go over exactly what they are looking for, and Silver wants to run up the steps and get to work.

"Patience, honey," Emily says gently. "We're looking for names, relatives, any information that has to do with her death."

Silver nods and then grins so widely that Emily can see all the way down her throat. "This collection is amazing," she shares. "I've only looked at it online, and if you make me sit here any longer I'm going to pee in my pants."

Emily surrenders. She throws her hands up in the air and then gestures for them to get up and go, and they immediately head through the doors and then up the well-worn marble steps leading into the Smathers Library, where special collections are housed. They turn right at the top of the steps and the moment Emily peers through the large glass doors she understands why Silver has been so excited.

There are libraries and then there are *libraries.* Her under-staffed and underfunded library has old metal filing cabinets, stuffed rooms, and so much unorganized material Emily can't imagine it every getting placed or displayed for public viewing before she dies. What she sees in front of her as she presses her nose to the cool glass, while Silver pushes an entrance button into the locked and guarded room, is a world of quiet, beauty, and elegance.

Someone electronically pushes open the door as Silver turns off her cell phone, forgets to check her messages, and the two women step into the huge room with their mouths open almost as wide as the lovely oak doors that have just swung open in front of them. Emily grabs Silver's left arm, squeezes it, and leans over to whisper, "Oh my God! I had no idea!"

The room has forty-foot dark-wood beam ceilings flanked by tall, church-like, oval windows, and is lined on three sides with bookshelves. The floor is covered with dark blue carpeting and the center of the room is full of long tables, surrounded by lovely patterned, upholstered chairs. There are seating areas where Emily imagines scholars sit and pore over papers, gorgeous tall, dark wooden doors at the back of the room, and when she turns, she sees that the entire wall behind her is covered with a bright, painted mural that she hopes someone will explain to her before they leave.

There's obviously more than one financial benefactor, and this is definitely a university, and a state, that understand the importance of securing and maintaining important documents. Before another thought can pass through her mind a thin, short woman pushes through a door on the side, claps her hands and hustles towards them swinging her arms so fast she looks like a small helicopter.

"Good Lord!" she says, not even close to a whisper. "If you two aren't the spitting image of Zora and Marjorie then I don't know who is!"

"Zora?" Emily has turned to look at Silver, who is extending her hand as the woman approaches.

"Zora Neale Hurston, the Afro-American writer and anthropologist who was also from this area, and who was a friend of Marjorie's," Silver explains quickly. "Their relationship was groundbreaking."

"Just like ours." Emily says, poking Silver in the ribs, and then smiling as the woman she correctly guesses is Mary approaches.

Within seconds, they are whisked over to a counter where they fill out paper work so they can peruse documents, and where Mary gives Silver a very hard time for not having access to a computer at home. She explains that many of the documents they can look at are online, and because she doesn't know what they are looking for it wasn't easy for her to pull things from the climate-controlled storage rooms.

"Things" being all of the private, personal and public documents that Marjorie willed to the university. There are letters, papers, magazine articles, photographs and the original manuscripts from her books. There are documents, legal papers, and folders stuffed with everything from faded hand-written notes to Western Union telegrams. It is a treasure trove from Marjorie Kinnan Rawlings' entire life.

Emily is glad Silver doesn't have a computer. If she had missed this opportunity she would never have forgiven herself. It's one thing to look at documents online, but something close to miraculous to hold them in your hand and run your fingers across them, smell them, touch the exact same spot where the author might have put her fingers.

Mary has filled an entire cart with original papers and documents that she guesses the women might like to see. Emily explains that she has a somewhat similar job, although she's not really in charge of anything, back in Ohio, and she appreciates the time and work Mary's already put into the project for them.

"I'm curious about what you're looking for," Mary says. Her long grey hair is tied in the back with a vibrant piece of cloth, and her tiny fingers are tapping on the counter. "Sometimes if I know, I can go right to it and save you a lot of time."

"If only I knew," Emily responds, not daring to look at Silver. "I'm sure you know how this works sometimes. When I find what I'm looking for, I'll know it when I see it."

"Of course," Mary exclaims, lifting her hands to her face. "I'm in charge of all things Marjorie and, as a professional courtesy, I'll be glad to show you behind the scenes, perhaps this afternoon or tomorrow. As you know, there's nothing like seeing stacks of material all lined up and preserved. And our Miss Rawlings was a busy thing. I'll also set aside some time in case you have any questions. I have absolutely no trouble at all talking about Marjorie. I suspect you are going to have a grand time when you see what I've pulled for you."

The grand time begins the moment Silver pushes the cart away from the registration desk and over to a table at the back of the room. Before Emily can get there, she looks at the wall behind the desk and almost falls over rushing to look at what's hanging there. "Oh my gosh!" she whispers breathlessly. "Silver, look at this!"

The first picture is a black and white photograph of Marjorie standing in a wooden boat. Her legs are spread apart, she's wearing a dress with what looks like a white collared shirt underneath it, and she's holding a long spear with a huge crab on the end of it. Silver's laugh bounces off the huge ceilings and dances throughout the entire room. The other three people doing research stop what they are doing and turn to look at her, as Emily silently mouths an apology.

"That's our girl," Silver chuckles into her hands. Then both women move a few feet to the left and lean in to see Marjorie's Pulitzer Prize. *"The Trustees of Columbia University in the City of New York to all persons to whom these presents may come greeting be it known that Marjorie Kinnan Rawlings has been awarded the Pulitzer Prize in Letters for* The Yearling, *'a distinguished novel' published during the year 1938 by an American author preferably dealing with American life."*

They remain silent, bent over, and unable to move for several minutes. Emily can't imagine that something like this would even mean anything to someone like Brett. But to her, it means years of struggle and hard work and a dedicated author writing from a place so deep and magical that the end result is a lasting masterpiece. It's not about money or fame, but about the string of moments that a talented person can link together that affects readers in such a way that emotions erupt, and perhaps lives are changed. All these years later, decades and decades, Emily knows that boys and girls and adults who read *The Yearling* are constantly touched by its story and the messages of love, life, and change that lie inside of its pages.

Eventually the Zora and Marjorie look-alikes tear themselves away from the wall, and spread out several stacks of material on the long wooden table. Emily is so smitten with everything she can barely get past the fact that the table and chairs and the lovely gold and white table lamps are nicer than what she has in her own home. Maybe she can transfer to this university. Wouldn't that raise a few eyebrows?

Silver sits at one end of the table and Emily sits at another. Before they begin, the women agree to try and be quiet and when they break for lunch they'll talk about what they have discovered. Emily reminds Silver what to look for and then remembers the jewelry. "Look at the photographs and see if she's wearing any of those pieces we found," she says, trying hard to whisper across the table before she starts working. She's about to say more when she realizes that Silver knows how to research too, and spends a great deal of time in libraries. Silver's already got her head down and Emily may as well be speaking to the wall.

The rest of the world quickly disappears. Suddenly, as if someone has switched on a light, it's the 1930s and 40s, and without a doubt Marjorie Rawlings is very much alive. Minutes and then hours begin to pass. Emily has to force herself not to read every word on every piece of paper. There are letters from Rawlings's publisher and from friends. She finds lively correspondence from Margaret Mitchell, an apparent friend of Marjorie's and the author of *Gone with the Wind*. Emily starts reading a letter and sits back, totally forgetting that she's supposed to be looking for specific information. When she discovers a letter on Metro-Goldwyn-Mayer Pictures letterhead dated 1940 from Victor Fleming, the infamous film director, her mind spins. Who didn't this woman know? Movie stars, writers, poets, publishers, fishing guides and local cooks. Emily rests her head in her hands for a moment and then looks at the letter and sees such a clear contrast in Marjorie's life. One day she would be having lunch in New York with her editor, and then the next, after a very long train ride home, she'd be gutting out fish on her back porch.

She turns to look again at the photo of Marjorie behind her and then rummages around in her pile of papers until she finds an identical photograph from a Saturday Evening Post newspaper article. Silver doesn't move when she gets up, takes the newspaper with her, and walks back over to stand next to the photograph. The bold headline reads, *Marjorie Rawlings Hunts for Her Supper* and Emily's glad to see that at least in one of the photographs, Rawlings is wearing pants as she hypnotizes frogs with a flashlight. Good Lord! The Post article talks about how Marjorie loved to go searching for food for her dinner table while characters were simmering in her mind.

Sitting back down, Emily holds the old newspaper close to her face and carefully examines each photograph while trying to balance her own desire to look into the past with her need to be a serious researcher. She learns so much in the next twenty minutes as she reads photo captions and the accompanying story that she can only imagine what else is in the piles on the desk and behind the locked doors.

Marjorie had four thousand orange trees and Phillips, a farm hand, to help her grow them. She could catch her own turtles and harvest their eggs, and eat almost every ounce of them. Then she could dress up, set the table as if she were entertaining in Manhattan, serve alligator steaks bedded on avocado leaves, swamp-cabbage salad and the crab a la Newburg from her own cookbook. Emily chuckles when she reads that Rawlings had "quiet friendliness", because she's certain Rawlings was about as quiet as the discharge from her shotgun. She does agree that her survival in rural Florida had lots to do with the fact that she called her neighbors "people of dignity."

Emily pauses to image the world she has just read about and to marvel, yet again, at her surroundings. She smiles when she sees Silver bent over a stack of papers with her eyes so close to the table it's a wonder she can see anything. She's also intrigued by Marjorie's relationship with Zora and she vaguely remembers how the author Alice Walker found her unmarked grave and gave it a proper headstone. Emily hesitates for a moment and is almost sidetracked by thoughts of adding research on Zora. She knows that parts of the south are still dicey, what with the confederate flags and active Ku Klux Klan groups and politicians who forget what year it is. Imagining what it must have been like for Zora and Marjorie, literary equals and contemporaries yet decades apart in real equality, is almost impossible.

Emily forces herself to go back to her newspapers and notices that Marjorie is rarely seen without a cigarette. She hopes she broke that bad habit if she lived past the age of fifty-seven, but back then she knows doctors actually prescribed cigarette smoking as a health benefit. The thought makes her shudder as if she's a wet kitten, and then she moves to the next photo where she sees Marjorie with yet another cigarette, sitting next to three men. She glances at the caption and sees that that man next to her is her husband, Norton, and he's busy opening either a bottle of whiskey or wine. Norton is dark-haired, handsome and with a sweater dangling over his shoulder looks almost as ridiculous in the swamp as Marjorie does in her belted dress. She looks at the next two men, Robert Camp and Cecil Clarke, and then almost falls off her chair when she sees who is also sitting in the circle.

"It's James Carlton!" Emily has risen out of her chair and she doesn't realize she's yelled his name very loudly.

Silver jumps up and rushes over and immediately puts her hand over Emily's mouth and shushes her as if she's a crying baby.

"Honey, you must remember where you are." Silver is also laughing almost as loud as Emily yelled. Emily works in a library, for crying out loud, and even if the rules here aren't strict, people have been talking and working together all morning. Yelling is probably not a good idea.

"Look," Emily holds up the article and points to a man who is clearly the father of Jimmy, the fisherman she met at Cross Creek, but Silver doesn't know what he looks like.

Emily explains and forces Silver to sit down for a few minutes. They talk with their heads pressed together. Emily admits it was silly to shout but it was exciting to see the connection, to realize how easy it is to access the past in this part of the world.

"Locked away in my room in Ohio, I guess I've forgotten how this part of my work, the touching and feeling and seeing, is so thrilling," she shares, remembering to talk softly. "It's just a photograph but it's the specific link. I met this man's son. Gosh, Silver, there's so much stuff here. This collection is amazing."

"I know. I hope I'm not drooling on anything. I keep looking up to see if she's walking through the door. It even smells like Marjorie in here and I don't even know what she smells like."

"Probably a mix of pine needles, raccoon flesh, oranges, butter and maybe a little hair spray, if they had the stuff back then."

Emily's head is touching Silver's but they are both looking at each other's feet and whispering. Could Marjorie and Zora have been this close? It must have been a test of openness and a challenge for them to be friends, especially if Zora ever visited her here. Blacks were still considered second-class citizens by so many people in the thirties and forties, and everything that Emily has read thus far shows that almost all of the men and women who worked for Marjorie were black.

Emily has rarely thought of that as an issue in her own life. It's almost if she's colorblind, and she feels lucky to have been raised in areas where there was a rainbow of races, nationalities, social classes, and genders. It feels uncomfortable for her to be thinking about it, because she sees people as people-men and women, perhaps, but that's as far as her mind can go.

"This Zora and Marjorie friendship, do you know much about it, Silver?"

Of course Silver knows about it and she tells Emily that it was a struggle at first for Marjorie to consider Zora as an equal, a contemporary, a woman on the same page, so to speak, in all aspects of her life. "It's easy to be critical about Marjorie and some of the things she wrote. Back then people still used the word 'nigger', and part of Marjorie's own journey was all about embracing not just Zora, but everyone."

"Seriously?"

Silver shakes her head up and down. "There've been books and articles written about this, about them. Marjorie was so much more than just an author."

Emily opens up her mouth to say something but Silver clamps her jaw shut with her left hand and says, "Focus. We can fill in the blanks later."

The women seriously try to concentrate and without realizing it, they work straight through lunch. Neither one of them notices when someone comes into the library or leaves and several hours pass before either one of them gets up or bothers to realize that the library will be closing within thirty minutes.

It's Mary who startles them both back to reality by leaning on the table and clearing her throat. Both Silver and Emily immediately look up.

"I was beginning to wonder if you two were still breathing," she says looking at her own watch.

Emily turns to look at the clock behind her and is shocked to realize it's close to closing time. "This is so fascinating. I had no idea the entire day had slipped away."

"Well, dear, it really hasn't slipped, but it looks as if you two are far from being finished." Mary has straightened up and is looking at the piles of documents spread out all over the table."

"I suppose we had better pick this up," Silver says, sounding as if she might start to cry. "I feel as if I've just gotten started."

Mary chuckles and crosses her arms.

Emily has her hands on a stack of unread letters to and from Marjorie and she's seriously thinking about stealing them. There are dozens and dozens more to read and she's already started a stack of correspondence to read through one more time because she noticed the names of several people she wants to ask Mary and Silver about before she files them away again.

She's read letters from World War II servicemen who dream about the food she talked about in all of her novels. There's one letter from a boy who was so touched by the father-son relationship in *The Yearling* that it allowed him to forgive the cruelties of is own father. Emily has been particularly drawn to letters Marjorie wrote to Norton. Their love was boundless and forgiving, but from she's learned so far, also incredibly modern, considering the time.

Emily turns to look at Silver and then they both look at Mary who is smiling and then closes her eyes and shakes her head back and forth.

"I know two addicts when I see them," she says. "I tell you what. Let's just leave all of this and I'll lock up what's left on the cart so you can resume tomorrow. I'd love to lock you two in here all night and I so wish we had evening hours, but budget cuts, you know."

Silver and Emily are both relieved and then overjoyed when Mary asks if they'd like to come in early tomorrow so she can give them a behind-the-scenes tour and answer questions before the library opens and gets busy.

Less than an hour later, as Mary locks the doors behind them and they turn to walk down the wide marble steps, the guard at the bottom is aghast when he hears one of them say, "Shit!" and the loudly-spoken word bounces off the high marble ceilings.

Silver has finally checked her cell phone messages and it's Emily's voice that is ricocheting through the halls when she reads a message from Getts: *Brett has been released. Call me ASAP.*

# 22

*"There was an unlikely woman, a beautiful young girl really, who took my arm one day when I was leaving the market. I never saw her before or after that, but she acted as if she knew me. I was almost on the sidewalk when I felt her warm hand on my arm, then her breath against the side of my face as she leaned in and said, "Don't be afraid." She startled me, but before she turned away I kissed her cheek, which was so unlike me. I closed my eyes, opened them quickly, and she was gone. My fears did not dissolve overnight but that woman gave me a place to start. I call her my angel."*
—*Lost Hearts in the Swamp of Life* - MKR - 1963

Emily and Silver are sharing a fourteen-inch white-sauce pizza piled high with vegetables and sausage, a half-pitcher of Yuengling beer, and a huge Caesar salad while dissecting the meal as if they are writing their own cookbook. Halfway through a discussion about pizza crust, sausage verses pepperoni, and the necessity of having anchovies in the salad, Silver points out the fact that the conversation is one Marjorie might have had with Zora.

Emily can only agree. She notices that half of the letters she's read in the library thus far are talking about hangovers, food, or Marjorie's notion that her second husband would be better off without her.

Both Silver and Emily decide, when they can't immediately get Getts on the phone, that the best way to handle their unease at the news of Brett's release is to eat. Not only did they agree that's what Marjorie might do, but they are also famished. The moment they walk into the Italian restaurant down the street from the library and smell the seasoned sauces floating through the dining room, it's as if their stomachs are in control of everything. They also realize how much they have been concentrating on their work. Their neck and back muscles ache from leaning over the work -tables.

While Emily orders, Silver frantically tries to get Getts on the phone and when one of the dispatchers finally tells her he is out on some kind of investigation, there is nothing to do but eat, talk about eating, and wonder what is going to happen next.

The women are in a quiet back corner of the restaurant, which has filled with gangs of students since they arrived. Emily has watched them file in, huddled in groups, as if they are litters of newborn puppies. The distraction is helping her get her mind off of the whereabouts of the recently freed stalker, even as she pumps her right leg up and down in nervous frustration.

She's watching the students as Silver checks and re-checks her cellphone, and thinking about how easy it is to feel alone if you are not a wild and free spirit like Marjorie Rawlings or her friend, Zora.

Silver takes a break and looks up. Then she kicks Emily's non-moving right foot. "Stop staring!"

Emily is unaware that she's focused on one particular group where the students are flailing around, probably looking for fake IDs so that they can order something stronger than water. She's also wondering if it's possible to recapture the carefree, cavalier attitude that the university years seem to bring to young lives.

"Did you get Getts yet?"

"No. This is driving me nuts."

"Do you remember being in college and how, in the end, no matter how hard the classes were, it was seriously one of the easier parts of life?" Emily has her elbows on the table and wistful look in her eyes.

Silver glances at the booth next to them and sees six students crowded against each other and eating a huge basket of garlic bread as if it's their last meal before a lethal injection.

She agrees that college is the easy part. How grand it was to know what one month and the month after would bring. There were parties and friends and yes, working hard, but she admits that there have been many times during the years when she's thought about how easy school was compared to the reality that came after it. Enrollment at a university offers a stretch of predictable nights and days that stave off the real world. Then it all ends, seemingly suddenly, and there are loans to pay, you get kicked out of the cheap housing, have to find a job and discover very quickly that the world is not a basket of butter-laced garlic bread.

Emily is listening and thinking about the teaching assistants, some professors, a handful of tenth-year seniors who figured that out a long time ago. The university world can indeed be very seductive. She glances at another table, this one filled with five girls, who are studying and exchanging notes as they wait for their food to be delivered. Two thoughts enter her mind at the exact same moment, and she blurts them out loud.

"I think I've missed a ton of opportunities by hiding out in the library and not taking advantage of everything that's offered on my own campus, and, Silver, have you ever thought about teaching?"

Silver looks startled. "What are you, a mind reader?"

"So have you?"

"I always wanted to," she admits. "That's why I got that fairly useless master's degree, but then you know the rest of the story and that's the path I took."

"You can change direction."

"A social worker and a mind reader?"

Emily laughs as she shrugs and they are both relieved when Silver's phone finally rings and Silver says that it's Getts. Emily leans across the table, hoping to hear what he's saying, but the noise inside the restaurant has increased along with the number of students. Silver is mostly listening and when she finally gets off the phone Emily is almost ready to scream with anticipation.

"What?" she says through her clenched teeth.

"Someone wired him bail money and Getts is trying to find out who, and Mr. Asshole took right off. Getts said because it's his first offense down here all he has to do is pay a fine and he's free and clear," Silver explains.

Emily isn't happy to hear the news, and she's realizing how dinner and watching the students have been a welcome distraction from the worry that has plagued her since Silver received the text message from Getts. "Now what?"

"There's a million-dollar question." Silver is drumming her fingers on the table and when the waitress comes flying past she stops her and asks her to bring another half-pitcher of beer to the table without asking Emily if she wants any.

"We're drinking to solve our problems?"

"Well, I prefer to say we are drinking because we're thirsty and we need to talk about this, and because Getts said we should carry on and try not to worry."

Once the beer arrives, Silver finishes telling her what else Getts told her. He called Auggie to let her know that Mr. Kinnan has been released, and to make certain the house doors are locked at night and when she comes and goes. He's also very sorry but he's extremely busy right now and he can't follow Brett because he's short-staffed. He promises to contact the cabin owner where he's been staying to make certain he can keep track of him that way. Silver says all of this with her face pinched up and looking like a visual description of the word "worry".

"So, we're on our own for a while and I'm thinking it's a good thing we aren't back there, or one of us might drive over and beat the living hell out of him to get some answers," Emily says. "What does he know that we don't know?"

"Getts made certain I realized how important it was not to do something crazy like that," Silver tells her, wishing she had ordered a whole pitcher of beer. "There's no way in hell he would find us here, so I think the smartest thing is to just keep looking for whatever it is we are looking for."

She also adds that Brett is bound to do something else stupid. "He's a dumbass. We have the boxes and we aren't even sure he knows what he's looking for."

"But maybe he does know," Emily tells her. "Maybe he has more then one letter. He's been to all the right places. He knows things."

Silver totally agrees, but then she lifts up her glass in a one-woman toast and says, "If he screws with us do you really think he has a chance?"

Emily's glass goes right into the air, even as she struggles not to adopt Silver's worried expression herself.

It takes them another thirty minutes to talk each other out of being dumbasses too. Emily imagines it would be easy to drive back, go to the cabin, and confront Brett, especially if Silver brought along her purse with the gun in it. Instead, they finish their beer, pay the bill, and then retreat to the hotel where they happily lock the deadbolt and spend the next three hours focusing on what they need to look for tomorrow when they are allowed into the sacred back rooms of the library.

"There are clues everywhere," Emily whispers across the room to Silver when they finally turn out the lights. But Silver is already asleep, almost before she hits the pillow and Emily lies awake again and wonders for a solid hour what it would be like to drink beer with Marjorie Kinnan Rawlings at a bar across the street from her Pulitzer Prize that is hanging on the wall of that magnificent library.



Crawford Langley is so much like her name-sophisticated, smart, knowledgeable and eager-that Emily finds it almost impossible to call her Mary, so she doesn't, and Crawford loves it.

"I've been missing my name," she says as she leads Emily and Silver into the library, locks the door behind them, and then orders them to follow her. "I'm named after my great-grandmother, who was apparently a wild thing and it's time I throw away my fake name and take on Crawford. This will turn Gainesville on its head, and I love it when that happens."

Silver and Emily exchange a smile as they walk through the door behind the library counter and Crawford warns them that they are about to enter a forbidden land where intellectual literary and library geeks would live 24/7, if such a thing were possible. Emily already knows this world and she slips behind the door and feels as if she's just been injected with a drug that makes every fiber in her body relax. This is home, this is where real work is done, this is where people who share her same loves and passions live and breathe and work, and save all the pieces of the past that keep worlds-past and present-linked together.

They follow Crawford past a jumble of desks and books and stacks and stacks of unopened boxes until they turn right and enter a hall that leads to a massive steel elevator that can only be entered by using a secret code tapped into the keypad outside its door. Emily is almost beside herself with excitement as the three of them enter, the door closes and they descend one, two, three and then four levels below the ground floor.

Crawford tells them they are going into the climate-controlled below-ground floors where actual documents are stored. None of this is news to Emily, who has a similar facility at her university library, but there are no Marjorie Kinnan Rawlings documents there. She also knows that if she would have gone on to get advanced degrees, including masters and doctorate degrees, that she might now have a position like the wonderful Ms. Crawford.

The elevator feels like a smooth ride in an expensive car and Emily can't help but imagine what Marjorie would think about all of this. She closes her eyes and imagines Marjorie standing next to her dressed in a long black dress, a double stand of pearls around her neck, her fingers laced together as she rocks back and forth in impatience. Marjorie was most likely polite, up to a point. Emily thinks that after the point had been passed, the author could probably take down half an army by herself. Emily can't wait to ask Crawford the questions she has hastily scribbled onto her notepad about Marjorie but in the meantime, she's having fun making things up based on what she has read.

Silver leans over as the elevator doors open and whispers, "I've never been down here. I'm kind of excited."

"Me too," Emily says as they follow Crawford off the elevator and into a Marjorie Rawlings materials aisle that is stacked floor to ceiling.

Crawford is easy-going and open, and she knows that Emily has been into places like this. So instead of talking about historic literary objects, and how crucial it is to correctly preserve and maintain them, she leans against the twenty-foot tall metal cabinet and says, "This is so flipping amazing that sometimes I just come here and stand with my head against one of these files and weep," she admits. "This is one of several collections that I administer and maintain, but I have to say that Rawlings… well, she was a broad in the truest sense of the word, and she's my hero."

She tells them that Rawlings donated everything but her doorknob-well actually, she did that too via Cross Creek-to the university, and that documents still come in from time to time. "Last week someone from Kansas sent me a signed copy of *The Yearling* that has been preserved all these years. She still has fans and followers, but there should be so many more," she tells them. "We have her original manuscripts, her letters, her grocery orders, you name it."

Emily knows they can't stand in the cold room very long and she has to fight an inner urge to start pulling the labeled boxes of writings and manuscripts off the shelves so she can sit down on the concrete floor to look at every single piece of preserved paper.

Instead, she allows Crawford to pull out random boxes. Silver stands behind her as Crawford takes a pair of white gloves out of her pocket, puts them on and then gently opens the first box. It's the original typed manuscript of *Cross Creek*, and Emily can feel her own heart surge when she sees the wild black editing marks, the way the dot of the *i* from Marjorie's typewriter leans a bit left, and the water, or perhaps whiskey, stains on every other page.

They next open memorabilia from the University of Wisconsin, and Emily is only mildly surprised to see Marjorie on the cover of a centennial edition of the Wisconsin Alumnus magazine wearing a black dress and a double strand of pearls just as she imagined. She's beginning to wonder if she isn't having one out-of-the-body experience after another, or if Miz Rawlings isn't standing next to her in some other dimension and giving her directions.

There are rows and stacks of material. Crawford tells them that Marjorie was a good saver of her papers and letters, unlike people now who throw away all the excess pieces of their lives to reduce clutter, or because they don't understand how important all the pieces of the puzzle might be one day. "I'm not saying we should be hoarders but the Internet and email and texting worry me sometimes," she says, looking towards the back of the room for a moment. "I don't care what they tell us, there's something sacred about paper and seeing words on the paper, and knowing that the paper was touched by someone like Marjorie Rawlings."

Emily has to hold back from throwing her arms around Crawford and kissing her face. She knows how much work went into the preservation of all the materials, and how researchers now and in the future will be able to use what's in this row and every other row to understand lives past, a world that no longer exists, and the workings of a literary giant's heart.

"You both know how one sentence, a story, a novel can change a person's life," Crawford continues. "It's been a unifying connection for thousands of years, and I suppose that's what has always drawn me to this work, to making certain it stays alive, even as its creator doesn't."

Silver reaches out to put her hand on Crawford's arm and Emily wonders if Crawford knows who Silver really is. She turns to look at Silver and wonders who's preserving her works, her contributions, the reams of correspondence she must send and receive. It's too much, all too much to consider, and as they walk around the corner and down the next aisle, Emily vows to ask Silver about creating her own files, just like these.

Crawford swings down the next aisle, grabbing other manuscripts, copyedited versions, proofs, notes and newspaper clippings until Emily feels as if she might faint. How will they ever find what they are looking for? Does she dare ask Crawford specific questions?

Finally, Emily asks her to pull several files that contain personal letters and several stacks of receipts that she thinks might offer some kind of clue, anything at all, and they follow Crawford back to the elevator and through the maze of desks, boxes and wild clutter to her office. Her office really isn't an office, but a small opening that looks as if it's been carved out of the side of a dark basement.

"It looks like hell in here but I can assure you that I know every inch of this cubbyhole and it works for me," Crawford explains, offering each of them chairs that look as if they came over on the Mayflower. "Sit. Talk to me."

Emily grabs her notes out of her purse as Silver's cell phone rudely rings. Silver quickly shuts it off, apologizes, and sits at attention.

There are so many questions Emily hardly knows where to begin. She realizes that Crawford, who has most likely gone through every Rawlings paper in the entire library and who has told her she's the president of the Marjorie Kinnan Rawlings Society, knows Marjorie in a way few others might. She follows her instincts, sets down her notes and asks her one seemingly simple question.

"Crawford, tell us what she was like, please? You must know her intimately, even if you've never met."

The floodgates open quickly and Crawford scoots back in her chair and unleashes a lecture so personal that Emily will wish that she had thought to record it. Instead, she feverishly takes notes, while Crawford Langley speaks about the marvelous Miz Rawlings.

She was self-confident, tenacious and a great listener. She was also a great mimic who had a wonderful linguistic ear-she could pick out subtleties, and was a total wordsmith who was also lively, stubborn, and introspective. Crawford doesn't move the entire time she is speaking, except once to turn to Emily and say, "Thank you for asking this question. Most people want to know other things, but this is what I want them to know, what is most important."

Marjorie was judgmental and liked to gossip too, she tells them, but she was also that way about herself, kind of like taking equal opportunity to wonder if everything people were saying was really true. She was always more attracted to writing about men than women, and often was not kind to women in her writing. Marjorie was without doubt a woman who knew what she wanted and she wasn't afraid to get it.

"She loved it quiet when she was writing," Crawford says. "She was very particular about her writing space and her needs. Coffee in bed, then getting dressed and then writing a lot while she was in bed, and she wrote a lot out on that porch of hers and all the while the people who worked for her would be tiptoeing around the house and hanging close to make certain she had everything that she wanted."

And Marjorie struggled with trying to create a balance of being happy in her relationship with her life partner, Norton, and her need to devote so much time to her work and writing. But how Norton loved her! He had a great sense of who she was and what she needed, and he worshiped her and wanted her to do well, even if he helped her party a bit too much. Norton, a hotel and restaurateur by trade, was very much a social creature and he was always a good time.

All three of the women chuckle and this is how Emily also imagined Marjorie, whose ever-present cigarette and talk of hangovers is well documented. Crawford agrees that Marjorie cultivated her independence and, yes, she was a drinker who loved rich hearty food, but she was also a hard worker.

"One of her greatest gifts was communicating a sense of place," Crawford tells them. "You can feel where she lived, there's almost a sense of taste about it too when you read her work. She made her readers feel special and *The Yearling* is classic in the sense that anyone who reads it can find themselves in the same place and find parallels in their own lives. It's what makes the book a enduring classic."

Silver has closed her eyes to take in every word of this lovely and spontaneous lecture. She's finally turned off her persistent beeping phone and has leaned back while Emily is now helping to guide the discussion. Ohio, it seems, is very good at this part of her work too.

"You know, after the huge controversy where her friend Zelma Cason sued her for invasion of privacy because she didn't like how she was portrayed in Cross Creek, it broke Marjorie's heart," Crawford says. "She never wrote about Florida again and I think of what a waste that was, how I wish she had taken better care of herself so she could have lived longer, written more, come back to this place she once loved so very much."

Silver and Emily turn slowly to look at each other and then Emily makes a note to try and find the files about the lawsuit. This must be what Tag was talking about when he mentioned Marjorie's sad heart. In both their minds it is also a very good reason to shut down, disappear, and thumb your nose at the entire world.

Crawford tells them she has placed the trial files on their stack of materials and asks them if they are finding what they are looking for or if need anything else. Because Crawford has been so honest, Emily decides to tell her they are trying to find letters or addresses or anything that might turn up some long-lost relatives.

Crawford looks puzzled. "There aren't many," she explains. "Norton's heirs ended up with what's left of Marjorie's estate, even though she has a nephew out there someplace from her wild brother."

"That's what I'm thinking," Emily says. "The wild brother. Is there a chance, and I'm asking this in total confidence, that the brother had more then one child? A secret relationship? Anything?"

Silver is stunned that Emily is asking these questions. She has to restrain herself from telling her to stop talking. Crawford is now leaning forward in her chair.

"Do you know something?" Crawford asks.

"Just a wild idea," Emily says, trying hard to act nonchalant. "I do this at my library also, you know, go through the files in hopes of finding something no one else has ever discovered and it's become a kind of vacation-induced hobby for me."

A vacation-induced hobby? Silver believes she may have totally underestimated Ohio's talents.

Crawford pushes back in her chair and admits that no one person has looked at every single piece of paper or document. Interns and part-time staffers have helped her for years and now with Florida's jackass governor acting as if it's stupid to fund educational pursuits they're lucky they can buy pencils. Then she turns and pulls open her slightly dented desk drawer, reaches in and pulls out two objects in clean plastic bags. "Someone found these in those very files last week," she tells them handing the packets to Emily. "I had no idea we even had these."

Emily is suddenly holding Marjorie's passport and a book of blue and white checks that are from the Phifer State Bank with an Island Grove, Florida address and Marjorie's name written across the top.

"Her checkbook and passport?" Emily asks, not as a question but more in astonishment as she slips the fingers of her right hand into the bag and runs them across the black lettering on the checkbook. She gently removes the passport and sees a stark black and white photo of Marjorie, her five feet five inch height, dark brown hair, blue eyes note and then her occupation boldly proclaimed: "WRITER."

She passes the treasures over to Silver who touches them just as tenderly while Crawford tells Emily she could spend a year looking through the files and folders and perhaps uncover something about a long-lost relative, but most likely there are no relatives, no more secrets, no hidden treasures.

"But there could be?" Emily remains hopeful.

"Well, if I didn't believe that I'd go jump off the bridge," Crawford says. "It would seem though, after all these years, that even an illegitimate relative might step forward."

Crawford tells them they are welcome to paw through every and anything she has in her files, and she also says, as a favor to a fellow librarian, that she'll make some calls if they want to drive to St. Augustine and perhaps see Marjorie's beach house and the hotel that she stayed in when Norton owned it. She tells them that a lovely woman now owns the Crescent Beach house where Marjorie lived part-time and that the house has changed little since Marjorie lived there. She tells them that when Norton purchased a hotel in St. Augustine and when finances permitted, they bought a beach home where Marjorie also worked and entertained.

The prospect of seeing yet another Rawlings house is too good to pass up and Silver agrees that they must go, and they ask if it's possible to arrange for visits the following day. Crawford promises to try and as they all stand, Emily asks one more question. "Is there anything you would love to ask her or say about her?"

A sweet smile opens up Crawford's entire face and she lets out a long sigh. "I so wish I had been one of her friends," she admits, her voice quivering as she speaks. "She made all of her readers feel that way but oh, to have been sitting on her porch, sipping whiskey with her, talking about the neighbors, and gazing at the stars would have been heaven, absolute heaven."

Emily can't help but think about Silver's porch and Auggie and jumping in the rain when they walk back to the beautiful library room and resume their own literary scavenger hunt.

Silver purposefully ignores her buzzing phone for as long as possible and then finally checks her text messages, looks up and sees that Emily is totally engrossed in her work, and decides to wait before she shares the latest news. They are both looking for names, a photograph that might show Marjorie wearing the gold jewelry Emily discovered, any reference to a Francis or a Kinnan that no one knows about or even a reference to something that may have happened long after Marjorie's death, especially anything in January of 1973, the date on all the newspapers found in Leslie's guestroom.

Several hours pass and Emily decides they should make photocopies of some of the files. She grabs some papers that Silver says she also wants copied and walks over the copy machine in the back corner. The papers shuffle through the machine and Emily has a moment to look around the big beautiful room again. Being in the library has also reminded Emily that she doesn't have a lot of time left before she must get back to her paying job. There's still so much to do here, so much to discover, and in spite of her obsession there's a ticking time clock in the basement library office back in Ohio that has her name on it.

Silver slips off to the hall to call Getts and check on the safety of her beloved dogs and her true-blue friend Auggie, while Emily thumbs through the last pile of papers. Following a series of phone calls, she decides to wait until they have checked out of the library, said their goodbyes to Crawford, and pointed the car toward St. Augustine before she tells Emily the news.

Emily is talking non-stop about Zelma's lawsuit, the possibility that there could still be some missing information about relatives or someone who helped Marjorie disappear, and Silver lets her go on and on because she's so excited that she's almost hyperventilating. It's entertaining, and Silver also believes she could be right and that there might be clues hiding inside one of the files.

"Anything's possible, isn't it, Ohio?" she says, as they leave Gainesville and Silver directs her to the same side-roads Marjorie may have taken all those years ago and they head a south towards Hawthorne. "We'll have to backtrack a little a bit but it will give us a feeling for what it was like when she drove from Cross Creek to the East Coast."

It takes Silver another thirty minutes to tell her that Brett has disappeared. She tells Emily that Getts told her that the cabin he was renting is empty, his truck is gone, no one has seen him and Getts has no clue where he has gone, or what he might be doing.

Both Silver and Emily know they should be happy about this latest development, especially if it means Brett has gone back to wherever it is he came from. But as they head through East Palatka, where the shaggy trees and dark swamps still look exactly the same as when Marjorie drove past them on the way to Crescent Beach, they wish that their complicated Marjorie was riding in the backseat, with her shotgun balanced on her left knee and a whiskey and water balanced on the other.

# 23

*"It was a glorious day, bright blue sky, the wind a soft caress that camouflaged the heat, waves sweetly serenading me when I saw the ocean for the first time. I thought about everything I had read and felt through the words that were meant to describe what I was viewing. But a remarkable thought plunged itself into my mind. Sometimes we must see and feel and touch what others see and feel and touch. It is the only way to truly know. The only way."*
—*Lost Hearts in the Swamp of Life* - MKR - 1963

Silver has more news. She waits until they are on the outskirts of St. Augustine before she grabs several papers she had Emily photocopy out of the stack of material they accumulated at the library. Emily glances sideways at her, and can tell something is about to happen.

They've already called the St. Augustine Chamber of Commerce and have been directed to a bed and breakfast in the historic part of town where, without asking, they've been told there's a Marjorie Rawlings room "that's very popular with the ladies."

"Come on!" Silver barked after she had called to reserve the room. "This is almost ridiculous. I really do think if those manuscripts aren't real, that I'm turning this into a novel. This is all too good to pass up."

What isn't ridiculous is the Florida Certificate of Death for Marjorie Kinnan Rawlings Baskin that Silver has decided they must talk about immediately.

"I found this in one of the folders and I didn't want you to go nuts in there but you have to listen to this," Silver says as Emily tries hard to see what Silver is about to share with her. "Keep your eyes on the road!"

Silver shares the recorded statistics of Marjorie's death as if she's telling a story. Everything happened in St. Johns County on December 14, 1953. Marjorie's occupation is listed as author, she's a white female who was born in Washington D.C. on August 8, 1896 and her father was Arthur H. Baskin. Marjorie was taken to Flagler Hospital on Route 1 after having fallen ill twelve to fifteen hours before she was admitted to the hospital. She died at 8:45pm.

Before Silver can continue, Emily is yelling, "Cause of death! What was the cause of death?"

"Ruptured aneurysm, circle of Willis," Silver reads and then hesitates.

"What?"

"Under 'other significant conditions contributing to death but not related to the terminal disease' is written, 'hypertension, chronic myocarditis, obesity,' and then the words, 'several years,'" Silver says.

"What the hell? Obesity?"

"I know," Silver says. "What's even stranger is I know about the circle of Willis because one of the characters in my novel had a brain aneurysm following a fall off a ladder years before. All the arteries that supply oxygen and other goodies to the brain are in a big loop that join in a circle-thus, the circle of Willis. The places where the arteries come together can weaken and rupture."

"The fall..." Emily whispers.

"What fall?"

"Marjorie fell off her horse. She wrote about it, and who knows how many other head injuries she had while living the kind of life she lived. She could have fallen fifty times."

Silver is shaking her head back and forth. She tells Emily that Auggie helped her do research for the novel where the characters had more than a few illnesses and that myocarditis has something to do with the heart, inflammation or infection or something similar, and that aneurysms are a dime a dozen when it comes to sudden deaths.

"What does that mean?" Emily is starting to think they are crazy to be chasing after a dead woman.

"It means that of course she could have died of those things and it also means she could have faked her death," Silver is talking slow, thinking out loud, and thumbing back through the files in her own mind. "A Dr. Norris signed the death certificate. Norton probably had drinks with him every other night at the hotel he ran. What I'm saying is that we have a death certificate, but we also have a box of manuscripts that sure as hell read like something Marjorie would write. It's her style, and that's terribly hard to reproduce."

Both women are quiet for a few moments. Emily is concentrating on making certain they stay on the correct road as she follows directions from the bed and breakfast hosts, and her mind is thumping with possibilities. Three minutes later, both Emily and Silver say the same thing at the exact same time.

"Obesity?"

"Did she look fat in any of the photographs you saw of her the past two days?" Emily is almost thinking of turning around and driving back to the library.

Silver tells her that Marjorie didn't age like women do now, who have facelifts, take vitamins, do not eat fresh cow's cream every day and realize the importance of exercise. Her face filled out and in a few photographs she didn't look well at all. Her eyes were puffy and she looked as if she were about to cry. Hard, Silver decides. Marjorie looked hard and almost deflated.

Emily can't stand it any longer and, as they approach the historic section of St. Augustine, she pulls over alongside of a long bridge so they are looking out across a sailboat-lined harbor and towards the rows of old brick homes in America's oldest city. The city looks like an ancient painting. There's a fort with canons, spots of color from painted tin roofs, tall palms swaying along the edge of the water. The women feel transported when they see costumed soldiers following the brick path alongside of the ancient fort that still guards the waterfront city.

"She probably saw all this too," Emily says softly while she rolls down the windows. "It's beautiful here, but from what I read she never felt as if this was her home. She was famous after she won the Pulitzer and there were tons of articles in the newspaper about events and book signings. I bet she craved all the quiet she had at Cross Creek."

Silver agrees, but she's distracted and can't get past the obesity, hypertension, and the bad heart. She knows from personal experience that there's hardly a working author alive who doesn't suffer from those same ailments. The stress and pressure of deadlines, always having to top the last book, meeting the expectations of readers, editors, and the publishing house accountants and also trying hard to follow the dictates of his or her own writing passions can kill a person. She believes that she might be alive today because she left that world and made a whole new one for herself. Perhaps Marjorie could have done the same thing. Silver knows it's totally possible.

Emily is watching the seagulls float through the air and wishing she had a time machine. It would take her three seconds to hop abroad and she'd come right back here, walk over to the big hotel where Marjorie lived part-time with Norton on the top floor, and look into her eyes and then demand some answers.

"I'm suddenly feeling deflated," Emily says, turning to look at Silver. "I mean, I knew there was a death certificate but now I feel depressed about the whole thing. Brett has disappeared and we've got a box of papers and yet..."

"Yet," Silver says, finishing her sentence, "there's the possibility that it did happen, that she did escape one life for another of her own design, just like I did."

Silver grabs Emily's hand and launches into a lengthy stream-of-consciousness lecture that is meant to convince both of them that they are not going crazy. She thinks that Marjorie must have known that her drinking and smoking and eating and stress would catch up with her and that she was ready to retreat into a new life. Sure, she loved company and entertaining and yet what she loved even more was writing. A month and then another one and then years away from the kind of life she had been leading could change everything, including Marjorie's rundown appearance.

She could have slimmed down, changed her hair, worked with a doctor to take care of her high blood pressure while still maintaining her relationship with Norton, who was always coming and going anyway. Then she could write all of the time, or half of a day, or not at all, because there would be less pressure. The world would not expect yet another book that was similar to *Cross Creek* or *The Yearling*. Silver confesses that there were bad reviews of Marjorie's novel *The Sojourner*, and stories she wrote after her bestsellers. Taking away the stress and pressure may have turned her into an author who could fill up more than six books.

Does it even matter if Brett disappears or hunts them down or they discover something they don't want to discover? A death certificate should not deter them, nor should the unanswered questions that keep popping up from their own wells of unease and uncertainty.

"We have something and we don't know what it is, and in order to find out we have to keep going, we have to finish this, we have to stop second-guessing the roadmap we have been following," Silver says with great conviction. "To hell with Brett, who I believe has not given up his search either. He has way too much at stake to stop now, even if he is a total fool."

Emily wants to be comforted and charged by the pep talk, but the same old feeling of surrender that has been her companion for so many years has jumped right on her back again. Who does she think she is? A literary archaeologist? Searching for a dead author? A brash woman following ridiculous leads all over the swamps? Emily drops her head onto the steering wheel and struggles to find a positive response.

Silver can tell that her companion, who just hours ago was a vision of power and poise, is fading and she's not about to let that happen. She gets out of the truck, walks over to the driver's door, pulls it open and orders Emily out of the truck. Stunned, Emily follows the instruction, and then stands in the hot sun while Silver restarts the pick-up.

"Babies cannot drive a big-girl truck," she tells Emily. "Get in, and make sure you lock your door."

Emily isn't certain if Silver is kidding or serious. She walks around the back of the truck, climbs inside, fastens her seatbelt and looks straight ahead.

Silver puts the truck in reverse, spins her wheels as she guns the engine and then stops before she turns around and pulls back onto the sleepy highway.

"Consider yourself spanked, missy," she says, as a smile opens up her face. "I'm not letting a little old thing like a death certificate stop me from finding Marjorie Rawlings and neither should you."

Before Emily can say one word, Silver squeals the truck tires down the usually quiet highway, crosses the long bridge, and then shouts out the window, "Come and find us, Brett. I dare you!"

Miles away, Sheriff Gettleman is pacing in his office, uncertain whether or not he should call Silver and spoil what he knows is a terribly important trip. He puts his hand on his phone three times before he decides not to call. The news about the location of Brett's birth mother and Brett himself can wait. Silver needs this break. She's come back to life and the sparkle in her eyes is worth the risk.

He'll tell her tomorrow, if she doesn't see him on the evening news doing something he knows he might actually arrest himself for doing.

Morning in St. Augustine is a beautiful event that includes a full breakfast for the lone occupants of the bed and breakfast where two women have spent the night in the Marjorie Kinnan Rawlings room. First there was a brisk walk to the edge of the water, the tossing of stale crackers to tourist-savvy birds, a discussion about the day's events and then banana pancakes, sausage, fruit cups and coffee so fresh it all but jumped up and slapped first Silver and then Emily.

The women are now waiting in front of their room for a local historian, William Oliver, to take them on a four-hour whirlwind tour of St. Augustine and all things Marjorie before they drive to Crescent Beach and then hopefully back to Silver's for the night.

Mr. Oliver comes to them as an unexpected surprise from Crawford Langley, who arranged for the tour after calling Silver and simply finding out where they had propped up their heads for the evening. He pulls up in a small sedan, waving with enthusiasm as they open the car doors and introduce themselves. Before they can utter a word he rattles off the agenda as if he's been working on it for a year.

William is Mr. History personified and a sweet man who has adopted St. Augustine and its past, and that definitely includes its most famous former resident and her husband. Emily is in the back seat, directly behind William so that she can make occasional eye contact with Silver, who is sitting in the passenger seat. William's shaggy hair bounces off his collar as he drives them out of the historic district and tells them that he's written several books about historic preservation, and that he feels a calling to maintain the past and keep his eye on local developers. Emily wants to kiss the back of his head when he talks. He's clearly a man who knows what's important, and as they start their lightening-fast tour she can't help but be sad that it's going to be a once-over-lightly tour and not the in-depth, three-day-long affair she'd love to experience.

He drives them all over town, pointing out where Marjorie's friends lived, where she liked to eat, and especially talking about his fondness for Norton who he said, "adored Marjorie with every ounce of his being."

"You knew Norton?" Silver asks him as he brings the car to a stop into front of a rather large historic marker.

"Everyone knew Norton," William says, with a hint of sadness in his voice. "He was a true gentleman, and the best storyteller I ever met in my life. He lived here after he retired and I don't think he ever got over the death of Marjorie. He adored her, he really did."

Emily is leaning forward and Silver is pinching the side of her arm as William speaks. Emily has to struggle not to yell, and also not to ask him the real questions that are bubbling up so close to her tongue she feels as if she may blurt them out at any second.

William is looking off into the distance and he keeps talking. He tells them that Norton lived into his nineties and that he had the honor of becoming one of his friends. Emily wants to hop inside of William's mind and know everything that he knows about Norton and Marjorie. But right now, she doesn't have to ask a thing. It's almost as if William knows what she wants to know. He keeps the car on, leans over to turn up the air conditioning, even though the windows are down, and reveals a string of sweet details about Marjorie and her second, and much beloved, husband.

Their lives were a tangled mess of differences that had a solid foundation made of true love. Marjorie loved her quiet and Norton, the hotel man, lived in a world that was based on entertaining. He was Mr. Fun, in every sense of the word. Marjorie never liked living in the plush top-floor apartment he built for her in his Castle Warden Hotel. She'd probably have a stroke right now if she saw that Norton's beautiful solid-brick landmark hotel had been turned into a Ripley's Believe it or Not Museum. Norton could barely stand to look at it when he became too frail to live on his own and was in a facility close to the hotel where the likes of Earnest Hemingway and Robert Frost might swing by for a chat and a drink.

The couple fought like cats and dogs, drank too much, loved to correspond via long, emotionally-honest letters when they were apart and when she died, he was strong and precise about everything having to do with his famous wife. This time Emily is the one who squeezes Silver's arm so tightly that Silver coughs, pulls away her arm and leans forward. Finally, Emily interrupts.

"It seems odd that he would be so strong, given how unique their relationship was and how much in love they were," Emily says as she releases her grip on Silver. "I'm thinking that would be the time for him to fall apart, be devastated, wonder how he was going to spend the next fifty years without her."

William pauses. He looks into the rearview mirror and catches Emily's eye. There's a giant pause and it feels as if someone put a shop vacuum inside the car and sucked out all the good air. William holds her gaze for almost thirty seconds, which feels like an absolute eternity.

"I was a baby back then, but people tell me he was a rock and that everything happened quickly so that one, two, three, there was a private burial and obits in every paper in the world, and a huge cloud of grief that swept over the entire world because she was so loved, so very much loved," William says, never taking his eyes off of Emily. "I think it was pure and true Norton. Always the strongest back, always the gentleman, always the one to pick up the last glass."

Emily senses something and she waits a moment. It almost feels as if a wild cloud has decided to lower itself and push a stream of cool air in through the back door window. She feels calm, strong, sure and she doesn't lower her eyes or move a muscle.

When William speaks again it's with a voice that seems octaves lower, almost as if he's sharing a sweet secret for the first time with someone that he trusts very much. He grabs the back of his neck with his left hand, does not move his head at all, and is still looking into Emily's eyes as if he's been hypnotized.

"People who were close to him, before I was even living here, tell me that he truly started to grieve in the 1970s," William says slowly. "It started at the end of January in 1973 especially, and seemed to last in varying degrees until he died. I'm not sure what happened, but he slowed down after that and even though he was a viable, terribly likeable man, it was as if something had shifted inside of him, something important, and I'm told that he was even more willing to talk about Marjorie and their relationship."

*January of 1973.*

Emily can feel her lovely breakfast rotating in her stomach as she once again grips Silver's arm, and then drops her eyes.

The rest of the tour doesn't seem to matter to either Silver or Emily as it should. The women can barely breathe, let alone concentrate on William's rambling dialogue, which swings quickly from his revelations about that important date and Marjorie's death, to the sign they have not bothered to read that has Zora Neale Hurston written across its top.

"You know Zora and Marjorie were friends, which is remarkable for many reasons, and this marker is in front of a house where Zora rented a room while writing and teaching here," Williams explains as he launches into a running narrative about Hurston's own literary talents, hard life, and horrid death in a welfare home from a myriad of problems including hypertension and heart disease.

"Hypertension? Heart disease?" Emily is leaning forward again and is almost in Silver's lap. "I don't suppose she had an aneurism too?"

William is about to roll up the windows and keep moving when he stops. "Zora had a tough life, and I doubt if they even did an autopsy. If Marjorie would have lived longer I'm guessing their friendship might have helped save Zora, but she died young too. Apparently it's an author's curse-you know, hard living and drinking and all that stress. It's a good thing you two, Marjorie and Zora look-alikes if I may say so, aren't authors."

Emily squeezes Silver one more time, pushes back into her own seat and then tries with great difficulty to enjoy the rest of the tour, and fails miserably as they glide past other Zora landmarks, the park where Marjorie loved to sit and look at the water, and the hospital where Rawlings was pronounced dead three days before Emily was born.


Silver is answering a text message from Getts, who for some reason wants to know exactly when he can expect them to arrive back at Silver's house. "He's driving me nuts," Silver announces, as they approach Crescent Beach. "He can't miss me this much. He's sent me more text message in the past two hours then he has in the past two years."

"Absence makes the heart grown fonder," Emily guesses.

"No. He's too damn busy to miss me. Something's going on, and I propose we ignore it until we get back there."

Emily doesn't argue, and she needs Silver's help to try and locate Marjorie's old beach house where she apparently spent loads of time following the lawsuit Zelma filed against her. The women have followed the beach-hugging highway south from St. Augustine and are just miles from Crescent Beach. They both know that the house became Marjorie's writing refuge and a halfway point between Cross Creek and Norton's job after he sold the St. Augustine hotel and ran the popular Dolphin Restaurant and Bar at Marineland, further south along the ocean.

Although Crescent Beach isn't technically that far from Cross Creek, Emily senses a major difference in terrain and climate. The sand is piled in heaps along the edges of the highway and sprawling beach houses rise like wooden storks everywhere she looks. Tall stands of sea grass, low palms, and hibiscus dot the landscape, and in mid-afternoon there's a lovely breeze blowing in off the Atlantic. The sultry inland swamps and fields near Cross Creek may as well be back in Ohio.

Silver is busy looking for the address of the home that several people have told them became a semi-refuge from Marjorie's adoring public and from the memories that settled heavily onto her heart following the long trial. "It's so different here than Cross Creek," Emily says out loud, as Silver admits they have just passed the entrance to the house.

"Secluded is the key word," Silver says, as Emily makes a U-turn and then drives into a small opening that is almost invisible.

The house is almost totally camouflaged by huge trees and plants that all but hide the long, yellowish wooden house that takes up two entire lots. Silver finally clicks off her phone as the two women jump from the truck at the same moment and all but race up a set of steps, cross a wooden walkway and are greeted by a limping woman and a large barking golden retriever who must have heard them slam the truck doors.

Dr. Ruth Streeter greets them as if they are old friends, hobbles to the living room chair where she is recovering from knee surgery, and assures them that the dog is just a big, hairy beast that will lick them to death before he would ever consider taking a bite out of them.

During the next hour, while both Silver and Emily rotate their eyes constantly around the living room, trying to guess what was and wasn't there when Marjorie sat in the same room, the lovely, open, and gracious Ruth tells them how her mother, Mary Elizabeth Streeter, purchased the home in 1989. Ruth, an oncologist, inherited it when her mother died and has been happily entertaining occasional Rawlings devotees ever since. Silver stops her and wants to know if she gets a lot of visitors.

Ruth says that most people are serious fans and respect her privacy and already know that the house is not a public museum. But occasionally someone is rude, expects her to come to the door during dinnertime, or be shown through the house simply because he or she pulled into the driveway. She shifts her bum leg, settles back into her big chair, and tells them it's funny they asked that question because a week or so ago, when she was out of town, a man was pestering the neighbors to let them into her house.

"Did he ever show up?" Emily asks, as Silver immediately excuses herself to go call Getts.

"I never saw him, and the dog and my husband are pretty darn good watchdogs," Ruth says with a laugh. "There's nothing to steal in here but memories, and if he ever does come back I'll run him off just like Marjorie would have. I can't even imagine anyone being crazy enough to cross her."

Silver is gone for a long time and Emily, whose blood pressure is now about as elevated as half the world's authors, finally helps Ruth hop to her feet so she can exercise her leg by giving a tour. When they swing through the living room to the far bedroom, Emily can see Silver on the front porch gesturing with her hands and pacing. This is not a good sign, but she feigns happiness and follows Ruth to what was once Marjorie's bedroom and bathroom, as Ruth explains how it was important for her mother to keep the house as close to the way it was when Marjorie lived there as possible.

She's explaining how there's only been minimal remodeling and how the house really needs to be sold to someone who also understands the importance of place and preservation, when Silver rejoins them.

"Everything okay?" Emily asks.

"Yes," Silver lies. Emily can tell and has to restrain herself from grabbing her by the neck. "Just checking in with the boss, but I don't want to miss this once-in-a-lifetime chance."

Silver is glaring at Emily. She wants to yell, "Focus on the moment! This is where greatness lived. Marjorie looked out these same windows and her feet touched this floor and this is an opportunity that you do not want to lose by worrying about what Getts told me."

Ruth, to her credit, ignores their non-verbal exchange and shows them the stack of Rawlings books that are on Marjorie's old bookshelf, the green and blue tiled fireplace where Marjorie warmed her feet in winter, and the remodeled kitchen where the author surely spent hours messing with her recipes and occasionally turning to watch a flock of birds head out to sea.

Emily stands by the kitchen window in silence while Ruth and Silver talk about cooking. She remembers a photo taken from this very spot that she saw in the library. Marjorie was sitting at a table, a cigarette in her hand, stacks of papers and books surrounding her as she wrote. Emily raises her fingers to the window and feels the cool glass and imagines that Marjorie must have leaned her head against it when she was thinking or needed a break. The kitchen still has remnants of what Marjorie might have looked at while she worked. There's a red and white brick fireplace standing against one wall that still works, and although the counters have been replaced, the sink, refrigerator and cabinets are in the same areas.

Silver and Ruth have walked into the room adjacent to the kitchen that Norton added as an office for Marjorie, and Ruth apologizes because the room has changed and is now used as a bedroom. It's when they step outside and see the sweeping view of the ocean, the horizon stretching to the other side of the world, and feel the rush of the wind rocking up the sand dunes and onto the long porch that both Silver and Emily feel the true spirit of Marjorie.

"Oh my God," Silver says, walking to the edge of the porch. "This view is amazing. It's breathtaking."

Ruth finds her way to a comfy chair, sits down, and is smiling. She understands what the view can do to a person's heart and soul, and she sits quietly while Silver and Emily take it all in.

There's a long trail of white puffy clouds strung together by tiny dots that looks as if they are occasionally tinted as blue as the sky that they are floating through. The waves pounding against the long, equally as white beach, are a constant reminder of the power of nature. The long green strands of grass that hold all the sand in place appears to be waving to all the passing birds. It's a rustic, powerful scene that must have been as inspiring to Marjorie as the long rows of orange trees and the thick forest across from her Cross Creek writing porch.

The women stand like that for a very long time, and they leave Ruth sitting in the sun and eventually say their good-byes and let themselves out through the front door. Silver all but runs down the long set of concrete steps that lead from the top of the house and down through a brightly-tiled concrete archway, but something makes Emily hesitate when she gets to the first step and pushes back the green tangled vines that she must pull back before she can descend.

Silver is already to the truck and is shouting at Emily to hurry so she can tell her what Getts has finally dared to share, before he sees them in person. But Emily can't move.

She has one hand on the metal railing and both feet on the third step when she realizes something that makes her knees buckle. These are the steps that Marjorie fell down the day she was supposed to have died.

# 24

*"It took me so very long to acknowledge this important life truth: the second you think you have everything figured out a strong wind will come along and blow all your notions, and perhaps even your own rear-end, right out to hell and back."*
—*Lost Hearts in the Swamp of Life* - MKR - 1963

The swearing starts when Emily is shifting from second into third gear and wishes out loud that Silver's truck had twelve gears so that by the time she was done shifting they'd be back at Silver's house where they could interrogate Getts until dawn. Instead, they have the winding back-roads that run from Crescent Beach to Cross Creek and beyond. They have open windows and no one but each other to hear their garbled arguments. They have the wind in their hair from the same beach the serenaded Marjorie through the writing of several books. They have the feel of her walls on their fingertips, the view from every window memorized, and a half-ass story from Getts who refused to elaborate until he saw the whites of their eyes.

"Well, pardon me, but that is just bullshit!" Emily says as the truck slips into third.

"He's not going to tell us anything until we get there, okay? He said he talked to Brett's mom and he said that Brett checked into a cabin that's, like, less than a mile from my house, like I told you—and that's it, that's all I know, for God's sake."

"So, we could go talk to Ruth's neighbors or something…" Emily is trying to remember look in the rearview mirror before she makes a series of right turns and heads west as quickly as possible.

"We are not cops!" Silver cuts her off because she's pissed off that she's not a cop and she had the exact same idea. Get more information from Ruth. Swing by the neighbors. Go through the underwear drawers. Whatever in the hell it took- but then again, they aren't cops.

"I know, but this is so frustrating," Emily has a tinge of anger riding up her spine and she thinks about pulling over and firing Silver's pistol into the bushes. "I mean, shit. Do you realize we were just in Rawlings heaven? It's like we are allowed to look at the candy but not taste any of it. I wanted to stay there for a week and sit in every room and ask Ruth a thousand questions. She was so damn sweet and nice to us, and how amazing that her mom was such a huge fan and taught literature, and that Ruth understands how important it is to keep the house. That place must be worth millions now. Sweet hell, Marjorie would laugh her ass off if she knew that."

Which is what Silver starts to do as Emily is talking and swearing and going on and on about St. Augustine and Crescent Beach and what in the world Getts could possibly have discovered that he doesn't want to share over the phone. She laughs so long and hard that Emily almost pulls over to make certain she's okay, but when she slows the truck Silver waves her left hand and says, "No, go, I'm fine, you-you-you're acting like Marjorie."

This notion, as Emily's taking a corner as she's doing fifty and forgets to downshift, just like she did all those years ago with her father, brings the truck onto it's two right tires which throws Silver, even in her seatbelt, almost onto her lap.

The truck drops back onto all four wheels and Emily stops in the middle of the road, the two women look at each other, and Emily can only think to say, "Holy shit, can you image doing this drunk, like she did?"

The unspoken *she* being Marjorie, who they know wrecked more cars than fifty average females, or males, in a lifetime. *She* being the woman they seem to be chasing down the shaded highway. *She* being the woman, who would be dead now, regardless of what happened on those concrete steps, unless she had a miracle drug to help her live past one hundred. *She* being the gift that has not only brought them together but who they both know is changing their lives in ways that will unfold for years and decades to come.

They sit in the road staring at each other and only half listening for the sound of approaching cars for one, two and then three minutes until Emily nods her head, shifts into first and starts slowly down the highway.

It takes another fifteen minutes for someone to speak, and it's Emily, talking so softly that Silver quickly rolls up her window so she won't miss a word.

"No one's going to believe us. I think we could tell this story, even as it's still unfolding, to the entire world and a few people would believe it, especially if we told your true story, but people would laugh at us. The thing is, I don't really give a shit if they laugh. I don't give a shit if people think I'm a washed up middle-aged whatever who wrote those pages by myself. I could care less if the academic and professional world revokes my tiny degree and re-evaluates every single piece of work I've ever documented. Marjorie didn't give a shit. She lived and wrote and followed her heart and she dared to believe in herself. She cared about herself and she knew that her work had to be done, no matter how hard, or what the world said, and that kind of courage is a powerful thing. You have the same kind of courage Silver, you do, and I am just a damn little baby."

Emily stops to take a breath and when she looks over she notices that Silver is crying. Her tears have left long streaks in her beautiful black skin and the tears are dripping off her face and forming a sweet river that has dampened the front of her shirt. Emily reaches over and catches a handful of tears and then gently wipes the left side of Silver's face.

"Oh, Silver. Don't cry!"

"Why not?" Silver says, sobbing so sweetly that Emily can't help but cry too.

"This is all good, what we have found, what might all come of it, whatever in the hell Getts tells us. One of us said something, Christ, a year ago it seems, that remarkable women aren't just remarkable for what they do, but for how they live. You live boldly, Silver. Marjorie did the same thing. Words are powerful tools, but so are actions."

Silver can't speak now. So many thoughts and choices and memories are rolling through her mind that she couldn't stop crying if someone held her own gun to her head.

Emily is now driving with one hand and she's keeping the truck in third gear. Her father would have a heart attack because the transmission sounds as if it's farting out screws and bolts. Her other hand is holding Silver's so tightly that Silver's arm is turning red.

Emily speaks in a whisper. She speaks for miles and miles as Silver cries out her past and parts of her present, and what might be tomorrow. She talks about ghosts and inspiration and how one woman's actions can ricochet down from generation to generation and be a powerful force that collects the spirits of other women who need a gentle push-or perhaps in her case, a shove over the side of a steep cliff. She imagines that Marjorie did die and came back as a blessed spirit to help random women who understand the importance of words and place and items like old fireplaces and the view from the writing table. She imagines that there could be more boxes of manuscripts and that Leslie knew so much more than she shared before she got so ill that she could no longer speak. She imagines that if people could have listened and watched and waited, that they would have been kinder to Marjorie, and given her more space and that she would have maybe done the same thing to herself. She imagines that Marjorie was so bold and so brave as to fake her death down those steep hard steps and that her beloved husband loved her so much that he let go of what they had and made something new.

This last sentence throws Silver into a much deeper and longer valley of tears. Emily lets her cry, because she knows now what she is thinking. She knows that Silver is wondering if she is strong enough to reverse her long-ago choice and re-create her life yet again.

And Emily is correct, and so is Silver, in thinking that Marjorie's magic has touched them both in such a remarkable way that even if she did die back in 1953, she will never really be dead at all.

By the time the women stagger out of the truck in front of Silver's house twenty minutes later, they both look as if they have been drug behind a tractor and they have agreed that they have not yet finished with what they will call the rest of their lives the Third-Gear, Daddy-Be-Damned Talk.

Getts has followed them down the highway and they don't even know it. When they pull into Silver's driveway and start swearing all over again because he's not there, he immediately drives up behind them and they disappear in a cloud of dust.

When he finally turns off his car and walks toward them all he sees are their backsides and all he hears is a litany of the words they were uttering as they headed back home. "Shit! Damn it! What the hell?"

"Girls! Your language!" he shouts emerging from the dust as if he's a living mirage. "I thought you'd never get here."

Silver takes one look at him and melts. She walks into his arms and he embraces her and then looks at Emily as if to say, "What happened?" Silver is melting into him and he raises his arms and begins rubbing her back and murmuring into her magnificent long hair.

Emily watches for a few moments and then quietly asks if Auggie is here. The sheriff shakes his head and says that she worked all day and that she called to say she wouldn't bother coming back out if they were coming home. Then Emily turns away and slouches toward the front door, hoping they will get on with it and let her in so she can use the restroom, and then find out what he has to say to them.

Silver gets the hint and asks him to unlock the front door, which she never carries a key for because it's usually never locked, and after the dogs are petted, fed and watered, they find Getts pacing in the kitchen.

It takes a few minutes for them to decide who should go first, and Getts realizes it's ridiculous to argue. Two against one in this house will never get him very far. Before he can start, Emily has the good sense to ask him if he's on or off duty.

"Off," he says with a very large sigh.

"Then unbutton your shirt, set down that silly gun thing, turn off your pager or whatever it is so they know you are off duty and sit down while I make you a drink."

"What happened to you?" he asks, without bothering to look at Silver.

"Oh crap, not much. We spent a lot of time in the library. Saw tons of great stuff. Slept in the Marjorie room. Meet the world's greatest historian, who actually was one of Norton's best friends, looked out the windows of her beach house and saw where she was supposed to have had a fatal spell right outside her back door, and then we had an epiphany in the car that has forever changed-or is about to change-our lives." Emily says all of this with a straight face as she rummages in the cupboards for three clean glasses.

Getts shrugs his shoulders and says, "Oh, thank God. I thought something remarkable happened. You both seem a bit... what's the word here? Um... changed? Exhausted? Crazy as hell?"

Silver slaps his arm. Emily smiles and finds the glasses, and something that she assumes is whiskey in a crystal decanter. Getts looks first at Emily then Silver, holds out his hand, sits down and begins to talk.

First, he says they must let him tell his story and then they can ask him questions. They both nod yes, sit down at the table beside him, and he starts with the release of Brett who they know disappeared shortly after that. Only he really didn't disappear. He drove ten miles down the road, found the first, and perhaps the most remote, fishing cabin in the area, and until Getts ran into the owner at the gas station, he was pretty much hiding in plain sight. He's been nowhere since. He hasn't caused any problems, and unfortunately Getts has been too busy to check on him.

Silver has her mouth open and is about to say something when Getts throws his left hand over her face and without saying a word shakes the pointer finger of his right hand back and forth.

Emily doesn't flinch as he apologizes for not being able to watch Brett and because he is still short-staffed having someone else sneak around to keep an eye on him won't work. Getts also says he didn't want to have to explain to anyone why they were going overboard to watch a tourist with a drinking problem. So the bottom line of the Brett story is that no one really knows why he's still around, and Auggie hasn't seen him or heard the dogs barking, but she's also worked some extra hours and has barely been back and forth to sleep a few hours and take care of the dogs.

Getts says he came past the house several times and all he saw was Emily's car parked like a good soldier guarding the front yard. He let the dogs out twice, because Auggie's been locking them inside so they don't lope off after the deer herd or a bear or a flock of wild birds.

He stops to take a sip of his drink and then looks first at Emily, then Silver. "I don't suppose you found any clues or solid evidence that would help us figure out why he's still here?"

"Not really," Emily says. "There are stacks and stacks of material in the library, and we have the same feelings we had

before we left that it's possible she didn't die and that the manuscripts we found are genuine."

Silver forgoes a sip and gulps instead, and can't help herself. "We also realize that we could want this so much that
someone might have us committed. We don't know for certain if Marjorie wrote those pages, but we have a feeling, you
know?"

"Ah!" Getts says with obvious amusement. "A feeling. So
nothing concrete popped up, but we do have this probable living heir prowling around, don't we?"

Silver and Emily put their glasses down and glare at him.
"Probable?" they both ask at the same time.

Getts shifts in his seat and tells them something they wish
they would have known before they left for Gainesville and St.
Augustine. He found Brett's birth mother, or rather his contact
in New Jersey found her, and through a series of missed calls
and a bit of begging he finally talked to her. Brett was indeed
adopted shortly after his birth. Getts stops for a moment and
looks at both women.

"You know this is all personal information and that she
spoke to me because I'm a law enforcement official, but I was
lying a bit in order to get her to even talk with me," he admits.
"So we will not be taking out an ad in the *Tampa Bay Times*
about this, now will we?"

Both women shake their heads. They've been doing a bit
of lying themselves.

Brett was adopted because his birth mother, the woman
Getts talked to briefly, was not in a financial or emotional position to raise a child as an unmarried woman. She did what
she thought was best, not just for her, but for her son as well.
She moved on, grieved, never forgot about him but honored

the adoption agency's rules that did not allow her access to records or contact unless her son initiated it.

That happened three years ago without any warning, when Brett simply showed up where she works. He wanted to know who his father was, and his birth mother had no idea.

"What?" Emily and Silver say the same word again at the exact same moment.

"First of all, we only talked for about ten minutes, and secondly, she was not eager to share anything in those ten minutes and I had to pry what I did out of her," Getts explains. "She was never sure who the father was because she was sleeping around. She was at loose ends. She was a mess, but when I asked her if any of the men had the last name of Kinnan she said no, but then again, maybe."

"Well, this tells us nothing," Silver says. "What about the adopted mother? Isn't she the one we're supposed to be talking to?"

The sheriff looks up and the women can tell what's coming next is not happy news.

"She died, and so did his adopted father. His life the past few years sounds like a tragedy ripped right out of the front pages. A car accident for the father, and breast cancer for the mom. No siblings. He apparently took an emotional nose dive and there are so many unanswered questions that I for one am thinking that we could spend the rest of our lives trying to find all of the answers."

The three of them start throwing all the unanswered questions out on the table. Wouldn't he have money from his parent's estate? Is there a chance there was no money, or there was money and he spent it all very quickly, as young people are apt to do? Did he discover the letter from Marjorie to Francis after they died, or was it something perhaps his mother shared when she knew she was going to die? Why did he change his name to Kinnan? If Marjorie pulled a Silver and disappeared, doesn't it make sense that she'd trust very few people with her? Leslie? What did she really know?

Silver is frustrated and still on an emotional ledge from her discussion during the ride home. Her impatience is showing and it's not pretty. She's thumping her fingers on the table, clenching her jaw, and her idea is not going to go over well, especially with the sheriff.

"Let's just drive over there to the damn fish camp and talk to him, honey. This has gone on long enough. Why can't we just ask him?"

"It sounds logical, I totally agree," Getts says, throwing his hand over Silver's noisy fingers. "But I could get into trouble because I've crossed about fifty inappropriate lines already, and now we're drinking and I'm going to be really brave here and say something that may upset both of you."

"Great," Silver snarls, pulling back her hand.

"Spill it," Emily says, acting as if she doesn't care.

Getts inhales as if it might be his last breath, sets down his glass, closes his eyes as if he's gathering up some courage, opens them and then looks mostly at Silver.

"Maybe we should just stop. Maybe it's time to just see this as a dead-end treasure hunt and let it all go," he says. "Sometimes you can want something so bad that it's hard to see what's real, and what isn't real. It's sort of like Cinderella's evil stepsisters trying to jam their feet into those tiny shoes. It's just not going to happen."

Silver looks as is she's just been stabbed in the heart. "Cinderella?"

Getts acts like he didn't hear Silver. "I spent some time last night after work reading up about Marjorie. After that lawsuit, it's as if she hated this area, and she went to Crescent Beach and then bought another house in New York. She struggled and her writing struggled and she didn't take very good care of herself."

He stops talking and Emily and Silver aren't moving. He's also stopped looking at Silver altogether and has his eyes fixed on the wall behind both women.

"I know you have those boxes with the writing and I know Brett had that letter, and I know that he probably knows more than we think he does, but what would finding out that she never died in 1953 change, or prove? My gut instinct tells me that sometimes it's the best thing to let sleeping dogs lie. And... well, hell, I'm worried about both of you running around like you have been and just damn, can we stop now? Please, can we get back to what it was like before all of this?"

Outside it's as if the world has suddenly come to a halt. The trees have stopped moving, the dogs must be slumped on the back porch because the sound of their toenails tapping as they run up and down the steps has vanished. There's an eerie stillness that's settled over everything and forced its way under the front door and into the kitchen as well.

Emily is afraid to move. She feels as if her heart has just dropped down past her knees and that if she hadn't thrown away her road map and turned off the main highway none of this would be happening. Getts would probably be loung-ing in his boxer shorts. Silver would be heating up leftovers, especially if you are bold enough to seize a grand day and get lost. Auggie might stop by after work for a drink and a chat on the porch. She'd be back in Ohio thinking about returning to work in a few days and everything would be just the way it's supposed to be.

Which would be absolutely horrible.

Silver is staring straight ahead and Emily is thinking she should excuse herself after she apologizes for ruining everything. Before she has a chance to say anything Silver turns slowly to Getts and asks him to leave.

He looks stunned. "You want me to leave?"

"Yes. I'm so goddamned angry I might hurt you and ruin everything, so it's best that you leave." Silver has both hands around her glass and Emily can see that her fingers are turning white because she's clenching it so tightly.

Getts isn't moving but something is passing between him and Silver that is palpable. "It's not what you think," he whispers.

Silver shakes her head back and forth and then closes her eyes and motions with her hand for him to go.

Emily feels like she did when she was a little girl and she accidentally walked in and heard her mother and father arguing. She would throw her hands over her ears, try and back out of the room, and make believe she was invisible. That's exactly what she wants to do now. But when she tries to get up, Silver reaches out, grabs her arm, and forces her to stay.

By the time Getts has picked up his gun belt and car keys, looked longingly at Silver, lowered his head and then slipped out the door, the wind has picked up and the dogs have scurried around the side of the house to bark their goodbyes to the back end of the police cruiser.

Befuddled, Emily sits and waits. A few minutes pass and then she gets up, refills their glasses, sits back down and asks Silver what just happened.

"He's scared," she says, tipping her glass so that the ice cubes clink. "We talked when we were at the library and I told him that Marjorie was inspiring me and that I was thinking of revealing my true identity. There's a part of me that's re-awakened since you've come into my life, Ohio. I'm thinking about travel, and setting up workshops. I want to build the Leslie museum and spin the literary world in a circle by telling my real story, and he's terrified that if that happens, he'll lose me."

"Oh, Silver!"

"I'm pissed that he doesn't trust what we have," she shares, pausing to take a drink. "He needs to think and I'm not about to sit here and prove to him how much I love him. I'm not a teenager, for God's sake. You and I will figure this manuscript business out ourselves. Everything will be okay. I know it."

Silver reassures Emily that she's not to blame for what's just happened. She gets up, walks into the living room and comes back with two CDs that she holds in front of her.

"I had Auggie pick up the movie *Cross Creek* and the original movie *The Yearling* that was partially filmed on Marjorie's property. I'm going to throw a frozen pizza in the oven and we're going to watch these and try to figure out what to do next, yes?"

Emily has a vague memory of watching *Cross Creek* back in the 1980s. Mary Steenburgen played Marjorie, Rip Torn was in it, and so was Peter Coyote. Halfway through the movie, Emily confesses that she's not just worried about Silver and Getts but about the fact that she's going to have to leave in a few days. It's hard to come up with a plan that has a satisfactory ending.

"Just watch the movie," Silver orders sweetly, leaning over to pat her feet.

"Good idea," Emily agrees, and before she knows it she's sobbing as the little boy in *The Yearling* pines away for something that he can call his own, something he can love, something that Emily can relate to as if she were the little boy herself.

Emily watches the movie not just to follow the story line, however. Both women are looking at the trees and swamps and some of the extras in the movie who they know were neighbors and friends of Marjorie. They know that portions of the movie were filmed on and near her property and both of them expect to catch a glimpse of her slithering through the tall grass and laughing at the absurdity of cameras and make-up artists mingled with the wild palms and terrified raccoons.

Thirty minutes later, they pause the movie and both run to the restroom. "Hurry," Silver yells as she jogs into her private bathroom. "Bring tissue too, I think the rest of the movie's a real tear jerker." Five seconds later Silver hears Emily scream and comes flying into her room with her pants unzipped.

"The boxes are gone," Emily yells. "Someone took all of the boxes!"

# 25

*"It would be so easy to lie, so that others might not be as terrified of life as they should be, but that doesn't help a soul. The truth of it all is that risk is part of the package. You can sit there watching the daylight fade and wonder what you might have seen if you would have gotten off the chair, or you can plunge into that first hint of morning light and stop being such a baby. Every day is a grand day to get lost and see what happens. Life is hard, but it's also a hell of a lot of fun."*
—*Lost Hearts in the Swamp of Life* - MKR - 1963

In a brief moment of denial, Emily thinks the missing boxes might be the end of it all. Now she'll simply sit back down on the couch, curl her legs underneath her and watch as Mary Steenburgen whips up a glorious life in the wilderness while she beds Peter Coyote and digs a few ditches. The pizza would burn in the oven and Silver would force her to eat it anyway and wash it down with a few beers. Then they would launch into a long discussion about how Marjorie might feel if she were still alive when the movie was released.

"She would laugh her ass off," Silver might say. "I don't think half of this stuff happened this way."

"Well, the spirit of her brazenness comes across," Emily would say in defense of the movie she remembers as inspiring the first time she watched it. "She seems a little crazy, a little fun, a little drunk, a little inspired, a little ahead of her time."

"Hell, Marjorie didn't even look like that skinny actress!"

"But the farm and the house seem close to the real thing."

They would go on and on and maybe watch the movie twice, but that's not what happens. What happens is that they both run all over the house looking for the boxes. They look under beds, in the kitchen pantry, in all of the closets and in Silver's surprisingly tidy office. They go outside and look in the storage shed, in Emily's car, and then they walk around the house looking for footprints and end up on the back porch.

The dogs are the only living things enjoying the search. They've obviously missed their human companions the past few days and when Silver and Emily bound up the back porch steps and the three dogs follow with tennis balls in their mouths, Silver has to apologize because she has no time for the tennis ball game.

"Shit," Silver says, pushing her face into her hands and then looking up at Emily. "The boxes were in your room. You left them there, right?"

"Yes!" Emily's heart is pounding so fast that she's out of breath. "They were on the floor and if I remember correctly, the papers were all over the place. Remember? We were reading when Getts called and we took off for Gainesville. We left everything on the floor. Didn't we?"

Silver nods her head and then turns around without saying a word and opens the back door.

Emily turns to follow her but then stops before she gets off the porch. "Silver, did you unlock the back door before we came outside?"

"No. Did you?"

"No."

Silver has already called Auggie by the time Emily has reluctantly thrown three tennis balls off the porch that had been dropped on her feet. Silver's on hold and pacing in the kitchen. Emily wants to lie down on the floor and have someone throw a blanket over her so that she'll disappear. Instead she goes back into her bedroom one more time to make certain she's not losing what's left of her mind. The floor is as bare as it was just a few minutes ago. She opens up the top dresser drawer to see if anyone has rummaged through her clothes but nothing looks disturbed. She's hidden the gold jewelry in the second drawer, and she's relieved when she finds it.

Emily can hear Silver talking and she spins in a circle, closes her eyes, and tries to imagine someone sneaking in through the back door without the dogs either licking them to death or scaring them away with their barking. Then again, if it was Brett who walked in and helped himself to the boxes, he'd know enough to bring dog treats or a few tennis balls. The dogs were probably inside the house if and when he came back.

She turns and walks to the front window where she was inspired just days ago to start thinking of herself as a literary archaeologist. Right now she feels like a literary fool. There's her car sitting out there like a flashing neon light. *Here's where the stupid woman from Ohio who discovered the manuscripts has parked her car. She's not home. So come on in, and help yourself.*

Emily now realizes that perhaps they were too naive about Brett and his capabilities. There was something oddly comforting about the boxes stacked up in her room. Emily loved leaning over and knowing that they were there. The yellowed edges were ragged and running her fingers over the raised typewritten letters made her feel connected to whomever it was who wrote them. It wasn't just the link to the past that excited her but the thrill of the mystery, the unknown author, the inspiration behind the creation. Several times when she was reading the manuscript she felt as if she could almost picture who had done the writing.

Emily leans against the window and feels a rush of sadness that surprises her. What if the boxes are lost forever? What if they've been destroyed, or are already halfway to New Jersey or Pittsburg or God knows where in someone's moldy trunk?

There's a sharp pain that is moving from the center of her stomach and up towards her heart that is turning into a long burning ache. Emily turns and sits down on the side of her bed and for a few moments can't bear to accept the fact that the boxes are gone. One part of her is totally devastated, and the other part of her is angry. How dare someone take her treasure! And Emily has come to think of it as her treasure, her ticket to a destination that doesn't yet have a name or an address.

Emily can hear Silver either yelling at Auggie, Getts, the dogs or all three. She hunches over to pull herself off the bed and sees something lying under the radiator. She bends down and fishes a bright green book of matches off the floor, flips it over, reads "Judson Fish Camp", and then wonders how long the matches have been hiding down there. She slips the matches into her pocket and arrives back in the kitchen just in time to see Silver hang up the phone.

"You look as if you might cry," Silver tells her.

"I might. What did Auggie say?"

"She left the door unlocked. She feels horrible, and she's handing off her last three appointments and rushing over here. I didn't try and stop her, because I'm thinking of smacking her upside the head."

"Shouldn't we call Getts?"

It's amazing how Silver's beautiful dark skin can turn almost as red as a ripe apple. "No, we cannot call Getts, and I don't want you to underestimate how pissed off I am at him."

Emily pauses, fishes out the matches, starts playing with them and nods her head because she's still wrangling with her own emotions. Something serious must have gone down during those library phone calls. It's so easy to assume that we know about a person's life and relationships by simply looking at them. Of course Silver and Getts' lives must be complicated not just by Silver's life, but also by his. Silver's past must call to her more than occasionally and it can't be easy to deal with the day-to-day stress of police work. And then there's wondering what might have been or what could be again. Who doesn't think like that?

Silver is still fuming. Emily feels at a loss for words mostly because she's pretty certain Silver's not going to listen to her anyway. In reality, Silver's a lot more like Marjorie than she is- feisty, determined, certain, and right now she looks as if she could kill a bear without having to use the gun in her purse.

"Stop looking at me like that," Silver barks. "This is what I get like when I'm angry and I don't know what in the hell to do about it. Let's do one thing at a time here. We have to find those boxes. Getts is in second place right now."

"But haven't we been robbed?"

"Well, think about what the report would look like. Two, or make that three, crazy women, worried about some boxes, who have been driving all over hell and back to find someone who died in 1953? If anyone's going to call me crazy it's ain't going to be the those fools who work with Getts. So we figure this out. We are women. We are smart. We are beyond able to handle this mess."

"We are also very stubborn." Emily doesn't smile when she says this.

"Yes, that is the truth, but your girlfriend Marjorie wouldn't have called for help, now would she?" Silver is clearly possessed. Emily can now understand why she was able to pack up and leave all those years ago and create an entirely new world and life for herself. Irritated, Silver suddenly grabs for the matches in Emily's hands and says, "What are you playing with?"

"A book of matches. These are rare up where I live but I've seen them all over the place in this part of the country. Then again, you can smoke inside of a church down here."

Silver looks at the match cover and then back at Emily. "Where did you get these?"

Emily tells her and then Silver explains that she cleaned the floors on her hands and knees just before Emily came. She sometimes does that when she's trying to work and nothing seems to be happening.

"You clean when you have writer's block?" There is no end to the surprises this woman can produce.

Silver can't take her eyes off the matches. She ignores Emily's question and tells her there's no way the matches were in that bedroom when she wiped up the floor. They both deduce that if someone had the matches in a pocket and bent over, say to pick up cardboard boxes and steal them, the matches could have fallen out.

And yes, Silver knows where the Judson Fish Camp is located. She also knows from snooping in Getts' logbook that it's where a man who has no intention of fishing or duck hunting is temporarily living.

His name is Brett Kinnan.


There's obviously a strict protocol in this part of the world for stalking people during the night. Who knew? Emily feels as if she's going on a six-month safari and she's thinking about leaving a final note in case something horrible happens to her during what she's been told might take twenty-four to forty-eight hours.

Emily wonders if something is not wrong with her for agreeing to do what she is about to do. Silver was like a caged animal until Auggie showed up. She paced in the kitchen, talked out loud about finding the tent, filling the cooler, stocking up, feeding the dogs, and preparing for something that sounded like a siege.

And yet, she couldn't say no.

The missing boxes were driving her half-crazy. She knew how to preserve them, how to make certain that the already yellowed pages didn't become brittle, how to examine the boxes, match the type style, delicately test to see what made the stains on the pages, how to check for fingerprints and even, as silly as it might sound, read between the lines.

Emily's aching heart has not receded and that is why she has been unable to run screaming from Silver's house and call in reinforcements. Instead, Auggie squealed into the driveway, spitting gravel all over the dogs, who had to run for cover. Auggie apologized for five solid minutes, she found out that Silver was not speaking to Getts, the dogs had most likely been seduced with cheap dog treats, and that Silver knew where Brett was staying. After that the plan they concocted seemed like a no-brainer, and took three minutes to design.

*The plan:*

*1. Have Auggie call the fishing camp and ask if Brett is staying there. Make up some story about medication or the hospital or some damn thing.*

*2. Locate all the camping gear as quickly as possible.*

*3. Put it all in Silver's truck, and oh yes, food, bring food. Maybe just a little alcohol in various forms as well.*

*4. Feed and water the alleged guard dogs and let them run wild to pay for their sins.*

*5. Dress accordingly.* (Emily had no idea what this meant.)

*6. Act as if you are one of three women going camping in the rustic campground adjacent to the fishing camp.*

*7. Do not forget the bug spray.*

*8. Do not forget the gaff hook.*

*9. Do not forget Silver's pistol.*

*10. Do not forget to lock the doors.*

The list was actually written down on a piece of paper and the truck was packed before Emily dared to ask what the appropriate attire might be. Jeans, shorts, shirt, jacket, bandana or head covering, socks, shoes, boots, anything black. As if Emily had this stuff in her small suitcase.

She rummages through her bag and finds jeans and a t-shirt and then quickly paws through the bags of clothing she has taken from Leslie's house, and picks out a bulky sweater, a moth-eaten jacket, a black felt hat, and what appears to be a man's dark blue buttoned-down shirt with pockets in front that the computer geeks seem to still love to wear.

They caravan to the campsite, with Auggie following Silver and Emily, in case she has an emergency call and needs to leave. This short ride gives Emily a chance to try and get a grasp on exactly what in God's name they are going to try and do.

Silver looks at her sideways as if she has just asked her something insane. Then she keeps driving and talks very slowly, as if Emily doesn't understand English.

"We are going to set up our camp next to the fishing cabins. Then one of us is going to sneak around and see if he's in there. Then we are going to wait it out and hope he leaves to get more beer or cigarettes or food or anything. Then we are going to go into the cabin and take back what belongs to us."

Emily thinks the plan is ridiculous, but there she is in her hot jeans, wearing a baseball cap, and trusting someone like she has not trusted someone in perhaps forever. Is that the missing link of her life? The inability to allow someone else to guide and instruct her, to help her move forward, to tell her what to do and how to do it and then to show her the way? Emily chooses to sit silently and think about this as they make a series of turns down unmarked roads, not even highways or streets really, until they are bumping along a dirt road that is littered with holes and rocks and not surprisingly, a variety of dead animals who must have been crazy to think they could cross the road and not get killed.

Holding on to the handgrips in the ceiling it's impossible for Emily not to feel as if she's looking out from Marjorie Rawl-

ings own eyes. Once the first glance of loveliness had vanished after she had first arrived here, here being less than
twenty miles away for God's sake, she must have felt like a
captive in many ways. First by the land itself, which has a
power that is uncontrollable, and then by the people who had
suddenly become her neighbors. She needed them to survive, to show her which roads to take, how to plant and where
to plant, the ways of the swamps and river and the blazing
sun and oppressive humidity. And with all of that must have
come some sense of humility, an acknowledgement that she
needed them in ways that a brash, self-confident, modern
woman really needed no one.

Silver has the windows open and the lights on even
though it's still light outside and late afternoon. Auggie has
faded into a cloud of dust behind them. It's as if they are
slowly disappearing into a jungle and when Emily turns her
head the unmistakable scent of sweetness, the perfume she
smelled the very first day she stopped at the side of the road
and discovered the leaf in her car, fills up her senses and she
feels transported.

The foliage closes in on them so that branches and
leaves are whipping Emily's face when she leans in close to
the window. When she looks off into the distance she can't
see anything but a deep blending of green. Nothing is certain;
everything is black, mysterious, and frightening. Emily feels
herself slipping past the present and into a place where she is
suspended, where uncertainty is a given, where she must surrender to a possibility that perhaps has always existed, and
that she has never before acknowledged.

She tips her head out the window, closes her eyes, breathes
in the damp scented air and wraps her heart around the notion

of falling and trust and most of all, risk. She wills her entire being to walk into the jungle as a follower and not a leader and to see what happens. Emily pulls her cap down another half an inch and the moment she does, a gust of wind slaps her face as if to say, "What took you so long?" She smiles, opens her eyes, and sees lights flickering at the end of the road.

"Almost there," Silver shouts, as the engine roars them past a series of holes that look as if they could swallow an entire house.

"We're sure he's here?"

"Auggie confirmed it."

"Let's do it, then," Emily says.

Silver looks at her with her head tilted, down shifts, turns right past a small sign that says *Primitive Camping*, and then the road all but disappears as they head even deeper into the heart of the jungle. There is absolutely no one else crazy enough to be camping when they can be inside watching television, sitting in front of a low fan, and eating a nice warm dinner.

An hour later they have set up the tent, positioned the lanterns, sprayed the living hell out of each other with high-octane bug repellent, gathered firewood, positioned the vehicles for a quick getaway and donned long-sleeved shirts to discourage the hungry insects. It's now time to decide who is going to sneak through the woods to see what Bret is doing in the cabin with the stolen boxes.

"Well, for God's sake, I'm black," Silver argues. "Ohio is nothing but a skinny-ass white girl and you, Auggie, you are a big-boned Caucasian with questionable heredity who would stand out like a floodlight on a night like this."

"I can do it," Auggie says. "You are not the most nimble person in the world."

Emily doesn't even try to volunteer. The argument is over before it has begun and within ten seconds Silver has disappeared into the night, and Emily and Auggie are left standing by the small fire, where they try not to worry. They have barely started a conversation when they hear Silver thrashing back towards them from the edge of the fish camp.

When she approaches, her hands are in the air, palms up, and she has a look of amazement on her face.

"He's reading!" she exclaims. "He's sitting on an old beat up couch, smoking, drinking beer and reading one page after another."

"Reading?" Auggie says as she throws a long on the fire.

"Yes. He looks about as menacing as an old shoe. There's not a gun in sight and because he's so engrossed I was able to walk around the entire cabin. His bag is packed as if he was ready to leave, and then decided to open one box and then started to read and couldn't stop."

"Does everything look okay?" Emily is terrified that something will happen to the papers and everything will be ruined.

"Nothing's been destroyed and the boxes are all sitting there behaving, if that's what you mean," Silver says. "I didn't expect this. I was ready to blaze in there and beat the shit out of him but now, now...let's think for a minute."

Auggie wants to know what he might be reading. She hasn't had a chance to look at any of the manuscripts, and Emily tells her about *Lost Hearts*, and before she can finish, Auggie chuckles and saying how that sounds like something Marjorie might write.

The wood pops and sizzles as all three women pull out campstools and circle the fire. It's gotten dark so fast that it's as if someone dropped a blanket over the entire world. When

Emily looks up she occasionally sees a set of wild white eyes blinking through the forest. Silver tells her it could be anything——a fox, raccoon, rabbits, even a wild hog or two. She also reassures her that none of the animals will approach or attack unless they are threatened. She says it's probably safer right where they are, in the middle of nowhere, than in every city in the world-even with Mr. Asshole next door.

The women sit and talk and decide that waiting is probably the best idea. Brett doesn't look as if he's going anywhere and maybe they'll figure out what to do sometime during the next eight-plus hours. Auggie, always the food queen, cooks up some frozen chili that she threw into the cooler. She soaps the bottom of a pan, clears a space on the coals and recruits Emily to keep stirring while she sets up bowls, crackers, and some vegetables on Silver's tailgate.

They've decided not to drink but cave in and have one beer each with the gut-burning chili, and just as they finish the sky opens up and is littered with more stars than Emily even knew existed. The air is still and within minutes a chorus of frogs starts singing so loudly it's as if they are sitting right next to the tent.

"Of course there's water here," Emily says. "It's a fish camp, there must be a lake?"

"It's a large section of the Ocklawaha River, with amazing holes for fishing," Silver says. "Back in the 30s and 40s, this camp was booked every single day of the year."

"Is there a pier out there?" Auggie asks, poking the coals down so the fire doesn't get too large.

"Yes, but it's a rickety old thing that sticks out halfway across the river. I was out there once years ago, and it's like floating in paradise. The fish jump, and the water is swirling and..."

Before she can finish Emily and Auggie are already getting up to make certain the fire won't spread, grabbing their jackets, ordering Silver to bring along her all-important purse and its contents because they are going to go sit on the pier. "Brett isn't going anywhere, and we can see the fire, the cars, and his door from the pier," Auggie says, as if she's done this a thousand times. "What can it hurt?"

They find one fairly dim flashlight, take two car blankets, and wobble through the woods, tiptoeing past an old rusty trailer, the backside of Brett's cabin, and a fish-cleaning shed before they step out onto the long wooden pier. The stars are so bright that Silver turns off her flashlight, the women stop for a moment to adjust their eyes, and then they creep to the very end where someone has built a new, and thankfully sturdy-looking, bench.

The night is Central Florida in all its glory. Bright sky, swirling water, the day's heat slowly fading into the soft cool arms of night. The stars are like reachable diamonds and the air feels like an open-air massage with every breath. Emily squeezes in between Silver and Auggie and for a long time no one has the strength or the audacity to say a word. There is no place like this on the face of the earth. No place at all.

Emily dares to speak first, talking in such a soft voice that Auggie and Silver lean into her and from behind it looks as if one very large person is sitting on the bench.

"She saw this, didn't she? She sat in a place just like this and watched these same stars and launched a canoe at midnight and imagined all the same worlds and times and places and people that we imagine?"

"Yes, she did," Silver whispers back.

"My God, she was brave and bold and so talented. Sometimes when I close my eyes, I see her driving past me like a bat out of hell, or casting her line across the weeds, or sitting on her porch with her maid, peeling potatoes and wondering which chicken they are going to kill for dinner."

Auggie laughs as quietly as a woman like Auggie can, and then reaches over to take Emily's hand, and then Emily reaches over to take Silver's hand. A huge white bird, spooked by another animal screeching across the river, leaps into the air and circles as the moon starts to rise above them.

"Oh my God!" they all say at once.

"This is almost ridiculous," Emily adds quickly. "But I'm thinking this is how it was. This beautiful moment, and right behind it danger lurking in the cabin, around the next bend, when the postman comes with a rejection letter or your agent calls with bad news."

"You nailed it, honey," Silver says.

There's a pause then as the bird disappears and the world is still again.

"Do you seriously think she could have done it?" Emily asks this and then tips back her head to focus on the stars.

Silver doesn't hesitate. "Without a doubt. Really, hello, here I am and I did the same thing."

"I'm not going to make a remark about how black you are and how I can't see you but I know you are there," Auggie says. "I have to say, if I was Marjorie Rawlings I would have scooped up Zora, found me a cabin like this, disappeared, and wrote and laughed in the sweet quiet until the day I really did die."

"Still," Emily says, sitting back up, "people will never believe us."

"Who gives a crap what other people think!" Silver says. "When we get the manuscripts back, isn't it your job to prove it's all real?"

Emily nods, forgetting they can't see her, and then leans into Silver and feels something in her shirt pocket crunch. She's wearing the old blue shirt she took out of one of Leslie's bags before she left the house. She sits up, reaches into the pocket and pulls out a crumpled and barely legible old cigarette package.

"Silver, turn on the flashlight for a second, okay?"

The light clicks on, Emily gently unrolls the brittle package, and stifles a shriek that would have frightened every bird within a twenty mile radius.

"What did you find?" Auggie asks.

With her voice shaking with emotion, she tells them it's an old Lucky Strike cigarette package.

"Where did you get that shirt?" Silver asks, already understanding the potential meaning of the old package.

Emily tells and them and tells Auggie that Marjorie was addicted to Lucky Strike cigarettes, in fact it's hard to find a photo of her when she's not smoking a cigarette.

"They just started making them again," Auggie says. "One of my old-fart clients told me, showed me his package, and said he started smoking them when he was eleven and now he can die smoking them."

Emily bends over to catch her breath and then holds the package up to the moon to make certain that it's real and that she hasn't imagined what she has just discovered.

"It could just be coincidence," she says. "But right this moment, I'm choosing to think it's not a coincidence, that this was Marjorie's and that we've been following a trail that will eventually lead us someplace…someplace wonderful."

Then she carefully slips the package back into the pocket so that she can keep it safe and dissect it properly as soon as possible. And suddenly there are no more questions, just the shimmering water, a flurry of anticipation and an endless string of stars that all three of the women wish could speak the truth of what happened below them all those years ago and then shout it out for the world to hear.

# 26

*"Good Lord! You think you know things and then just like the last eighty-mile-per-hour wind that tails a hurricane, something happens that you should expect, but do not. Something always happens and that something can either throw you back sixty paces or push you so far ahead that the rest of the world is nothing but a blur. That's why life is so exciting, and it is also why I drink every day, and occasionally stop to look in the mirror to see if I can recognize myself."*

—*Lost Hearts in the Swamp of Life* - MKR - 1963

The unmistakable wailing of a loon is a beautiful and constant echo that signals the beginning of a new day on the Ocklawaha River. The pre-dawn serenade has left Auggie, Emily, and Silver speechless. The distinctive and warble-like trill bouncing across the water and into the woods is as haunting as it is lovely.

There's a light wind picking up from the east and the gentle slapping of the waves against the banks of the river, the loon song, and the fast departure of the cool morning air have all combined to give the early morning a surreal feeling and appearance.

Silver is standing guard over a very small fire while Emily and Auggie struggle to get out of the tent, stretch, and face a day that has clearly been kick-started by nature's magic hands.

No one wants to speak first and break the spell, and all three of them are wishing that this moment could last way past sunrise, especially given what they have decided to do.

They watch the sky for hours and then wait for the lights in Brett's cabin to go out before they crawl into the tent, certain that he is not going to take off in the middle of the night with their precious boxes and so many unanswered questions.

The women whisper in the dark for another hour, trying to decide what they are going to do when the night ends and their plan becomes obvious, once they decide to be realistic. They can either wait him out and approach him, if and when he decides to leave, or they can surprise him and take their chances.

There really is no choice. The loon calls are starting to fade by the time all three of them are moving nervously around the fire. They only have one decision left to make-should Silver bring her purse, which also means, should she bring her gun?

"It's not like the three of us couldn't take him," Auggie says, swaggering just a bit.

"We are not trained for this kind of thing," Emily says, trying to inject some sense of reality into what might happen next. "But I agree that bringing the gun is sort of stupid."

The women are whispering, not because they think Brett or anyone but the loons might hear them, but because it feels like the right thing to do. It's as if the semi-quiet morning demands it. There's a feeling of sacredness that's hanging in the air and the women are speaking softly, moving gently, waking up as slowly as the world around them.

"The simplest thing would be to hold the gun on him, take the boxes, and get the hell out of here," Silver finally says as she pushes the last log in the fading coals. "But that would also be acting like he's acted. We all know that desperate people get more and more desperate as the days roll by, and he was desperate enough to break into my house and steal something."

"So you're saying just because he acted like that doesn't mean we should?" This from Auggie, who has always wanted to kick in a door, and beat someone up.

"No," Silver says, looking up and directly at Auggie. "I'm saying that we have no idea what he might do and I'm not in the mood to have someone lunge for my gun. He's bound to freak out, and he's obviously not rational."

"Which means we should be, I suppose." Auggie sounds beyond disappointed.

It's Emily who squares her shoulders and tells them exactly what they should do. She wants them to be nice. Silver and Auggie look at her in bewilderment and don't say a word.

Knock on the door before he gets up so he's sleepy, and maybe even shocked. Someone stand by the back door, just in case. Someone else linger on the side with the gaff hook. Leave the purse locked up in the car. Get the boxes. Load them into the car. Go home and cook breakfast. Figure out what to do next.

"That would be sort of nice, you know?" she adds, waiting for one of them to flip out and start cleaning the pistol.

But instead, they agree. Emily almost doesn't believe it but Auggie immediately starts rolling up their sleeping bags while Silver pulls out tent stakes. She watches them for a moment in disbelief and then gathers up their dishes, trash, and boldly tucks Silver's purse behind the driver's seat. It takes them twenty minutes to pack everything and when they finish the sky above the river is just beginning to brighten.

Dozens of birds start chirping and singing from every direction and the women stand and listen for a moment. The waking world is a pleasure to see and hear and all three of them smile as they stand half-dumbstruck next to Silver's truck. The contrast between this moment and what is about to happen is not lost on them.

"It's like the calm before the storm," Silver offers.

"And so lovely," Emily says with a big sigh.

"It's so easy to forget about all of this, even for someone like me who lives in the midst of it all," Silver admits. "Half the time I keep my windows closed, or the air conditioning is running. It's silly, really."

"No, what we're about to do is silly," Auggie says, hands on hips, eyes to the slowly brightening sky. "I have a feeling even your wild Marjorie would think we are foolish."

"Foolish suits me," Silver says. "Are we ready?"

Auggie and Emily shrug, because how can you be ready for what is about to happen?

Silver takes over again, because she really can't seem to help herself. Given her size, Emily's been ordered to stand guard off to the side of the house with the gaff hook. Auggie is to head to the back of the cabin, which some would think is the front because it's facing the river, and Silver gets the pleasure of knocking on the door.

The women walk silently towards the dark cabin, kicking through tall grass and past a small gulley that separates the campground from the cabins, until Silver motions for Auggie to go around back. Emily slips into the dark shadows and Silver walks to the cabin door.

Silver knocks three times on the old wooden door as hard as she can and then takes two steps back. She also looks over to make certain Emily is ready for whatever is going to happen next.

They wait, and when nothing happens Silver walks back to the door, pounds again, and steps back again.

"What?" They hear Brett rumbling from inside, his feet hit the floor, and then stay there. "Is someone there?"

Silver knocks again.

The feet start to move, and when the door creaks open Silver is smiling. Her beautiful white teeth are almost glowing in the dark and Brett, in his stripped boxer shorts, leans out of the door until he sees her and then tries to step back and slam the door.

"I don't think so," Silver barks, lunging forward with her considerable weight and pushing into the cabin and past Brett.

He stumbles to the side and looks as if he might faint. Emily is right behind her and he looks over her shoulder as if he's checking to see how many more people are coming inside.

Emily closes the door, switches on the light, and as if by magic, Auggie walks in from the kitchen. "The door was unlocked," she says matter-of-factly, and suddenly the three women have him surrounded.

"You know why we're here, Brett?"

He looks as if he might faint. He's tall, pale, and the same scraggly man Emily saw at Cross Creek. He's got dark circles under his eyes, it looks as if he hasn't shaved in days, and the menacing look he has been throwing all over the county has been replaced by taut lines of fear that make his face look absolutely sad and pitiful.

"Brett?" Silver says his name and takes a step forward.

"I know," he says with his voice shaking.

"You broke into my house and took something that wasn't yours and we want it back."

Brett appears frozen in place and then the strangest thing happens. He starts to cry.

This is the absolute last thing they thought would happen. They haven't planned for this, talked about what they would do if he simply cooperates, or if he has a nervous breakdown in front of them. Thank God Auggie is a doctor. Emily and Silver are standing like statues when Auggie gives them both a dirty look, steps forward, and puts her hand on his arm. He flinches, drops his head, and cries like a hungry baby.

Silver fights an urge to smack him as Auggie gently walks him over to the couch where Silver spied him reading. That's when she sees all the boxes stacked in the corner, papers all over the floor, and a pile of empty beer cans next to that.

"We aren't going to hurt you," Auggie says, much to the displeasure of Silver. "Sit down. It's going to be okay."

Brett stumbles onto the couch, sobbing so deeply, that it looks as if he might not be able to sit upright and Auggie reaches into her jeans pocket and hands him a wad of tissues. He blows his nose, while still sobbing, and mumbles, "Everything's right there. I was just reading it all. I didn't hurt nuthin'."

*Oh dear God*! Emily and Silver exchange a glance as Auggie motions to them to pull up some chairs.

He looks up, and snot is running down his nose. The man looks so pathetic and sad that Emily sets down the gaff hook, sits down, and nods her head so that Silver gets the hint and sits down too.

"Is the Sheriff out there?" he asks. "He scared me. Is he out there, waitin'?"

Emily and Auggie look at Silver. Neither of them can wait to hear what she says.

"Yes, he is," Silver lies. "He wants us to talk with you first and find out what you are doing here, why you have been following her, and why you took the boxes."

Brett starts to cry even harder. Emily walks into the kitchen, finds a glass, fills it with tap water and brings it over to him. He drinks the entire glass, wipes his mouth with his hand, blows his nose, and then asks if he can put on his pants.

"I'll get them," Silver says, not convinced that his little boy act is sincere. Instead, she grabs the small blanket off the back of her chair, hands it to him and says, "Just cover yourself, and talk, please."

"You want to know everything?"

"Everything would be good. We have all day, but I'm not sure how long the Sheriff is going to wait. So it would be good if you start talking now."

"Okay. Okay, I will." Brett pulls the blanket around his spindly legs, blows his nose one more time and shrugs his shoulders in defeat. He takes a breath before he begins and the women take turns looking at each other in disbelief.

Emily lets her mind stop for one moment and wishes she could take a photograph of the scene. Three half-crazed women, a man on the couch in his underwear, a cabin right out of the last century, the fading calls of the loons, stolen boxes of who-knows-what next to the dirty couch. It's a scene out of a novel or a made-for-TV horror movie, and she wonders if Silver is taking mental notes like she is. Her own heart has finally slowed and she's wondering if there isn't something wrong with Brett. He's surely not menacing now, and the way he talks, slow and as if he's trying to remember exactly how to speak, make her wonder if he doesn't have some kind of disability. He's been smart enough to follow the trail of breadcrumbs she's unwittingly laid out for him but there's something else and of course, a well of sadness that's turned him into a blubbering fool.

He begins by apologizing for stealing the boxes, but quickly adds that he didn't know what else to do.

"Thank you for that, but please start at the beginning," Silver interrupts him before he can continue. She must stay in control.

"I'll try," he promises. "There's so much to remember and I'm so tired, so tired of being here and trying to find something that might not even be real."

*Oh, great.* Silver crosses her legs and urges him through a very direct gaze to get to it. And his story is as unexpected as his tears.

Brett Kinnan comes from a family steeped in secrets, or so it seems. He grew up listening to stories that he now believes may not be true. Brett learned he was adopted only after his parents both died and he was going through their papers. The discovery devastated him and made him wonder if anything they had every told him about his past, their pasts, or anything at all was true. He was an only child, his parents were good to him, and he felt loved but the lie of his birth, how they adopted him, everything that springs from wondering where the truth lies, turned him into an angry young man.

And then there was his grandpa.

His grandpa, Francis.

The grandpa who adored Brett and who was already so old when he was a little boy, but who loved to spend time with him. Grandpa Francis had once worked in the hotel business and he traveled a lot. He showed Brett postcards and ashtrays and trinkets from lots of hotels but the hotels he loved the best were in Florida.

Emily is now sitting so close to the edge of her chair if she breaths heavily she may fall right off of it. Silver is the picture of calmness, but Emily catches her lip quivering a bit when Auggie clears her throat.

Francis talked about his special friends, famous friends, movie stars and writers and politicians who he would help with hotel arrangements and, near as Brett can figure, his grandfather was a consultant for the rich and famous and the hotel owners who loved the rich and famous. His grandpa lived to be ninety-nine years old, and Brett helped his mother clean out his house and joked to her about how he was so like his grandpa that he would live to be that old too.

"All a lie," Brett says, trying hard not to cry again. "All lies."

But before Grandpa died his arteries were freezing up, and he liked to talk a lot, and some of it made sense and some of it didn't. Brett was recruited to sit with him because he wasn't going to college, couldn't seem to hold a job, and had absolutely no idea what to do with what he is now calling his fake life. So babysitting grandpa was just the ticket.

Grandpa talked about creatures flying in through the window that gave him pink and green pills but he also talked about a secret friend in Florida. "Some day you will find out the big secret," he would chuckle, while Brett wondered if anything his beloved grandfather was saying was true. But then he found things. Old envelopes with Florida postmarks. Tons of newspaper clippings all about someone named Marjorie Rawlings. Then all of her books, with her autograph, and all in perfect condition. Little clues about the big secret, he decided, were everywhere.

Emily must now sit on her hands to keep from jumping up and asking him where all this stuff is being kept. She also feels a bit woozy. Could this be true? She prays he is telling the truth.

The last thing he found was a key to the safety deposit box, which he dutifully handed over to his mother and promptly forgot about during the next few years following all those deaths, all those lies.

"I'm not stupid or anything," he almost shouts. "It's just that I'm like one of the few people in the world who can say they fell off their bike in fifth grade, hit their head on the concrete, and something got confused up there. It takes me a while, and that makes me angry a lot of the time, but eventually it all slips into place."

He stops, looks up, and then smiles.

"What's so funny?" Silver is starting to melt. Brett would be pathetic if he wasn't so helpless and sad.

"I sort of ended up like my grandpa after all. He was just like this when he was an old fart. Forgetting things, having to focus really hard, and he would get mad too. Maybe he's my real grandpa."

Auggie has all she can do but to throw her arms around him and start crying herself. Emily is already sniffling. This is definitely not the ending Silver would expect, or perhaps even write.

"So," she finally asks, "then what happened?"

Brett found the safety deposit key after his mother died and with everything he had to take care of, including the financial mess his parents had left, he forgot about it until he was in his own financial mess. And of course, with his "thinking problem", as he prefers to call it, everything took longer, was harder, and often didn't make sense. "All those people and no one had any money or was smart enough to even have life insurance," he laments. "I'm no Einstein, but if I loved some-one, I'd have life insurance."

Brett shivers under the little cover-up and says he finally remembered to go to the safety deposit box and it took him a long time to figure out what he had discovered. There were several letters signed by a Marjorie, and some with just an M, and they looked old. There was a wad of cash, all dated prior to 1970, some old coins that he still hasn't bothered to have valued, and a note that said, *I took my secret to the grave.*

What in the world?

Brett looks around and can see that they are as confused as he was. He tells them that he put all the pieces together after he spent months researching Marjorie's life. This hap-pened because he remembered his grandfather going to the funeral of Norton Baskin and Norton, he learned, had been married to Marjorie. It was a clue! It actually made him want to go to college to become a historian. He thought if his grandpa had somehow been involved with Marjorie, and if the letters were real, that she really didn't die in 1953, and maybe she wrote some more and maybe there were still things she wrote that would surely be worth money. He would sell them, and use the money to go to college.

"I remember when Grandpa went to that funeral because he was so old himself," Brett tells them. "I thought he was going to fall and die and I think it was the very first time that I realized how important Florida and all those people he mum-bled about had been to him."

Now, Emily is the impatient one. "How did you know to go to that house and look for those boxes?" She blurts out the question and then wants to slap herself, but she has to know and so do Silver and Auggie.

"Go in the back bedroom and get the papers that are on the dresser," he says. Then he sits with his head down, like a guarded prisoner, and waits.

Emily retrieves the papers and thumbs through them while everyone waits. She sees records about his search for his birth mother, her address and phone number, his adoption papers, photo copies of other documents that all focus on the adoption. Everything seems to be about his adoption. There are addresses for his birth mother, and someone has written a big "no" over almost every page, as if they were angry.

"These don't tell me anything," Emily says, shuffling through the papers again.

"Give them to me," Brett says and then quickly adds, "please."

"Emily hands them over and he touches them gently. This is not the menacing man they have seen everywhere. Finally, he comes up with one page that Emily must have missed. He hands it back to her.

It's a photocopy of an old *New York Times* article about Leslie, and on the very bottom someone has written in her Florida address with exact directions on how to get there from the highway. Emily feels a chill run up her back. These directions could have been in her GPS if she had one.

Emily hands the paper to Silver. "Where did you get this?"

"It was in the safety deposit box, and I thought it was a clue," he explains, shrugging his shoulders. "It took me so long to figure things out and I ran out of money because I was always in the library and I never worked. And then I tried to find my real mother..."

He trails off and drops his head.

Silver wants to lie down on the floor and sob. This boy-man needs someone to rock him like a baby and perhaps a bit of counseling, a warm meal, and closure.

"It's okay," Auggie tells him, reaching out for a moment to touch his arm.

Emily is not feeling as kind. "So you were essentially on a wild goose chase? You were guessing about coming here and finding something?"

He nods his head.

"You have no idea what's in the boxes do you?"

He shakes his head back and forth. "I was just going to all the places from the books and then I kept seeing you and I thought you looked smart and that you might know about the secret. That's all."

"What about your last name?"

He looks up. "I know! When I saw it on those books at my Grandpa's I was like, wow!"

Now Emily feels as if she might cry. She squeezes her eyes shut, opens them, and then looks at Brett. He's thinking. Hard.

"There's one thing kinda strange, though."

"What?"

"My mom, you know, my birth mom in those papers I found, it was like she looked and looked for someone with my last name to adopt me. She rejected like so many couples. I don't get it, and I'm going to ask her. I am. And…"

They all wait. Brett definitely needs moments to space out his thoughts. He's no dummy, but Auggie can clearly see the effects of his youthful injury. Everything is up there, it just takes a while for him to search around and find what he's looking for.

"I looked a lot like my grandpa. People said it all the time. But I don't know. I'm just confused now."

The women take turns looking at each other and Emily wants to run out the door and go to a genealogy library immediately. But instead Silver lowers her voice and talks as gently to Brett as she can. She tells him that they are not going to press charges if he agrees to leave and stay away and get on with his life.

He shakes his head and then she says she's going to go outside and tell the sheriff so that he can leave. Brett watches her get up and Emily and Auggie act as if that's exactly what Silver is going to do. He looks up at Auggie and asks if he can say something.

"Of course," Auggie says.

"I don't know who wrote that stuff, but it's kinda good, isn't it?"

"I'm not sure," Auggie says. "I haven't read it."

"Maybe that Leslie woman wrote it because I read about her and what she did there and everything. I think I could use some creative recovery myself."

He tries to smile but something else is pulling at his heart. He looks as if he might start to cry again.

Silver is standing at the door but he doesn't see her as he drops his head again and continues to talk. But Silver can hear him. She can hear every word.

"I watched you all, you know, and I saw how you all care for each other and how that sheriff guy takes care of her out there and after that... well, all I could think about was my birth mom back there, and how hard it must have been to give me away and now everyone is dead and really, she's my family now."

He stops to let his thoughts gather and Silver isn't moving.

"I was going to bring the boxes back, really, I don't know what to do with them," he admits. "I'm going to go back and see my mom. She told me it was okay. Maybe I can help her and maybe she can help me."

An hour later Brett is already heading north, the boxes are loaded into the back of Silver's pick-up truck and Auggie has disappeared down the dirt road toward her morning appointments.

Emily assumes they are going back to Silver's so she can throw herself on the floor and try to figure out what in the holy hell to do next. But that doesn't happen.

"There's something you need to see," Silver tells her, as they crawl down the dirt highway trying to avoid the weather-beaten glaciers. "It's not too far, but the road is totally a washboard, so brace yourself."

If only such a thing were possible, Emily tells herself, as she straps on her seatbelt, Silver turns on the four-wheel drive, and they turn right and drive even deeper into the heart of the jungle.

# 27

*"The mysteries of life have always given me such great pleasure. Parentless children, scientific quandaries, disappearing bodies and broken hearts—life is indeed filled with one mystery after another. Isn't that exciting? Isn't that why we search and question and roam the world with our magnifying glasses? Sometimes the answer is close, right within us, and that, of course, is the greatest adventure of all."*
     —*Lost Hearts in the Swamp of Life* - MKR - 1963

The washboard of a road has reminded both Emily and Silver that it's way past time to purchase new bras. Emily is also glad that the ruts in the road are shaking the truck so violently that everything is rattling and it's impossible to have a conversation. Her mind is spinning as if it's been ripped out of her head and thrown into the wind.

Who could have foreseen this day and the night before it? She was certain that Brett held all the answers and although he had some of them, there were still so many unanswered questions. Even though she's half-exhausted, Emily's also wondering if she'll ever be able to sleep again. What is she going to do? The mere idea of going back to Ohio to work makes her want to fling herself out of the window.

Silver watches as Emily turns around every five seconds to make certain the boxes are still in the back of the truck. Maybe she thinks something or someone is going to swoop down and take them, or that they will magically disappear. Her own attention is totally devoted to Getts at this moment. How she wishes he had been there! She already knows she'll be telling and re-telling him every detail of the last twenty-four hours, that is if he will ever speak to her again. Silver puts her hand on her heart to make certain it's still there. His missing shadow in her life, even for this short period of time, has made her feel empty in a way she has never before experienced. Compromise, she thinks, that's what this will have to be. She knows that she would feel equally as empty if she didn't move forward and into a new, frightening, but terribly challenging phase of her own life, but she wants him there. What that will look like is anyone's guess but it has to happen. It does.

Silver is gripping the wheel to keep the truck steady, and stops suddenly in the middle of the road. Emily can't wait to hear what she has to say.

"Grab us a couple of beers out of the cooler, will you?"

"We haven't eaten anything yet! It's like eight o'clock in the morning!"

"What does that have to do with anything? I'm thirsty. There's protein in beer. "

Emily doesn't bother to argue. She hops out of the truck, opens the cooler and fishes out two ice-cold beers, and gets back in the truck. They haven't seen one car and the chances of a cop, Getts perhaps, prowling around back here are slim to none. The first sip totally converts her. It's the most delicious drink she's ever had in her life.

"Cheers!" Silver says, holding up her beer so they can bump cans. "In case you haven't noticed, I'm not that big on following rules."

"That's putting in mildly," Emily says, taking one more drink before Silver starts back down what poses as a road.

They drive for a very long time. Emily occasionally sees a house, backed up against what she assumes is a river or creek. There are dead orange and grapefruit trees everywhere, a few living ones also, an occasional trailer placed as if someone threw it down in the middle of a field and then ran away. Emily is now thinking of this as true Florida. Almost untouched, survivable if you have what it takes, exceptionally beautiful, and really hot.

She thinks about Tag and Jimmy and the fabulous tour guide at Marjorie's home. Silver and Auggie and the pearl-laden librarian-everyone so real and true and in touch with what it takes not just to survive, but to live. Maybe the grass is greener in some places, but the people who lived here, Marjorie's neighbors, the hired help and the locals-they all knew better. Emily can see how this scraggly, always green, humid hunk of the country can seduce someone. She feels as if she's gotten addicted to the sweet air, the waving palms, the way the sky pushes and pulls itself and then scatters those puffy white cottonballs everywhere. Maybe it's like this too in Ohio, not that she's ever bothered to pay attention.

Emily steadies her beer on her thigh, turns again, and stares at the boxes. What is she going to do? There are suddenly more than a few choices. She turns back around and smiles. Emily's certain that if she looked at herself right now in the mirror that's behind the visor she wouldn't recognize herself.

A few moments later Emily is still smiling when they come to their first intersection. The road going left narrows, and the washboard road continues to the right. That's the road they take, and then they bounce another few miles until Emily notices a fairly new looking metal fence on the left side of the road, a farm off in the distance and then a small sign near the fence. Silver slows the truck and then backs it under a stand of trees across the road.

Emily leans across the dashboard and stares across the street. They are at a cemetery. *Antioch Cemetery.* This is where Marjorie Kinnan Rawlings is buried! Well, perhaps this is where Marjorie Kinnan Rawlings is buried. And Norton Baskin.

Silver shuts off the truck, finishes her beer, and turns to face Emily. "Even if she didn't die in 1953, this is where she'd be. This is where Francis, or whoever in the hell, buried her. I know that. And don't ask me how because I couldn't tell you. This is where she was finally buried. They would never keep her apart from Norton."

"Have you been here before?"

"Yes. It's kind of a ritual here. You have to find this place and pay homage. It was one of the first places I came to visit when I moved here, but I'm not your average, run-of-the-mill transplant."

"No kidding," Emily says, turning to jump out of the truck.

The women cross the gravel road and walk in silence to a gate at the end, pop it open, shut it behind them and then start walking. Emily loves cemeteries for many reasons, the least of all being how much information she can get from them when she is doing research. But it's also what people leave when they visit, the chairs in front of some gravesites, the trees someone cared to plant, notes and letters, the simplicity or gaudiness of the markers. It's a world and place unlike any other and what strikes her immediately about this cemetery is not just it's location, but how simple everything is-markers, signs, flowers.

She begins weaving in and out of the gravesites, head bowed, being careful not to step over them because her mother told her not to fifty years ago. "It's out of respect," her mother said. "Never, ever step on top of where the bodies were buried." Silver is just paces away when Emily asks her if she remembers where the graves are located.

"Not totally, but when you see it, you'll know immediately."

Emily doesn't bother to reply but keeps walking and then, seconds later, comes across the first of many similar markers. First she sees a plain granite marker for *Tom Morrison, Age 80 Plus.* Then, next to it, a much fancier marker: *Tom Morrison—Immortalized in the Writings of Marjorie Kinnan Rawlings.*

Emily has never seen anything like this before. She keeps walking, and it seems as if every three feet there's another marker just like the Rawlings marker next to Tom's grave.

Silver's way ahead of her. Emily spins in a circle and realizes that probably half of the people buried here knew Marjorie or knew of her. Many of the people who lived in this area were mentioned in Cross Creek. Marjorie was famous and very much loved, and also occasionally feared. The simplicity of everything she sees is so fitting. Life here demanded it, and for good reason. Emily stumbles forward and has to laugh at the irony of discovering Zelma Cason's grave marked in the same way. She was the woman who changed Marjorie's life with her lawsuit, compelled her to head for New York and

Crescent Beach, and perhaps a lonely cabin a mile away from this very spot.

How ironic that they are buried in the same cemetery; but then again, how absolutely perfect.

Emily looks up and sees that Silver is watching her and has stopped moving. She walks quickly to where Silver is standing, looks down, and clasps her hands over her mouth. "Oh!"

"Here she is," Silver says, moving back a few feet to give Emily room.

Emily can't speak. The grave is a long slab of simple white concrete. It reads: *Marjorie Kinnan Rawlings 1896-1953, wife of Norton Baskin, Through Her Writings She Endeared Herself to The People Of The World.* At the very top of the grave there is a statue family of miniature deer-a buck, doe and a fawn. There's a spot by the fawn where people have placed dozens of pens and pencils in tribute, of course, to Marjorie and *The Yearling.* Norton is four inches away. His marker reads *Beloved Husband.*

Emily drops to her knees, places her hands on the sun-warm grave, and feels a rush of emotion that brings tears to her eyes. No matter what we do, how we hide, what we discover-this is how it ends up. The irony of it all is surely something Marjorie must have thought about. She wrote about death and life and tragedy in such way that it was as if she were living through every character, every loss, every heartache, all those pages of grief and laughter and challenge. People loved her writing because it was real and true, and so was she.

Silver kneels down beside her and puts her hand on Emily's shoulder. "Are you okay?"

"I didn't expect to be so emotional, so moved by seeing this."

"The first time I came here the same thing happened," Silver admits. "I'm not big on the spiritual stuff and whatever happens after we die, but it feels as if she's here or was here or is watching us from some unseen place."

"What do you think she'd say if she knew people like us come here, put pens and pencils at the top of her grave and cry into the wind?"

Silver rocks back on her heels and plants her elbows on her knees. "She would have been touched for sure, but don't you think she'd also say something like, 'Don't those damn fools have something better to do?'"

Emily laughs softly and then pauses to think about Marjorie's terribly complicated life.

"I can see how she was always torn. The consummate party girl who needed her quiet time, and was always wondering if she should please herself or everyone else. When she was working I bet she thought about the luncheon or party she might be missing, and when she was at a party, most likely drinking too much, she was thinking about writing."

Emily rocks back so she is squatting next to the grave like Silver. They look as if they are waiting for her to rise from the dead. Silver agrees by shaking her head up and down. They both sit quietly; lost in a parade of thoughts that are so similar they could be sharing the same brain. There's Marjorie, attending more than one gravesite ceremony right here. The old black and green and dark blue cars parading down the road at a snail's pace so that no one would choke to death in the billowing dust. Norton, with his arm across the back of her seat if he was driving and Marjorie going too fast if she was behind the wheel. Flocks of birds vanishing in the clouds that caught her eye, and made her think of a paragraph or a sentence she would write the second she got the hell out of there. A nip on the bottle that was in the glove box, or her purse, or Norton's back pocket on the way home.

They would stop for dinner in Island Grove and half of the customers at the restaurant would recognize Marjorie and the other half would recognize Norton from his work at the hotel. After dinner, Marjorie would ask him to drive all the way home with the lights off and she would sing a bit and he would laugh. Then she would make up stories and hold his hand and then she would wonder out loud what their lives might be like if things were different.

If she didn't have to go to New York to meet her editor, the legendary Max Perkins, sign books and hobnob with book reviewers.

If he didn't have to run a large hotel and be present at a reception next Thursday.

If she could let down her guard and realize that he loves her, no matter what she says or does.

If he could slip away and let the assistant take over and surprise her once in a while in a place and with a plan so that she wouldn't have to beg for his company.

If the world would stop for just a few seconds or maybe a week or perhaps for several decades so they could just *be*.

Or if they could jump off and create a whole new world.

The Marjorie and Zora look-alikes sit for a long time, rocking from heel to toe, occasionally touching the ground when they move too fast, watching as the clouds disappear and the sky turns so blue it almost looks black.

Silver finally pushes herself up, reaches down for Emily's hand, and asks her if she wants to go get a pen to put by the grave.

Emily doesn't say anything at first. She turns in a circle and lifts up her hands and then waves to all the dead people.

"She's got such great company here, doesn't she?"

"Yes, these are her people."

"If I thought I would never be back here, yes, I would put a pen and a note on her grave to satisfy my own soul, but I'm coming back," Emily says firmly. "Let's just consider this my first visit."

The women turn and walk carefully past Norton's grave and they say goodbye to Zelma and Tom. Silver makes certain the gate is locked and then invites Emily to sit on her tailgate as they dangle their feet, look across to the cemetery, and Emily grabs two more beers without bothering to ask if Silver wants one.

The heat is already beginning to intensify and the birds and flying insects are finding places to rest in the trees and bushes until late afternoon. That creates a sense of stillness and quiet that is fitting for such a place. Emily tells Silver that it could be any year right now. It could be 1934 or 1950 or 1978. The cemetery, albeit for some new markers and shiny plastic flowers, is as timeless as Marjorie's writing.

The women talk about the past two weeks, what they have discovered, the risks they have taken and the challenges that are now spread out in front of them. Emily knows she must leave, perhaps even today, but where will she go and what will she do? Silver must find Getts and reconstruct a life that just days ago seemed to her to be planned and set for the rest of her life. It's obvious to both of them that something is ending and something else is beginning.

"What are you going to do, Ohio?" Silver has set down her beer can and is leaning against the side of the truck, staring intently at her friend.

"I can leave the boxes here, take them with me and keep searching, or forget about these past two weeks and what might be."

Silver smiles, knowing already that two of those possibilities really are not so possible.

"And?"

Emily totally changes the subject. "What happened to Zora?"

"Girl, she had a hard life, but what a life it was! She traveled and wrote and fell on hard times and got very ill and did so many remarkable things. Zora and Marjorie were like two shooting stars who I like to think are still out there, zinging through the sky, sipping whiskey on one of those wild planets, and discussing all the characters from their own books and lives."

"I would love to have known her."

Silver turns to look into Emily's eyes. "Don't you think you do?"

"Almost," Emily whispers, "almost."

Emily will leave Silver's house in a matter of hours with new bracelets, taken directly off Silver's arm, dangling on her own wrists, her truck loaded with cardboard boxes, and a hastily drawn map for the route to New Jersey, and not Ohio.

Four weeks after that, three jars of pickles will be delivered to Silver's house along with a framed copy of a grocery list that once hung on Leslie Kincade's kitchen wall. In the bottom of the package there will be a bottle of whiskey and a package of Lucky Strike cigarettes. There will also be a note from Ohio in the box, along with a photograph of her in her new Manhattan apartment, surrounded by all the papers and manuscripts she is researching and cataloging. "Getting closer," the note will read.

Silver's next novel will be published the following year and cause a sensation because it will be published using the name Jenka Armador. The story will be a fascinating mix of reality and fiction and will parallel two lives-one hers, and one a famous author's, who died in 1953 after falling ill at her Crescent Beach, Florida home.

Silver will close her eyes when she hears the sound of the approaching cars for her first press conference about her life, her disappearance, and some mysterious boxes. The reporters will gather on her front porch where Silver waved goodbye to Ohio, and where Ohio stood with the car door open, tears running down her face and said, "Holding those manuscripts is like holding a possibility and I can't let go of that, I can't."

Silver will remember how Emily finally got in the car, drove off, and then stopped before she left the driveway. Her hand came out of the window and she was waving a sweet scented leaf that had magically appeared on her front seat.

And then she was gone.

# The End

## 1953
## *Crescent Beach, Florida*

*It is so damn hot today. And I am so damn tired.*

*The top of these concrete steps offers me a glorious view of so many things I love-the palms that fan out toward the river, the bluest sky in the world meeting the water on the horizon, white birds rotating in unison as if they are in the middle of a Broadway dance rehearsal, and a slice of quiet so my addled brain can recover from yet another week of hard work, sleepless nights, and all those empty glasses.*

*Sweet Norton will be here very soon. We planned this for much earlier, kind of a first glance at morning light kind of thing, but alas, I couldn't prepare in time. Soon, I may have all the time in the world. It will be "a grand day to get lost," he keeps telling me.*

*When I called to tell him I needed a bit more time he was his usual ho-hum self. That man is unequaled and I must tell him when he arrives that if everything goes as planned all of his wishes will come true, and then some.*

*Unfortunately there is an uneven heaviness in my heart today. It's an odd mixture of excitement, and a real physical pain that has left me with a blinding headache, which could be the payment for our misbehaving last night.*

*Standing here I can see his car approaching. Norton is wearing his favorite black hat, and I think I can hear him whistling. He's pulling in now, waving and out of nowhere a beautiful green leaf, smelling like lemon, sweet perfume, and this salty air, lands at my feet.*

*When I bend to pick it up the world spins, and when I look up Norton is coming up the stairs. My laugh disappears into the morning air, past his wide smile and beyond all, to time.*

*—Lost Hearts in the Swamp of Life* - MKR - 1963

# Author's Note

More than twenty years ago I sat up late one night and watched the movie *Cross Creek*. I was captivated and mesmerized by the bold life of Marjorie Kinnan Rawlings, infamous for her Pulitzer Prize winning book, *The Yearling*, and I vividly remembering feeling some kind of cosmic connection with her.

When I moved to Florida and fell under its tropical spell it was almost as if I could hear her whispering to me, "Bring me back, Kris!" I finally visited Cross Creek and ran my fingers across her writing table, looked through the screen door where she sat and wrote, and hiked through the thick brush on the same path she walked through her orchards while chasing ducks and chickens. After that spiritual experience I had no choice but to resurrect this remarkable woman.

My greatest muse, guide, and source of information about her life was Marjorie herself. I read all of her books, spent hours reading the letters and newspaper articles she wrote and that were written about her, drove the back roads in Central Florida where she often skidded off the highway, cooked her recipes, and imagined what was in her heart, soul, and mind.

I am extremely indebted to Florence M. Turcotte, Literary Manuscripts Archivist in the Department of Special & Area Studies Collections for the George A. Smathers Libraries at the University of Florida. She is a kind genius, a Rawlings expert, and a woman I know MKR would have hand-picked to guard her legacy.

I must also thank historian David Nolan, who was more than generous with his time and knowledge about all things Marjorie, Norton, and Zora.

There really is a Dr. Ruth Streeter, and I will always cherish the day she allowed me to spend time inside Marjorie's Crescent Beach home and patiently pointed out every single object that once belonged to the famous writer.

Like Marjorie herself I took liberties meshing fact and fiction, but I did so with Marjorie looking over my shoulder. I would love to have been her friend and there's a part of me bold enough to think that somehow we are kindred spirits fighting against the judging eyes of a publishing world that seems to have gone mad.

And how can you not love a woman who saluted the day with a great glass of whiskey, a lovely swear word, and a Lucky Strike, coupled with the passion of all those beautifully-placed words rising inside of her like a gorgeous pink-feathered roseate spoonbill?

In my world all things are possible, and Marjorie Kinnan Rawlings remains as alive and vibrant as she was the day she first stepped on my now beloved Florida's exotic soil.

# About the Author

—

Kris Radish is a former journalist, nationally syndicated columnist, and the author of The Elegant Gathering of White Snows, Dancing Naked at the Edge of Dawn, Annie Freeman's Fabulous Traveling Funeral, Searching for Paradise in Parker, P.A., The Sunday List of Dreams, The Shortest Distance Between Two Women, Hearts on a String, Tuesday Night Miracles and two non-fiction books, Run, Bambi, Run and The Birth Order Effect. She lives near St. Petersburg, Florida where is also co-owner of a wine lounge, the Wine Madonna, and where she hosts book clubs and reading groups from across the country when she's not working on her next two novels.

Made in the USA
Lexington, KY
06 July 2014